P9-CFE-049

Feels Like Family

SHERRYL WOODS

Feels Like Family

MIRA®

MIRA®

ISBN-13: 978-0-7783-2436-2
ISBN-10:   0-7783-2436-2

FEELS LIKE FAMILY

www.MIRABooks.com

Printed in U.S.A.

10 9 8 7 6 5 4 3 2 1

Dear Friends,

I'm so delighted you're back for one last visit to Serenity. And though I have dearly loved writing about Maddie and Dana Sue, I have to admit that Helen holds a special place in my heart with her yearning for a child and her sudden awakening to the fact that it might be too late for her to have one.

To be honest, I had another hero in mind for Helen when I began writing about the Sweet Magnolias, but suddenly in midstream I realized exactly how perfect she and Erik would be together. Because of his history and her belated desire for a child, there were bound to be high-stakes consequences for these two wonderfully strong-willed people. I hope you'll enjoy the twists and turns they take on their path to the altar.

As always, I owe a huge debt of gratitude to Margaret Marbury, a wonderful editor who can see far deeper into a story than I and show me ways to enrich it. She embraced this series from the beginning and made me want to make it the best yet. And for years now—almost from the beginning of my career— I have trusted agent Denise Marcil not only to cheer me on, but to show me the error of my ways when I'm about to leap off the proverbial cliff that every author clings to from time to time. She's amazing. Both women are among the smartest in the business.

And while I'm thanking the two people who keep me on track with each and every book, my thanks as well to the wonderfully supportive Harlequin sales team. My respect for them is boundless. I couldn't be happier that I found a home at Silhouette Books and then MIRA Books, years and years ago.

All best,

Sherryl

1

For a woman who prided herself on being cool and competent, who relied on her wits to win a case, Helen Decatur walked away from the Serenity courthouse with a strong desire to pummel some sense and decency into a few of South Carolina's good old boys.

Not that she could have proved—weekly golf outings aside—that the judge, the opposing attorney and her client's soon-to-be ex-husband were in cahoots to deprive her client of what she deserved after the nearly thirty years she'd devoted to her husband, his career and their children. Nonetheless it was clear that the ongoing delays and postponements were designed to wear down Caroline Holliday until she settled for a pittance of what her husband owed her.

One of these days Caroline would fold, too. Helen had seen the defeat in her eyes today when the judge had allowed Brad Holliday's attorney yet another postponement. Jimmy Bob West claimed they hadn't seen papers Helen had filed with the court weeks ago. Helen's production of a signed courier receipt for the delivery of those papers on the same date they'd been filed with the court had done

nothing to dissuade Judge Lester Rockingham from grant-
ing her opponent's request.

"Now, Helen, there's no reason to be in a rush," the
judge had said, his tone condescending. "We're all after the
same thing here."

"Not exactly," Helen had muttered under her breath,
but she'd resigned herself to accepting the decision. Maybe
she could use the extra time to do a little more digging into
Brad's finances. She had a hunch that would wipe that
smug smile off his face. Men who provided such extensive
records as quickly as Brad had often buried financial secrets under the avalanche, hoping they'd remain buried.

If Brad's smug expression annoyed her, at least she
could take some pleasure in Jimmy Bob's careful avoid-
ance of her gaze. He'd known her long enough to be leery
of her temper once she snapped. On his own, he would only
push her so far. Spurred on by a client, he was sometimes
tempted to take risks—as he was now.

Jimmy Bob, with his slicked-back hair, ruddy complexion and ribald sense of humor, had tangled with Helen on
so many occasions that she pretty much knew what to expect from him. He was a born-and-bred South Carolinian
who'd been talking his way out of jams since high school.
While he'd never crossed an ethical line to Helen's knowl-
edge, he danced right on the precipice so often it was a
wonder he hadn't lost his balance and fallen into some legal
quagmire by now.

"I'm sorry," Helen told Caroline as she gathered up her
files. "They're not going to get away with this forever."

"Sure they will," her client replied wearily. "Brad's in
no hurry. He's too busy popping Viagra and sleeping with
any female who crosses his path to be worried about when

the divorce actually goes through. In fact, this is giving him the perfect excuse to avoid making a commitment to another woman. He's in hog heaven right now, free to do whatever he wants without any consequences. He figures that any woman hooking up with him does so at her own, fully informed peril."

"What did you ever see in a man like that?" Helen asked.

It was a question Helen found herself asking her clients a lot lately. How did smart, attractive women wind up with men who were so unworthy of them? To her mind, marriage was something to be avoided. Her friends told her she was simply jaded from handling too many nasty divorces, and while she couldn't deny that, she could list on the fingers of one hand the number of successful marriages she'd seen. Her friend and business partner, Maddie Maddox, had one—though only after recovering from a lousy first marriage—and her other friend and partner, Dana Sue Sullivan, had recently reunited with her ex, and even to Helen's cynical eye it looked as if this time things would last for her and Ronnie.

"Brad wasn't always that way," Caroline told her, a faintly nostalgic expression in her eyes. "When we met, he was thoughtful and considerate. He was a great dad, a terrific provider and until a few months ago I'd have said we had a solid marriage."

Helen had heard the rest before, or some version of it. Brad had had a brush with prostate cancer that had threatened his virility. After that, he'd lost his grip on reality. All he could think about was proving he was still a man, and he did that by sleeping with a succession of younger women, never mind that a real man would've stuck by the family who'd stayed by his side during his treatment and recovery.

By the time Helen left the courthouse, she felt even

more cynical than usual. She would have given anything to head to The Corner Spa, the business she'd started with Maddie and Dana Sue, and spend an hour working out, but she knew she had a full schedule back at the office. Normally a jam-packed calendar would have reassured her, but lately she'd begun to wonder what she was working so hard to accomplish.

She had professional success, she had money in the bank—quite a lot of it, in fact—and she had a lovely home in Serenity she rarely had time to enjoy. She had good friends, but the family she'd once envisioned for herself had never materialized. Instead she played doting surrogate aunt to Maddie's children—Tyler, Kyle, Katie and Jessica Lynn—and to Dana Sue's daughter, Annie.

It was her own fault, she knew. She'd always been too driven, too dedicated to the clients depending on her to take the time for the kind of serious dating that might actually lead to a relationship and marriage. And as the divorces had piled up in her caseload, she'd grown less and less enchanted with the idea of risking her own heart, especially on something that came with no guarantees.

When she reached her office, a small cottage on a side street near downtown Serenity, her secretary handed her a thick stack of message slips and nodded toward her office.

Barb Dixon was almost sixty and unapologetically gray-haired, and she'd come to work for Helen the day she'd opened the office. A widow who'd raised three sons on her own and gotten all of them through college, Barb was endlessly patient and compassionate with the clients and fiercely loyal to Helen. She also felt it was her right and duty to take Helen to task from time to time, which made her one of the few people on earth who dared.

"Your two o'clock's been waiting in your office for an hour," she chided. "Your three o'clock will be here any second."

Helen glanced over Barb's shoulder at the calendar the woman maintained with careful detail, instinctively knowing when to allow extra time for a client and when to keep the appointment to a fifteen-minute session that wouldn't try Helen's patience.

"Karen Ames?" Helen questioned. "She works for Dana Sue at Sullivan's. What's she doing here?"

"She didn't tell me, just said it was urgent she speak with you. You had a cancellation for this afternoon, so I called her yesterday and confirmed her for that slot. If you can keep it short, maybe you can catch up a little."

"Okay, then, let me get started. Apologize to Mrs. Hendricks when she gets here. Give her a cup of tea and some of those cookies from Sullivan's. She'll say she's on a diet, but I know better. I caught her diving into a strawberry sundae at Wharton's the other day."

Barb nodded. "Done."

Helen stepped into her office, with its antique furniture and pale peach walls. Karen was seated on the edge of a guest chair, nervously biting her nails. Her blond hair pulled back into a ponytail that emphasized her fragile cheekbones and large blue eyes. She didn't look much older than a teenager, though she was, in fact, in her late twenties with two very young children at home.

"I'm so sorry I kept you waiting, Karen," Helen said. "My court case didn't start on time and then it took longer than I anticipated to agree on a new hearing date."

"It's okay," Karen said. "I appreciate you seeing me at all."

"What can I do for you?"

"I think Dana Sue's going to fire me," Karen blurted, her expression tearful. "I don't know what to do, Ms. Decatur. I have two kids. My ex-husband hasn't paid child support in a year. If I lose this job, we could wind up on the streets. The landlord's already threatening to evict us."

Helen's heart went out to the pale, obviously frazzled young woman seated across from her. There was little question that Karen was at the end of her rope.

"You know Dana Sue and I are friends, as well as partners in The Corner Spa," Helen said. "Why did you come to me? I can't represent you, but I'd be happy to recommend someone who could."

"No, please," Karen protested. "I guess I was just hoping you could give me some advice because the two of you *are* friends. I know I've bailed out on her way too often lately, but it's only because of the kids. It's been one thing after another with them—measles and then their babysitter quitting. I'm a mom first. I have to be. I'm all they have."

"Of course they're your first priority," Helen said, even though to her increasing regret she'd never experienced the need to juggle kids and a career.

"The thought of being homeless with two kids scares me to death."

"We're not going to let that happen," Helen said decisively. "Have you sat down with Dana Sue and explained about your ex and the threats of eviction?"

Karen shook her head. "I'm too embarrassed. I think it's unprofessional to bring my financial problems into the workplace, so I haven't talked to her or Erik about this. When I call to say I can't come in, I tell them the truth, but hearing about one problem after another involving the kids has to be getting old by now. I made a commitment to be there, and Dana Sue has every right to expect me to honor that commitment."

"Then you can understand her position," Helen said.

"Of course I can," Karen replied at once. "It's not as if she has a huge staff to take up the slack. In fact, it's almost too much for us when we're all there. I've been trying to find another sitter for the kids, but do you have any idea how hard it is to find someone willing to take care of two sick kids under five during the hours I need to work? It's almost impossible. And day-care programs don't run late enough and wouldn't have taken them when they were sick, anyway."

Her shoulders sagged with defeat. "Until all this happened, I was a good employee. You can ask Dana Sue or Erik how hard I worked. I love working at Sullivan's. Dana Sue gave me a fabulous opportunity when she hired me away from the diner, and I hate that I'm blowing it."

"You haven't blown it yet," Helen consoled her. "I know Dana Sue thinks the world of you. But you're right. She needs staff who're reliable."

"I *know* that," Karen said miserably. "And she deserves it, too. I guess I'm just feeling completely overwhelmed right now. Is there anything you can do to help? How should I handle this?"

Helen considered the situation. Though employment issues were not her area of expertise, she was fairly certain Dana Sue could legally fire an employee whose absenteeism was intolerable, especially if there'd been repeated warnings about the absences. At the same time, she also knew that her friend would never kick someone when they were down. Sullivan's was a huge success in part because Dana Sue had always thought of the relatively small staff there as a family. It was one of the reasons she'd been reluctant to expand.

"Why don't we sit down with Dana Sue and see if we can't brainstorm some solutions?" Helen suggested. "Dana Sue is a compassionate person. I'm sure she's no happier about the prospect of firing you than you are. In addition, I know she's invested a lot of time in training you to become her sous-chef eventually. Compared to the man who had the job when she first opened, you've fit in perfectly. I also know you've taken a lot of initiative in creating new recipes for Sullivan's. And you *were* there when she had a family crisis of her own. Maybe I can mediate some kind of compromise to buy you time to pull things in your life together."

"That would be incredible," Karen said.

"Unfortunately, it only solves part of the problem, not the part about finding a reliable sitter," Helen reminded her. "But between Dana Sue and me, we know a lot of people. I'm sure there's someone out there who has time on her hands and would be thrilled to be needed."

Hope sparked in Karen's eyes, but faded quickly. Clearly she was someone who'd come to accept defeat as the norm.

"I'm so sorry if I'm putting you in an awkward position," she said.

"Nonsense," Helen returned. "If it were a matter of you wanting to sue Sullivan's for wrongful dismissal, I wouldn't be able to help you because of my close ties with Dana Sue. This is just three reasonable women sitting down for a little heart-to-heart. I think being straightforward and honest with Dana Sue is the only option here."

Karen gave her a worried look. "I have no idea what your fee is, but I promise you I will pay you as soon as I possibly can. You can check my credit. As tough as things have been since my husband left, I've worked really hard to pay my bills on time. I got behind one month on the rent and the landlord went ballistic, even though he got his money a week after the due date. He's just waiting for me to slip up again so he can kick us out and charge more rent to the next person."

"Let's not worry about any fee right now," Helen said. "As I said, we're going to look at this as an informal chat among friends, okay?"

Tears welled up in Karen's eyes and spilled down her cheeks. She swiped at them impatiently. "I don't know how to thank you, Ms. Decatur. I really don't."

"First, call me Helen. And before you thank me, let's wait and see if we come up with some way to make this a win-win situation for everyone, okay?"

Helen didn't think there was going to be any problem once Dana Sue understood the whole story. Sullivan's was successful enough that she could afford to hire someone else part-time, if need be, to fill in when Karen had another of the inevitable family crises that came with having kids. If worse came to worst, Helen herself could step in to help out. She'd done it before when Dana Sue had a crisis that took her away from the restaurant.

Helen had discovered that working with Erik was actually fun. He was probably the only male on the planet who wasn't the least bit intimidated by her. She'd found that to be both refreshing and frustrating.

In addition, she'd found chopping and dicing to his very precise expectations oddly soothing. After a tough day in court, it had relieved some of her stress to envision a particularly thorny witness or cantankerous judge on the chopping block as she worked. After today, taking a knife to an imaginary Judge Rockingham, Jimmy Bob or Brad Holliday would have been particularly soothing.

"Are you working tomorrow?" Helen asked Karen.

"Assuming my sitter shows up, I go in at ten to prep for lunch, then stay 'til seven so the early part of the dinner rush is covered."

Helen nodded. "I'll check Dana Sue's schedule to see when she'll be there and get back to you, okay? We're going to work this out, Karen. I promise you."

If she had to be a volunteer substitute in Sullivan's kitchen on a regular basis for a while, she would do everything she could to save Karen's job. Maybe she could even do something about that deadbeat husband of hers, though Karen hadn't asked for her help with that. She'd happily do the work pro bono.

Karen left Helen's office feeling a lot better than she had when she'd called out of sheer desperation to make the appointment. She knew enough about the attorney to know she worked hard for her clients—worked hard at everything she did, for that matter. If ever Karen had met a type-A personality, Helen was it. She made Dana Sue's perfectionism in the kitchen at Sullivan's seem like a cute little eccentricity.

When Karen got back to her two-bedroom apartment in a charmless rectangular building, she knocked on her neighbor's door. Frances Wingate, who had to be over eighty but wouldn't admit to it, had agreed to keep the kids for a couple of hours, which was about all she could manage with rambunctious, five-year-old Daisy and three-year-old Mack. Two hours were about as long as Daisy was content to make pictures with her crayons or read her books, and twice as long as Mack usually stayed down for his nap. Even as Karen waited for Frances to answer her knock, she could hear Mack crying.

"You big baby, look what you did to my picture!" Daisy yelled just as Frances opened the door.

Karen regarded her apologetically. "I am so sorry I took so long."

Frances didn't look nearly as frazzled as Karen had expected. "Oh, don't mind them. This just started. Mack woke up a minute ago and made a beeline for the table where Daisy was coloring. He tore her favorite picture, the one she'd colored for you. I was just about to get both of them some cookies and milk—that should settle them down. Why don't you come in and have some, too? They're chocolate chip. I baked them this morning."

"Are you sure you can stand this commotion another second?" Karen asked worriedly. "You must be ready for some peace and quiet."

Frances gave her a wry look. "At my age peace and quiet aren't the boon you'd think. I like having the kids around. They remind me of mine, though I hate to tell you how long ago it was when they were as young as Daisy and Mack. I have great-grandchildren older than these two." She drew Karen inside. "Now, you sit down and get off your feet. I'll get the kids settled and then you and I can chat."

When Karen had asked Frances if she'd mind watching the kids, she'd said only that she needed to talk to someone about some problems at work. The older woman hadn't hesitated. "Of course," she said. "You go do whatever you need to do."

Now, while Frances bustled off toward the small kitchen, Karen stepped into the dining room where the kids were still engaged in a noisy dispute over the destroyed picture. The instant Daisy spotted her, she ran to Karen and lifted her arms to be picked up.

"Mommy, Mack tore my present for you," Daisy said with an indignant huff, her big blue eyes shimmering with tears.

Though Daisy was getting much too heavy for Karen to hold for long, she cradled her precious little girl in her arms. "Sweetie, he's only three. I'm sure he didn't mean to hurt the picture."

"But it's ruined," Daisy wailed.

"I bet you can draw me another one that's even more beautiful," Karen suggested. "You're very good at drawing pictures."

Even as she spoke, Mack latched on to her leg, shoulders heaving with great hiccuping sobs. "Mommy!" he wailed. "Up!"

Karen felt the start of a pounding headache. Torn between her two distraught children, she managed to sit down at the table while still holding Daisy. Settling her on one knee, she hauled Mack into her lap. Daisy immediately struggled to get down, clearly feeling betrayed by the shift in attention to her little brother.

"Not just yet," Karen told her firmly. "Let's talk about this."

"He's a baby," Daisy said sullenly. "He never listens."

"And isn't that the point?" Karen asked. "If he's too little to understand that something is important to you, then you need to be the big sister and keep important things where he can't get at them. Can you try to do that?"

"I guess," Daisy said, sounding resigned.

"Thank you," Karen told her solemnly.

"Who's ready for cookies and milk?" Frances called cheerfully.

Both kids immediately abandoned Karen, scrambling down and heading toward the kitchen, the disagreement forgotten. Frances's cookies were always a huge hit with her kids, who preferred them to the fancier desserts Karen sometimes brought home from Sullivan's.

"Why don't we make it like a picnic?" Frances suggested. "I'll put a big tablecloth on the floor in front of the TV and you can have your cookies and milk in there."

"I love picnics!" Daisy said enthusiastically.

"Me, too," Frances confided. "And you know the best part of having it indoors?"

"What?" Daisy asked.

"No ants."

Daisy giggled.

Karen helped Frances spread out a plastic red-checked tablecloth, where she then set down a plate of cookies. "Two for each of you," Frances said emphatically. "Mack, here's your sippy cup with milk in it, and Daisy, here's your glass of milk."

She flipped on the TV, then handed the control to Daisy. "Find that cartoon channel you both like, okay?"

That was something else the kids loved about visiting Frances. She had cable TV, which gave them a whole range of channels Karen couldn't afford. At home they had only the three major networks and one local station that carried ancient reruns.

"That should keep them busy for a while," Frances said. "I've made some tea for us to have with our cookies. You sit down at the dining-room table and I'll bring it right in."

"Please, let me help," Karen said.

"The day I can't carry a plate of cookies and two cups of tea to the table is the day I'll check myself into that nursing home they built up the street a few years back," Frances said.

Karen knew better than to argue. Frances was as strong-willed and independent as anyone she'd ever met. It was probably the reason she was still doing so well on her own. Every now and then one of her children would come for a visit and drop in on Karen to see if she thought Frances was getting too feeble to be left alone.

Karen had never felt a need to shade the truth even slightly. Frances still had a sharp mind and plenty of energy for a woman her age. She was active at her church and made a trip to the library at least once a week to pick up something to read. Until a few months ago, she'd even volunteered at the regional hospital, but the long drive had gotten to be too much for her. Now she spent an hour or more a day checking on local shut-ins, calling or visiting them just to chat and to see if they needed anything more than a few minutes of company.

Though Frances's apartment was the same dimensions as Karen's, it was cozy and welcoming in a way Karen's was not. Maybe it was the lifetime of memories on display in pictures and collectibles. Every knickknack crowded onto every surface in the living room had a fascinating story behind it. Surprisingly the kids—even Mack—had learned to look, and not touch. On the one occasion when, to Karen's chagrin, something had gotten broken, Frances had waved off the incident.

"One less thing to dust," she'd said, sounding as if she meant it.

Now, as she poured tea into mismatched chintz teacups, she studied Karen intently. "You still have that worried look in your eyes. Did your meeting not go well?"

"Actually it went better than I'd expected," Karen admitted. "But the real test is going to be tomorrow. The attorney I saw thinks we should sit down with my boss and work out a solution to the problem I've been having getting to work lately. She's optimistic everything will work out. I'm not so sure."

"Surely you don't think Dana Sue would fire you," Frances said, clearly startled. "Is that what this is about?"

Karen nodded. "I wouldn't blame her if she did."

"Honey, she's one of the sweetest gals I've ever known. It's not in her nature to fire someone just because they've hit a rough patch. Did you know I taught her back in second grade?" She shook her head, a smile crinkling her face. "Oh, my, she was something back then. She made your Daisy look like a little angel."

Karen grinned. "I can't imagine that."

"I knew her mama and daddy real well because of it," Frances said. "And Dana Sue spent a lot of time-outs inside during recess, so I knew her real well, too. She reminds me of that every time I go to Sullivan's for lunch with my group from church. She says I was the last person who ever managed to keep her in check. I could speak to her, if you think it would help."

"The only thing that's really going to help is me finding someone to take care of the kids so I can get to work when I'm supposed to be there," Karen said.

Frances regarded her with regret. "You know I'd help if I could. I might be able to manage Daisy for a few hours, but I'm too old to be chasing after Mack."

"Believe me, there are days when I think *I'm* too old to handle Mack," Karen told her honestly. "I appreciate you taking them for a couple of hours every now and then. I would never ask you to deal with them any longer than that."

Frances gave her a sympathetic look. "Have you heard from their daddy lately? Has he made any of his child-support back payments?"

Karen shook her head. Just thinking about the way Ray had left her to fend for herself and their kids when he ran off made her head throb again. "I can't even think about that right now," she said, not trying to hide her bitterness. "I've gotta focus on keeping my job so I don't lose the roof over our heads."

"If that happens, you'll just move in here with me 'til things get straightened out," Frances said at once. "I will not let you and those babies be on the street, and that's that, so quit your worrying on that score."

"I couldn't," Karen protested.

"Of course, you could. Friends help each other out. I may not be able to watch those kids for you all day long, but I can certainly see that there's a roof over your heads."

Karen just sat there, stunned into silence. Though she prayed she would never have to take Frances up on her offer, that Frances had even made it was the most wonderful, generous thing anyone had ever done for her. Combined with Helen's willingness to help her fight for her job, a day that had started with nothing but worry was turning into one filled with blessings.

2

It was nearly seven when Helen finished with her last client. Barb had left an hour earlier, so she turned off the lights and closed up the office, relieved to have the workday behind her.

Outside she weighed the prospect of going home to her empty house against dropping in at Sullivan's for a decent meal and a few snatched minutes of Dana Sue's time. Anytime she could see one of the Sweet Magnolias, as they had once called themselves, she grabbed it. Maybe she could lay some groundwork before she and Karen met with her formally tomorrow at the restaurant. Barb had already set up that appointment for two o'clock, after the lunch crowd thinned out.

The restaurant, which specialized in what Dana Sue called new Southern cuisine, was packed, as it was most nights. Though Serenity's population was only 3500 or so, the restaurant's reputation had spread through the entire region thanks to excellent reviews in the Charleston and Columbia newspapers.

Helen was greeted at the door by Brenda, the harried waitress. "I should have a table opening up in a few minutes," she told Helen. "Do you mind waiting?"

"Not at all. Do you think I'll be risking life and limb if I stick my head in the kitchen to say hello to Dana Sue?"

Brenda grinned. "I'd say that depends on whether you're prepared to pitch in and help. She and Erik have their hands full tonight. It's been crazy ever since that review in the Columbia paper. If it's going to stay this busy, she needs to hire some additional prep staff for the kitchen and some more waitstaff. Paul and I have just about run ourselves to death tonight, even with the busboys pitching in. And just so you know, we ran out of all the specials an hour ago."

"I'll keep that in mind," Helen said, then headed for the kitchen.

When she pushed open the door and stepped in, she saw Dana Sue at the huge gas stove. Face flushed from the heat, Dana Sue juggled half a dozen different sauté pans, then slid the contents onto waiting plates, added the decorative sauces and spicy salsas, and moved them to a pickup area for the waitstaff.

Her expression filled with relief when she spotted Helen. "Grab an apron," she ordered. "We need you. It's nuts in here."

"Looks to me like what you need is more trained help. Where's Erik?" Helen asked as she whipped off her suit jacket, hung it on a peg in the pantry, then found an apron and put it on over her two-hundred-dollar designer silk blouse.

"Right behind you," a deep voice rumbled. "Watch your step. I'm loaded down."

She turned and found him carrying a tray laden with pies fresh from the oven. She could smell the heady aromas of peaches, cinnamon and vanilla.

"If you'll give me a slice of that, I'll be your slave for the rest of the night," she said.

Erik grinned at her. "I'll save you a whole pie, but you don't have time to eat it now. I need you to mix up another batch of the mango-papaya chutney for the fish." His gaze skimmed her outfit and he shook his head. "You realize that blouse is heading straight for the dry cleaner's after this, don't you?"

Helen shrugged. She had a dozen more in her closet. It wouldn't be a huge loss. "Not a problem."

His dark eyes warmed. "That's what I love about you. No pretensions. Underneath that icy courtroom demeanor that I hear you possess lies the soul of a woman ruled by a passion for food and a willingness to help out a friend in distress, no matter the personal cost."

The compliment caught her off guard. When the usually taciturn Erik popped out with something unexpected or insightful, as he occasionally did, it made her wonder what his story was. She winked at him. "I'm only this cavalier because I figure with the size of tonight's crowd, Dana Sue's good for the cost of another blouse."

"Don't," he protested. "You're ruining my illusions. Do you remember how to make the chutney?"

Helen shook her head. "But don't worry. I know where the recipes are. I'll get that one and find the supplies in the storeroom. I'll have another batch whipped up in no time. You don't need to supervise."

"As if," Dana Sue called out from her station by the stove. "Erik is so thrilled to have someone to supervise for once, he's not going to pass up the chance."

Within moments, Helen had fallen into the frantic rhythm of the kitchen. When she could, she snatched glances at Erik, admiring the efficiency with which he moved almost as much as she craved the desserts which he

excelled at making. Though he'd been hired primarily as
a pastry chef right after graduating from the Atlanta Culinary Institute—which he'd attended after apparently leaving some other career he never mentioned—his role in
Sullivan's kitchen had been expanded over time. Dana Sue
relied on him as her backup and had officially named him
as assistant manager just a few weeks earlier.

In his late 30s or early 40s, he had a wry wit, a gentle demeanor and was fiercely loyal to and protective of Dana Sue.
Helen liked that about him, almost as much as she liked
his pastries and occasionally lusted after his six-pack abs
and competent hands. That she lusted after him at all was
a surprise, because she'd always preferred polished ex-
ecutives over the strong, silent, athletic types.

Helen was relegated to the most basic duties for the next
two hours, but she liked being part of the hustle and bustle of the kitchen. The aromas were delectable, the excitement and stress palpable. If cooking at home were half this
much fun, she might do it more often. Instead her culinary
endeavors ran to scrambled eggs, when she remembered
to buy any, and the occasional baked potato. She did make
a damn fine margarita, though, if she did say so herself.
That was the result of a few summers in Hilton Head working as a bartender during law school. She'd made great tips,
great contacts and learned a lot about human nature.

By the time the last meal had been served and only a
few customers were lingering over coffee and dessert, she
was exhausted from being on her feet for so long, to say
nothing of being half-starved.

"Okay, you two, that's it," Erik said, hustling them toward the door to the dining room. "Get in there and sit
down. I'll bring you both dinner in a few minutes."

Dana Sue shook her head. "Only if you're going to join us," she told him. "You haven't had a break all night, either."

"Sure," Erik said. "But you need to eat now and Helen needs to kick off those ridiculous heels she insists on wearing."

Vaguely miffed by the comment, Helen stuck out her foot in its sexy high-heeled sandal, her most extravagant indulgence. "What's wrong with my shoes?"

Erik's gaze lingered on her foot with its perfectly manicured pink toenails, then traveled slowly up her leg to the hem of her skirt, now hitched up to show a couple of inches of thigh. "Speaking as a man, there is nothing wrong with those shoes," he told her, regarding her with amusement. "Speaking as someone who's watched you hobbling around in here for the past couple of hours, I'd say they're inappropriate for being on your feet for very long."

Mollified, she grinned. "You may have a point. If me pitching in around here is going to become a habit, I should probably keep some sneakers in Dana Sue's office."

Dana Sue gave her a startled look. "You own sneakers?"

"Don't be snide. What do you think I wear when I work out?"

"Oh, yeah, those customized things you created online in colors to match your workout clothes," Dana Sue said.

Erik looked at Helen in amusement. "What's wrong with the sneakers you buy at the mall?"

Helen gave him a disdainful look. "Everyone has them," she replied. "Come on, Dana Sue. I can't possibly deal with a man in faded jeans and a grease-stained T-shirt who doesn't understand fashion, no matter how sexy he thinks he is."

Erik chuckled, while Dana Sue said, "Right now, all I

care about is that he understands food." She gave Erik a
wink as she and Helen headed for the dining room and a
corner booth away from the few remaining customers.

As soon as they were seated, Helen groaned and kicked
off her shoes under the table. "Please don't tell Erik, okay?
These things *are* torture if I'm on my feet too long. They'll
definitely never be my dancin' shoes."

"Still, it's a small price to pay for looking sexy." Dana Sue
grinned. "I haven't worn shoes like that in years. I'd break
my neck."

"Next time you want to knock Ronnie's socks off, I'll
let you borrow a pair of mine," Helen said.

Dana Sue's eyebrows rose and fell. "I knock his socks
off no matter what I wear."

"Then the honeymoon's still not over?"

"You can stop asking me that, you know," Dana Sue said
smugly. "Ronnie and I expect to be in the honeymoon phase
for months and months. Maybe years. And this time around,
I'm going to do everything in my power to see to it that the
marriage never ends, even if the glow does wear off."

Helen regarded her wistfully. "I never thought I'd say this
about you getting back together with Ronnie, but I envy you."

Dana Sue regarded her with compassion, but she quickly
shifted to impatience. "Then what are you doing about it?
When was the last time you went on a date, and I don't
mean sitting down with some male attorney to discuss torts
or writs or whatever else it is you talk about over coffee."

"Who has time?" Helen said defensively. "Between
work, keeping up with things at the spa and trying to exercise more regularly, I don't have five spare minutes a week."

"Really?" Dana Sue said skeptically. "You just spent two
solid hours in my kitchen. That's enough for a quality date."

Helen shrugged. "That's fun. There's no pressure in there."

Dana Sue lifted an eyebrow. "Really? No pressure? Not even with Erik's exacting orders flying at you? He scared off the last two prep guys I brought in for a tryout."

"He's a perfectionist, that's all. Lord knows, I get that and respect it. And there's more at stake in there for you and for him. I'm just a volunteer worker bee from time to time. If I mess up, what are either of you going to do about it?"

"I'd probably banish you forever, but I can't speak for Erik," Dana Sue said. "By the way, was there some reason you came by tonight other than the chance we'd put you to work?"

"To be honest, I was hoping for a few minutes to talk to you," Helen admitted.

"About...?"

"Karen."

Dana Sue's eyes widened. "You want to talk to me about Karen Ames? Why? Is that why Barb called to set up an appointment for tomorrow afternoon? I thought it was about the spa." She held up her hand. "Wait. Here comes Erik with our food. If it involves Karen, he probably needs to hear this, too. And he should be at any meeting we have."

Erik set three plates of grouper, with its garnish of mango-papaya chutney, wild rice and a side of baby carrots in a brown sugar glaze on the table. Everything was as artfully arranged as it was for the paying customers.

"Where's my pie?" Helen asked immediately.

"Not 'til you've cleaned your plate," he teased, sliding into the booth beside her. "Pie's your reward, not your meal."

Helen frowned at him. "Who says?"

"The chef," he told her. "So. Dig in."

All three picked up their forks and started eating. After a

minute, Erik asked, "What were you two talking about when I got here? You looked awfully serious for a couple of women who were supposed to be kicking back and relaxing."

"Karen," Dana Sue told him, her expression somber. She took another bite of food. "Helen brought her up."

Erik stared at Helen, his expression immediately shifting into something far more cautious. "What do you have to do with Karen?"

"She came to see me today. She thinks she's about to be fired."

Dana Sue exchanged a rueful look with Erik that spoke volumes.

Helen sighed. "I see she was on target. It's because of the amount of time she's missed lately, right?"

Dana Sue nodded. "It makes me very unhappy, but I don't have a choice, Helen. I can't operate a kitchen if one of my key employees is absent half the time. Even if I do find the right prep person, as busy as we are I need an assistant I can count on."

"Do you know why she's absent?"

"Every time she calls in, it's always about the kids," Erik volunteered.

"And I sympathize with that, I really do," Dana Sue added. "But it comes back to my ability to keep this place running the way it needs to. It's not fair for Erik and me to have to pick up the slack all the time. I have to have an employee who's reliable." She studied Helen worriedly. "Is she going to make a legal issue out of this? Is that why she came to you?"

"No," Helen said, putting down her fork. "I don't think it needs to come to that and I wouldn't represent her if it did. I just want you to sit down with Karen and me tomorrow and see if there's not another solution, something that will enable you to run this kitchen the way it needs to be run, yet keeps her from losing her job."

"You're putting Dana Sue in an impossible position," Erik said protectively. "Come on, Helen, she's not the bad guy here."

"I know that," Helen said. "But Karen's not some irresponsible kid, either. You've spent a lot of time training her. Just let her explain and see if we can't come to some kind of solution."

Though Erik looked less than thrilled with the idea, Dana Sue nodded. "I can do that much."

"Thank you," Helen said, then turned to Erik and added sternly, "And you, reserve judgment, okay?"

"I'll do my best, since the champion of the underdog requests it, but I'm not happy about it. I intend to be at that meeting. And so you know, I'm a little surprised that you would take Karen's side over your best friend's."

Helen bristled. "I'm trying *not* to take sides," she retorted. "Successful negotiating means making this a win-win situation."

"Then tell me exactly what Dana Sue is getting out of this," he demanded.

"She gets to keep an excellent, well-trained employee," Helen replied, determined to keep her tone reasonable, though his attitude was starting to grate on her. He wasn't the only one who felt protective about Dana Sue. She'd been looking out for her friend a lot longer than he had. Her appetite fading, she said, "You know Karen's good. I've heard you say it more than once."

"Doesn't matter if she's never here," Erik said.

His refusal to give Karen a break riled her. "That's an exaggeration," she snapped, losing patience.

"Whoa," Dana Sue protested. "It's a meeting, Erik. We owe Karen that much. Helen's right. When Karen's here, she's been terrific."

"Just as long as you don't let your pal here railroad you into doing something that's not in the best interests of the restaurant," he said.

"I've never railroaded anyone in my life," Helen said, annoyed. Her appetite for her food completely vanished.

"Really?" Erik scoffed. "Whose idea was it to get Ronnie Sullivan out of town when he and Dana Sue split up? That really worked out well for their daughter, didn't it?"

Dana Sue regarded him with dismay. "Old news, Erik. Annie's fine now, and so are Ronnie and I."

"No thanks to Helen's interference," he said.

Helen glowered at him, stung by his accusation. When Dana Sue would have responded to his comment, Helen stopped her with a look. "I can fight my own battles," she said tightly. She faced Erik. "You weren't here. You have no idea what was best at the time."

"No," he agreed, leaning forward, his gaze intense. "I came along just in time to see all hell break loose when Annie landed in the hospital."

"That was *not* my fault," Helen said fiercely.

"Really? Her eating disorder was brought on to some degree because her father abandoned her, or did I get that part wrong?" He didn't wait for an answer before charging, "You made that happen."

"That's a little simplistic," Dana Sue said, though neither of them even looked at her.

Helen was practically nose-to-nose with Erik. "Where do you get off making an accusation like that?"

"Just calling it like I see it, sweetheart."

"Go to hell," Helen said, nudging Dana Sue until she moved out of the way so that Helen could slide out of the curved booth on the opposite side. She glanced at Dana Sue as she grabbed her shoes out from under the table. "I'll see you tomorrow," she said, then scowled at Erik. "I suggest you skip the meeting."

"Not a chance," he said. "Somebody has to make sure common sense reigns."

"And you have to be that somebody?" Helen asked. "How do you feel about that, Dana Sue?"

"I'm pretty much shell-shocked by the way this entire conversation has spun out of control," Dana Sue responded. "What is wrong with you two? I've never seen either of you act like this before."

"I guess know-it-all attorneys bring out the worst in me," Erik said stiffly.

"And judgmental men, who won't even listen to reason, bring it out in me," Helen said.

Erik gave her a once-over that made her blood almost as hot as her temper. "I guess that means you won't be wanting your pie, since I baked it."

The reminder of that peach pie, which had been all she could think about as she'd worked in the kitchen, created a major dilemma. Her mouth still watered when she thought about it. Her pride dictated she not let him know that.

"I never said that," she said huffily, then stalked into the kitchen and picked up the entire pie from the counter.

One bite, she thought as she drew in a deep breath and savored the aroma. What could it hurt? She put the pie down, grabbed a fork and dug into the fragrant peach mixture and flaky crust, then sighed as her temper simmered down a notch. Maybe two bites, she decided. Erik would never know. She ate the second mouthful, then picked up the pie again, marched straight back into the dining room and, before she could talk herself out of it, threw the remainder straight into his shocked face.

Beside him, Dana Sue sucked in a startled breath, then fought to contain laughter. Helen watched as the pie oozed down Erik's face and onto his T-shirt. She was so intent on watching it spread across his impressive chest that she apparently missed the wicked glint in his eyes until it was too late.

Before she could make a dash for it, he'd wiped most of the pie off his face and was on his feet. In an instant, he had his arms around her, his hot, demanding mouth on hers and the remains of that incredible peach pie crushed indelibly into her silk blouse.

Helen figured she could always buy another blouse, but it was going to take a whole lot longer to erase the memory of Erik's breath-stealing kiss from her head, especially with Dana Sue as an obviously fascinated witness. Dana Sue wouldn't let her forget it in this lifetime. And since there were still a couple of diners left in the restaurant and this was Serenity, it would be all over town by morning. Helen Decatur, the Sweet Magnolia with the most common sense, the one who got people out of trouble, had just landed in a pile of it.

When Erik finally released Helen from that ill-advised kiss, he cast Dana Sue an apologetic look, then headed for the kitchen. He needed to figure out what kind of insanity had possessed him to first taunt and then kiss a woman like Helen Decatur.

She *was* a pushy, arrogant, know-it-all attorney, but she was also his boss's best friend and a regular customer at Sullivan's. Moreover, on more than one occasion including tonight, she had willingly pitched in to help them out of a jam in the kitchen.

Maybe that was the problem, he concluded. It was one thing to disapprove of the fancy clothes and pretensions, but in the kitchen at Sullivan's he'd seen another side of her. He'd seen a woman who cared more about her friend and what she needed than she did about such superficial things as her designer clothes. She also checked her ego at the door and did whatever was asked of her without complaint. She did it damn well, too, if he was being totally honest. He actually liked her, most of the time, anyway. Tonight she'd just gotten under his skin for some reason. Despite what he'd said, he *did* know she'd never choose someone else's side over Dana Sue's.

Baiting her, he could understand. Kissing her, well, that was a whole other story, one destined for an unhappy ending. He'd crossed a line, a move for which he'd have to apologize eventually.

Of course, he couldn't help remembering that she'd kissed him back. In fact, she'd kissed him with such unexpected heat and passion, it had sent him running for cover. He hadn't run from a female since Susie Mackinaw had planted an unwanted kiss on him in third grade to the accompaniment of jeers from his friends.

No, he amended, pouring himself a cup of coffee and drinking it as he methodically began to clean the kitchen. The truth was he'd been running from women since his wife had died in childbirth. An EMT in Atlanta at the time, he'd been with Samantha in the ambulance after she'd gone into premature labor and begun hemorrhaging. The ride to the hospital had taken an eternity, and even before they'd arrived in the emergency room, he'd known it was too late. Sam had lost way too much blood, her vitals were fading and the baby was too early to be saved.

That was the day his heart had been ripped from his chest, right along with his ability to function in his job. If an EMT couldn't do something to save his own wife, how could he ever trust himself to help anyone else?

After a month's leave, during which he'd drunk himself into a stupor every single day, he'd walked into his boss's office and quit. Gabe Sanchez had argued with him, pleaded with him to get some counseling and then come back, but Erik had known that his days in any career tied to health care were over.

He might have drifted aimlessly after that, but a friend of his wife's had suggested he go to the Atlanta Culinary Institute. Erik had laughed at the idea at first, but Bree had kept badgering. Her husband had added his support for the idea as well.

"Out of our entire crowd, you're the best cook, hands down," Bree had told him. "More important, you enjoy it. If nothing else, taking the classes will get you out of this funk you're in. Once you graduate, who knows? Maybe you can open your own restaurant or become a caterer or just come to my house once a month and cook for Ben and me and the kids. It doesn't matter. The distraction is what's important. Sam would hate what you're doing to yourself. She wouldn't want you to grieve forever."

Erik might have dismissed the whole idea if Bree hadn't shown up on his doorstep a few days later with application forms. She'd sat right there while he filled them out, then written a check herself, tucked it all in an envelope and taken it with her to mail. Obviously she hadn't wanted to leave anything to chance.

"Consider it a gift toward your future from Ben and me," she said. "When you're running your own restaurant, you can pay us back with free dinners on our anniversaries."

A few weeks later, he'd been accepted and shortly after that he'd taken his first classes. By the end of the first month, he knew it was the best decision he'd ever made, next to marrying Samantha. By the time graduation rolled around, he wondered how he'd ever considered, much less worked in, any other field.

Then Dana Sue had contacted the school to find a pastry chef, which was Erik's specialty. He hadn't been convinced he wanted to move to a small town in South Carolina, but after he'd visited Serenity and seen Sullivan's, he'd been hooked. It was just the change he needed, a chance to get away from Atlanta and all of its memories. Moreover, Dana Sue had created something special in a community that was trying to turn itself around after some hard knocks to its economy. As all of the reviews had glowingly stated, Sullivan's was a rare culinary treasure and he was glad to be a part of it.

As for Dana Sue, she was something special, as well. He'd even harbored a vague notion that someday their relationship might move from professional to personal, but it had quickly become clear that the shapely blonde was still in love with her ex-husband.

Even so, Dana Sue, her daughter, Annie, and even the annoyingly unreliable Karen had become his family. And as hard-hearted as he'd obviously sounded to Helen, when it came to Karen what he most cared about was the toll her problems took on Dana Sue, who simply didn't need the added stress.

Unlike Dana Sue, Helen was not a woman who needed anyone to look out for her, which was yet another reason Erik was at a loss to explain why he'd kissed her so thoroughly a few minutes earlier. He was by nature a nurturer, a self-proclaimed knight in shining armor. The idea of tough-as-nails Helen needing nurturing was laughable.

Then again, maybe the kiss had been inevitable. She was a gorgeous woman, a little too uptight for him, a *lot* too opinionated. But sometimes just such a mix guaranteed an explosion sooner or later. Now that the kiss was behind him, the steam was released, and odds were it would never happen again.

He was just congratulating himself for making it all seem reasonable when Dana Sue came into the kitchen and joined him at the sink, where he was scrubbing pans. Picking up another pan from the sudsy water, she nudged him with her hip.

"So, what was that kiss all about?" she asked, keeping her gaze on the greasy pan in her hands.

"Pure impulse," he said, dismissing it.

"Something tells me the impulse has been coming on for some time. There's something in the air every time you two are in the same room."

"Tension," he suggested.

"*Sexual* tension, I think," she retorted, a glint in her eye. "Why haven't you done anything about it before?"

He rolled his eyes. "Helen and me? Are you crazy?"

"I don't think so. You're an incredible man. She's an incredible woman. Both of you deserve someone special in your lives."

"I don't know about Helen, but I'm not looking for a relationship," he said.

"You used to say you wanted me," she reminded him.

He grinned. "Because I knew there wasn't a chance in hell you'd say yes."

"So you claimed to want me only because I was unattainable?"

"Exactly."

"Not buying it. If you like the challenge of the unattainable, then Helen's an even better bet. Think of the fun you could have trying to change her mind."

"And then what? Tell her it was all just a game?"

"No, you idiot. Then you fall madly in love and marry her."

Erik laughed. "I don't see that happening. Somehow I just can't picture Helen's designer duds hanging next to my Levi's in the closet."

"After that kiss tonight, I can see it," Dana Sue told him. "And judging from the way Helen ran out of here, I think she can see it, too."

"Stop meddling, Dana Sue. She's your friend and that alone is reason enough for me to stay away from her."

"Why? I'm giving you my permission to pursue this. In fact, I'm encouraging it."

"And what happens when one of us gets our heart broken? Whose side do you take?"

She looked vaguely disconcerted by the question. "It would never come to that," she declared.

"Really? You can see into the future?"

"No, but I have faith in both of you, and I saw something tonight, a spark, that hasn't been there before in either one of you. Passion—the real deal that leads to love—is a rarity.

I'm here to tell you that a spark like that shouldn't be ignored."

"Well, I'm ignoring it," he said flatly.

"We'll see," she taunted. "I'm sure I can think of some way to change your mind." She shrugged. "Or Helen's. It'll only take convincing one of you to get this ball rolling."

"It's not up to you," he said, even though he could see he was wasting his breath. He was just going to have to be on high alert from now on.

Damn. That meeting tomorrow. He'd have to be in the same room as Helen and Dana Sue when the memory of that searing kiss was just a little too fresh in his mind.

3

Karen's heart was in her throat all during the first part of her shift prior to the meeting Helen had scheduled for two in the afternoon. Erik kept shooting daggers at her, as if he was really ticked off about something. She got the impression he'd been against the meeting. Dana Sue was trying to overcompensate by being extra nice, but the tension in the kitchen was really beginning to take a toll on Karen.

Added to that, they'd had one customer from hell, who'd sent her meal back three times. Erik and Dana Sue had finally drawn straws to decide which one of them would go into the dining room to deal with her and take a stab at making sure she left Sullivan's happy. Dana Sue had drawn the short straw. Free champagne and dessert for everyone at the table finally soothed the woman, but the whole exchange had ruined Dana Sue's mood. It was now as dark as Erik's.

At precisely two o'clock, Helen sashayed in, wearing one of those power suits she favored, a pair of Jimmy Choo shoes that probably cost more than Karen made in a week, maybe even a month, and designer sunglasses that she didn't remove.

Pointedly ignoring Erik, she smiled at Karen, then

turned to Dana Sue. "Where do you want to meet? It's going to be a little crowded in your office, unless Erik has decided to skip the meeting."

There was a cool, antagonistic note in her voice that Karen didn't recognize. Something told her it didn't bode well for the discussion to come.

"Not a chance," Erik replied tightly, adding to the tense atmosphere.

"The last of the customers have gone. We can sit in the dining room," Dana Sue said briskly. "Karen, you want a soda or something? Helen?"

"I'm good," Karen said, too nervous to even try to swallow something while her future was at stake.

"Nothing for me," Helen said.

"Then let's get started, shall we?" Dana Sue said with obviously forced cheer, leading the way.

"Could I see you for a minute first, Helen?" Erik asked, his expression grim.

Dana Sue tucked her arm through Karen's and immediately steered her through the door into the dining room. "We'll give you a minute alone," she said to the two of them.

"What's that about?" Karen asked in a hushed voice.

Dana Sue grinned. "They had a little disagreement last night. Trust me, it'll be a whole lot better if they work it out before this meeting."

Almost before the words were out of Dana Sue's mouth, though, Helen appeared right behind them, her expression as grim as Erik's.

Karen leveled a worried look at Dana Sue and leaned close to whisper, "That's not a good sign, is it?"

Dana Sue sighed. "Not especially," she said, frowning

when Erik emerged from the kitchen right on Helen's heels, his own expression even stormier than before.

"Okay," Helen said when they were all seated. "Remember, this is just a conversation among friends. The goal is to work out a solution all of you can live with. Karen's well aware that her absences lately have put a real strain on the two of you. Karen, why don't you tell them what's been going on and why you haven't spoken up before now?"

Swallowing hard, Karen avoided Erik's unyielding expression and focused on Dana Sue as she explained about the kids having the measles, the babysitter quitting and the financial stress she'd been under with Ray not sending child-support payments.

"I haven't told you before because *my* personal problems shouldn't be your problems," she said. "I know I've been unreliable and that it's unacceptable. But I swear to you if you can just bear with me a little longer until I can make permanent arrangements for someone responsible to watch the kids for me, I will be here every single minute I'm supposed to be. I won't have to hunt for someone new every day."

Helen held up a hand. "Don't make promises you can't keep, Karen. Let's face it, being a single mom is unpredictable. Dana Sue, you certainly know all about that. Here's what I suggest, especially after being here last night. Isn't it time you considered hiring another chef, or at least some prep staff who can be trained just the way you've trained Karen? That way if Karen *does* have another one of these inevitable crises, you'll have some backup."

"Why should Karen's problems force Dana Sue to hire additional staff?" Erik demanded.

"Because you need the help, anyway," Helen said before

Dana Sue could answer. "Karen wasn't scheduled last night and it was crazy in the kitchen. If I hadn't shown up—"

"We'd have managed," Erik interrupted. "We always do."

"Come on, Erik, Helen's right," Dana Sue cut in. "We really are understaffed for the size of the dinner crowd lately. I've interviewed half a dozen people for prep work and given two of them a trial run, but neither one was right for us. I really need to accelerate that search. I've been putting off doing anything about it, because I wasn't sure the popularity of this place would last. That sometimes happens after rave reviews. The kitchen can't keep up for a few weeks and then people go back to their usual routine and you've got more staff underfoot and counting on you than you need and you have to let people go."

"Hiring someone to do prep work is one thing," Erik conceded. "But as long as we're still counting on Karen to be here, how does that solve the problem if she bails?"

"Another trained person can come in if Karen has an emergency," Helen said.

"And be paid overtime wages?" Erik asked. "How is that fair to Dana Sue? She has to think about costs, you know. And prep work is a far cry from being her assistant or sous chef. We need someone who can move into that position, now that I'm assistant manager."

Karen studied Erik and Helen and knew there was something going on between them that had nothing to do with her. It was clear, though, that this discussion wasn't going to work in her favor unless she stepped in with a solution of her own. Fortunately sometime in the middle of the night she'd actually come up with one. Until now she'd been hesitant to offer it, but it was beginning to seem as if she had nothing to lose.

"I have an idea," she said quietly.

All three of them looked at her in surprise, almost as if they'd forgotten she was there.

"Go ahead," Helen encouraged.

"I worked with another cook at the diner 'til she had to leave. She had the same problem I'm having now. She was a single mom and her kids had to come first. Doug fired her, just the way I know you two have been debating about firing me. Anyway, Tess was really, really good, but she took a job telemarketing, so she could work at home. I know she hates it and would love to get back to work in a restaurant."

Erik's scowl deepened. "If she's already been fired for being unreliable, why would we ask for more problems by hiring her?"

"Because, frankly, she's got exactly the skills you need," Karen told him, determined not to back down in the face of his skepticism. She needed to fight for herself. To do that she had to convince them to at least give Tess a try. "She's fast. She's a quick learner. She's creative. She doesn't get rattled in a crisis. And she already knows her way around a kitchen."

"That still doesn't address the key problem," Erik said.

"Let her finish, for goodness' sakes," Helen snapped.

"Well, pardon me all to hell for wondering how this solves anything," Erik retorted, his gaze locked with Helen's.

Suddenly Karen got it. Whatever tiff those two had gotten into, it was because something personal was going on between them. She hadn't heard anything about them dating, but that didn't mean it hadn't happened. There were enough sparks bouncing around to set the tablecloth on fire.

Biting back a grin, she waved a hand to catch their attention. Dana Sue looked equally amused.

"Here's my idea," Karen said. "Let me and Tess share the job as sous-chef."

Helen looked startled, but to Karen's relief Dana Sue looked intrigued.

"How would that work?" Dana Sue asked. "Don't you both need a full-time job?"

Karen nodded. "But you're open six days a week, right? And you're open more than eight hours a day. One of us could work three days, the other four, and you could schedule our shifts to overlap. You need the extra help anyway on weekends. The sharing part would be that Tess and I would adjust that schedule between us if one of us had an emergency, so you'd never be left without a sous-chef. You'd have two trained people and you'd be covered all the time. The odds of both of us having an emergency on the same day are slight."

"I like it!" Helen said eagerly. "Dana Sue, what do you think?"

Karen held her breath.

"It could work," Dana Sue said slowly. "We do need the extra coverage. I'd have to meet Tess and see if she can handle the job or if she even wants it, but it would solve a lot of problems. Erik, what do you think?"

Though his expression remained grim, he nodded. "It has potential, as long as at least one of you shows up, no matter what," he conceded grudgingly. For the first time, he actually looked at Karen. "That's one of the traits I've always liked about you. You do think outside the box and you're not afraid to try new things."

Karen smiled at him. "Thanks. This time it was mainly out of desperation, but I really do think you're both going to love Tess. She's bright and energetic and loyal. She'd fit in perfectly here. And I know she and I can work things out so you're never short staffed."

"Okay, then, have her call me," Dana Sue said. "We'll get her in here and give her a try."

Helen sat back, a satisfied smile on her face. "A win-win solution. Good job, Karen. Thanks, Dana Sue."

Karen noticed she pointedly ignored Erik as she stood up. "I need to get back to the office," Helen said.

This time Erik shot out of the booth. "I'll walk with you," he said in a determined tone that silenced any argument. "Back in ten minutes, Dana Sue."

Dana Sue stared after him. "Take all the time you need."

After they'd gone, Karen met Dana Sue's amused gaze. "Are those two…?"

"Not yet," Dana Sue said. "But I predict it won't be long."

"My, my," Karen murmured, laying on a thick Southern drawl, "I do believe I could use some iced tea. It's gotten a little warm in here and I'm parched."

Dana Sue laughed. "Isn't that the truth? Come on. I'll join you. Something tells me we're going to be on our own for a while in the kitchen."

Helen was sorry she'd walked over to Sullivan's from her office. If she'd driven, she could have gotten in her car and slammed the door in Erik's face. Instead, he was walking along beside her in an increasingly awkward silence. Finally she could stand it no longer.

"If there's something on your mind, just say it," she demanded. "Otherwise, leave me alone."

"I'm trying to figure out what to say," he admitted.

"'I'm sorry' has a nice ring to it. Or 'I was wrong.' That's a good one."

"Okay, both of those," he said, his lips twitching.

She stopped and whirled around to look him in the eye. "That's it? I throw you a couple of options and you don't even repeat them or put your own pitiful spin on them?"

"But you're the one who's so good with words," he returned dryly. "I figured you put it exactly the way you wanted to hear it."

Helen rolled her eyes. "Oh, for heaven's sake, do you even know what you're apologizing for?"

"The kiss?" he suggested uncertainly.

The hint of vulnerability in a man who'd always struck her as supremely confident cut through her defenses. "That would be a good place to start," she agreed.

"There's more?" he asked.

Though his tone was perfectly serious, she thought she detected a hint of teasing. "You're darn straight, there's more. How about the fact that you were behaving like a horse's behind about Karen?"

"I was trying to look out for the restaurant's best interests," he said. "Something I thought would matter to you, you being Dana Sue's good friend and all."

"Of course that matters to me," she retorted. "So, don't you think the solution we worked out in there is the best thing for everybody?"

"Possibly," he said. "But by Karen's own admission, her friend was fired for being unreliable. In my book, that's not a terrific recommendation, no matter what her skills are."

"Not only a horse's behind, but stubborn as a mule, too," Helen muttered under her breath.

"I heard that," he said.

"As I intended," she replied, then studied him curiously. "I thought you liked Karen."

"I like a lot of people I don't want working in my kitchen," he said. "Not if they're not going to show up when they're supposed to."

Helen's lips curved in a small smile and she resumed walking. "Does that also mean you don't mind having someone you dislike working in your kitchen?"

"If they do the job well," he said, his gaze narrowing as he strode beside her. "What's your point?"

"You don't seem overly fond of me at the moment."

"Because you're annoying the hell out of me right now."

"And last night?" she teased.

"And last night," he agreed.

"And yet we worked so well together. Interesting," she said thoughtfully.

"What's so interesting about that?"

"The way your mind works. Can I ask you something else?"

"I don't imagine I can stop you, interrogation being one of your primary work skills."

"How did the kiss fit in?" she asked, clearly catching him off guard. Color bloomed in his cheeks.

"I apologized for that," he reminded her.

"I know, but what sparked it? A sudden attack of lust, the heat of the argument, a desire to get even because of the pie I'd tossed at you?"

"I wish to hell I knew," he said.

"Come on. Think about it," she prodded, stopping to look at him. "I just want to know so I can avoid triggering that particular response again."

"You and me both," he said, then studied her intently. "You seemed to be into it at the time."

"I most certainly was not!" she replied indignantly.

"Bet I could prove what a liar you are."

Now there was a challenge that was best avoided. And since she seemed to be increasingly off balance around Erik, maybe it was time to turn the tables. After all, the man was seriously cute when he was befuddled. Feeling downright daring, she reached up and pressed a kiss to his cheek, hoping to throw him even further off-kilter.

"Let me know when you figure out how we wound up with our lips locked," she said. "We walked past my office five minutes ago and I need to get back there. See you."

"Hold it!" he commanded before she could leave. "What about the apology you owe me?"

Helen frowned. "Excuse me?"

"That pie you tossed in my face," he reminded her.

"You deserved it," she said.

"Maybe you deserved that kiss," he said. "Maybe I should take back that apology. After all, it could happen again."

Helen gave him a hard look. "Don't even think about it."

There was a daring gleam in his eye as he took a step in her direction. She backed up and nearly tripped over a crack in the sidewalk.

"Okay, okay, I'm sorry about the damn pie," she said hurriedly. "Now I really do have to go."

She spun around and took off in the direction of her office as fast as she could, given the three-inch heels she wore. Viewed from Erik's vantage point, her haste probably wasn't a pretty sight, but impressing him wasn't real high on her priority list right now.

"Women!" Erik muttered as he watched Helen cut across the grass in an awkward gait and run up the front steps to her office.

But it wasn't women in general who made him nuts. It was *this* woman. He needed to stay as far away from Helen as humanly possible. Maybe he could figure out some way to get Dana Sue to ban her from the kitchen at Sullivan's. No, that was impossible, given Dana Sue's apparent match-making scheme, which, now that he thought about it, had probably kicked into gear months ago, when Helen had first been drafted into kitchen duty. If he suggested now that Helen didn't belong in the restaurant kitchen, he could all but guarantee that's where she'd turn up. Better to keep his mouth shut.

When he got back to Sullivan's, Karen and Dana Sue both avoided looking at him. He figured that wouldn't last, either. Dana Sue's curiosity would eventually get the better of her. When it came to cross-examining, she came in a close second to her attorney pal.

Thankfully he still had to finish the preparations for tonight's dessert special, an apple bread pudding that had become a customer favorite. It was on the menu every Friday night. Working quickly, he assembled the ingredients, filled two large baking pans with the bread-and-apple mixture, then poured the blended liquid ingredients over the top and popped both pans in the oven. After baking, it would be cut into squares, then served warm with a caramel sauce, whipped cream or cinnamon ice cream, according to the customer's preference.

Just as the pans went into the oven, he noticed Dana Sue studying him intently, but before she could accost him with questions, her husband walked in and her attention immediately shifted to him. Erik figured he owed the man a beer for his excellent timing.

"Hey, Erik, Karen," Ronnie said as he made a beeline

for his wife and pulled her into his arms. "Hey, you. How's my favorite chef?"

Dana Sue glanced pointedly in Erik's direction. "Actually I was about to suggest to Erik that we take a break before the dinner rush."

"Too busy," Erik said, heading toward the pantry in search of the ingredients for walnut brownies he could make now and freeze for later.

"Doing what?" Dana Sue asked, regarding him suspiciously.

"I thought I'd get a head start on next week and make up some brownies," he told her.

Dana Sue beamed at him. "Sounds like an excuse to avoid talking to me." She linked an arm through his. "Let's take a break. Ronnie, how about bringing some iced tea out for all of us?"

Ronnie regarded Erik with sympathy. "Sorry, pal. She's the boss."

"At home, too?" Erik asked.

Ronnie grinned. "At home there's a delicate balance of power that's ever-changing," he replied. "Unfortunately, for your sake, we're in her restaurant now. I have zero standing here."

"Pitiful," Erik said. "I thought men were supposed to stick together."

"Normally, yes," Ronnie agreed. "But in this instance, I have to admit to being a little curious myself about why the prospect of talking to my wife has you as jittery as a june bug."

"Are you two through yet?" Dana Sue was impatient. "At this rate, there won't be any time left for a nice long chat."

"Now *there's* a reason to celebrate," Erik muttered.

Across the kitchen, Karen giggled, then buried her face in a paper towel in a futile attempt to smother her laughter.

"Another traitor," Erik noted. "Okay, let's get this inquisition over with."

Dana Sue frowned at him. "It's hardly an inquisition," she said, leading him to a booth in the dining room. "Just one friend catching up with another one."

Erik smiled despite his deteriorating mood. "How much catching up can we possibly have to do?"

"You were gone half an hour," she said. "A lot can happen in half an hour." She sat and patted the seat beside her. "Sit right here."

"I think you should reserve that spot for your husband," Erik said. "I'll sit over here." He sat on the edge all the way around on the other side of the table, as far away as he could possibly get and still be in the same booth.

Dana Sue regarded him with amusement. "How did your chat go with Helen? Did you two kiss and make up?" she asked just as Ronnie joined them.

Ronnie's eyebrows shot up. "You and Helen? Now that's something I never would have imagined."

"Be quiet," Dana Sue ordered.

"There is no me and Helen," Erik assured him. "It's all in your wife's imagination."

"I did not imagine that kiss last night," Dana Sue told him. "That kiss was hot enough to solder steel."

"How much do you know about soldering steel?" Erik asked.

"Beside the point," Dana Sue retorted. "You get the picture. Now, answer me. Did you kiss and make up when you walked her back to her office?"

"We walked. We talked. End of story. May I go now?" Erik said. "My bread pudding is probably burned to a crisp."

"It's not due out of the oven for another ten minutes and you know it," Dana Sue said without hesitation. "I want details about what happened between you and Helen."

Erik slid out of the booth. "Then call Helen. The doors of this place open in less than an hour and I have work to do, something I would think that you, as the owner, would remember."

He walked away without looking back.

"I won't forget about this," Dana Sue called after him.

Sadly, he knew that was the truth. Like most women, Dana Sue had a long memory. Worse yet, she had a streak of determination that could rival a wartime general's. Something told him her full-throttle campaign to get him hooked up with Helen had just begun.

4

Helen hadn't been able to forget the way her evening had ended at Sullivan's a few days earlier. Nor had she been able to forget the speculative glances Dana Sue had given her and Erik during their tense meeting with Karen the next day. She knew that kind of look. Her friend thought there was something going on between Erik and her. Or maybe she just *wanted* something to be going on so she could feel good about her matchmaking skills. Either way, Helen was not looking forward to her next encounter with Dana Sue and the questions that awaited.

Unfortunately, she couldn't put off seeing her any longer. She, Dana Sue and Maddie were scheduled for one of their morning get-togethers at The Corner Spa today. Since Helen had been all for these regular meetings to discuss spa business, she could hardly skip one. Her absence would just bring Dana Sue's curiosity to a boil.

Besides, what with Maddie's increasingly hectic schedule—a new husband and a new baby took up most of her time—and Dana Sue's demands at Sullivan's and her remarriage to Ronnie, the three of them hardly had any time to themselves anymore. Helen missed their leisurely chats.

She'd started to feel a little like an outsider in their busy lives, though both of them would be appalled if they knew she felt that way.

Filled with a peculiar sense of dread, she braced herself as she walked through the bustling workout room. Personal trainer Elliott Cruz waved to her, as did several of the women who were sweating through a spinning class. The instructor was really putting them through their paces on the stationary bikes.

Helen paused to stick her head into the lavender-scented spa area where Jeanette was busy giving a facial to a blissful customer. The relaxing aroma reminded Helen that she'd been promising herself a massage for weeks now, hoping it would ease the constant tension in her shoulders.

"Everything okay with you?" she asked Jeanette, whom they'd stolen from a very upscale spa in Charleston. With her very short black hair and huge dark eyes, there was something exotic about Jeanette that made most of their clientele think she'd come from Europe. At least until they heard her speak. Her accent was as slow and sugary sweet as any South Carolinian's.

"Perfect," Jeanette told her. "Be sure to ask Maddie about the idea I had the other day."

"Will do," Helen promised.

Jeanette had more ideas, most of them excellent, than everyone else combined. She'd brought a lot of experience and creativity with her when she'd come to work for them. Their day spa services had increased in revenue at an even faster clip than their gym memberships. The days of Helen thinking of her investment in The Corner Spa as a tax shelter were long past. The place filled a surprisingly large niche in the region and business was booming.

Jeanette had already justified the expense of adding another technician to help handle the ever-increasing number and range of beauty treatments and massages they offered to a clientele who wanted to be truly pampered. Even the women of Serenity, who'd never even considered the extravagance of getting a massage, were signing up to treat themselves on special occasions. And, thanks to Jeanette's word-of-mouth promotion, they'd sold a dozen gift certificates in the past week alone before Maddie had even had a chance to make their spa package marketing plan. If this kept up, The Corner Spa was single-handedly going to turn the previously well-kept secret of Serenity's small-town charm into a tourist destination.

When Helen couldn't put it off a second longer, she wandered onto the patio and spotted Maddie in the shade with her eyes closed. Obviously she'd seized the opportunity for a little catnap. Helen hesitated to interrupt her.

Maddie had only recently told them that she was pregnant for the second time since her marriage to Cal, something she claimed had taken both of them by surprise. Still, her previous pregnancy had gone so smoothly and she and Cal were so delighted with their daughter that she'd taken the fact of her second pregnancy in stride, though Maddie admitted she'd kept it to herself through the first trimester just in case there were complications.

Helen was the one who'd been thrown. Why did it seem to be so easy for Maddie to have a baby while she herself continued to wrestle with the decision about whether to take measures to have a child of her own? Sometime during the past year, watching Maddie breeze through her pregnancy with a doting husband by her side, holding baby Jessica Lynn in her arms and breathing in that powdery, just-bathed baby scent, Helen had become increasingly obsessed with the idea of having her own child. The depth of the yearning had caught her completely off guard. Up until then, she thought she'd been content and fulfilled with her single lifestyle and playing doting aunt to her friends' children.

Once the yearning had surfaced, though, it had taken over most of her waking moments, at least when she wasn't drowning in a sea of court documents. Lately she'd been working hard to get her high blood pressure in check, as the two high-risk pregnancy obstetricians she'd visited had advised. She'd made a dozen lists of the pros and cons about seizing her dream by whatever means necessary. But when it came down to actually taking the next step, she'd hesitated. She didn't know what to make of her un-characteristic indecisiveness. Something was holding her back, but she had no idea what.

Pushing aside her own doubts and her envy of Maddie's pregnancy, she plastered a smile on her face and went to join her friend.

"Are you sure you're only a few months along?" Helen asked, waking Maddie from her nap. She patted the mound of her tummy. "Seems to me you weren't showing this much this early with any of your other kids. Maybe you're having twins this time."

"Bite your tongue," Maddie said. "One baby at a time is more than enough. I hate to think how exhausted I'd be if there were two of them."

Helen regarded her with concern. "If you're that tired, shouldn't you be at home with your feet up?"

Maddie grinned. "I work for these tyrants," she ex-plained. "This place gets busier and more demanding every day. I can't get any time off. Besides, the baby's not due for months."

Helen sat down and studied Maddie's glowing face. With four children already—three from her first marriage to pediatrician Bill Townsend—forty-two-year-old Maddie hadn't been nearly as anxious as Cal to try again, but looking at her now, Helen knew that she was as excited about the new arrival as her husband.

Maddie studied Helen with a knowing look. "You haven't said much about it for quite a while now, but you're still thinking about having a baby, too, aren't you?"

Helen nodded. "I had no idea I'd ever feel such a strong maternal yearning, but every time you hand me Jessica Lynn and she looks up at me with those big blue eyes and blows those tiny little bubbles or smiles at me, it makes me realize just how much I've missed in my life."

"And?" Maddie prodded. "Did you ever follow through and talk to a doctor about whether your high blood pressure presents too much of a risk? When you didn't mention it, Dana Sue and I figured that you'd dropped the whole idea."

"To be honest, I'm a little surprised you haven't pestered me about it long before now," Helen said. "You're usually not that hesitant to poke about in my life."

"This is one of those decisions that's yours to make. Neither of us wanted to sway you one way or another. So, did you follow through or not?"

Helen wasn't sure why she'd kept those doctor visits a secret, but when confronted with a direct question, she saw no reason to lie. "I've seen two high-risk pregnancy experts," she admitted. "Both of them have said that if I promised to take extremely good care of myself and stay in bed at the first sign of blood pressure problems, I could go ahead with a pregnancy."

Maddie's brows drew together. "Then why do you look so unhappy? Isn't that exactly the news you were hoping for?"

Helen nodded. "Then I bumped straight into reality. Getting pregnant isn't the slam dunk I thought it would be. I mean, some women get pregnant just by going to bed with somebody once, but somehow I don't see myself going out and having some casual fling, hoping to get a baby out of it."

Maddie smiled. "Yes, I imagine you'd want to know the man's entire medical history and his pedigree, which pretty much rules out the whole casual thing."

Helen frowned at her because the remark hit a little too close to the truth. "My point is that this should mean something, you know? I can't imagine telling my son or daughter someday that I met their dad in a bar and never saw him again."

"Okay. What about artificial insemination?"

"I've thought about it," Helen said. "Even did some research on fertility clinics that do the procedure. There are very reputable ones. I could either bring in a donor or use one of their anonymous ones." She struggled to put her feelings into words. "It just seems so, I don't know, *artificial*. To be honest," Helen went on, "my reaction threw me. You know me. I take charge. I don't think I need anybody for anything, but the idea of having a baby that way seemed too cold and impersonal."

"So you've just given up?" Maddie asked, clearly surprised.

"No," Helen protested. "I've just taken a step back. I've been thinking about it."

"Making lists?" Maddie asked.

"Yes, I've made lists," Helen replied. "If more people did that, they'd make fewer mistakes."

"Whoa!" Maddie said. "On any level whatsoever, do you see having a child of your own as a mistake?"

Helen winced at the heat in Maddie's voice. "Don't say it like that. I told you that getting pregnant was only one of my concerns. What if I'm too selfish, too self-absorbed, too busy to be a really good mom?"

"Ah, so that's it," Maddie said. "Self-doubts plague just about everyone contemplating having a baby for the first time. You're not unique."

"I'm trying to be responsible," Helen said defensively. "I'm older. I'm alone. Is that going to be the best thing for a child? By the time my child's in kindergarten, the other kids will have grandmas my age."

"You're exaggerating," Maddie said.

"Only a little bit."

"Do you want to know what I think?" Maddie asked, then went on without waiting for Helen's reply. "I think you're just plain scared. This would be a huge step, a big change in your life and for all of your claims to being a modern, totally independent woman, you're terrified that you'll finally find something in life at which you can't excel."

Miffed at Maddie's perceptiveness, Helen said, "Well, you have to admit it would be a really bad thing to mess up."

"Okay, let's go back to basics," Maddie suggested, studying Helen intently. "Are you really sure you want a baby? Or do you just like the *idea* of having a baby?"

Helen regarded her miserably. "I wish I knew."

"Have you ever known yourself not to go after something you really, really wanted?" Maddie pressed.

"Are you saying you don't believe I want a child at all?" Helen asked, startled by the thought.

"I'm only suggesting that your biological clock started ticking loudly when I got pregnant with Jessica Lynn and you realized it was now or never." She reached for Helen's hand. "Maybe it's never, sweetie. Not every woman has to have a child to be fulfilled. Maybe what you're really longing for is a powerful connection to another person."

"A man?" Helen asked incredulously. "You're suggesting I forget about a baby and just find myself a man? Now there's an enlightened point of view. Come on, Maddie. I think I know myself a little better than that. Besides, of all people, I know that relationships don't always last. Why would I want to set myself up for heartache?"

"I'm just telling you that maybe what you're feeling is an emptiness in your life that could be filled in some other way. If you haven't taken steps by now to have a baby, then perhaps on some subconscious level, you know that's not really what you want."

"Or maybe I just want one the old-fashioned way," Helen retorted, annoyed that Maddie was questioning her determination, even if she was asking questions Helen had asked herself a million times. "Did you ever think of that? Maybe I want a man and a baby and the whole family thing that you and Dana Sue have."

"But you just said…" Maddie began, obviously confused.

Helen could hardly blame her. She was confused herself. To her dismay, tears welled up in her eyes and spilled down her cheeks. "Excuse me. I need to get out of here."

"Helen?" Maddie called after her. "Come back here. Let's talk about this."

But Helen made a clean getaway—which she'd hear about

later. In fact, she'd probably find Maddie and Dana Sue on her doorstep before the sun set. Although, maybe by then she'd somehow figure out what the hell was really going on with her and why this decision about a baby was the only one she'd ever been incapable of making.

Erik had come to work early, hoping to get enough done to cut out the second Dana Sue arrived and thereby avoid another conversation about his love life, or lack thereof.

He was surprised when the back door inched open and Annie Sullivan, Dana Sue's daughter, stuck her head in. "Is it okay to come in?" the seventeen-year-old inquired. "Are you really busy?"

"Just getting a head start on my day," he said, gesturing for her to come in. "Shouldn't you be in school?"

"Not for another hour," Annie told him, dropping her books by the door and climbing onto the stool beside his prep area. "My mom's not around, is she?"

"No. Why?" he asked. "Were you hoping she would be?"

"No. Actually I wanted to talk to you."

Erik regarded her suspiciously. "Why?"

"Because you're a guy and you're not my dad."

"An unbiased male point of view is what you're after," he concluded. "Are you sure I'm the right person? I'm not exactly a relationship expert. I assume this is about Ty."

She grinned. "Of course."

Ever since Annie's hospitalization with severe complications from anorexia, she and Maddie's son Tyler had gotten closer. They'd always been family friends, but Annie had wanted more, and Ty seemed to be showing some interest at long last. They'd been on half a dozen "real" dates, as Annie liked to call them, before Ty left for college, though both of them stopped short of saying they were actually a couple.

"What's your question?" Erik asked, studying her closely for signs that she'd fallen back into her old harmful eating patterns. It didn't matter how frequently he saw her, he couldn't seem to stop himself from checking. Fortunately her complexion had a healthy glow, her hair was shining, and even more telling, she was wearing clothes that fit and showed off a figure that was still a little on the thin side, but far from the skeletal form it had been a year ago.

"You know Ty's at Duke," she began.

Erik bit back a grin. "You've mentioned it a time or two since he left for school last fall."

Annie frowned at his teasing. "I mention it so much because it's amazing that I actually know a guy who's at Duke and who's the star of their baseball team, even though he's only a freshman. What's even more amazing is that we go out once in a while to movies and parties. He's even…" She blushed furiously.

Erik's gaze narrowed. "He's even what?"

"Kissed me," she confessed shyly. "It was totally awesome."

Although he wasn't her father, Erik felt like it sometimes, so close was he to the family. And like a father he did not want to hear about any guy, even a responsible young man like Tyler, kissing Annie. For sure Ronnie wouldn't be thrilled about it, either, even if kids their age often did a whole lot more than kiss. Still, maybe it was a good sign that Annie was talking about it. If things had gone beyond the kissing stage, he suspected she'd keep it to herself. He was so out of his depth with this stuff!

"You know there's nothing amazing about Ty liking

you," he told her, opting for a lesson in self-esteem. "You're a terrific young woman. You could have a dozen boyfriends at a dozen different colleges if you wanted them."

"You're just biased, like my dad," she scoffed. "Anyway, my question is whether I should ask Ty to come home to take me to my senior prom or whether that would be totally lame."

"Isn't prom coming up soon?" Erik asked. "I think your mom mentioned something about taking you to Charleston to shop for a dress."

"It's three weeks away," she said. "So it's practically last-minute if I ask him now."

"Why have you put off asking him?"

"It feels weird. It's not like we're exclusive or anything. Don't guys like to do the asking?"

"As a general rule, yes," Erik told her. "But this is your event, not his. My guess is that Ty's probably wondering why you haven't already asked. You said yourself you're not dating each other exclusively. What if he thinks you're going with some other guy?"

"But I would never do that," Annie said, her expression dismayed. "I don't even want to see other boys."

"Then, if you want him to go, ask him. A man appreciates a woman who's direct with him." He winked at her. "Unlike women, we're pretty simple creatures. Be straightforward and honest with us and we'll go along with the program. Women are the mysterious, complicated ones."

"I wonder if Ty thinks I'm mysterious and complicated," Annie asked, looking intrigued with the idea.

"I can just about guarantee it. He's nineteen. I doubt he gets anything about women yet. I'm still working it out and I'm twice that age."

Annie hopped down off the stool and hugged him. "Thanks."

"Why didn't you just ask your dad or your mom about this?" he asked.

She shrugged. "They're parents. They get all worked up thinking I might wind up disappointed and I get a half-hour lecture on not counting on too much where Ty's concerned. That usually turns into a conversation about disappointment leading to depression and bad decisions and eating disorders, yada-yada-yada."

"You mean I just blew this entire conversation by not including a lecture?" Erik demanded, mostly in jest, of course, though he did find these little tests of his untried parenting skills to be disconcerting.

"For which I am very, very grateful," she assured him. She grabbed a brownie off the tray he'd just taken from the oven and took a bite as if to prove a point. "Have a good day."

"You, too, sweet pea. Let me know how it goes when you talk to Ty."

She smiled, looking more carefree than she had when she'd arrived. "I'll call you tonight right after I talk to him."

No sooner had Annie exited through the back door than Dana Sue pushed open the door from the dining room. "Was that my daughter I saw sneaking out the back?"

Erik regarded her with his most innocent expression. "Was it?"

Dana Sue rolled her eyes at his pitiful attempt at evasion. "What did she want?"

"To talk to me."

"About?"

"Sorry, confidential."

Her gaze narrowed. "You and my daughter are having

confidential conversations? I'm not sure how I feel about that. It was bad enough when she was having them with Maddie."

"I don't think this was something she felt she could ask Maddie," Erik said.

"Then it was about Ty," Dana Sue guessed at once.

"I never said that."

"Is she inviting him to prom or not?"

"I know nothing," Erik insisted.

"We could talk about you and Helen instead," she suggested.

"Sorry. Gotta run."

"Run where?" she demanded.

"Someplace where you're not," he said readily. "But don't take it personally. You know I love you."

"I think you love Helen," she countered. "Or at least like her."

"What was that?" he asked, already closing the door. "Can't hear you."

The door snapped open before he could make his escape. "I said that I think you're crazy about Helen," she shouted after him. "And just so you know, I think she likes you back! Can you hear me now?"

Unfortunately, Erik figured half the people of Serenity had heard her. And if they had, his life had just gone from peaceful and quiet, the way he liked it, to downright complicated. There was no more popular sport in town than watching, and then discussing, a cat-and-mouse game between a man and woman.

Erik had barely walked to the outer fringe of downtown Serenity when he literally bumped right into the woman who'd become the bane of his existence. Helen was strid-

ing purposefully along with her head down and her
thoughts obviously somewhere else.

"Hey, where are you heading in such a hurry?" he asked,
steadying her as she blinked up at him.

To his shock her makeup was streaked and her eyes
were swimming with tears. "Helen, what's wrong?" He
dug in his pocket and found a fistful of clean tissues. He
handed them to her.

Even as she accepted them and mopped her eyes, bright
patches of color bloomed on her cheeks. She tried to push
past him. "I'm fine," she muttered.

"Sure you are," he scoffed. "The strongest, most in-
control woman I know is walking around town crying her
eyes out and claims to be fine. Not buying it, sugar. Talk
to me."

"Erik, please," she pleaded. "Just leave me alone."

"Sorry. It's not in my genes to walk away from a woman
in distress."

"I'm not in distress. I'm just confused, and before you
ask about what, it's not something I want to talk about."

"Okay, then, we'll just go to Wharton's and get one of
those hot-fudge sundaes I hear you Sweet Magnolias turn
to whenever you're upset."

She regarded him with surprise. "You know about those?"

"I've worked with Dana Sue long enough to know a lot
of things," he said.

"She blabs?"

He laughed at her indignation. "No, I have amazingly
astute powers of observation for a man. Plus, I hear things."

"You eavesdrop?"

"I remain attuned to my surroundings," he contradicted.

"How is that any different from eavesdropping?"

"If you come with me, I'll explain it to you."

"I don't want to come with you," she murmured.

He fought a grin. "Do it anyway. Just think about what I'm offering—a hot-fudge sundae and someone willing to sit quietly and listen to all your woes. Do you know how many women would beg to be in your place?"

"I'm not one of them," she claimed. "I just want to be left alone."

"I'm sure that's your usual way of coping with things," he agreed. "Doesn't seem to be working out so well today. How about trying something new?"

"Spilling my guts to you?"

He nodded.

She actually seemed to be weighing the offer. When she finally nodded, he felt a far greater sense of relief than he should have. He attributed that to having been spared tossing her over his shoulder and carrying her into Wharton's.

"Let's go, then," he said, tucking her arm through his. "I'll do my best to make this painless."

"Whatever," she said, sounding a little like a petulant child.

"Think of it this way. If you had to spill your guts to a shrink, you'd be paying a hundred dollars or more an hour. I'm a bargain."

"And you're throwing in a hot-fudge sundae, too," she said grudgingly. "Is this my lucky day or what?"

"Told you so."

It remained to be seen if it was going to be Erik's lucky day or if this was going to be just one more step down a very slippery slope.

5

Helen avoided Erik's concerned gaze and dug into her hot-fudge sundae. It might only be 9:00 a.m., but Erik had been right. The combination of rich vanilla ice cream, thick fudge sauce and whipped cream was just what she needed. She could barely remember what had thrown her into such an emotional tailspin and sent her fleeing from the spa and Maddie.

What the sundae wasn't accomplishing, Erik was. He was a very disconcerting man. Few other men would have dragged her out for ice cream at this hour or even guessed that it was what she needed. In fact, most men would have been put off by her tears and run the other way.

"You ready to tell me what's going on?" he asked eventually.

She took another overflowing spoonful of the sundae to avoid speaking and shook her head.

"Sooner or later you're going to finish the ice cream and you won't have an excuse not to talk," he reminded her as he lounged on the seat across from her, seemingly content to sip his coffee while she made a total pig of herself.

"I'll have to leave as soon as I finish this," she said, pleased with the perfect excuse. "I'm already running late for work. Barb will send out a search party if I don't show up soon."

His mouth curved into a smile. "Okay, then. You'd better start talking now."

"Look," she said, "I skipped breakfast. That's the only reason you were successful at persuading me to come here. My blood sugar must have been low."

"And is that what made you cry in public?"

She shrugged. "It can have all sorts of weird effects."

"Trust me, that's usually not one of them," he said.

He sounded very sure. She studied him curiously. "What do you know about it?"

"You have no idea how many pieces of miscellaneous information I have stored away here." He tapped his head.

"But you said that with some authority," Helen countered. "Is that because you read up on diabetes so you could keep an eye on Dana Sue?"

"Yeah, that's it," he said, but his expression had become shuttered. Helen sensed this was far from the whole story. Pushing aside the sundae, she put her elbows on the table and leaned toward him. Maybe she could avoid his probing questions by asking a few of her own. "I just realized that I know very little about you. Who are you, Erik Whitney? And what were you before you became a chef?"

"What makes you think I was anything before that?" he inquired.

"Because you'd just graduated from the Atlanta Culinary Institute when Dana Sue hired you. Unless you're a very slow learner, which I doubt is the case, you must have done something before you went there."

He seemed increasingly uncomfortable with the direction of the conversation. "Look, the only reason we're here in Wharton's is so you can get whatever's bothering you off your chest," he reminded her. "This isn't supposed to be about me."

"But you're so much more interesting, or at least your reaction is. What are you hiding, Erik?"

He regarded her incredulously. "What makes you think I'm hiding something? And what exactly do you think I'm hiding? Some nefarious past as a bank robber, perhaps? Or maybe you think I'm AWOL from the marines?"

"I'm an attorney. I deal in facts. I try not to have any pre-conceived ideas, which is why I'm asking you." She tilted her head and noted the closed expression on his face. "You know what I find absolutely fascinating?"

"Not a clue."

"You've gone all secretive and strong, silent type all of a sudden. Why is that, especially if you have nothing to hide?"

"No particular reason other than not liking to dwell on the past," he said, his tone indifferent, but a tic in his jaw suggested he was anything but indifferent.

"Well, just so you know, it's the kind of thing that kicks a lawyer's curiosity into high gear. The art of a successful cross-examination depends on being able to read body language and expressions." She surveyed him lingeringly, then added, "I'm considered to be very, very good at it."

"It's hardly the big deal you're trying to turn it into," he said. When she continued to pin him with her gaze, he finally shrugged. "Okay, here's the condensed version. I was an EMT. I decided it was time for a change. There's not a lot of drama in that."

Helen was less surprised by the revelation than she probably should have been. It explained a lot about how observant he was when it came to Dana Sue's monitoring her diabetes and the close eye he always kept on Annie and her eating patterns. Still, it didn't seem as if it were something he'd want to hide, yet he'd obviously been very reluctant to reveal it. She couldn't help wondering why.

"Did you like the work?" she asked.

"For a long time, yes," he said, his expression still guarded. "Look, if you're feeling better, I need to get back to the restaurant."

"Running out on me just when things are getting interesting?" She shook her head. "It intrigues me that a man who was trying to dig around in my psyche just minutes ago can't handle the idea of me asking personal questions."

"I wasn't the one having a public meltdown," he said. "If you spot me having one, feel free to ask all the questions you want." He tossed some bills on the table and was gone before Helen could formulate a response.

She stared after him, then distractedly picked up her spoon and ate the last few bites of her now-melted sundae.

"Now there goes one very sexy man," Grace Wharton declared as she joined Helen. "How'd you let him get away?"

"I think I scared him off," Helen admitted, vaguely unnerved by how guilty that made her feel. He'd been kind to her and he'd given her an excuse to take a few minutes to gather the composure she'd lost after her conversation earlier with Maddie. What had she done in return? She'd cross-examined him as if he were some kind of criminal.

"A man like that doesn't scare too easily," Grace said. "You didn't mention marriage or something like that, did you? That's the only thing I can think of that scares a confirmed bachelor."

"The subject of marriage most definitely did not come

up," Helen assured her. "What makes you think he's a confirmed bachelor?"

"I've seen just about every single woman in town throw themselves at him at one time or another," Grace said. "He flirts right back, but that's as far as it ever goes. For a while I thought he might be hung up on Dana Sue, but then Ronnie came back and that put an end to that."

"Interesting," Helen murmured. She wondered what Grace would think if she knew about the kiss Erik had laid on her not that long ago. Her lips still burned every time she thought about it. He hadn't shown any real interest in repeating it, though. If he was a confirmed bachelor, and that kiss had shaken him as badly as it had her, maybe that alone was enough to make him cautious around her, especially when the conversation took a more personal turn.

Before she could pick apart her own theory, her cell phone rang. She snatched it out of her purse.

"You planning to come to work anytime today?" Barb asked wryly. "I have a waiting room filled with clients and they're getting restless."

"Oh, my God," Helen said, glancing at her watch. It was going on ten. "I got sidetracked."

"By Erik Whitney, if the rumors are true," Barb said, proving that the Serenity grapevine was faster than the speed of light.

Helen didn't fall in to her trap. "I'll be there in five minutes."

"Make it four," Barb retorted. "Your nine o'clock looks as if he might start breaking things."

"On my way," Helen said.

When she'd turned off the phone and jammed it into her purse, she looked up into Grace's fascinated gaze. "Never known you to be late for work," the woman commented. "Must have been something about the company."

Helen frowned at her amused expression. "Don't even go there."

"Can you think of any other reason you'd lose track of time like that?" Grace teased.

"Too much on my mind," Helen said, "that's all. Nothing to do with Erik."

"If you say so," Grace said, but she sounded skeptical. "Maybe you were hoping he'd kiss you again, the way he did at Sullivan's a few days ago."

Helen nearly groaned. So, Grace knew about that, after all. Unfortunately Helen didn't have time to stick around and debate the subject with her. And what would be the point, anyway? It would only add fuel to the fire. Grace had more than enough fodder for her lunch-hour gossip mill as it was.

"Mommy, I got a tummy ache," Daisy told Karen when it was time to get out of the car at the day-care center.

She'd picked her up from kindergarten five minutes before and spotted her climbing a jungle gym when she drove up. She regarded her daughter with dismay. "You didn't look sick when you were playing with your friends on the playground."

"Because I wasn't sick *then*," she said, clearly exasperated. "I want to go home."

"You can't go home. There's nobody there to take care of you and I have to go to work. I'm working the late shift today."

Daisy's lower lip quivered. "But I'm sick," she wailed. "I can stay with Frances."

"Frances can't take care of you all afternoon and evening, Daisy."

"Please!"

Karen felt her own stomach twist into knots. She'd thought she'd put these crises behind her. She'd found a new day-care center that kept both kids 'til five, and thanks to Helen and Dana Sue, she'd found an excellent sitter to pick them up and watch them until she got home. For a week now things had gone smoothly.

In addition, Dana Sue had interviewed Tess and scheduled an on-the-job evaluation for tomorrow. Karen knew Tess would pass that with flying colors and then Karen's backup plan could be set in motion.

She reached into the backseat and put a hand to Daisy's forehead. No fever, thank goodness. "Sweetie, do you have a pain in your tummy? Or do you just feel sick?"

"Sick," she said miserably, then promptly threw up to prove the point.

Karen wanted to weep. It wasn't Daisy's fault. She needed to keep reminding herself of that. Kids picked up a million germs at school, particularly at Daisy's age. Karen grabbed some tissues and packets of baby wipes, then got out of the car and opened the back door to clean up her daughter.

"I'm sorry, Mommy," she said with a sniff.

"It's okay, baby. You can't help getting sick." The thought of calling the restaurant to tell Dana Sue and Erik what was going on made her feel sick to her stomach, as well.

"Do I still have to go to day care?" Daisy asked pitifully.

"No, sweetie. I'm going to take you home."

"And stay with me?"

"Yes, I'll stay with you." Maybe she could go to work once the sitter got there, assuming she still had work to go to.

Half an hour later she had Daisy settled on the couch in

front of the TV with a glass of ginger ale. She was about to brace herself to face Erik's reaction, when it struck her there might be another solution. She dialed Tess.

"Tess, I know you're not supposed to have your on-the-job evaluation 'til tomorrow, but I've got a problem," she explained. "Daisy just threw up in the car. The sitter's not due for three hours. Is there any chance at all you could work today, if Dana Sue agrees?"

"Hold on and let me check with my mom. She came in early from picking vegetables because the heat was bothering her. If she's up to babysitting, I can do it."

Within minutes she was back. "It'll work on my end," Tess said. "Call me as soon as you've spoken to Dana Sue. I'll get ready in the meantime, just in case. Tell her I can be there in half an hour."

"Thank you! You're a lifesaver." As soon as she'd hung up on Tess, she called the restaurant. Unfortunately it was Erik who answered. "It's Karen," she said.

"You're late," he said, obviously exasperated.

"I know. I was running right on time, but then Daisy got sick. I had to bring her home."

"Then you're on your way?"

"Actually I need to stay here with her," she admitted.

"Not again," he said, now sounding beyond annoyed. "Karen, things can't go on like this. I thought these last-minute absences were going to end."

"I know. I thought so, too. But it's not as bad as before. I've already spoken to Tess. She can come in for her evaluation right now and take my place. She said she could be there in thirty minutes, if it's okay with you guys."

"Fine," Erik said tightly.

"I'm sorry," she apologized. "I really am, but at least this proves that my suggestion about having two of us in this job will work."

"That remains to be seen," he said, then sighed. "Tell Daisy I hope she feels better. She's had a tough time lately."

"Thanks," she said. "Maybe you could come by some-time and have a tea party with her. She loved that." And Karen had gotten a huge kick out of watching the very mas-culine Erik holding one of Daisy's delicate, tiny teacups and drinking pretend tea.

"Sure," he said. "We'll work it out."

She hung up and called Tess back, then called the sitter to tell her she wasn't needed tonight. She'd either have Frances keep an eye on Daisy for a few minutes while she went back to the day-care center to get Mack, or she'd take Daisy with her.

In the meantime, she sank onto the sofa next to the now-sleeping Daisy and closed her eyes. Thank heaven for Tess. Without her pitching in, Karen knew that her job would have been history and there would have been nothing Helen or anyone else could have done to save it. Erik's fragile pa-tience was obviously at an end. And though Dana Sue owned Sullivan's, Erik had a lot of clout when it came to decisions about what happened in the kitchen.

Not for the first time, Karen was nearly overwhelmed by just how close to the edge she was living. She had hardly any savings and very little reserve of energy for these constant emergencies. Sometimes when the kids were screaming and she was juggling bills, she wondered just how much longer she could cope without snapping.

Then she glanced over at her sleeping daughter, her long, dark eyelashes a smudge on her pale skin, and the force of her love for Dasiy flowed through her. She would do anything—*anything*—to protect her babies and give them the kind of loving home and security she herself had never known.

Helen wasn't one bit surprised when she opened her front door at eight that night and found Maddie and Dana Sue on the doorstep. The only surprise was that it had taken them so long.

"Shouldn't you be home?" she asked Maddie, then regarded Dana Sue just as inhospitably. "And shouldn't you be at work?"

"We would both be where we belong, if you hadn't taken off from the spa in tears this morning," Maddie said.

"And then landed at Wharton's with Erik, who was so concerned he dragged you over there for a hot-fudge sundae," Dana Sue added.

"I see it didn't take long for that piece of news to make its way around town," Helen commented sarcastically.

"It didn't have to travel far," Dana Sue said. "Erik told me."

"Really? I'm surprised. He doesn't seem inclined to talk much about himself," Helen said.

"In this case, he was talking about you," Dana Sue retorted. "He thought I should know my friend was upset. When Maddie called and confirmed it and said she was worried, too, we agreed that we needed to come by and check on you."

"Here I am, not upset," Helen said. "You can go home now."

"I don't think so," Maddie said, pushing past her. "I need to get off my feet. So does Dana Sue. It's been a tough night at the restaurant." Maddie headed for the sofa and sank into its cushions. "I hope you two can drag me up when it's time to go, but right now this feels heavenly."

"We'll manage," Helen assured her, then studied Dana Sue and saw that she did, indeed, look more frazzled than usual. "What happened at the restaurant tonight?"

"Karen bailed again. Fortunately she was able to get that friend of hers, Tess, to come in, but in some ways that just complicated things."

Helen's stomach sank. "How so? Isn't she any good?"

"She's great. In fact, I think she's going to work out just fine, but on-the-job training in the midst of the dinner rush is not exactly ideal. It took more time to explain how we do things than it would have for me or Erik just to do them ourselves."

Helen regarded her with concern. "But you're still going to give Karen's idea a chance to work, right?"

Dana Sue nodded. "I promised we would, didn't I?"

"I should call Karen and let her know," Helen said. "I'm sure she's terrified that you're fed up with her and her problems."

"I spoke to her a little while ago to tell her that we're definitely hiring Tess and that things are okay," Dana Sue told her. "You're right. She was relieved."

"Now let's get back to you," Maddie said, reminding Helen that she could be as single-minded as anyone on earth when she needed to be.

"How about something to drink?" Helen said. "Bottled water? Juice? Decaf coffee?"

"You're not going to distract us," Dana Sue said, looking amused. "You know us better than that. Maddie filled me in about the whole baby dilemma. Why don't you get one of the million and one lists you've no doubt made and go over it with us? Maybe we can help you sort things out."

"No," Helen said flatly. "Maddie was right this morning, when she said this was something I need to work out for myself."

Both women frowned at her.

"That was then," Maddie said. "This is now."

"You were *crying,*" Dana Sue said. "In public. That is so not like you. Obviously this is too much for you to deal with on your own."

Helen sighed. "I'm stronger than you think."

"I would have agreed with that before this morning," Maddie said.

"Okay, look," Dana Sue began. "Maddie mentioned that maybe you want more than just a baby. She says you've been reexamining your whole life and that you think you might want the whole family thing."

"So what? You're going to snap your fingers and get it for me?" Helen retorted, sorry she'd ever opened her big mouth.

"We could," Dana Sue said. "In fact, if you would just open your eyes and see what's staring you right in the face, you could have it all."

Helen sighed. She'd seen this one coming a mile away. "Erik, I assume."

"Well, of course, Erik," Dana Sue said. "He's smart. He's gorgeous. And he's hot for you."

Maddie stared at her with obvious surprise. "Really? How did I miss that?"

"You've had other things on your mind," Dana Sue said to Maddie. "You missed the kiss."

"What kiss?" Maddie asked, clearly fascinated.

"Long story," Dana Sue said. "Trust me, though it made me go home and throw myself at Ronnie."

Helen moaned. "I am not having this conversation with you. And stop matchmaking. Erik and I are friends," she said, then corrected herself. "Not even friends. We're acquaintances."

"Sweetie, if a man kisses you like that, you're more than acquainted," Dana Sue replied. "You're about ten minutes away from falling into bed together."

"Grace Wharton says Erik is a confirmed bachelor," Helen countered.

"Nonsense," Dana Sue said dismissively. "Just because she doesn't have a line on his social life doesn't mean he doesn't have one."

"If he has one, then what makes you think he has any interest in someone new?" Helen asked. "You can't have it both ways. I think it would be best if you get over the whole idea of trying to shove Erik and me together. I know that's why you've been coming up with all those excuses to have me pitch in at the restaurant. It's not because you discovered I have hidden culinary talent."

Dana Sue's face was the picture of innocence. "We've been swamped every single time you've helped out, and you know it."

"Then how come you never asked Maddie to pitch in? She actually knows how to cook. So does Ronnie, for that matter. You used to ask him."

"Yes, why haven't you asked me?" Maddie demanded.

"Because you've been pregnant off and on for most of the past two years," Dana Sue answered. "You shouldn't be on your feet. As for Ronnie, what little spare time he has now that his hardware store has taken off, he needs to spend with Annie."

"Yeah, right," Helen said skeptically. "Face it, Dana Sue. I know what you're up to and I'm telling you right now to cut it out."

"But I think—" Dana Sue began.

"Don't think. Go home to your husband and drag him off to bed. Maybe if you're not feeling sex-deprived, you'll stop worrying about my love life."

"Trust me, not an issue," Dana Sue said, her cheeks flushed. "You're my friend. I want you to be as happy as I am."

"Me, too," Maddie said.

"Then, please, just lay off about Erik and about me having a baby. I'll work this out for myself when the time is right."

"We just don't want you to wake up when you hit fifty and realize that you have all these huge regrets," Maddie said. "The saddest question of all is 'What if…?'"

"You mean like what if I'd never mentioned to the two of you that I thought I wanted a baby?" Helen said testily.

Maddie frowned at her. "No, I mean like what if I'd realized how much I wanted one before it was too late. You can't go back, then, Helen."

The aching emptiness deep inside Helen, the ache she'd been trying so hard lately to pretend wasn't there, came back with a vengeance.

"Believe me, I know that," she said quietly. "It's not something I'm ever likely to forget, which is why I'm under so much pressure. I know I can't take forever to make this decision."

"Then get those lists of yours and let's talk about all the pros and cons," Dana Sue prodded.

"But…" Helen began, only to sigh when both woman regarded her with unyielding expressions. "Okay, fine. I'll get the lists."

She grabbed her briefcase and fished through it 'til she found the legal pad she'd reserved for just this particular topic. Page after page had been covered with her notes, including everything she'd been told by the obstetricians she'd consulted. Though she was filled with reservations about this entire conversation, she handed her notes to Maddie, whose eyes widened as she flipped through the pages.

"You could write a Ph.D. thesis with this much research," Maddie said.

"I thought it was critical to be well-informed," Helen replied defensively.

Dana Sue looked over Maddie's shoulder. "You consulted medical textbooks?" she asked incredulously.

"Well, of course, I did," Helen replied. "You don't think I'd rely on only two sources for something this important, do you?"

Dana Sue sat back down. "I think you're overthinking this whole thing. That's the problem. It comes down to this, Helen. Do you want to have a child of your own or don't you?"

"It's *not* that simple," Helen protested. "I can't just wave a magic wand and be pregnant."

Dana Sue regarded her with a wicked grin. "Well, the right guy could."

Maddie swallowed a laugh. "Dana Sue!"

"Well, isn't that really the bottom line?" Dana Sue retorted.

"No!" Helen said. "I have to know with every fiber of my being that I want this, that I can make the kind of changes in my life that having a baby will require. You were both a lot younger when you got pregnant for the first time. You were married. It was the natural order of things, the right time in your lives. Now, especially for someone who's spent her life so far married to her career, it's not that easy. Heck, Maddie, even you wrestled with the decision to have another baby when you and Cal got married, and you had him to support your decision."

"True," Maddie conceded. "But I'm still trying to pin down what has you worried. Is it a fear that you're incapable of devoting the time required to raising a child? Are you concerned just about the process of getting pregnant— natural versus artificial insemination? Are you wondering what will happen to your child if something happens to you? Or are you just afraid that you don't want this enough to disrupt your life? If that last one is it, then you're right to worry. This is not something to undertake unless you're totally committed to it."

Dana Sue reached over and took her hand. "You do know that we'll both be around to support you every single step of the way, don't you? You and this baby will have a big extended family. If you hit any kind of rough patch, you won't be in it alone, even if you do decide not to do things in the traditional way. You would be an incredible mom. Annie thinks so, too."

"My kids feel the same way," Maddie added. "They adore you."

Helen's eyes swam with tears for the second time that day. "I know that," she whispered, swiping at the annoying evidence of what she perceived as weakness. "I guess I never thought I'd find myself in this position. I thought I'd do it all the traditional way. Time just…got away from me."

"Well, it's not too late yet," Dana Sue said firmly.

"From a medical standpoint, I know that," Helen said. "But you touched on something that does worry me. What if something happens to me? Knowing I'm the only parent could make a child feel incredibly insecure."

"Which is why your child will always know they can

turn to any of us," Dana Sue reminded her. "Now let's get down to business. We can stay here all night and go through those lists of yours item by item, if that will help."

Already somewhat relieved by their reassurances and their commitment, Helen shook her head. "No, but thanks. I'll work this out."

"Soon," Maddie said.

"Soon," Helen agreed, though she immediately felt the pressure starting to build again. She hated knowing that there was no time to waste, that a decision of this magnitude couldn't be put off forever.

Maddie struggled up from the sofa with an assist from Dana Sue. If she was this awkward now at only four and a half months, Helen couldn't begin to imagine how ungainly she'd be by her ninth month. For some reason the image made Helen want to weep all over again. She *did* want that for herself. The awkwardness, the belly out to here, the kick of her baby keeping her awake at night.

It was the aftermath that terrified her—the middle-of-the-night feedings, pacing the floor trying to soothe a crying baby, letting go of a tiny hand on the first day of school, having to make excuses to the court when her child had chicken pox, making sure homework was done, teaching her son or daughter the dangers of alcohol, smoking and premarital sex. The litany of things that could make the difference between raising a happy, well-adjusted child and a kid destined for disaster scared her out of her wits. Despite the accolades from Dana Sue, Maddie and their children, what if she was lousy at all of it? What then?

"You're overthinking it again," Maddie said, interrupting Helen's thoughts. She tapped her chest. "Listen to what's in your heart. It won't steer you wrong."

Helen hugged both of them fiercely. "Thank you for not listening to me when I told you to go away."

Dana Sue grinned. "Not a problem. We've spent a lifetime ignoring your orders. We enjoy it."

"That's true," Maddie agreed. "Now get some rest. Maybe this will all be clearer to you in the morning."

Helen doubted that, but she did feel better for having these two old, and very dear, friends offering her unconditional support. It was the one thing she should have realized she could count on long before tonight.

6

Erik had been predisposed to dislike Tess Martinez, mostly because he resented the way Helen had manipulated the whole situation to convince Dana Sue to hire someone else for the kitchen. He also had major reservations about hiring another single mom after the problems they'd been having with Karen.

Yet he'd discovered it was all but impossible not to like a woman who was little bigger than a bird and whose sheer perkiness and good-natured eagerness to work commanded his respect and approval. After only a few days, he'd grudgingly conceded to himself—though not to Dana Sue and definitely not to Helen—that Tess was a real find.

Right now, nearly an hour after the restaurant had closed, Tess was hovering beside him, watching every move he made as he finished decorating a wedding cake for a reception Sullivan's was catering on Saturday.

"So many flowers," she whispered reverently. "It's like a picture."

"What was your wedding cake like?" Erik asked.

"Not so beautiful as this," she said sadly. "We had no money for such things."

Born in the United States, and the daughter of Mexican immigrants who'd come into the country legally to work harvesting sugar in Florida, Tess spoke with a charming mix of Spanish and Southern accents. The family had worked hard, saved their money and had eventually started a small vegetable farm in South Carolina a few miles outside of Serenity. They sold their produce to local grocery stores and restaurants and at weekend farmers' markets, including the one started last summer in Serenity's town square. The instant Dana Sue had met Tess, she'd realized that much of Sullivan's produce came from Tess's family farm. Erik had known at that moment during the interview that Dana Sue would hire Tess even if the young woman could do nothing more than boil an egg.

If that alone hadn't been enough, though, Tess had also told them that her husband, Diego Martinez, had been picked up on a job for not being able to produce a valid green card and been deported back to Mexico before they could establish in court that he was here legally and that, even had he not been, his three-year marriage to Tess would have qualified him to stay.

Erik had a hunch it was a case Helen would want to be involved in, once she heard the details. Fighting the system to reunite two people in love might be a welcome change from the divorces she usually handled. And lately she seemed to be sticking her nose into all sorts of things that were none of her business, so why not this one?

In the meantime, though, Tess was struggling to make ends meet with two children under three. She'd tried making it on her own, but after being fired from the diner, she'd moved back home with her family. Though they helped some with child care, they had their own long, hard days in their fields. Tess worked to help them and to put money away for the legal fight to get her husband back to South Carolina. Erik sympathized with her plight, but what had won him over was her quick grasp of any task assigned to her in the kitchen. In less than a week, she'd learned many of the recipes and executed them to perfection.

"Would you like to do this?" he asked now.

"Really?" she asked, awestruck. "You would teach me to make a cake so beautiful?"

"Sure. With the number of catering requests we're getting for wedding receptions, it would be wonderful to have someone to help out. Dana Sue had to turn down someone just this week because we had a conflict for that date."

"I could come in early," she offered at once. "I should not learn while I am being paid."

Erik smiled at her. "I think we can find the time during your regular hours, Tess. I'll talk it over with Dana Sue and we'll figure it out."

"But I'm willing to be here early," she said. "Please tell her that, so she doesn't think I am taking advantage of her."

"No one would ever think such a thing," he assured her. "You work as hard as anyone here. We're lucky to have found you."

A brilliant smile spread across her thin face, which was dominated by large brown eyes that sparkled with humor. "No. I am the lucky one, to have found a job I love. I am so grateful to Karen for recommending me and to you and Dana Sue for giving me a chance. I will not let you down."

Erik decided to broach the subject he knew weighed heavily on her mind. "You know, Tess, Dana Sue has a friend who's an attorney," he began. "She might be able to help you with Diego's case."

Tess's eyes immediately filled with regret. "I do not have enough saved yet to hire another lawyer. The last one took my money and did nothing."

Erik bristled at the thought of anyone taking advantage of her situation like that. "I'm sure Helen would be glad to work something out with you about the money. In fact, she might even be able to get it back from this lawyer who did nothing." He had a hunch Helen would enjoy that.

"Do you really think so?" Tess said solemnly. Then she glanced at her watch. "I'm late, as usual. My parents will be worried. Do you need me to do anything else before I go?"

"Not a thing. I'll see you tomorrow."

"And you will speak to Dana Sue about the cake decorations?"

"Absolutely," he promised.

"Muchas gracias," she said. *"Adios."*

Tess had been gone only a few minutes when Dana Sue came in. Erik frowned at her. "I thought you'd gone home hours ago."

"Paperwork," she said, pulling up a stool and sitting next to him. "The cake is beautiful. The Lamberts will be thrilled."

"Tess thought so, too. She wants to learn how to do this."

"She's eager to learn everything, isn't she?" Dana Sue said with a smile. "I like her. How about you?"

"She's working out a whole lot better than I expected," he admitted. "And it's certainly improved the situation with Karen, too. For the past few days she hasn't looked nearly as stressed out as she did before."

"So Karen and Helen did a good thing for us, didn't they?" she suggested slyly.

"Yes, Dana Sue. Your friend did us a good deed. Want me to pin a medal on her?"

"Nope. I just want you to stop keeping her at arm's length."

"I'm not doing that," Erik argued, though he knew Dana Sue was right. Ever since he'd found Helen in tears, he'd avoided her whenever possible. That hint of vulnerability in such a strong woman had cut right through his defenses. Okay, that and the still-vivid memory of locking lips with her.

"Have you spent two seconds alone with her since *the kiss?*" Dana Sue asked.

"I took her to Wharton's for a hot-fudge sundae, remember? That was just last week."

"Ah, yes, I seem to recall something about you running out the second she started asking you about yourself. Okay, since then? Have you seen her? Asked her out?"

Erik frowned at her. "The opportunity hasn't arisen," he replied. "Which reminds me, have you spoken to Helen about what's going on with Tess's husband?"

Dana Sue shook her head. "I wasn't sure it was my place. Tess might not want us meddling in her private business."

"I think you should. Sounds as if the case might be something Helen could really sink her teeth into, especially if some other lawyer cheated Tess out of a lot of money."

Dana Sue regarded him with dismay. "I hadn't heard about that part. That's really rotten."

"I thought so, too," he said. "I figured it would get Helen's dander up."

"It would," Dana Sue agreed. "Why don't you talk to her?"

He gave a nonchalant shrug. "You see her. I don't."

"You could," she countered. "Pick up the phone and call her. Invite her out for coffee to discuss a legal matter, since you're too chicken to ask her on a real date."

Erik scowled at her. "I'm not chicken. I don't want to date her."

"Oh, please," Dana Sue said scornfully. "Try telling me something I can believe. You're hot for her and that scares the daylights out of you. What I don't understand is why."

Erik had given that more thought than he probably should have, so he had an answer ready for her. "We're complete opposites, for one thing. Barracuda attorneys give me hives, for another. The list goes on."

"Haven't you heard? Opposites attract. And Helen's only a barracuda in the courtroom."

"Yeah, I noticed that when I got a pie in my face because she was a little ticked off at me."

Dana Sue's lips twitched. "You have to admit that was pretty unpredictable and funny, especially coming from Helen. She's usually so darn proper."

"Did you see me laughing?"

"No, I saw you planting a kiss on her, also unpredictable, but way too hot to be even remotely amusing."

"Whatever."

Dana Sue seemed to be even more tickled by his feigned indifference. "Well, it's up to you. I think you're right about Helen being the perfect person to handle that legal case for Tess, but I'm going to leave it up to you."

He saw right through her scheme and he wasn't falling for it. "Come on, Dana Sue. You talk to her."

"I don't think so. Not about that, anyway."

"You'd risk letting Tess twist in the wind, just so you can stick it to me and Helen?"

"I prefer to think of it as motivation for the two of you to get together. I know what a wonderful, compassionate man you are. You won't let Tess twist in the wind for long. Eventually we'll all get what we want."

"You're almost as annoying as Helen," he muttered. "You know that, don't you?"

"Of course, I do," she said cheerfully. "But I suggest you not kiss me to shut me up the way you did her, or Ronnie will have something to say about it."

Erik chuckled. "Yeah, I imagine he would. Go home, Dana Sue. It's late. Get your things and I'll walk you to your car."

"I think I can walk the twenty yards to my car unprotected," she said.

"Not on my watch, you won't, not even in relatively crime-free Serenity," he said. "Get your purse or whatever. I'll meet you at the front door."

When he'd finally tucked her safely in her car, she rolled down the window. "Helen needs someone like you," she told him. "Every woman does."

"Someone like me? What does that mean?"

"A knight in shining armor," she said.

"I'm afraid you've got the wrong man," he replied. "My suit of armor got tarnished a long time ago."

"I'll buy you some polish first thing in the morning," she said, "but believe me, the result will only be cosmetic. The truth runs much deeper. Good night, Erik. Sleep well."

He stared after her as she drove off into an inky darkness brightened only by a scattering of stars.

It astounded him that she saw him that way when it was so far from the truth, so far from the way he'd come to view himself ever since that night his wife had died. Even if

Dana Sue bought all the polish in the local Piggly Wiggly, he doubted it would be enough.

Helen sat in the courtroom and looked across the aisle at Jimmy Bob West and Brad Holliday.

"What excuse do you think they'll come up with this time to get another postponement?" Caroline Holliday asked her, already sounding resigned to another delay in her divorce proceedings.

"Actually I was thinking we'd turn the tables on them," Helen said. "If it's okay with you, of course."

Caroline sat up a little straighter. "What do you have in mind?"

"I had a detective I use do a little digging around. I think I have enough evidence to show the judge that Brad's been trying to hide some of his assets from us. I'd like to ask for a continuance so we can find every penny that man has tucked away."

Caroline regarded her with amazement. "But they gave us financial statements, and those pretty much matched all the records I had."

"Of course they did. They handed over everything they knew they couldn't hide. Unfortunately for them, there was an interesting little paper trail they weren't so clever about concealing. Brad's a partner in some out-of-state real estate ventures that add up to a tidy little sum."

"You're kidding me!" Caroline said, her mood improving considerably. "And I'm entitled to some of that property?"

"Or the cash from the sale of that property," Helen said. "And in my experience, if a man works that hard to hide some of his assets, it's probably only the tip of the iceberg." She studied the woman next to her, who finally had some color back in her cheeks and a glint of determination in her eyes. "So, do we go for it?"

"Absolutely," Caroline told her. "If only so I can see the look on Brad's smug face when he realizes we're on to him."

Helen chuckled. "I'm looking forward to that myself."

When the judge entered the courtroom a few minutes later, Helen was on her feet before Jimmy Bob could even shove back his chair.

"Your Honor," she began, shooting a quelling look at Jimmy Bob that had him sitting right back down. "We'd like to ask for a continuance."

For an instant Brad looked as if he'd just won the lottery. Jimmy Bob, however, was studying her with a narrowed, suspicious gaze. He obviously knew that she was up to something and that it didn't bode well for his client.

"I'm sure you plan to explain why," the judge said. "Especially seeing as how you've been against every delay the opposing counsel has sought."

"Indeed I will explain," Helen said. "May I approach the bench? I have some papers here to support my request."

She handed one set to the judge, another set to Jimmy Bob. He took one look at the first page and scowled at his client.

"What is it?" Brad demanded.

Helen tried not to smirk. "I'll be happy to explain, if you'll allow me to, Your Honor."

"Be my guest."

Helen proceeded to outline the detective's findings. "These papers lead me to believe that Mr. Holliday has deliberately tried to mislead his wife and this court about the extent of his financial holdings. We'd like time to explore this further so we can be sure that whatever settlement this court ultimately reaches will be based on *all* the assets and not just those Mr. Holliday has very selectively revealed."

The judge peered at the papers, then looked over the top of his reading glasses at Brad Holliday and Jimmy Bob. He was clearly unhappy about the position they'd put him in.

"You have any objections?" he asked Jimmy Bob.

The attorney sat back with a sigh. "None," he mumbled.

"Well, I do," Brad said, leaping to his feet, his eyes sparking with anger. "I have plenty of objections. What right do they have to go snooping around?"

Judge Rockingham slammed his gavel on the desk, then speared Brad with a look that had him sitting right back down. "Every right," he said.

"Thank you," Helen said sweetly, delighted to see Brad put in his place for once. "I don't suppose I could make one more little request of the court?"

The judge gestured for her to continue.

"Could you order Mr. Holliday and his counsel to give us another accounting of all financial assets? A complete one this time. Not that I'll take it at face value, but it'll be interesting to compare it to what we discover."

"So ordered," the judge said. "I'll see all of you back here in two weeks. Mr. West, see that Ms. Decatur has that revised financial disclosure by the end of business this Friday."

"But—" Jimmy Bob began.

"Do it!" the judge snapped, his patience at an end.

Outraged by his friend's ruling and angry at being one-upped by Caroline and Helen, Brad stormed past them and out of the courtroom almost before the door to the judge's chambers closed behind him. Jimmy Bob cast an admiring look at Helen.

"I guess you won that round," he said.

Helen bristled at the idea that this was some sort of game, though she knew divorce often turned into a competition of strategy and quick wits. "If you and your sleazebag client would play straight with us, we could get this over with instead of dragging it out interminably." She shrugged. "Then, again, maybe you like the way the hourly billings are adding up. Will you have enough for a down payment on some beach-front cottage if they go high enough?"

She snapped her briefcase shut and walked past him, while his mouth was still flapping like a fish on the end of a hook. Caroline was right on her heels.

Standing in the hallway, Caroline looked at Helen with pleasure. "That was almost fun. A divorce would be better, but watching Brad turn green had its moments."

"I predict we'll end this next time we're here," Helen told her. "They've been counting on us just sitting by passively while they play their games. They don't seem too pleased about the shoe being on the other foot. I suspect Brad will be anxious to get this over with before we discover any more of his dirty little secrets."

Caroline's expression sobered. "He's really furious right now. I've never seen him like that."

Helen frowned. "Are you worried about him retaliating?"

Caroline immediately shook off her gloomy expression. "No, of course not. I was married to him for years, for goodness' sakes."

Though her tone was firm, Helen thought she detected a trace of doubt. "You sure?"

"I'm sure," Caroline said, then glanced at her watch. "It's almost noon. Do you have time for lunch? My treat. We can go to Sullivan's."

"I wish I could," Helen told her. "But I have to run. My calendar's booked solid all day today. Another time, though."

She reached into her briefcase and extracted a gift certificate for The Corner Spa. She, Dana Sue and Maddie had each taken half a dozen of the complimentary gift certificates to use for promotion. Given to the right people, they were excellent for spreading the word about the spa's services. "Tell you what. Why don't you go over to the spa and have a massage or facial to celebrate today's victory? I'll call Jeanette and make sure she fits you in."

Caroline's eyes lit up. "I'd love to do that. I've been dying to try the spa because all my friends have been talking about it, but since all of this mess started with the divorce, I've had to cut out anything that wasn't an absolute necessity."

"That'll change once we get the final divorce decree," Helen promised. "You and the kids will be well provided for."

"After today, I'm actually beginning to believe that," Caroline said. "Thank you."

"Just doing my job," Helen said.

Karen gave the gazpacho she'd made for the lunch soup special another lackadaisical stir, then put it in the refrigerator to chill. She was so exhausted she could barely put one foot in front of the other, but she'd come in to work, anyway. She hadn't dared to ask for any more time off, not even knowing that Tess could back her up.

Her exhaustion must have been showing, because Erik came into the kitchen and asked, "You okay?"

"Just tired," she said. "Daisy's still sick, but the sitter was able to spend the day with her today."

"She keeping you up at night?" Erik asked.

Karen nodded. "But I'm fine. The gazpacho's made and the salads are chilling, as well."

"Then why don't you take a break for a few minutes?" he suggested. "Have a little of that gazpacho. Last time you made it, it was outstanding. The customers have been clamoring for it ever since, especially on these hot days."

"You know, I think I will," she said, then ladled some of the chilled soup, with its spicy mix of tomatoes, green peppers and onions, into a bowl. She pulled a stool up to the counter and tasted it. To her shock, it almost took off the roof of her mouth.

"Oh, my God!" she said, spitting it back into the bowl. "We have to throw it out."

Erik regarded her with dismay. "What's wrong with it?"

Karen winced. "I must have put in too much hot sauce, thinking it was the Worcestershire," she said. "I'm so sorry. I don't know where my head was."

"Probably trying to catch up on the sleep you missed," Erik said. "It happens. Fortunately there's time to make another batch. I'll help you chop the vegetables."

"Maybe you'd better add the seasonings," she said. "Obviously I can't be trusted."

Erik studied her worriedly. "Karen, is there more going on here than you're admitting? Are you getting sick, too?"

"No," she said firmly, panicked that he might insist she go home. Not only would that be another black mark against her, but she needed the income. Her last two paychecks had suffered from all the unpaid leave she'd had to take. "I'll have another cup of coffee and I'll be fine by lunchtime."

"If you're sure," Erik said, his skepticism plain.

"Look, I know you're not happy with me or with my

work, but I'm trying," she told him. "Please bear with me a little longer."

"We're trying to do that," he told her. "But you know there's a limit. We can't afford to have the quality of the food we serve suffer because you're only half-awake."

Tears welled up in her eyes. "I know that. It's just that there are days when everything gets to be too much, you know. I'm not getting enough sleep. And I don't see any end in sight. On top of everything, I'm worried about bills." She stopped herself. "I'm sorry. I have no business whining to you. These are not your problems."

Erik regarded her with unexpected compassion. "But you are a part of this team," he reminded her, his tone gentle now. "And even though I'm tough on you, I do care about what's going on in your life. If Dana Sue and I can help, we want to."

"Unless you want to babysit my kids, so I can sleep for a week, I don't know what else you can do, except be patient with me. I'm doing everything I can to stay on track."

"I know you are," he said.

Maybe it was the gentleness in his voice or the fear that she was way too close to blowing everything, but Karen burst into tears and ran from the kitchen, leaving behind a bewildered Erik.

In the restroom, she splashed her face with cold water, then clung to the edge of the sink to steady herself. She was so close to being completely out of control it terrified her. Thanks to her mother's total irresponsibility, she'd learned at an early age that she had only herself to rely on. Half the time her mom had been too busy with her boyfriends to even notice Karen was around. Even when her marriage had fallen apart, she'd kept it all together. Lately, though, the least little thing seemed to overwhelm her.

"Get a grip," she muttered, studying her pale face in the mirror. "You cannot afford to lose this job."

She drew in a deep breath, then another, until she was finally feeling calmer and more together. She pulled a lipstick from her pocket and touched up the glossy shade of pink on her mouth. The color helped.

Just as she was about to go back to the kitchen and apologize, Dana Sue came in, a worried frown creasing her brow.

"Are you okay? Erik is beside himself that he made you cry."

"It wasn't his fault," Karen assured her. "I'm a mess." She forced a smile. "I'm all ready for the lunch rush, though, I promise."

She started to brush past Dana Sue before she had another meltdown, but Dana Sue stopped her.

"Do you need time off?" she asked. "I'll figure out a way to pay you for a week or two, if it will help."

Karen shook her head. "I have to learn how to handle everything that's going on in my life. If I don't, a couple of weeks off won't make any difference."

"You'd be able to get some rest. Things always look a lot worse when you're exhausted."

"I appreciate the offer, I really do, but no."

"Karen, don't turn your back on help when it's offered," Dana Sue said. "You won't be any good to us or your kids, if you fall apart."

"There are plenty of single moms who have it tougher

than I do," Karen insisted. "You've already done more for me than I have any right to expect."

"Because when you're on top of things, you're an excellent candidate to become a sous-chef," Dana Sue said.

"And I'm going to prove you're right to have faith in me," Karen said. "I'm going to get my act together, I swear it."

Dana Sue sighed. "Just let me know if you change your mind and want that time off."

Karen nodded. "Now I'd better get back to work. I have another batch of gazpacho to make."

She also had a whole lot to prove to these two people who were bending over backward to accommodate all her crises. Failing them just wasn't an option.

7

"What is wrong with you?" Dana Sue demanded when Helen walked onto the patio at The Corner Spa a few mornings after she'd tried to push Erik into calling her.

Helen frowned at her. As much as she relished confrontation and sparring in the courtroom, she didn't want to deal with it with her friends. "Excuse me? What have I done to you?"

"Not me. Erik. The sexiest, nicest man to cross paths with you in years kisses you senseless and you do absolutely nothing about it," Dana Sue accused. "I thought you wanted a real relationship in your life. Wasn't that on that endless list of goals you set awhile back? That and having a baby? And learning to kick back and relax? You're about as relaxed these days as a cobra poised to strike. I can't help wondering what Doc Marshall and those pricey obstetricians you saw would have to say about that."

Helen looked from her to Maddie. "I suppose you agree with her?"

Maddie shrugged. "Pretty much."

"Haven't we had this conversation before?" Her scowl

deepened as she squared off with Dana Sue. "I really, really don't want to have it again."

"Do I look like I care?" Dana Sue retorted. "You're throwing away what could be your best chance to get everything you claim to want because you're stubborn."

"I am not…" Maddie's smile and Dana Sue's incredulous look stopped her from completing the thought. "Okay, I am stubborn, but that's not the issue. This is my life. I make my own decisions."

"Then make one!" Dana Sue snapped. "Stop dawdling."

"I can't rush a decision about having a baby," Helen said. "There's too much at stake."

"Then at least go out on a date with Erik," Dana Sue pleaded. "Surely that's not a difficult decision to make."

Helen shrugged. "He hasn't asked."

"Then ask him," Dana Sue said. "Since when are you some shy, retiring wallflower who waits to be asked? Aren't you the woman who prides herself on being direct, on going after what she wants?"

"I second that," Maddie said, then rested a hand on her stomach. "And as fascinating as it is to watch you trying to wriggle off Dana Sue's matchmaking hook, I think maybe we ought to table it for this morning. We need to start thinking about our plan for running this place while I'm on maternity leave."

Helen took a deep breath, relieved by the change of topic. She grinned at Maddie. "You do like to plan well ahead, don't you? By my calculations, there's plenty of time left."

"I'll feel better if we get a plan down on paper," Maddie said. "I'll be able to check one thing off my list. Cal seems to have a list of his own that requires my attention."

"What's on his list?" Helen asked curiously.

"He wants to turn the attic into some sort of playroom. It sounds like something out of a Jane Austen novel to me. You know, lock all the kids away upstairs with a nanny." She shook her head. "Anyway, he's determined. He thinks Jessica Lynn and the new baby should have a special place. Yesterday he came home from Ronnie's store with enough wallpaper samples and paint chips to decorate the entire town. It'll take me days just to sort through them."

"I could help," Helen offered. "It would be fun."

"Be my guest," Maddie said. "In the meantime, though, focus, you guys. We need a plan."

Dana Sue shrugged. "I figured you could run the spa from home," she teased. "Isn't that what you did last time, even though we officially left Jeanette in charge?"

"That's what I remember, too," Helen concurred.

Maddie scowled at them. "Okay, we all know I'm a control freak. And maybe I could keep tabs on everything with one baby in the house, but with two we're talking a whole new ball game. Kyle insists he's changed his last diaper. Ever since Jessica Lynn's arrival, Katie resents not being the baby anymore. She's not exactly ecstatic about yet another baby coming along. I doubt I can count on her for much help. It's spring, so Cal has baseball practice and games just about every day. And Tyler's away at Duke for another two weeks, not that he'd be that much help, anyway. He's determined to get a summer job."

Helen glanced at Dana Sue, who nodded. "It's a little early for this, but we thought you might be feeling a little overwhelmed," she said, reaching into her briefcase and extracting a flat, rectangular package. "Which is why we got you a little something, since you refused to let us give you another baby shower."

Maddie took the package, eyeing it with suspicion. "What is this?"

"You'll see," Dana Sue told her. "Just open it."

Helen watched her as Maddie carefully undid the bow, then removed the wrapping paper and folded it neatly. "Will you hurry up," she prodded.

Maddie grinned at her. "I love to draw out the suspense," she said as she extracted a gift certificate from the folds of tissue paper. She studied it for several seconds, then stared at them with a stunned expression. "You hired a nanny service for me? For a year?"

Helen and Dana Sue exchanged high fives at the shocked note in her voice.

"You get to do the interviewing and hiring," Helen assured her. "But it's all paid for. We need you to be happy and serene and we thought a nanny might help you to accomplish that. Cal agreed it was the perfect gift."

"Perfect?" Maddie echoed. "It's amazing and generous. Too generous, in fact."

"Don't be ridiculous," Dana Sue said. "Think of it as one of the perks of the job, to say nothing of being our friend. This place has become a gold mine, thanks to you. Besides, we love you."

Maddie sat back in her chair, the gift certificate clutched tightly in her hand. "I'm...I'm overwhelmed."

"Not too overwhelmed to hear us when we tell you we don't want you to even think about setting foot in this place for at least six weeks after the baby arrives, longer if you can stand it," Helen told her. "You've trained Jeanette to handle every single detail. Let her do it."

"And we'll check on her," Dana Sue promised. "If there's a problem, she can come to either one of us. You rest, enjoy your family and take advantage of the free personal training Elliott is offering to give you at home whenever you're ready to get back your girlish figure."

"My figure hasn't been girlish in twenty years," Maddie said ruefully. "But you know, for once I might just listen to you and do absolutely nothing for a few weeks at least."

Dana Sue regarded her with amusement. "Two little ones under two and you honestly think you'll get away with doing nothing? You're delusional."

"But the nanny will help," Helen said. "And Dana Sue and I are only a phone call away if you need backup."

Maddie studied her with a narrowed gaze. "Are you thinking you could use the practice?"

"Don't go there," Helen pleaded. "I'm still wrestling with all my options, and no, I do not want to talk about them in case you were thinking I might have changed my mind about that in the last three minutes."

"Then I guess there's nothing fascinating to be learned here," Dana Sue said, resigned. "I need to get to the restaurant. Karen hasn't exactly been on the top of her game lately, so I need to keep a close eye on her."

Helen frowned. "You're still having problems with her? I thought bringing Tess on board would solve everything."

"It's certainly helped," Dana Sue said. "But this is about Karen's state of mind. She's thoroughly sleep-deprived, if you ask me. She's been showing up, but she's not all there. Don't worry about it, though. I'm sure it's just going to take a little time for her to learn how to juggle everything going on in her life. Being a single mom is never easy, even in the best of circumstances."

"Amen to that," Maddie said. "Those months I was on my own with Ty acting out, Kyle all closed off and Katie sobbing her heart out for her daddy every night were among the worst months of my life. And that was even with their dad only a phone call away, my mom pitching in, *and* after Cal came along. I can't imagine how I would have coped without all that support and you guys around to listen to me."

"I could speak to Karen again," Helen offered, feeling somehow responsible for the younger woman. Maybe, deep down, she even feared that Karen's apparent inability to cope with her kids and her job was a warning about the struggles she herself would face if she did decide to have a baby on her own.

"Come on," Dana Sue protested. "This isn't your problem to solve."

"Maybe not, but Karen obviously doesn't have the kind of support system we all have," Helen said. "Maybe we could figure out a way to get that for her."

Dana Sue shook her head. "No, right now I think our butting in, especially me, will only add to the pressure she's feeling."

Helen considered that, then sighed. "You're probably right. But let me know if you think I can help."

"Sure," Dana Sue said. "There *is* another situation I'd like you to look in to, but Erik promised he'd fill you in."

Helen studied her with a narrowed gaze. "His idea or yours?"

"Does it matter?" Dana Sue asked.

"More than likely," Helen muttered.

Oddly, though, she felt a little hum of anticipation speed through her at the prospect of crossing paths with him again, no matter the reason.

Probably not a good sign.

* * *

Erik tried to get out for a walk every afternoon between the end of the lunch crowd and the beginning of the dinner rush. At one time he would have run, but recently his knee bothered him if he did. Walking wasn't the same, but at least it gave him time to collect his thoughts, which lately had been chaotic. Helen Decatur seemed to inhabit his head a whole lot more than he was comfortable with.

Picking up his pace on the warm, sticky afternoon, he passed through downtown Serenity, if it could be called that with only Wharton's Pharmacy and its soda fountain and Ronnie's hardware store anchoring the main square. A lot of empty storefronts remained and probably would until a few more people showed a willingness to take the sort of risk Ronnie had when he'd revived the old hardware store and added the kind of creative spin that made it economically viable. Working with local developers to fill their construction-supply needs had been brilliant.

When Erik reached the town park, where swans swam on a small, sparkling lake, he was grateful for the shade provided by the old oak trees, heavily draped with Spanish moss.

Intent on keeping up his pace, he was almost on top of Helen before he saw her. She was seated on a bench, an oddly pensive expression on her face.

"Hey," he said, stopping in front of her. "You playing hooky from the office again?"

Clearly startled by the sound of his voice, she glanced at him and color rose in her cheeks. "Something like that," she said.

"Same thing troubling you that was on your mind the other day?"

"I suppose," she said tonelessly. "What are you doing

out at this time of day? Shouldn't you be chopping and dicing and marinading for dinner by now?"

"Soon," he said, then sat down beside her. "Actually I've been hoping to bump in to you."

"Oh? Why is that?"

He grinned at the suspicion in her voice. "Do you always suspect an ulterior motive when someone wants to talk to you?"

She shrugged, her expression rueful. "Mostly."

"Well, my motives are pure. This is about Tess, Karen's friend."

"Ah, yes," Helen said. "How's she working out?"

"Surely Dana Sue has told you," he said.

"She has, but I'd like your perspective."

"Well, she's amazing," he said, then cast a sideways glance at her. "Dana Sue says we owe you for that."

"I didn't find her. Karen did."

"But you opened us up to the possibility of some solution other than firing Karen and replacing her," he said.

"If Tess is working out so well, why did you want to discuss her with me?"

Erik took a deep breath. "She could use some legal help, but she's not making a lot of money. I don't think it's the kind of problem that should be held up until she can afford to hire the best, especially since some other lawyer took her money and never did a thing to help her."

Helen immediately sat a little straighter. "Explain," she said briskly.

He told her what little he knew about Diego Martinez's situation and Tess's previous attorney. "Is there anything you can do?"

"At the very least I can pin this jerk's tail feathers back

a little and get her money returned. And I can certainly look into her husband's case, even though immigration law is a far cry from what I normally do. Does she know you're talking to me?"

"I mentioned that a friend of Dana Sue's might be able to help, but Tess was reluctant to ask because of the whole money thing."

"Tell her not to worry about that. Make sure she calls me." She glanced at her watch. "Is she working now? If she is, I'll walk back over to Sullivan's with you and speak to her right now."

"No, she's off today, but she'll be there tomorrow," Erik told her. "Can you come by then?"

"I'll try, and before you remind me, I'll avoid coming during peak hours."

"Tired of being drafted into working in the kitchen?" he teased.

"No, to be honest, it's one of the few things that seems to relax me lately."

He regarded her with surprise. "Really? What do you have to be uptight about? You're smart. You're successful. You're beautiful."

"Thank you, but it has recently come to my attention that there's more to life."

He laughed at that, though he gave her a commiserating look. "Dana Sue been filling your head with notions, Helen?"

"She and Maddie," she confirmed. "I suspect you've fallen victim as well."

"I have," he said.

"Any advice?"

"Hey, you've known Dana Sue longer than I have. You could probably give me a few pointers."

"I seem to have run out of arguments that work with her, especially since she's back with Ronnie and thinks the world should operate like Noah's ark, you know, in pairs."

Erik's gaze locked with hers. He couldn't seem to look away from that hint of vulnerability he saw once again in her eyes. "I guess we both just need to stick to our guns."

"I suppose so," she said, though with surprisingly little enthusiasm.

"We could go out for coffee sometime, plan our strategy for keeping Dana Sue from meddling in our lives," he suggested. "How much misery can she stir up if we're both on the same page?"

Something that might have been disappointment streaked across her face, but she recovered so quickly, Erik was certain he'd been mistaken.

"That sounds like a plan," she finally agreed with a forced note of cheer in her voice. "I guess Grace was right about you."

"Grace? How did she get involved in this?"

"She says you're a confirmed bachelor."

"Not always," he said, clearly taking her by surprise.

"You've been married?"

He nodded.

"Divorced?"

He shook his head. "She died." Before Helen could pester him with a lot of questions he had no intention of answering, he was on his feet. "Thanks for agreeing to look into Tess's situation, Helen."

"Not a problem. See, even barracuda attorneys have their good side."

Erik winced. "Sorry about calling you that."

"Hey, you're entitled to your opinion. And frankly, I'm

rather proud to be called that. If you have to go into court, a barracuda attorney is exactly who you want fighting for you."

"So, we're still friends?"

She grinned at him. "Of course we are, though it would help if you'd answer some of my questions, instead of stonewalling me. Real friendship is all about conversational give-and-take."

"So I hear," Erik said.

"Then you'll tell me all your deep, dark secrets?" she asked.

"Nah," he replied. "What would be the fun in that? I think I like the idea of you being frustrated and wanting more."

"Is that an ego thing?"

"Nope. It's a guy thing. See you around. Come by and chop and dice sometime," he invited. "We miss you in the kitchen. And we will have that coffee one of these days."

Even as he walked away, he realized that the offhand comment about missing her was absolutely true. He'd enjoyed having her underfoot in the kitchen. When Helen was on his turf, the whole barracuda thing disappeared and she was just an intelligent, attractive woman who made his hormones sit up and take notice. It had been a very long time since any woman had done that.

And *that* was something he hoped to hell Dana Sue never found out or she'd make both their lives a matchmaking nightmare.

Three-year-old Mack had barely closed his eyes for the night when he woke up screaming. Karen, who'd fallen asleep in front of the TV, jolted awake and ran into the bedroom to find Mack trying to climb out of his crib and Daisy trying to shove him back in, which only made Mack cry harder.

"It's okay," Karen told Daisy. "I've got him."

"If he gets to stay up, I do, too," Daisy said, her face setting stubbornly.

"No," Karen said, holding on to her temper by a thread. "You need to get some sleep. You have school in the morning."

"It's not fair," Daisy wailed.

"I don't care if it's fair or not. It's the way it is," Karen told her, even as Mack continued to sob in her arms. "Please, sweetie, let me try to get your brother to settle down. Go back to sleep."

"He's making too much noise," Daisy protested.

"Which is why I'm taking him with me into the other room," Karen explained patiently. "Now, crawl back into bed and put your head down. You'll be asleep in no time."

After giving her mother one last mulish look, Daisy finally did as she'd asked. Karen bent over to press a kiss to her forehead, then carried Mack into the living room.

"Okay, sweetie, what's up with this?" she asked, resting a hand against Mack's damp, satin-soft cheek. "Do you have a fever? Or did you just have a bad dream?"

Mack whimpered and stared back at her, his dark blue eyes swimming with tears. He clung to Karen's neck with a viselike grip. When Karen tried to loosen the hold, Mack started sobbing again.

"Oh, baby, what is it? Please calm down. Mommy's here. Everything's fine." She settled into an old wooden rocker she'd found at a flea market before Daisy was born and tried rocking Mack back to sleep. It used to work like a charm, but tonight every time Mack's eyes started to drift shut, he'd yank himself awake and starting crying loudly all over again. Nothing Karen tried seemed to soothe him.

With each new round of sobs, Karen's nerves stretched a little tighter. When Daisy appeared, begging for a glass of water, something inside her snapped.

"No!" she shouted. "I want you back in bed right this instant!"

Her daughter stared at her for a heartbeat, obviously startled by her sharp tone, and then she began to cry, too. The sound of the two of them rose to a pitch that left Karen shaking with rage and dismay. Completely overwhelmed, she all but ran out of her apartment and across the hall, with Mack still in her arms and Daisy trailing behind. Oblivious to the late hour, she knocked frantically on Frances's door.

"What on earth?" Frances said when she responded to Karen's knock wearing a bathrobe, her hair in curlers. She took one look at Karen and the two squalling children and led them inside, where a TV was tuned in to a late-night talk show. Taking Mack from Karen's arms, she began patting his back, then sent Daisy into the kitchen for a glass of water.

Her soothing, matter-of-fact tone accomplished what Karen had been unable to. Both children quieted down almost immediately.

"I can't do it," Karen told Frances, swiping at her own tears. Never in her life had she imagined herself as the kind of mom who could snap in an instant and hit one of her children or even yell the way she had at Daisy. "I can't handle this another minute. I'm afraid of what will happen if I try."

"Come now," Frances murmured, soothing her as if she were one of the distraught children. "You're a good mother. You brought them over here, didn't you? You would never hurt these babies."

"Oh, God," Karen said. "It makes me sick to even think I could."

"Then we'll see what we can do to fix this," Frances told her in the same calm, matter-of-fact tone. "You just leave these two with me for now, okay? Go back to your place and take a little nap."

"I can't leave them with you! It's too much."

"We'll be fine. You need a decent night's sleep. I don't want to see you back here before tomorrow afternoon. I'm going to speak to Dana Sue and explain what's happened."

"You can't do that," Karen protested. "It will be the last straw. I know it will."

"Don't be ridiculous," Frances admonished firmly. "She'll understand. I'll make sure of that. Now, go. The kids and I will be fine tonight and I can get them off to school and day care in the morning. I have a key so I can get their clothes and I know the routine."

"Are you sure?" Karen asked halfheartedly. The idea of sleeping through an entire night lured her like some kind of lighthouse showing her the way home. Uninterrupted sleep would be a godsend.

"I'm sure," Frances said. "We'll talk some more tomorrow. You come over here when you wake up and I'll fix you a nice, big breakfast."

Impulsively, Karen went back and threw her arms around Frances and the now sleeping Mack. "Thank you. I honestly don't know what I would have done if you weren't here. And thanks for offering to speak to Dana Sue."

Even if Dana Sue did fire her in the morning, an entire night in bed when she didn't have to listen for the sound of the kids waking and a morning when she might actually awake refreshed, rather than exhausted would be worth it. She couldn't go on as she had been. Tonight had proved that.

Defeated, she dragged herself back across the hall and

climbed into bed. Clutching her pillow, she started to sob, letting out all the frustration and fear that had been bottled up inside for weeks now. She didn't know what tomorrow might hold, but it had to be better than this emotional roller coaster she'd been on.

8

The phone call woke Helen out of a sound sleep. Used to snapping awake to deal with legal emergencies that occasionally befell her clients, she was sitting on the edge of the bed with the light on and pen in hand to take notes before she even picked up the receiver.

"Helen, it's Dana Sue. We have a situation," she said, sounding shaken.

"What kind of situation?" Helen inquired, her stomach dropping. The last time Dana Sue had had a middle-of-the-night crisis, her daughter had been taken to the hospital with complications from anorexia. Fearing the worst, she asked, "Is it Annie?"

"No, it's Karen."

"Karen? I don't understand. What's going on with her at this hour? And why call me?"

"Please, can you just come over to her apartment now? I'm already here and I'll explain when you get here."

Never one to waste time asking unnecessary questions in a crisis, especially when it was one of the Sweet Magnolias asking for her help, Helen jotted down the address. "I'm on my way. Give me ten minutes."

"Thanks."

Helen yanked on a pair of slacks and a blouse without bothering to tuck it in. She shoved her feet into a pair of expensive backless slides that were about as casual as any shoes she owned. Grabbing her briefcase out of habit on the way out, she was on her way in under five minutes.

When she arrived across town at the apartment building where Karen lived, she noted that lights were blazing in both of the downstairs apartments despite the lateness of the hour. As soon as she entered the building, Dana Sue greeted her and pulled her into an apartment on the right.

"Karen's had some kind of breakdown," she said, her voice low and her gaze directed at a closed door to what was most likely a bedroom in the cramped unit. "Her neighbor called me after Karen knocked on her door and woke her up, pleading with her for help. She told me Karen was afraid she was going to hurt her kids. Frances—you know her, right? Frances Wingate…?"

Helen nodded. Frances had taught them all when they were in school. She'd been strict, but fair, and she definitely wasn't prone to exaggeration. If she was afraid for Karen and the kids, then there was reason to be afraid.

Trying to keep herself from overreacting, she asked, "Did she hit them? Shake them?"

"No, they're both fine," Dana Sue said. "But Karen's in the bedroom. She's pretty hysterical. Frances was going to wait to call me in the morning, because she thought Karen would go to bed and get a good night's sleep. But she came over to check on her and Karen was locked in her bedroom, sobbing. Frances called me to ask what I thought she ought to do. She thought Karen might need medical attention or something."

"So naturally you came running over," Helen said.

"Of course. What was I supposed to do? Karen's my employee and a friend. She's obviously completely distraught. She wouldn't open the bedroom door for me. I thought about getting Ronnie over here to break it down so we could take her to the hospital, but I was afraid to do that. I wasn't sure if social services would have to come and take the kids. That's why I wanted you here before we did anything."

Helen nodded. "Let me talk to her. Are the kids okay across the hall for now?"

Dana Sue nodded. "You know Frances. She's completely unflappable. Apparently the kids stay with her a lot when Karen has to run an errand or something. At her age, she can't keep them all the time, but she obviously adores them. She's like a grandmother. I don't think either Daisy or Mack understand what's going on. They're both asleep now."

Satisfied that the children were unharmed and safe for now, Helen knocked on the bedroom door. "Karen, it's Helen. Please let me in so we can talk. Whatever's going on, I want to help."

"Go away," Karen pleaded. "I don't want anyone to see me like this. I'll be okay if I just get some sleep."

"It doesn't sound to me as if you're even close to falling asleep. Talking things out will unburden you, help you to relax," Helen said. "I know I can never sleep when my mind's racing a hundred miles an hour."

Her comment was greeted with silence, so she tried again. "I hope you're not worried that if you talk to me, I'm going to go running to Dana Sue. She's already gone back to Frances's apartment. This will be just between the two of us."

"Just go away," Karen pleaded again. "I need to figure things out for myself."

"Figure out what?" Helen coaxed. "Tell me. Two minds are always better than one. Whatever's going on, I can help you sort through it."

"Dana Sue should never have called you," Karen said. "I don't need a lawyer."

"How about a friend?" Helen asked gently. "Please let me be a friend."

A long minute passed before a key finally turned in the lock. The door remained closed, but when Helen tried the knob, it opened. Inside the pitch-black bedroom, she felt for a switch and turned on the overhead light. Karen was sprawled facedown on the bed wearing an old chenille bathrobe, her hair disheveled and her face blotchy from crying. She regarded Helen apologetically, then buried her face in the pillow.

"I'm so sorry Dana Sue dragged you out in the middle of the night," Karen said, her words muffled. "I'm sorry she got dragged into this, too. I hate having my boss all caught up in my personal drama."

Helen sat down gingerly on the edge of the bed. "Stop worrying about that. It's not important. Can you tell me what happened?"

Karen nodded, her expression bleak. "I've been feeling more and more overwhelmed, you know. About my job. About money. Ray's still not paying child support, and even though Tess and I worked out that plan with Dana Sue, I'm still not pulling my weight at the restaurant. Dana Sue's been great about it, but I know Erik thinks I'm taking advantage of her. And, face it, she can't pay me when I'm not there, so my salary's not what it was. And it seems like every time I turn around one of the kids is sick again. It's too much. I can't cope anymore."

"What happened tonight?" Helen prodded carefully.

"My three-year-old—that's Mack—woke up crying," she began, her voice catching on a sob. She swiped at the tears on her cheeks with the sleeve of her robe. "Nothing I did calmed him down." Again, her voice hitched. "And then Daisy got mad because Mack was getting all my attention, so she started acting out."

The look she directed at Helen begged her to understand. "They've both had tantrums before, but not at the same time, and not when I was already at the end of my rope. I could feel myself losing control. When I realized I just wanted to shake Mack to make him stop crying and then I yelled at Daisy, I knew I had to do something, so I went across the hall and asked Frances for help. She insisted on taking them, but they can't stay there indefinitely. I have to figure out something else, at least until I can trust myself with them again."

"You did exactly the right thing by taking them to Frances," Helen soothed her. "Recognizing that you were at your wit's end is a good thing, Karen."

Karen suddenly regarded her with alarm. "Nobody will try to take them away from me because of this, will they?"

"Not if I can help it," Helen stated. "But you do need to get some help, you know that, don't you? You can't just tough it out and hope all these feelings will disappear."

Karen nodded, looking defeated. "But I can't check in to a hospital. I'll lose my job and my kids for sure, if I do that."

Helen knew that was a strong possibility, so she couldn't disagree with her. "How about this?" she said. "We'll arrange for some counseling sessions. Dana Sue knows a psychologist, a Dr. McDaniels, who helped her daughter conquer her eating disorder. Maybe she can make arrangements for you to see her first thing in the morning and schedule some regular sessions every day for a couple of weeks."

"But that's bound to be expensive," Karen protested.

"You have health insurance at the restaurant, right?" Helen asked. "That should cover it. If it doesn't, we'll figure something out. The main thing is to see someone who can help you calm down and get some perspective. Maybe Dr. McDaniels can offer you better ways to cope with your stress. Then we'll see where we stand."

"And the kids could stay here with me?" Karen asked hopefully.

Helen was less sure about the wisdom of that. "I'm not sure that's such a good idea. Right now, they're just adding to your stress. I think you need some time to get yourself strong again. That doesn't mean I think you're a bad mother, Karen. Not at all. I just think you're worn out and need a break."

"But what about the kids?" Karen asked worriedly. "Frances and the sitter could help some, but they can't keep them."

"There's foster care," Helen began, but practically before the words were out of her mouth, Karen was shaking her head.

"Absolutely not," she said fiercely. "I don't want my kids with strangers. Besides, once they get into the system, it'll be hard to get them out. I know that firsthand. I was bounced around foster homes most of my life because my mother couldn't get her life together. I swore I'd never repeat that pattern." She buried her face in her hands. "God, I feel like such a failure. I always judged my mom for not being able to cope and here I am, exactly like her."

"Okay," Helen said, "how about this? I'll take them temporarily." The words were uttered before she could talk herself out of the crazy, impulsive idea, but surprisingly she had no inclination to take them back. "They can stay with me. We'll keep the same sitter and I'll make sure Frances comes by for a visit every day so they won't feel too uprooted. You can come over, too, as much as you want to."

"But I can't ask you to do that," Karen said, looking stunned. "They're a handful. You've never had kids. You have no idea of what you'd be letting yourself in for."

"Oh, I have some idea," Helen said, thinking of the times Maddie's kids had stayed overnight with her. Of course, this would be more than a one-night sleepover, but surely she could manage, especially with the help of the sitter and Frances. And she could see just how adept she'd be at juggling work demands with caring for children. Maybe that was the real reason she'd offered, not out of some burst of generosity, but out of selfishness. If fear of failure was holding her back from making a decision about having her own child, this would be a good test. She didn't have time now, though, to analyze her motives further. The offer was on the table.

"Well?" she asked Karen. "Would you be okay with that?"

"Of course," Karen said with obvious relief. For the first time since Helen's arrival, her face lost its pinched, desperate expression.

"Then that's what we'll do," Helen said decisively. "You pack up a few things for them. I'll speak to Dana Sue about setting up those appointments with the psychologist for you first thing in the morning. Maybe you should come with me tonight and stay over at my place, too. It'll make the transition a little easier for the kids. Or we can let the kids sleep tonight and I'll get them tomorrow."

"That would be best, especially if they're finally asleep,"

Karen said. "Are you really sure about this? I don't want to disrupt your life any more than I already have. I already owe you for saving my job."

"It'll be okay," Helen assured her, then went in search of Dana Sue, who'd returned to Karen's apartment and was waiting in the living room for Helen to emerge.

When she'd explained the plan, Dana Sue stared at her incredulously. "You're taking them in? All of them, including Karen?"

"Karen will come with me tonight," Helen said. "I don't think she ought to stay here alone. Tomorrow, she'll help me get the kids settled and I'll take them to school. She'll come back here, if the doctor says it's okay. She just needs some time to get her bearings. She also needs to get back on track at work. This will give her a little freedom to do that without worrying about her kids."

"Do you have any idea what you're letting yourself in for?" Dana Sue demanded. "Are you even equipped to have an instant family under your roof, even for a couple of weeks? You've got a house filled with breakable antiques, for heaven's sake!"

"I'll manage," Helen said. Her organizational skills kicked in. "As soon as I get home, I'll stuff the breakables into a closet or something. I'll make a list of everything I need from the store and have it delivered first thing tomorrow. You can help me with that. I'll get their schedule from Karen and make sure they get to day care and school. Her sitter will come to my house. I'll have Frances visit every afternoon, too."

Dana Sue shook her head. "I should have known you'd come up with a thorough strategy in ten seconds or less," she said wryly. "One thing you ought to consider, though."

"What's that?"

"Kids tend to make mincemeat out of plans. They're not predictable."

Helen heard the concern in her friend's voice, but shrugged it off. "Then this will be a good test of my flexibility, won't it?"

Dana Sue gave her a worried look. "That's my point, sweetie. You're not flexible."

"If I'm ever going to have a child of my own, I'll have to be," Helen said. "This will be excellent practice, even better than having Maddie's kids or Annie underfoot for a night."

"You're really sure you want to do this?"

Helen nodded. Mixing with her carefully banked fears, she felt a faint stirring of excitement.

"Okay, then," Dana Sue said briskly. "I'll help Karen pack up their things. You might want to at least peek at the kids. If you're going to take them home tomorrow, it'll help if you can at least recognize them."

"Not funny," Helen said, though she was filled with trepidation as she crossed the hall and went in to speak to Frances, who guided her into a guest room where both children were sleeping soundly.

One glance at those sweet, innocent faces and Helen knew she was doing the right thing. She would care for and protect them 'til Karen could take over again. How hard could it be?

"They look like little angels, don't they?" Frances asked.

"They do," Helen confirmed.

"Don't believe it," Frances said, her voice threaded with amusement and affection. "They're little hellions, same as all kids that age. You come by first thing tomorrow and I'll go with you to drop them off at school and day care. I'll be by your place tomorrow afternoon just in case you're tearing your hair out."

"But the sitter—" Helen began.

"Isn't worth one thin dime of what Karen is paying her," Frances said with disgust. "I know you found her for Karen, but she doesn't know how to handle those children. *I* do. Between you and me, we can get the job done. Getting rid of the sitter will save Karen some money."

"But I have to work," Helen started to protest, then sighed. She had a hunch that was just the first of many compromises she was going to have to make. "I'll call my secretary and reschedule my afternoon appointments."

Frances gave her an approving look. "Now we have a plan."

Helen had the oddest sensation that fate had just handed her not just two children to test her mettle as mom material, but a wise and experienced guide to help her when the going got rough.

Erik stared at Dana Sue as if she'd just announced that Helen had been abducted by aliens.

"You're telling me that Helen is taking care of Karen's children for the foreseeable future," he repeated, still not certain he'd heard correctly.

"That's what I'm telling you," Dana Sue confirmed. "You could have knocked me over with a feather, too."

"Does she know anything at all about children?"

"Well, she always returned Annie to me in one piece. The same with Maddie's kids."

Erik shook his head. "The woman is full of surprises, isn't she?"

"She is," Dana Sue concurred. "But this one's a doozy,

even by my standards. The good news for us is that Karen's already feeling less stressed now that she knows the kids are safe and being well cared for. She's had her first appointment with Dr. McDaniels and she'll be in on time today. She's determined to use this respite to get her life back on track."

"But what happens the minute the kids go back home again, which they will eventually, right?"

"That's the plan. Helen's convinced that all Karen needs is a little breather. We'll see if Dr. McDaniels agrees. I hope so. I like Karen. I want this to work out."

"But you won't mind if I remain skeptical," Erik said.

"I don't blame you, but I'm determined to remain optimistic. Look, I'm going out for an hour, okay? Hold down the fort."

Dana Sue was barely out the door when the phone rang. Erik almost ignored it, since the restaurant wasn't open yet, but when it continued ringing, he finally grabbed it.

"I need Dana Sue," Helen announced without so much as a greeting for him.

"She's not here," he said. "Can I help?"

"Only if you have some idea who or what Elmo is," she said. "Mack seems to be obsessed with getting his hands on one."

Erik bit back a chuckle at the panic in her normally confident voice. "It's a toy," he explained patiently. "From *Sesame Street*."

"How do you know that?"

"I have nephews," he said. "You know, it's not necessary that you provide a child with every single toy he asks for."

"You try telling that to a three-year-old who has the single-minded determination of a pit bull," she grumbled.

"Distract him," Erik advised. "He's three. It shouldn't take much."

"Distract him how?"

"Cookies," he suggested. "Ice cream. A TV cartoon show. If *Sesame Street*'s on now, you can kill two birds with one stone, a distraction *and* Elmo."

"There are kids' cartoons on in the afternoon?"

Erik laughed at her bewildered tone. "Darlin', you've just entered a whole new world. That's just one of the joys of cable TV."

"I'll try it. Thanks."

"Hey, Helen," he said, oddly determined to keep her from hanging up.

"What?"

"What you're doing is pretty amazing," he told her, not even trying to hide his admiration.

"Maybe you should wait before paying me a compliment. I still have plenty of time to screw this up."

"You won't," he said confidently.

"How do you know?"

"Because I know you. When was the last time you screwed up anything you set your mind to?"

Her silence was answer enough.

"I rest my case," he told her quietly. "Call back if you need any other advice, okay?"

"Will do. Thanks, Erik."

He replaced the phone, then stood there like an idiot staring at it. She really was an amazing, unpredictable woman. He'd met Daisy and Mack on the couple of occasions Karen brought them to the restaurant, and knew what Helen had unwittingly let herself in for. He'd give anything to see her chasing down those kids in her designer suit and stiletto heels. Come to think of it, maybe he'd bake some chocolate chip cookies before leaving Sullivan's tonight. He could take them by first thing in the morning so she could pack them in the kids' lunches. It would give him a firsthand look at the ever-in-command Helen in a situation she couldn't possibly command. It'd probably make his day.

Getting two kids ready to leave the house before eight in the morning left Helen winded, frazzled and right on the edge of throwing in the towel. When the doorbell rang, she left Mack under Daisy's watchful eye and raced to answer it, praying for the calvary in the form of Maddie or Dana Sue. Instead, it was Erik, his expression oddly smug as he took in her hair, which was sticking out in every direction, her lack of makeup, her untucked blouse and bare feet.

"I thought you might need a little help," he said. "And I brought cookies."

"It's seven forty-five in the morning and you brought cookies?" she demanded. "Are you crazy? The last thing those two need is more sugar."

"Save the cookies for a treat after school," he said. "Or tuck one into their lunches."

Helen stared at him with a bewildered expression. "They need lunches?"

"I imagine so," he said, barely containing a grin.

"I was thinking lunch money for the school cafeteria," she said, then recalled the paper sacks Frances had given them the day before. "Are you sure they can't get lunch at school?"

He shook his head. "Not likely. Where's Daisy? We can ask her."

"Daisy's watching while Mack decides what he wants

to wear today," Helen said. "He stubbornly resisted all my selections."

Erik chuckled. "You left a three-year-old to decide on his own?"

"Of course," she said huffily. "Well, with Daisy's help, anyway. Children should develop their own sense of style at an early age."

"Maybe I'll go help him out," Erik suggested. "You make the lunches. I suggest peanut butter and jelly sandwiches. They're not complicated."

Helen frowned. "Okay, I have that leftover from Katie's last visit, but aren't some kids allergic to peanut butter? I read an article—"

Erik cut her off. "Not these two. They've been at the restaurant once or twice, and Karen's brought PB and J sandwiches for them."

"You're sure?" she asked worriedly.

"I'm sure. Now go or Daisy will be late for school and you'll be trying to explain why you have her instead of her mother. I imagine that would not be a good thing."

"You're right. That would be awkward. I'll hurry. I can check on them and have myself pulled together in two minutes," she assured him.

She winced at the skeptical expression on Erik's face. "I can," she repeated, then darted off to make good on the promise. Maybe later she'd think about why Erik's arrival struck her as salvation, rather than an annoying intrusion.

Erik wandered through the spacious house until he found Mack in a bedroom probably the size of Karen's entire apartment. The toddler looked a little lost, sitting on the floor in his bright red shorts and sneakers, surrounded by a pile of inside-out T-shirts. Daisy was poking through them.

"His Superman T-shirt's not here," she explained. "That's what he wears with his red shorts." She frowned, then added emphatically in case Erik had missed the point, "Always!"

Erik looked over the pile of discarded shirts and honed in on the Spider-Man shirt. "This would look pretty cool with the red shorts," he suggested. "In fact, Spider-Man is so totally awesome he goes with anything."

Daisy studied the shirt skeptically. "You think so?"

"I *know* so," Erik confirmed, already pulling it over Mack's head. "Now, let's hustle, pal. You need to get to day care."

"How am I going to get to school?" Daisy asked.

"Helen's going to take you."

"Can you come, too?" she asked.

"If you want me to, I can. Any particular reason you want me along?"

"So you can make Helen stay in the car and not walk me to the door holding my hand. I can get to the door by myself."

Erik bit back a grin. "I'm sure you can."

"So, will you tell her not to do it again?"

"You could tell her yourself," Erik suggested.

"I don't wanna hurt her feelings. Mom said we need to be nice to her."

"Okay, then. I'll tell her," he promised.

Within minutes Helen had Daisy and Mack belted into their respective car seats, which she'd borrowed from Karen. She was about to open the driver's-side door when she noticed Erik opening the passenger door. She stared at him.

"You're coming with us?"

"By special request," he said softly, gesturing subtly to

indicate Daisy. "She wants me to make sure you don't take her hand and lead her to the door."

Helen gave a small gasp. "I thought that was what moms did. I could tell by the look on her face that she hated it, but she didn't say anything."

"She didn't want to hurt your feelings."

She sighed. "Do you suppose I'll ever figure all this out?"

"You're doing fine, especially for someone with no experience."

"But you don't have kids and you seem to know what to do. You knew about the toys and cartoons and peanut butter and jelly."

"Like I told you on the phone, I have nephews. This isn't rocket science, Helen. It just takes practice."

"I hope so," she said, sounding resigned.

In front of the school, though, she pulled to the curb, then turned to Daisy and gave her a smile that hardly looked forced at all. Only her white-knuckled grip on the steering wheel gave away her tension. "You have a good day, okay? Frances will pick you up this afternoon."

Daisy beamed at her. "Okay. Uh, don't let Mack go by himself, 'cause he doesn't know anything. He'll get lost."

Helen regarded her solemnly. "I'll keep that in mind."

After Daisy was safely inside the building, she turned to Erik. "So that went well, didn't it? And I'm not even a parent," she said.

He studied her. "Ever want to be?"

"I've thought about it," she said in a tone that warned him away from asking any more questions. "You?"

"Once, a long time ago," he admitted.

"Before your wife died," she said.

He nodded. "Yeah, that dream pretty much died with

her." He somehow managed to inject a lighter note into his voice as he peered into the back to check on Mack, who gave him one of those brilliant smiles that could melt a man's heart. "Let's get this little tough guy to day care. It's only a few blocks from here. Something tells me he's regressed to his pre-potty-training days. Unless you want to deal with it, we need to make a quick getaway."

Helen grinned at his conspiratorial tone, then began to chuckle. "I am so with you on that. Think you can hustle him inside while I keep the motor running?"

"Oh, yeah," he said. "We can be across town before they catch on."

For the first time since he'd arrived at her house, Helen looked relaxed.

"How about I buy you that cup of coffee and some breakfast when we've made a clean getaway?" he suggested, giving in to an impulse that it would have been smarter to ignore.

"I don't suppose I could talk you into making the coffee at Sullivan's?" she suggested. "It's the best anywhere in town."

He grinned. "You angling for one of my omelets, too?"

She regarded him with unmistakable gratitude. "Please."

"You going to help?"

"After two cups of coffee, I'll do anything you want me to do," she said fervently.

Erik stared at her 'til bright patches of color rose in her cheeks. "An interesting offer," he commented. "I'll keep it in mind."

In fact, he suspected it would be quite a while before he could shake the thought.

9

"I just need to establish a routine," Helen said, pulling a notebook out of her briefcase and setting it on the table next to her empty plate. She'd finished every bite of Erik's ham-and-cheese omelet, along with enough home-fried potatoes with bits of onion and green peppers to keep her stuffed for a week. She was also on her third cup of his fragrant French roast coffee. She was feeling pretty darn invincible compared to the way she'd felt an hour earlier.

As she wrote "Routine" and underlined it at the top of the page, she caught Erik's lips twitching. "What?" she demanded.

"You are talking about Daisy and Mack, right?" he asked in amusement. "Two little people about so high?"

She frowned at him. "Yes. What's your point?"

"I think aiming for a routine is just a little optimistic," he said.

"But children need routine," she said, regarding him with puzzlement. Routine had certainly been lacking in her childhood. It was at the top of her list of things she'd do differently if she ever had children of her own. She expanded on her point for Erik's benefit. "They need to know there are certain things they can count on. They need goals and expectations."

"At five and three?"

"It's never too early to start teaching them these things," she insisted. "It's important to be clear about what you expect and the consequences of not living up to those expectations. You have to be totally consistent. Mixed messages confuse them."

"You've been reading parenting books, right?"

"Well, of course I have," she said. "And I do have some experience to draw on."

"Annie's occasional sleepover at your place or a visit from Maddie's kids?"

"No, it's more than that. My childhood was chaotic, to put it mildly. I never knew when one or both of my parents would show up. I never had a curfew. Meals were catch as catch can, especially after my dad died and mom worked two, sometimes three jobs."

He nodded. "Ah, that explains it."

"Explains what?"

"The obsession with organization and routine."

"You're just not getting this," she accused. "If Daisy and Mack are going to be with me, even for a few weeks, I need to handle things the way they're *supposed* to be handled. What if I do something stupid and scar them for life? I need to be prepared for every eventuality. That's the responsible thing to do."

"So how many books *have* you read, Helen?" he taunted.

Avoiding his gaze, she replied, "I don't know exactly. A few."

Under Erik's increasingly amused scrutiny, she was beginning to feel embarrassed about her obsessive need to read everything she could about parenting. Other people apparently approached parenting instinctively. She was clueless. Her own parents could have used a few books. Volumes, in fact.

Of course, it was hard to find five minutes to read them with two very active children around, which was why she'd been up past midnight last night. She blamed the lack of sleep for being so frazzled this morning. Now it was easier to understand why Karen had been so stressed out.

"What did you do, send that efficient secretary of yours to a bookstore and have her buy out the entire parenting section?" Erik asked.

She frowned at him. That was exactly what she'd done. How annoying that he could read her so well. "I wanted a variety of opinions."

He nodded. "Fair enough. How about listening to one more?"

"You don't have kids," she protested. "You told me you weren't even thinking about having kids."

"No, but I was one. So were you. You said yourself that that kind of experience counts. And I do have all those nephews. You have Annie and Maddie's kids. They didn't come to any harm staying with you, did they?"

"No, but they never stayed for more than a night. I don't think you can ruin a child in one night just by indulging his every whim. That's what I did, you know. Pizza, candy, popcorn, ice cream, videos for half the night—you name it. My house was a no-rules environment." At his incredulous look, she shrugged. "What can I say? I wanted to be Auntie Helen, the fun one. I wanted them to like me. Even I'm smart enough to know you can't live like that on a regular basis. If I try that with Daisy and Mack, I'll return them to Karen with a whole lot of very bad habits. I don't think that's the way to go."

Erik nodded. "Okay, you have a point. Maybe the real answer is finding a routine for you, not the kids. My hunch is you're the one making the biggest adjustment here."

Helen regarded him with astonishment. "You're absolutely right," she said at once, seizing on the notion like the lifeline he'd intended it to be. "If I'm organized and on track, then everything will go a lot more smoothly. Obviously today's schedule didn't work. I'll need to be up at 4:30 a.m., not five."

She jotted that down and noted that extra half hour as her time to fix lunches, her own breakfast and coffee. Lots and lots of coffee.

"How did you do with bathtime last night?" Erik asked.

Helen regarded him with dismay. "Baths?" she echoed. "My God, they never had baths, Erik. I sent those children off to school totally filthy."

"Don't panic," Erik consoled her. "I'm sure they were ecstatic, which is probably why Daisy, at least, didn't remind you. You might want to make a note to yourself, though. Make sure they brush their teeth, too."

Helen had remembered to make them brush their teeth, but she wrote down "Bath" in bold letters, then gave Erik a considering look. "I don't suppose you'd want to come by and help," she suggested hopefully.

"I don't get out of Sullivan's 'til nearly midnight," he reminded her. "They need to be tucked in bed long before that."

Helen sighed. "Of course they do."

Erik regarded her with pity. "I am off tomorrow, though. How about I come by then to help out? We can

take them out for burgers, then I'll help you get them settled for the night."

"Take them out?" she repeated incredulously. She hadn't
taken Maddie's kids or Annie out to any kind of restaurant
until the youngest was at least six. "Won't they disrupt the
other diners. There's nothing more annoying than having
other people's children running wild when you're trying to
enjoy a pleasant dinner out."

"Which is one of the joys of the fast-food restaurant,"
he said. "You'll be surrounded by other people with out-
of-control kids of their own. They won't pay any attention to yours."

"Fast food, of course," she said, jotting it down.
"That's perfect."

To his credit, Erik managed to keep a straight face. "I'll
be by at five-thirty tomorrow afternoon," he promised.
"Now I'd better get to work before Dana Sue decides to
dock my pay."

Helen regarded him with a grateful expression. "I don't
know how to thank you for helping out this morning. I was
on the verge of a full-fledged panic attack when you
showed up."

"Hey, no big deal. You could have managed."

"I'm not so sure about that. These two kids don't seem to
be falling in line the way I anticipated. I don't scare them."

"You wanted to rule by intimidation?"

"I considered it," she admitted. "But it seemed like a bad
idea."

"See, you are capable of making smart choices where
the kids are concerned," he said.

He spoke with such confidence that Helen left Sullivan's
feeling as if she had things back under control. It was prob-

ably an illusion, but at least it would get her through the day 'til the next test came along.

Helen had barely left and Erik was still gathering up their dishes, when Dana Sue came flying into the dining room at Sullivan's.

"Was that Helen I saw driving away from here?" she asked.

"Hard to say," he said evasively.

She frowned at him. "Don't you dare try to trip me up on one of those technicalities you enjoy so much. Do you realize when you do that, you sound exactly like Helen when she's cross-examining a witness?"

"Then I'll stop it immediately," he said, amused.

"Don't try to sidetrack me, either. Was Helen here or not?"

"She was," he conceded reluctantly.

"And you had breakfast together," she surmised, her gaze on the plates, cups and silverware he was holding.

"We did."

"Interesting," she murmured, then studied him intently. "How did that happen?"

Now there was a can of worms Erik really didn't want to open with the resident matchmaking queen. He shrugged. "No big deal. We ran into each other."

"Where?" she persisted. "And why would you bring her here, instead of going to Wharton's, which is actually open for breakfast?"

He shrugged. "What can I say? She likes our coffee better. Now, if you don't mind, I need to get to work."

"And I say you have time to answer a few more questions."

"If I have that much time, I could leave and run a few errands," he countered.

"You just want to avoid my questions," she accused.

Erik grinned at her. "Gee, you think?"

"I'll ask Helen."

"Feel free."

"She'll tell me whatever it is you're hiding," she warned him.

"I doubt it. I don't think she's any more interested in encouraging this scheme of yours than I am."

"What scheme is that?"

"To throw us together 'til we stick."

She frowned at him. "I wouldn't put it exactly that way."

Erik laughed. "No, I'm sure you wouldn't. You'd tie it up in some pretty, romantic bow, but it all amounts to meddling in something that's none of your business."

"You're both my friends. That makes it my business," she said as he brushed past her and headed for the kitchen.

It was too much to hope that she'd just give up. She followed him.

"Have you mentioned Tess's problem to her yet?" she asked.

"The other day," he said, relieved by the switch in topic.

"Then this morning wasn't about that?" she said, her expression thoughtful. "What did she say when you told her?"

"That she'd follow up with Tess. I didn't remind her about it today because with Karen's kids under her roof she has enough on her plate at the moment." He scowled. "Go away, Dana Sue. I mean it. Baking takes concentration."

"Oh, please, you could do it with one hand tied behind your back while you're listening to music on your iPod."

"Neither of which is as distracting as listening to you go on and on and on," he said. "I have to do today's baking, plus tomorrow's, remember? Or do you want tomorrow's customers to discover the only dessert on the menu is ice cream from the Piggly Wiggly?"

Dana Sue sighed, but she backed off. "Fine. I'll be in my office if you need me, or if you decide you want to talk."

"I won't," he assured her.

The entire encounter was a warning, he told himself after she'd gone. If he was ever foolhardy enough to decide to ask Helen on an actual date, he might as well invite Dana Sue and Maddie along, as well. Otherwise he'd just have to fill them in on every detail later.

He wondered how the devil Ronnie Sullivan and Cal Maddox had done it, courted their wives with the other two women overseeing every single second. Dating Helen would be tricky enough. Having the other two chiming in every other minute would drive him completely nuts. No way. Next time he got that tingly feeling in the pit of his stomach or had the sudden urge to haul Helen into his arms and kiss her, he needed to remember that.

And then he needed to run like hell in the other direction.

Karen missed her kids like crazy. When she got back to her apartment after working at Sullivan's, it was way too quiet and lonely. She should have been eager to fall into bed and catch up on some of the sleep she'd missed in recent weeks. Instead, she paced from room to room, switching on the TV in one, the radio in another, just to have some background noise.

She spoke to Mack and Daisy every afternoon when they got home from school and again before they went to bed. They were clearly adjusting well to living with Helen, but in some ways that was hardest of all to bear. She wanted them to miss her, at least a little. She'd spoken to Dr. McDaniels about her mixed feelings that morning.

"It's perfectly normal to worry that you're becoming extraneous to your children's lives," Dr. McDaniels told her. "But, trust me, that's not happening. You're still their mom. Helen is not going to replace you in that role, no matter how effective she is at filling in for the time being. Be glad that Mack and Daisy are adapting and use this time to figure some things out for yourself, to get strong again. In fact, I recommend that you start working out at The Corner Spa. The exercise will be good for you."

When Karen had protested that she couldn't afford a spa membership, Dr. McDaniels had waved off the objection. "I'll work it out if you promise me you'll go."

Though Karen had played sports under duress back in high school phys-ed classes, she'd never undertaken any form of organized exercise activity as an adult. "You really think this will be good for me?" she asked. "I sucked in gym class."

The psychologist had laughed. "So did a lot of us," she told Karen. "But there are plenty of studies that show that rigorous or even moderate exercise not only keeps the body in shape, but increases serotonin in the brain, which makes a person feel happier."

"No kidding?" Karen had said, skeptical, but willing to give it a try. "If you can work it out, I'll go. You said there were two things you were recommending. What's the other one?"

"I want you to sit down with a financial counselor and get yourself on some kind of plan to straighten out your finances. I think that'll relieve a lot of your worries if you can clear up any debts and budget your money wisely."

Karen hadn't been able to argue with that, either. "Is there anyone you recommend?"

She'd taken the business card Dr. McDaniels had given her and called for an appointment as soon as she'd gotten to work. The financial counselor had scheduled their first meeting for next week. And while she was working, Dana Sue had told her she was arranging for a free membership at The Corner Spa.

"Dr. McDaniels talked to you?" Karen had protested, humiliated. "I am so sorry."

"Don't be," Dana Sue responded. "Business is booming at the spa. We can afford to let you use the gym at no cost, and Elliott said he's happy to help you get started."

Karen had gotten a glimpse of the sexy personal trainer a time or two. Looking at him up close was definitely no hardship.

Karen sat on the edge of the sofa and considered all the good things that had happened since she'd finally started to face the mess her life was in. She was actually beginning to believe she could take charge of her life again. And with all that Dana Sue and Helen were doing to support her, she owed it to them to make sure she didn't waste this opportunity.

Still, there was this huge empty place inside where her kids should be. She wanted them back home. No one had set an exact timetable for when her babies *would* be coming back, but she hoped it would be sooner, rather than later. Talking to them on the phone or even spending an hour with them every few days wasn't nearly enough.

Spotting Mack's favorite stuffed bear on the other end of the sofa, she reached for it and held it tightly. The bear's coat was matted, the ribbon around its neck bedraggled and stained with baby food, but it smelled of baby powder and shampoo and Mack. She was a little surprised that Mack was falling asleep without it, but Helen hadn't mentioned any problems with getting Mack to bed. Even so, Karen resolved to drop it off first thing in the morning, maybe catch a glimpse of her kids before she headed to her first workout session at the gym. It was almost impossible to imagine that just a few days ago, her children had been too much for her to cope with.

The light tap on her door startled her. Relieved at the prospect of a visitor, she dropped the bear and rushed to open it. Frances stood on her doorstep, a container of soup in one hand, her expression filled with compassion.

"I heard you come in a few minutes ago. I thought you might be feeling a little lost," she said. "Want some company?"

"Oh, yes, please," Karen said fervently, drawing her into the apartment. "It's way too quiet around here."

Frances patted her arm. "I can understand that. I remember how completely bereft I felt when my last child went off to college. The empty-nest syndrome is no myth. I had a full life teaching and my husband was still alive, but I almost went stir-crazy without a bunch of teenagers underfoot demanding food every hour of the day and night. My children left one by one after eighteen years of me watching over and worrying about them. Yours are still little more than babies and they left practically overnight. There's no way you could be prepared for something like that."

"I want them back now," Karen admitted, taking the soup from Frances and putting it in the kitchen. "I had to turn on the TV and the radio just so there was some commotion in here when I got home from work."

Frances nudged her toward a seat at the table. "You sit

and let me warm up that soup. I imagine you haven't eaten, have you?"

"I pick at food all day long at the restaurant," Karen said, then realized she was hungry. "But the soup sounds good."

Frances found a pan and poured the thick split-pea soup into it, then turned the gas element on low. "How about a sandwich to go with it? If you don't have anything, I can run across the hall. I have some honey-baked ham that's delicious."

When Karen started to protest that she was going to too much trouble, Frances waved her off. "Nonsense. I'll be right back. Keep an eye on the soup. Don't let it boil."

Karen nodded, hiding her amusement that Frances thought she needed cooking instructions. What she did need, though, was this bit of mothering, something that had been sadly lacking in her life.

When Frances bustled back into the kitchen, she'd already piled the ham high on thick multigrain bread from a bakery in town. "I wasn't sure if you'd prefer mustard or mayo, so I didn't add either," she told Karen.

"I like mayo. I'll get it," Karen said.

"No, you sit and relax. You're on your feet all day long, while I do nothing but sit around."

Karen laughed. "Frances, I have never seen you stay still for more than a few minutes at a time. You're on the go every day of the week."

Frances shrugged. "Only way I know to keep mind and body active," she conceded. "But there are plenty of hours when I'm across the hall with my feet propped up. Now, tell me about your day."

Karen told her about the plan for financial counseling and for the spa membership.

"That's wonderful," Frances said enthusiastically. "Exercise will do you a world of good. I know my aerobics class at the senior center always makes me feel better—not that they have us doing too much for fear we'll drop dead."

She set a bowl of soup in front of Karen, then pulled up a chair for herself. "You know," she began, her tone conspiratorial, "I hear there's a personal trainer at that spa who looks like a Greek god. I'm tempted to get a trial membership just to check him out myself."

"Frances!" Karen said, laughing. "I'm shocked."

"Any woman who tells you she doesn't like looking is lying," Frances said. "Sneak a camera in there and take pictures for me. I can live vicariously."

"I most certainly will not," Karen said. "But I will check in to taking you along as a guest one day, if you think your heart can take it. I've seen him. He *is* pretty gorgeous."

"Then it might be worth my winding up in the hospital just to sneak a peek at him." She patted Karen's hand. "Now, let me get out of here, so you can finish that meal and get some sleep. You want to look your best when you go to the gym."

"I'm going for the exercise," Karen reminded her piously.

"Well, of course you are," Frances said. "But there's no harm in exercising your libido at the same time, is there? You could use a man in your life."

"I could say the same about you," Karen returned. "I know there are at least half a dozen men at the senior center who are interested in seeing you."

"Oh, piddle," Frances said dismissively. "Who wants to listen to a bunch of old fools sit around and talk about their aches and pains? I've got enough of those myself."

"Still, you might want to consider the benefit of having

some companionship," Karen said. "I'm sure you must get lonely, too."

"I have my moments," Frances admitted, "but I'm never bored, not for a second. There's plenty to do, if you just get out there and look for it. And then there are you, Daisy and Mack. You occupy a huge place in my life, where my own kids and grandkids would be if they lived close by. So, you see, my life is full. I have nothing to complain about."

"You're remarkable," Karen told her with total sincerity. "I hope I grow up to be exactly like you."

"You'll be your own person," Frances corrected. "There's no one else on earth just like you. You need to remember that, Karen, and use this time on your own to figure out exactly who you are and who you want to become. Your children will be that much happier if they have a mom who's confident and knows where she's headed and how she plans to get there."

"Do you really think I'll figure that out?" Karen asked wistfully. "I was barely out of high school when I met Ray. He thought community college was a waste of time, so I didn't go. I just put in my time at the diner. Then I got pregnant with Daisy, we got married and the kids came along. I didn't plan any of that. Right now it seems like my only goal is keeping my head above water."

"I know you'll get past that," Frances said. "Now get some sleep. Be sure you stop over tomorrow and tell me every single detail about that sexy trainer at the spa."

"I love you," Karen said, impulsively wrapping Frances in a hug. "I am so lucky you're my neighbor and my friend."

"Same goes for me," Frances said. "You kiss those babies for me if you see them in the morning. Tell them I'll be by in the afternoon. I'm baking oatmeal raisin cookies for them."

"They'll love that."

She waited in the hallway until Frances had closed the door to her apartment and locked it, then went back into her own unit and tidied up the kitchen. Feeling one hundred percent better than she had earlier in the evening, she switched off the TV and the lights, then changed into her favorite pajamas and crawled into bed. She set the radio on a timer and turned it down low, the sound of oldies lulling her.

To her amazement, the instant her head hit the pillow, she felt herself drifting off to sleep, a smile on her lips. Deep inside was a tiny little seed of optimism about the future, something that hadn't been there for months, perhaps even years.

10

Karen had been inside The Corner Spa on several occasions to deliver some of the salads, muffins and other light menu items that Sullivan's prepared for the spa café, but she'd never gone into the workout room. Dressed in a pair of shorts, old sneakers and a T-shirt, she approached it warily, stunned by the variety of equipment and the crowd of women, most of whom seemed to know each other.

The walls were a cheery shade of yellow. Sliding doors opened to a spring breeze and a tranquil view of a wooded area. There was music playing low in the background, something classical and soothing, but the predominant noise was conversation and laughter.

Too intimidated and uncertain to try any of the equipment, Karen stood where she was trying to decide what to do. She regretted not going back home after she'd stopped by Helen's to drop off Mack's stuffed bear and spend a few minutes with the kids before school. Here, she felt as awkward and out of place as she had in high school when she'd been expected to get excited about playing field hockey.

"You must be Karen," a low male voice said, approaching her from behind.

That sexy rumble, which would have triggered an instant response in bed, was especially unexpected amid the higher-pitched female voices. She turned and stared into dark brown eyes the color of espresso. It was the first time she'd seen Elliott Cruz up close, and she couldn't seem to tear her gaze away. With his long, coal-black hair pulled back from his face in a ponytail, those incredibly soulful eyes, broad chest and shoulders and impressive thighs, she understood why the personal trainer was the talk of Serenity's females.

"I'm Elliott Cruz," he told her. "Dana Sue told me to watch for you."

A grin tugged at her lips. "And my neighbor told me to watch for you," she said.

Surprise flickered in his eyes. "Oh? Is she a member here?"

"No, but she wants to be, just so she can get a look at you," Karen blurted before she could censor herself. "She's in her eighties. I don't think the shock would be good for her."

To her surprise, his olive complexion reddened. "I'm sorry. I didn't mean to embarrass you."

He chuckled. "I could never work around this many women if I couldn't handle a few stares and a whole lot of teasing. I'm pretty much immune to it."

Karen thought otherwise. His embarrassment was unmistakable and suggested he was still taken aback by overt female appreciation. He led her through the gym toward a treadmill.

"Why don't we start here?" he suggested, his hand resting on the machine.

"You're going to put me on *that?*" she asked.

"Unless your idea of exercise is standing around watching everyone else sweat, you have to start somewhere," he said. "This is just walking, the most basic exercise of all. You can do that, can't you?"

"On a sidewalk, not a machine."

"Pretty much the same thing, except this gives you a way to control your pace and challenge yourself," he said, pointing out all the dials and the calculations visible in the digital readouts. "You'll be able to determine your pace, your distance, calories burned and so on. Hop on, and let's see what you can do."

Karen stepped up and placed her feet where Elliott told her to as he turned on the machine.

"When you're ready, just step onto the treadmill and start walking," he said. "I've set the speed fairly low for now."

She did as he'd instructed and immediately clutched the bars in front of her in a death grip as she tried to walk at the measured pace of the machine.

"It's going a little fast, isn't it?" she asked as she felt herself sliding backward as she struggled to keep up with it.

He grinned. "That just means you need to walk a little faster," he said, refusing to slow it down. "You can keep up. It's not exercise if it doesn't push you a little."

She picked up her pace and felt herself falling into a more natural rhythm. It wasn't so bad after all. "How long do I have to do this?"

"We'll do ten minutes today and see how you hold up. I'd like to see you up to thirty minutes eventually."

Ten minutes didn't sound too tough. Once she grew accustomed to the machine, it'd be a breeze. "How long have I already done?"

"Two minutes."

She frowned. Was that all? Surely she'd been at it longer. As if to mock her, her legs suddenly felt heavy and her

breath hitched slightly. "And you want eight more minutes?" she asked.

He regarded her solemnly. "Yes, I do."

"Are you sure you didn't set the speed higher?"

"Nope. Same speed. You can do this. I hear you have
kids. They must keep you on the go. Surely you're fit
enough to do a brisk walk."

There was something in his gorgeous eyes that made her
want to do whatever he expected of her. She had a hunch
that was why he was so good as a personal trainer. Every
woman in the spa probably wanted to live up to his expectations, no matter how impossible they seemed to be.

Feeling an impish desire to torment him just as he was
tormenting her, she looked him straight in the eye and
asked, "If I finish the whole ten minutes, will you do something for me?"

His gaze narrowed with suspicion. "Such as?"

"Take off that shirt so I can see if your abs live up to
all the hype," she said in the same solemn tone he'd just
used on her.

His low laugh washed over her. "Now, if I did that for
every woman who asked, this place could wind up with a
reputation as a strip club." His gaze locked with hers. "You
want to see my body, Karen, you're going to have to work
much harder than this."

Karen sucked in her breath at the suggestive note in his
voice. Anticipating amusement, she was surprised to see
something darker and far more serious in the depths of his
eyes. It was so totally male it made her knees weak. She almost stumbled and pitched off the back of the treadmill. He
flipped the off switch in the nick of time and steadied her.

"You okay?" he asked.

Was she? It had been years since she'd flirted with a man, years since a simple sexual innuendo could make her blood run hot and her body tremble. Her marriage had lost that spark long before it had ended. Maybe that was why something that probably meant no more to Elliott Cruz than hello or goodbye sent her hormones into overdrive.

She plastered a smile on her face. "I'm fine," she said. "What's next?"

The slow warming of his smile melted the last of her defenses.

"Something told me you were going to become an eager student," he said.

Karen was eager, all right. Unfortunately, it had less to do with whatever torture Elliott had in mind for the next hour than it did with anticipation of what might happen in a more private setting.

"Idiot," she muttered under her breath. No doubt every woman in here thought she would be the one to capture his attention. She'd have to be a fool to think he'd singled her out after only a few minutes in her company.

"Did you say something?" he asked.

"No, nothing," she said. "Just talking to myself."

And, with any luck at all, maybe her rampaging libido would get the message. She had a feeling the pleasurable sensations she was experiencing weren't exactly what Dr. McDaniels had been talking about when she'd discussed one of the side benefits of exercise.

Helen was extremely proud of herself. She had both kids bathed and dressed in neatly ironed clothes by the time Erik rang the doorbell at 5:30 p.m. to take them out for supper.

"My, my, don't you two look good," he said to Daisy

and Mack, swinging Daisy up in his arms to give her a smacking kiss on the cheek that had her giggling and Mack holding out his arms for a turn.

Then his gaze landed on Helen and his expression changed. He seemed to be struggling to contain a laugh.

"What?" she asked.

"Have you checked a mirror lately?" he inquired delicately.

"No." Since she arrived home from work, she'd been too busy getting Mack and Daisy ready for their outing. Erik had arrived before she'd had a chance to check her makeup, much less think about changing her own clothes.

"You might want to do that," he said. "Not that I don't think you look terrific, because I do." A wicked grin spread across his face. "Believe me, I do."

Helen frowned because his gaze seemed to be lingering on her chest. "I'll be right back."

In the bathroom, she took one look in the full-length mirror on the back of the door and groaned. Her silk blouse had gotten completely soaked when she'd had the kids in the tub. It was plastered to her chest, revealing the pattern in her lacy bra and a whole lot more. No wonder Erik had gaped.

Her skirt, though not as revealing, was every bit as drenched. She ducked into her room, grabbed another blouse and a pair of linen slacks, and slid her feet into more sensible shoes. Her hair and makeup took two seconds to fix.

Satisfied she was more presentable, she returned to find all three of them on the sofa watching cartoons. Erik seemed as absorbed as the kids.

"I hate to tear you all away from your entertainment, but shouldn't we be going?" she asked.

Daisy protested, but a look from Erik was enough to silence her. Mack seemed perfectly content to do whatever Erik suggested. He was especially delighted when Erik swung him up on his shoulders to carry him piggyback.

"Go!" he ordered imperiously.

Erik laughed. "He's taking after you already," he said to Helen as he headed for the door.

"Something tells me you didn't mean that as a compliment." She followed him out and locked the house behind them.

They piled into Helen's car because it had the kids' seats, but when Erik offered to drive, Helen accepted. She could hardly keep her eyes open. She'd had no idea how exhausting it would be trying to keep up with kids for several days running.

The fast-food restaurant Erik drove them to was in the next town, and it had an indoor play area. Daisy spotted it at once.

"Can we go play?" she pleaded.

"Not until we've eaten," Erik said. "Why don't you guys find a table and I'll get the food? Daisy, you want to come with me to help?"

"Sure!" she said, obviously delighted to be the object of Erik's attention.

Helen settled Mack in a booster seat, then watched Erik bending down to consult Daisy as they ordered. She was amazed by how at ease he was with the kids. Though she'd relaxed considerably over the past few days, she was still awkward with them. She told herself it was because they'd been thrust into her life with no preparation. She hadn't even met them before. Truthfully, though, it was more than that. It was the responsibility of keeping them safe and making them feel secure 'til they could be with their mom again. Much as she hated to admit it, she needed a support system as desperately as Karen had. Frances was pitching in, but they needed backup. Maybe Annie would be willing to babysit or just come by to give Helen a break in the evenings. She was still pondering the options when Erik and Daisy approached.

"Why the frown?" Erik whispered in her ear as he set the tray that was piled high with food on the table. "Are you overthinking all this again?"

She forced a smile. "More than likely."

"Sugar, they're people. Enjoy them." He divvied up the huge order, then suggested, "Daisy, why don't you tell Helen about that story your teacher read in school today?"

Daisy regarded her hopefully. "You wanna hear?"

"I'd love to," Helen said.

Daisy began with what had to be the very first page and told the whole long, rambling story of a dinosaur, adding some embellishments Helen suspected hadn't been in the original. Her telling, though, was filled with enough drama and enthusiasm to keep Mack spellbound and Helen laughing.

"Brava!" she enthused when Daisy had concluded. "You're an excellent storyteller."

"I could read it to you tonight," Daisy offered eagerly. "I brought the book home from school. My teacher said it would be okay."

"I'd love that," Helen said, and realized she meant it.

"Now can Mack and me go play?" Daisy begged Erik after they'd eaten.

Erik glanced at Helen. "Okay with you?"

She looked at the indoor equipment where several other young children were already playing. "Are you sure it's safe?"

Erik nodded. "I'm sure."

She gave her approval. "Just stay where we can see you."

After they'd gone, Erik studied her. "Letting them go wasn't so hard, was it?"

"No, I'm trying to get better at it." She sighed. "I know I'm too uptight, but this parenting business is scary."

"I imagine that's how everyone feels when they bring their first baby home from the hospital. You came home with two kids who already have personalities, a vocabulary and who are mobile. It's no doubt been a shock to your system. You'll get the hang of it, though."

"What I don't get," she said, regarding him with curiosity, "is why someone who's as comfortable with children as you are isn't interested in having a whole crew of them."

His expression suddenly shuttered as if she'd ventured into an area so personal that any considerate person would have known it was completely off-limits.

"Did I say something wrong?" she asked, not sure why he was so sensitive on this subject.

He shook his head. "Of course not. I just don't have any plans to have a family. I told you that."

"But you'd be—"

He cut her off. "Not going to happen, okay?"

If he hadn't looked so shaken, she might have persisted. Instead she let the subject drop. "I'm sorry."

He rested his hand on hers. "No, *I'm* sorry for snapping at you. It was a perfectly reasonable question. I'm just a little touchy. All my plans to have kids were tied up with my wife. When she died, that part of my life died with her."

He sounded so sad that Helen couldn't help wondering if the loss was recent. "How long ago did your wife die?"

"Six years and seven months ago," he said tonelessly.

Helen knew there wasn't any strict timetable for grief, but that seemed like a long time to be mourning someone's loss.

"Before you went to culinary school?" she guessed.

He nodded. "I needed to make a complete change after she died. A friend suggested culinary school, mainly as a distraction because she knew I enjoyed cooking. It turned out I loved it. The instructors said I was a natural. And it eventually brought me back to life."

"But not all the way," Helen said before she could stop herself.

Erik stared at her, his expression hard. "Meaning?"

"Please don't take this the wrong way, but it still seems as if some part of you died with your wife," she suggested.

Rather than snapping at her again, he merely nodded. "I suppose that's true."

"You must have loved her very much," she said.

"She was amazing." His eyes filled with a sorrow that looked as raw as it must have on the day she died. "Not perfect. Not by a long shot, but amazing just the same."

Helen couldn't turn away, even though witnessing that much pain seemed intrusive. Forcing herself to seek out the children in the play area, she thought what a shame it was for a man as decent as Erik to have shut himself off emotionally.

"Why are you suddenly so pensive?" Erik asked. "I didn't mean to bring you down."

"I guess I'm a little envious," she admitted. "I've had a few relationships, if you can call them that, but no one's ever meant as much to me as your wife obviously did to you. I'm not sure I even believed until recently that love could run that deep."

"What happened recently to convince you it's possible?"

"Seeing Cal and Maddie together," she told him. "And

lately even Dana Sue and Ronnie are making a believer out of me."

"I suspect it's your line of work that's made you so cynical," Erik said.

"You're not the first to tell me that," she returned.

"Ever thought about practicing a different kind of law?"

She shook her head. "Not really. I like sticking up for women whose marriages have crumbled. They're usually so emotionally shattered that they need someone in their corner who's strong enough to fight for what they deserve."

"But look at the toll it's taken on you," he said. "By your own admission, you've shut yourself off emotionally."

"So have you," she retorted.

He gave her a rueful smile. "Touché. But at least I loved once with everything in me."

She nodded slowly. For the first time she really understood what Tennyson meant when he wrote that it was better to have loved and lost than never to have loved at all. She glanced back at the play area to see Mack and Daisy starting to squabble. "Right now, I think there are other issues in my life. Looks as if those two are getting tired. We should probably get them home."

As Erik gathered them up and Helen waited for them, the oddest sensation stole through her. For just a fleeting instant, it felt as if she were part of a family.

And it felt really, really good.

Erik couldn't seem to shake the dark mood that Helen's questions had stirred in him. He knew it was only her natural curiosity that had made her pry into his past, but every reminder of what he'd lost when Samantha and his unborn child had died always took him right back to the night it had happened. He'd gone over that night a thousand times, wondering if there had been anything at all he could have done differently, anything that would have changed the outcome. Every doctor and EMT he'd asked had assured him that he'd done everything exactly right, but their reassurances hadn't been enough. He still blamed himself.

If it had been entirely up to him, he would have dropped Helen and the kids back at her place and headed straight home, but Daisy had other ideas.

"I'm going to read a story, remember?" she told him when he tried to make his excuses at the front door.

"I think Mack and Helen will be a great audience," he told her. "You don't need me."

"Please?" she begged, regarding him with such a plaintive expression that he couldn't say no.

"I'll stay for half an hour," he agreed reluctantly.

"Yea!" Daisy proclaimed. "I'll get the book."

"She's got you wound around her finger," Helen commented, shaking her head in amusement.

He shrugged. "What can I say? I'm a sucker for a woman who begs."

"Just one more reason why you and I would be a disastrous match," she responded. "I *never* beg."

He laughed. "Add that to the list and tell Dana Sue next time she starts meddling." He reached for Mack and took him from her. "He's down for the count. I'll put him in bed."

Helen relinquished the boy. "Daisy's going to be crushed that her audience has dwindled to just us."

"I think it's *us* who're most important to her. Mack's just her baby brother. She can read to him anytime."

"Well, I'm looking forward to it. I can't recall the last time I read a good dinosaur book."

Erik settled Mack into his bed. It was made to look like a car and painted bright red. "You bought him a bed?" he asked Helen. "Why, if he's only here for a short time?"

She flushed. "I wanted him to have something special. I thought it would turn this visit into more of an adventure."

"He's three. He could fall asleep on a rock."

She chuckled. "I doubt that's recommended, though."

Erik tucked Mack under the covers, then turned to catch an oddly wistful expression on Helen's face. "You okay?"

She nodded. "Seeing him like that, looking so innocent and sweet, just reminds me of what I've missed."

It wasn't the first time tonight she'd come close to admitting that her life hadn't turned out the way she'd anticipated. Just proved that people were more complicated than they appeared.

"You wanted kids?" he asked.

"I took for granted that I'd have them, but time just slipped by," she admitted. "I've been regretting that lately."

"It's not too late," he said, even as he added her desire for children to the list of reasons they were unsuited. "Women with careers are having kids at your age all the time now."

"I know."

"Well, then?"

"I'm still weighing my options," she said. "I have to say that having Mack and Daisy here has been eye-opening."

"In a good way?"

Her gaze still on Mack, she nodded. "Yeah, in a good way."

Just then Daisy appeared in the doorway. "Are you *ever* coming to hear the story?"

Erik chuckled at her impatience. He swung her up in his

arms. "How about we tuck you in and Helen reads it to you?" he suggested. "Mack's already asleep."

Daisy regarded Helen somberly. "Would you? I like it when Mommy reads to me."

Helen seemed vaguely startled by the request, but then her lips curved into a smile. "I would love to read it, but only if Erik makes all the dinosaur noises."

"Done," he said at once, surprisingly eager to share this experience with her.

He was seeing more and more sides to Helen these days and with each new one, his preconceptions were toppling like pins in a bowling alley. For a man determined to keep her at arm's length, that was not a good thing.

11

Several days after the supper outing with Erik, on Saturday morning, Helen woke up to the sensation that someone was watching her. Cracking open one eye, she saw Mack standing beside the bed, a thumb stuck in his mouth. He looked as weary as she still felt, even after a full night's sleep, the first she'd had since the kids had come to stay. For the second time in the past week, she told herself to find some backup ASAP.

She glanced at the clock and saw that it was already 8:00 a.m. She never slept that late, not even on weekends. No wonder Mack had come to find her. She listened intently and heard the TV going in the living room, which was apparently keeping the self-sufficient Daisy occupied.

Mack removed his thumb from his mouth long enough to ask hopefully, "You up?"

"I am now," she confirmed. "Are you hungry?"

He nodded emphatically.

"Seems as if you could use some clean clothes, too," she suggested. "You must be getting tired of that Spider-Man shirt."

"No!" Mack said.

"Okay, then. How about I wash it this morning?"

"No!" he repeated.

Oh, well, it was hardly worth fighting about. First thing Monday she'd send Barb out to see if she could find a few more identical Spider-Man shirts.

In the meantime, she dragged on a robe and headed for the living room, Mack toddling along behind. Daisy was sitting in front of the TV—and she was crying! Helen felt her throat catch at the sight of her. She looked so lost and alone despite her cheery pink T-shirt, orange shorts and bright red sneakers. Her silky hair was tangled and tears stained her cheeks.

Helen immediately crossed the room and sat down beside her, gathering her close. "Oh, sweetie, what's wrong?"

Daisy lifted her damp face to Helen and inquired pitifully, "Are we ever going to live with Mommy again?"

"Of course you are," Helen said at once.

"When?"

"Very soon."

"But when?" Daisy persisted.

"As soon as the doctor says she's okay," Helen said.

"Is she really, really sick?" Daisy asked. "When I'm sick, I only stay home from school for a little while. Mommy's been sick for a long time now." She glanced at Helen hopefully. "She didn't look sick last time she came to see us. Maybe she's better."

How on earth could she explain this so a five-year-old would understand? Helen wondered. "I know it must seem like a long time, but you've only been with me for a couple of weeks," she said, though she sensed that to a child two weeks could seem like an eternity. "And what your mommy has isn't like a tummy ache or the measles," she explained carefully. "It doesn't just go away."

"Then how can she get well?" Daisy asked, looking more perplexed than ever.

"She needs to rest and talk to some people and then she'll be strong again."

"But she's really strong now," Daisy protested. "She can lift all sorts of stuff."

Helen concluded she was only making things worse. "How about this? Why don't we call her right now, so you and Mack can talk to her? Maybe she'll even have time to come by before she goes to work."

Daisy's eyes lit up, even though they were still shimmering with tears. "We can call her?"

"Of course you can," Helen said, regretting that she hadn't told Daisy that much sooner. Instead, she'd relied on Karen to call and stop by. Obviously Daisy needed to know she could make a call herself if she wanted to. "You get the portable phone and I'll help you make the call."

Daisy scrambled off the sofa and ran to the table where the phone rested in its base.

"Talk," Mack commanded.

"In a minute," Daisy said to him, then added proudly to Helen. "I know my phone number."

"Then you can punch it in," Helen said.

A moment later, Karen obviously answered because a smile broke across Daisy's face.

"Mommy! It's me."

"I talk to Mommy, too!" Max wailed.

Helen gave Daisy an imploring look that had her handing over the phone. Mack babbled happily for a minute, then Daisy yanked the phone back.

"Mommy, can you come over?"

Whatever Karen said caused Daisy to frown and hold the phone out to Helen.

"She wants to talk to you," she said, sounding betrayed.

Helen took the phone. "Hi, Karen."

"Is everything okay?" Karen asked worriedly. "Daisy seems upset. Is she crying?"

"Yes, but everything's fine, really. Daisy was just missing you a lot. I thought maybe you'd like to join us for breakfast if you have time."

"Really?"

The surprised note in Karen's voice puzzled her. "Of course. I told you you'd be welcome here anytime."

"I know," Karen said. "But the last time I was over, I had the feeling I was disrupting their new routine. Since you've been so great about keeping them, I didn't want to make things more difficult for you."

"Oh, Karen, I'm sorry," Helen said, chagrined. "I had no idea I'd made you feel that way. Though no one's a bigger fan of routine than I am, I've discovered that sometimes the best things in life happen unexpectedly. Please come over. They need to see their mom."

"I'll be there in fifteen minutes," Karen promised, sounding as eager as Daisy. "And don't cook. Let me do it. The least I can do is fix breakfast for all of you."

"That would be wonderful," Helen admitted. Her repertoire of cereal or scrambled eggs had worn thin days ago. "See you soon."

"She's coming?" Daisy asked the instant Helen clicked off the phone.

"In a few minutes," Helen confirmed, picking up Mack. "Why don't you wash your face and brush your teeth while I get dressed? I'll braid your hair for you, if there's time."

"All right!" Daisy enthused, taking off.

But rather than going back to her room to change, Helen patted Mack's back, loving the feel of his warm little body in her arms. For now he was perfectly content to have her hold him, something she knew wouldn't last once he spotted his mother. It was getting harder and harder for her to accept that these two amazing children were merely on loan to her for a few more weeks at most. They already had a mom, one who was doing everything possible to be able to care for them again.

Helen couldn't help admiring how hard Karen was working to get her life in order, but a tiny part of her—one she wouldn't acknowledge to another breathing soul—hoped it would take a long, long time. Despite her initial bouts of uncertainty and periods of utter and complete exhaustion, motherhood—albeit *temporary* motherhood—was turning out to be more rewarding than she'd ever imagined. .

Helen seemed to have vanished off the radar. Erik hadn't seen her for several weeks. He'd finally risked asking Dana Sue if the kids had locked her in a closet or something.

"No, but she's definitely in way over her head, though she'd never admit it," Dana Sue told him. "Annie's been going over there practically every evening to help out. She says Helen's in her pj's and ready for bed five seconds after they get the kids to sleep. For a night owl like Helen, that's very telling."

"Does she regret taking the kids in?" he asked.

Dana Sue regarded him curiously. "Why so interested, Erik?"

He feigned indifference. "It's just unusual not to have her around here at all."

"You could always call to check on her," Dana Sue suggested.

"Don't start with me," he said. "I asked about her. No big deal."

Dana Sue grinned. "I think it is. I think you've missed her."

He rolled his eyes and headed toward the storeroom. Dana Sue called after him.

"No, she doesn't regret taking the kids. She says it's the best thing she ever did."

Erik wasn't sure how he felt about that. Sure, he was glad she was enjoying the motherhood experience, but if it had solidified her desire to have a child of her own, it meant there was no future for the two of them. That bothered him more than he wanted to admit. What bothered him even more was the realization that Dana Sue was right. He *did* miss Helen.

A few days after his conversation with Dana Sue, Erik was still stewing over the discovery that Helen's absence was getting to him when he ran into her at Wharton's. She was staring despondently into a cup of coffee she'd barely touched. He slid into the booth opposite her. Given her apparent mood, he was surprised there wasn't an empty sundae dish in front of her.

"Tough court case today?" he asked.

She shook her head.

"Kids acting up?"

She sighed heavily. "No, they're great."

"Then why do you look as if you've just lost your best friend?"

"I spoke with Dr. McDaniels today about Karen."

He stiffened. Was there more trouble on that front he

hadn't heard about? Dana Sue might keep it from him, since she knew he was still maintaining a wait-and-see attitude about Karen.

"Oh?" he said casually. "What's going on with her?"

"Dr. McDaniels says Karen's doing great, better than expected, in fact. She says the kids can go back home to live with their mom in another week or two. She's convinced Karen's back on track."

She looked at him with an expression he couldn't quite read. It was almost as if she didn't want to believe that the psychologist had gotten it right.

"What do you think?" she asked.

The question confirmed his suspicion, but he knew his reply wasn't going to be what she wanted to hear. "I know she's been showing up at work when she's supposed to. She's working harder than ever and her mood's vastly improved. I'd have to agree with the doctor. It's about time for her to be reunited with the kids."

Helen sighed. "That's the way it looks to me, too. I think at first they may only stay with her on her days off, but it won't be long before they go home for good."

"I would have thought you'd be thrilled to be getting your life and your house back," he said.

"I'd have thought the same thing a month ago," she admitted. "I had no idea I'd start to care about them so much. Letting go is going to be harder than I expected."

"They belong with their mom," he reminded her.

"Believe me, I know that," she said. "That doesn't make it any easier."

"No, I don't imagine it does, but what you've done for all of them has been incredible. That should leave you with a tremendous sense of satisfaction."

"Oh, I'm a real saint," she said with an edge of bitterness that surprised him.

He stared at her. "Okay, what's going on? Is this about the whole baby thing?"

To his shock, when she lifted her gaze to meet his, her eyes were swimming with tears. She nodded.

Erik told himself he shouldn't let her get to him, but how could he help it? She looked totally miserable. Instinctively, he reached across the table and took her hand in his. "Helen, you can do something about that if it's what you really want. Mack and Daisy aren't the only kids out there who need a temporary home or a permanent one, for that matter. Become a foster mother. Or adopt. Do whatever it takes to fulfill that need if it's that important to you."

"You don't think I'm being selfish?"

"No, I think adopting kids or becoming a foster parent is tremendously generous. You do realize it will change your life, though, right? From the beginning you've known that Daisy and Mack would eventually go home again, but adopting a child of your own will be forever. It won't always be a lark."

She gave him a wobbly grin. "I've been digging Cheerios out of the sofa cushions for a month now. The guest bathroom is usually under water and littered with rubber ducks. I know every song in half a dozen children's movies by heart. I think I'm starting to grasp the impact of having a child in my life."

"You've been lucky. They haven't gotten sick. Your schedule hasn't been turned upside down. Kids are unpredictable and you like to lead a very predictable life. The past couple of months have been an adventure for you, but there's been an end in sight."

She frowned at his caution. "I know that. I get that I can't just turn a kid in if he gets to be too much trouble. I get that it's a lifelong commitment."

"Do you really?"

"Why are you so supportive one second and so negative the next?"

"Because I've been around you enough to know that you like order, not chaos. And by your own admission, you've never made a commitment to a relationship that's lasted for more than a few dates."

"Are you saying you don't think I'm cut out to be a mother?" she asked.

"I would never presume to say that. I'm just saying that you're anticipating Mack and Daisy leaving and feeling the loss right now. It's natural to want to grab on to a replacement to fill that empty spot in your life. Just be sure you're doing it because it's the right thing for you for the long haul and not as some temporary fix because you're going to be a little lonely without Mack and Daisy underfoot."

Her scowl suggested that his comment had hit a little too close to home.

"I need to get to work," she said stiffly, starting to edge out of the booth.

He reached for her hand. "Hold on," he commanded. "I didn't say any of that to be mean."

"I know you didn't. You just think I'm too selfish and self-absorbed to be a mother."

He stared at her incredulously. "I did *not* say that. I think you're an amazingly competent woman and capable of doing anything you set out to do. You can multitask with the best of them. I was just playing devil's advocate. If you're going to jump into parenting, you need to know exactly what you're in for. Kids need a parent who's totally committed to giving them what they need and what they deserve."

"I know that, probably even better than you do," she told him. "I've been weighing the pros and cons for this for so long I'm practically dizzy from it."

Suddenly her feisty attitude faded and she gave him a resigned look. "But that was all theory, you know what I mean? Having Mack and Daisy was real. Taking them in was kind of an experiment, to see if I could handle it. I didn't expect to get so attached. I didn't expect them to turn my life upside down, to make me want so much more than what I already have. It scares me how much I want children. I've always been so independent. I liked it that way. Now it feels as if I've spent the last twenty years just going through the motions, not really living at all."

Erik could understand that. Real life always tended to be a whole lot messier than you expected. He saw that all the time with the wedding receptions that were planned with such attention to detail, only to have a supplier fail to deliver something they'd been counting on, or the bride suddenly have a change of heart about the menu one week ahead of the date.

People with kids or in the restaurant-and-catering business pretty much needed to have a go-with-the-flow attitude or they'd wind up with ulcers or an early heart attack. Embracing change and unpredictability wasn't easy, though. Helen, with her previously well-ordered existence, had just bumped up against that truth and discovered she could cope, after all. She seemed as surprised as he was.

"I know you didn't ask me what you should do, but I'll tell you anyway," he said. "I know all too well how short life can be and how unexpectedly things can change. If you really want something, you need to grab it. Don't wait until it's too late and wind up living with regrets."

"The way *you* have?" she asked.

Erik nodded. "The way I have."

He would regret to his dying day that he hadn't agreed to having children when Samantha had first broached the subject right after their marriage. They'd been in their twenties then, just starting out, struggling to make ends meet. He'd wanted to get their marriage and their finances on a solid footing before having a baby. Samantha had reluctantly agreed to wait.

Maybe if they'd tried sooner, when they were both a little younger, things would have turned out differently and he'd have both his wife and a family.

The sad truth was, though, that he couldn't go back and change that and he'd never know if it would have made a difference or not. He'd go to his grave wondering about that, about the night Sam and his child had died, about so many things.

He met Helen's troubled gaze. "If you want a child, if you've considered it from every angle, then do it, Helen. You've got a terrific support system. You won't be in it alone. And you've got the financial resources to hire all the help you need. Don't let your life be ruled by doubts and uncertainty. That's not who you are."

The smile that broke across her face was startlingly radiant. It reminded him of the smile on Sam's face when he'd finally agreed to start trying for a baby of their own.

"Thank you," Helen said quietly. "You have no idea how you've helped me crystallize everything I've been thinking."

She stood up and this time he let her go. When she bent down and pressed a kiss to his cheek, he felt a surprising burst of longing. It was more than the sexual desire he'd felt before around Helen. It was partly a need to be included in this new life she was planning for herself, and partly regret that it would never happen. She was heading in a direction he would never again dare to go. He'd accepted that he would never have a family of his own. He'd convinced himself he didn't deserve it.

Even knowing that, though, he couldn't seem to stop himself from making an outrageous suggestion just to see how she'd react. It would be a test of just how flexible and daring she'd become.

"I have an idea," he began innocently before she could walk away.

"Yes?"

"Why don't I come by later tonight and bring some camping gear?"

She stared at him. "Camping gear?" She sounded as if she were testing very unfamiliar words.

"Sure, a tent, a grill to cook some burgers or roast marshmallows. The weather's perfect for camping out in the backyard. The kids will love it." He had to fight a smile at the horrified expression she was trying hard to mask. "You game?"

He could tell from her expression that she'd never been camping in her life, that the idea held no appeal now.

"You really think it would be good for the kids?" she asked doubtfully.

He nodded. "Mack and Daisy will be fine. What about you?"

She seemed to be waging a debate with herself, but finally she smiled. "I think you've lost your mind, but sure, why not?" she said gamely. "It'll be another adventure."

Erik admired her bravado. "Great. I'll stop by after lunch and put the tent up in your backyard. You guys can start enjoying the campout before I get there. It's Friday, so I could be late."

"I'll manage 'til you get there. The kids can take naps—that way they can stay up later." She gave him a warning glance. "But just so there's no misunderstanding, I draw the line at ghost stories."

"I figured as much," he said. "How do you feel about bugs?"

"I try to avoid them at all costs," she said with a little shiver.

Erik swallowed a laugh. "I'll bring spray."

"What was I thinking?" she murmured as she walked away.

"It's going to be fun," he called after her.

She turned back, her expression doubtful. "If it's not, I'll be in my silk pj's and tucked into my own comfy bed five seconds after you get there."

Erik very nearly groaned. That image was not what he'd needed to have planted in his head just hours before he intended to spend a friendly, totally platonic night with her. Then again, from the moment he'd uttered the suggestion, he'd pretty much known the night was going to be torture.

Helen gathered up her briefcase and a stack of legal papers at four-thirty that afternoon and headed out of her office. Barb glanced up from the computer on her desk, her expression startled.

"You're leaving?" she asked incredulously.

"No more appointments," Helen said. "Check your calendar."

"But even so, you never leave here before six."

"I never had two kids at home before, either. I'm adapting to that. And Frances needs to leave early because she's going to visit her son and his family. I said I'd take over no later than five."

Barb regarded her with curiosity. "How's the whole instant family thing? Everything still okay? You haven't said much the past couple of weeks, so I assumed everything was going smoothly."

Helen sat down beside the desk. "It's been going surprisingly well. Mack and Daisy are so curious about everything. They're smart and energetic. I'm worn out by bedtime, but it's the good kind of exhaustion, you know?"

"Oh, I know," Barb said. "To be honest, I never thought you'd last this long."

"What choice did I have?" Helen replied. "I had to adapt."

"No, you didn't have to. You *chose* to. There's a huge difference. You actually volunteered to give those kids a home while their mother got the help she needed." A worried frown creased her brow. "What's going to happen when they go back home to their mother? Are you going to be okay?"

"Of course," Helen said. "That's been the plan all along."

"Plans are one thing," her secretary told her. "Emotions tend to be less tidy. These kids have managed to sneak into your heart, haven't they?"

Though she'd admitted it to Erik just that morning, Helen wasn't sure she wanted to tell Barb just how attached she'd become in such a short time. Once she'd come up with some semblance of a routine and realized that Daisy and Mack were pretty adaptable, she'd started to enjoy having them around. She'd explored a whole new world of games and television and family movies. In fact, the best part of her day wasn't the time she spent in the courtroom winning a case for her client; it was the end of the day, when she, Daisy and Mack snuggled on the sofa and watched a DVD together just before bedtime. Being with them had solidified her desire to have a child of her own. It hadn't, however, given her the first clue about the best way of going about that.

Unfortunately, just as Barb suggested, there was a down-side to her newfound maternal instincts. She was starting to resent just a little the time Karen spent with Mack and Daisy when she came by. Helen knew her attitude was not only unfair, it was a warning flag flapping so noisily it could have been heard throughout town. Letting them go, not just for a couple of days with their mom, but perma-nently, was going to tear out a little piece of her heart.

"Well?" Barb prodded. "You like having them there, don't you?"

"Well, of course, I do," she said.

"What happens when they go home?"

"I guess I'll be able to tell you that on Monday," she said, forcing a note of cheer into her voice. "Karen's pick-ing them up on Sunday for a two-day visit back home. It's her day off and everyone agrees she's ready to have them back, at least part-time."

Barb's expression immediately turned sympathetic. "Oh, Helen, I'm sorry."

"Don't be. They should be with their mother. They be-long with her." She said the words by rote, trying to mean them, but failing miserably.

Furthermore, Helen had doubts about whether the tran-sition would go as easily as she implied. Last night after her conversation with Dr. McDaniels, she'd sat beside Mack's bed and then Daisy's, watching them sleeping, and trying to imagine her life without them in it. Her heart had ached at the prospect of all that silence once again greeting her at the end of the day, at the absence of fierce hugs and sticky kisses.

"Helen, I worry about you," Barb said. "I can see it in your eyes. This visit to their mom is one thing, but letting go of them for good is going to break your heart."

"Well, we're not there yet. For now, they're still at my house and I need to get home to them. Erik's coming over as soon as he can get out of the kitchen at Sullivan's and we're going to camp in the backyard."

Barb gaped at Helen. "Excuse me? Did I hear correctly? You're going to camp in the yard, in the dark? In what? A tent?"

"Yes, a tent," Helen said. "Erik has one."

"Well, that should be cozy," Barb said, amusement dancing in her eyes. "Does he know you've never stayed in anything less than a four-star hotel?"

"Probably," Helen said, recalling the glint in his eye when he'd made the suggestion. She'd recognized the whole thing for what it was—a poorly concealed dare. "I think he's counting on me panicking at the sight of the first bug."

Barb laughed. "I just hope he catches it on video."

Helen frowned at her. "I'll ban cameras from the premises. The two of you would get entirely too much enjoyment out of that."

"Enjoyment?" Barb shook her head. "I was thinking about enough blackmail money to secure my retirement."

"You are so not funny," Helen said.

"I don't need to be funny. I'm efficient and I'm about to be rich."

Helen cast one last scowl in her direction, but as soon as she was out the door, she grinned. The whole idea of her camping, even in her own backyard, was pretty ludicrous. Lately, though, she'd been lured into trying lots of new things, not all of them bad, either. In fact, spending the night with Erik, even if it was in a tent with two kids as chaperones, struck her as more intriguing than most of the dates she'd had in the past few years.

When he'd suggested the campout, she'd bitten back the negative response that had immediately come to mind. She needed a few more memories like this to store away. She could use more of Erik's sane, rational advice, as well. Things always went more smoothly with the kids, too, when he was around. They obviously adored him. She'd wondered on more than one occasion lately why he and Karen hadn't drifted together, since it was obvious his connection to the kids wasn't something recent. Maybe she'd ask him that tonight. She had a hunch his reasons ran deeper than some noble objection to a boss dating an employee. Maybe it had more to do with his flatly stated intention never to have kids.

Maybe it was a question best not asked. He'd just tell her his love life was no more her business than it was Dana Sue's. And it seemed clear after their conversation this morning that he was still a long way from moving on from his past. Grace Wharton had gotten it right, after all. Erik was pretty much a confirmed bachelor. That he hadn't always been one didn't really matter. If friendship was all he was willing to offer, she'd take that. She'd never really been friends with a man before, at least not with one who seemed able to see into her soul the way Erik did from time to time. It was nice. More than nice, in fact.

Of course, if it came along with the occasional kiss that could rock her world, so much the better.

12

To Erik's relief, Helen was not wearing anything resembling silk pajamas when he arrived around nine-thirty that night for the campout. When Dana Sue had heard what he was up to for the evening, she'd insisted he take off the instant the dinner rush had slowed. He figured he'd pay for that big-time by having to answer a slew of questions in the morning.

He took another look at Helen and dismissed Dana Sue and her nosiness from his mind. Helen had on formfitting jeans and a pale pink T-shirt that flattered her complexion. She was actually wearing sneakers in the same shade of pink with white accents. He instantly recalled Dana Sue teasing Helen about ordering custom sneakers to match her outfits. Still, custom designer shoes aside, she looked far more down-to-earth and approachable than she usually did.

Erik dropped a kiss on her cheek, then checked out her attempt to start the charcoal in the grill he'd put on the patio. There were glimmers of red at the edges, but it was a long way from hot enough to do any effective cooking.

"You ever barbecued before?" he asked.

"No. Why? Am I doing something wrong?"

"Well, you need some heat."

"I didn't want it to burn itself out before you got here," she claimed. "You're early. How'd that happen?"

"Dana Sue sent me packing."

She gave him a questioning look. "Why would she do that?"

"She knew I was coming here."

"Are you crazy? Why would you tell her that?"

"I needed her key to your place. Didn't you see the tray of burgers I left in your fridge earlier?"

"There are burgers in my fridge?"

"And a few other things I thought we'd need," he said, ignoring the patches of indignant color in her cheeks. "I'll go get the food."

Her gaze narrowed as she followed him inside. "Exactly what did you tell Dana Sue that convinced her to give you a key to my house?" she asked in an icy tone that suggested she wasn't pleased about the conversation or his invasion of her home.

Erik shrugged off her annoyance. He was confident she'd get over it—eventually, anyway. "The truth," he said. "That I was cooking you dinner and spending the night and needed to do some advance preparations. Worked like a charm."

"So she thinks you're over here seducing me?"

"Something like that," he said unrepentantly. "She seemed pretty thrilled."

"I'm sure she was. Imagine how overjoyed she's going to be when I tell her just how differently tonight went."

She looked so thoroughly flustered and exasperated he couldn't help baiting her. "You can't be sure of what's going to happen once the kids are asleep." He dropped a kiss on the end of her nose as he passed by on his way outside with the food.

"Oh, I can be sure," she said, evidently regaining her confidence. "And just so you don't have any further illusions, it's not going to be pretty. You'll be lucky if you don't leave here in handcuffs."

"We'll see," he said smugly, not the slightest bit intimidated by her threat. He glanced around the yard. "Where's Mack, by the way?"

"He's in the tent. He fell asleep waiting for you." She glanced pointedly toward Daisy, who was lying down on a blanket, her eyes drifting closed. "Something tells me she's going to miss those burgers, too."

"No way," Daisy murmured sleepily. "I've been waiting and waiting for them. And the marshmallows."

"Then I will speed this production along," Erik promised, fanning the charcoal and stirring the embers to life. "And when everything's ready, we'll wake Mack up."

"Over my dead body," Helen muttered. "Do you know how hard it is to get him back to sleep once he's awake?"

"But that's the fun of a campout," Erik told her. "Staying awake all night is what it's about."

"Yea!" Daisy cheered, fully awake now. "I never stayed up all night before."

"Come on, sugar, get with the program," Erik told Helen. "We could use some music."

"There's a stereo system set up just inside the back door. Keep the sound down, though. The neighbors might not appreciate having classical music blaring at this time of night."

Erik gave her a chiding look. "Classical music? I don't think so. Forget the CDs. I'm going in to grab the bowl of potato salad. When I get back out here, we'll sing."

"Sing what?" Helen asked.

"'Row, Row, Row Your Boat' comes to mind," he said. "Everybody knows that one, right, Daisy?"

"*I* do," she said at once and began to sing loudly and tunelessly.

Erik grinned at Helen. "Now we have a campout!"

Judging from the sour look she gave him, she wasn't all that impressed.

Two hours later, they'd run through all the songs he knew. Helen had chimed in from time to time, but it was evident that campfire songs were not her forte. Now the coals had died down and the kids were sound asleep inside the tent, despite their best efforts to stay awake. They'd filled up with hamburgers and burnt, gooey marshmallows and cherry Kool-Aid. The menu had been pretty disgusting by Erik's culinary standards, but Daisy and Mack had loved it. Even Helen had gotten in to the marshmallow thing. She had the sticky residue at the corners of her lips.

Before he could stop himself or think about consequences, Erik impulsively cupped the back of her neck and moved in to savor the sweet marshmallow taste of her mouth.

When he released her, she swallowed hard and stared back at him. "What was *that* about?"

"Couldn't resist," he said with a shrug.

"Are you sure you weren't trying to prove a point?" she asked.

He grinned at her suspicious expression. "Such as?"

"That you weren't lying to Dana Sue when you implied that you were going to seduce me tonight."

"There are two children in that tent," he reminded her, injecting a self-righteous note into his voice. "I would never try to seduce you practically in front of them."

"Would you ever try to seduce me at all?"

At the surprisingly wistful note in her voice, blood rushed to a part of his anatomy he'd been trying to ignore all night. "Are you saying you'd want me to?" he asked in a voice that had turned husky.

"I'm not sure," she confessed. "I've thought about it, though."

"Me, too."

"Maybe we should keep thinking about it," she said.

He nodded slowly. Given where they both were in their lives—on very different pages—her comment wasn't a huge surprise. "Keep me posted on what you're thinking, okay?"

Her lips curved slightly at that. "You'll definitely be the first to know if I reach any conclusions."

Erik forced himself to look away from the heat in her eyes. He stared at the dying embers of their barbecue and wished the heat roaring through his blood would fade as quickly. No, what he really wished was that it had never been ignited. The talk of seduction, the kiss, all of it was leading him down a road he'd vowed not to travel ever again, least of all with Helen.

"You go join the kids," he said gruffly. "I'll stay out here."

"You're not sleeping in the tent? Why?"

"It's better that way," he said.

Helen gave him a look that said she saw right through him. It wasn't better. Just safer.

When the doorbell rang on a Sunday afternoon a few weeks after the campout, Helen's heart seemed to stop. Even as Daisy and Mack ran toward it screaming, "Mommy! Mommy!" she was trying to come up with some way not to open the door at all.

It wasn't as if it was the first time Karen had come to take the kids away. They'd been home for two-day visits half a dozen times now. This time, though, it would be for good. The brief visits had been such a success that Dr. McDaniels thought the time had come for the move home to be permanent. It was the day Helen had been dreading for a couple of months now.

Even so, she forced herself to open the door. But rather than finding Karen on the other side, she found Maddie and Dana Sue, laden down with grocery bags.

"What's this?" she asked.

"We know today is going to be hard on you, so we brought supplies," Dana Sue announced. "I brought the makings for nachos and a huge container of my spiciest guacamole."

"And I brought the ingredients for margaritas," Maddie said.

"You can't drink," Helen reminded her. "You're pregnant."

"No, but you can. And a nice frosty glass of limeade will make me feel as if I'm partying with you."

Daisy stared up at Helen accusingly. "You're having a party? How come? Is it 'cause we're leaving? Are you glad?"

Helen scooped her up. "Absolutely not. I'm going to miss you and Mack like crazy."

"Then can we stay for the party?" Daisy asked. "I love nachos."

"Nachos!" Mack echoed enthusiastically.

Dana Sue grinned. "I'll make them right this minute and you can have some before your mom gets here. Maddie, sit down before you tilt over. Your tummy's the size of six watermelons. I don't know how you stay upright at all. Something tells me that baby is going to come out fully grown and ready for college."

"Obviously the doctor and I figured the due date all wrong. After my last sonogram, he told me this baby was going to be here a whole lot sooner than we'd expected," Maddie said. She put a hand on her stomach. "I was so relieved I almost kissed him. I was beginning to think I'd explode if I really did have another month to go." She eyed her favorite easy chair with skepticism. "There's no way I'll get out of that once I'm down."

Helen grinned, thoroughly enjoying the spectacle of the girl who'd been the star of their ballet production when they were ten, now too cumbersome to move with any grace at all. "Not to worry. We'll pull you up."

"How? With a tow truck?"

"If need be," Dana Sue said. "Now sit. I'll be back in a minute. Helen, you can make limeade for Maddie and the kids and the margaritas for us, while I fix the nachos."

As she was about to leave the room, Helen spotted Daisy inching shyly toward Maddie. When she was close enough, she put her tiny hand on Maddie's stomach. "Is there a baby in there?"

Helen's heart clenched at the awe in Daisy's voice and the gentleness of her touch.

"There is," Maddie confirmed. "You're very smart."

"Mack used to be inside my mommy. I remember."

"You were inside your mommy, too," Maddie told her. Daisy looked intrigued. "I don't remember that."

"That's because when babies are born there are so many new things to discover all around them that it makes them forget the warm, safe place they were before," Maddie explained, her gaze lifting to meet Helen's.

In that instant, Helen knew with absolute clarity what she wanted. Not just any baby, but her own baby. One

she'd sheltered and nurtured for nine months before bringing it into the world. She felt a need so powerful it nearly
overwhelmed her. Afraid of what her expression might be
revealing, she quickly followed Dana Sue into the kitchen
and busied herself with making the drinks.

Dana Sue's upbeat chatter washed over her without reg-
istering. All she could think about was that instant when
everything had come together in her mind with startling
clarity. A feeling of serenity stole over her then and stayed
with her even after Karen arrived. It was still with her
when Karen, Daisy and Mack walked away from the house
for the last time.

Though she went back inside with tears in her eyes, her
heart wasn't nearly as heavy as she'd expected it to be. And
that was because of the epiphany she'd had.

"Are you okay?" Maddie asked, studying her worriedly.
"I know letting them go must have been hard, even though
you've been preparing for it for a few weeks now."

Helen nodded. "I just kept telling myself they'd be okay
and that I'd see them soon. It's not as if they're moving to
the other side of the world. They'll be right across town. And
Karen's promised to bring them by whenever I invite them."

"You're calmer than I expected you to be," Dana Sue
said, her brow furrowing. "Why is that? Are you relieved
to have your house to yourself again?"

"No, it's not that at all," Helen swore. "I just made peace
with them going home."

"I'm not buying it," Dana Sue persisted, but then her expression turned sly. "Or did having Erik spend the night
here a few weeks ago give you something else to think
about? Has he been around more than I realized?"

Maddie stared at them. "Erik spent the night?"

"It was one night. We camped in the backyard," Helen corrected. "With the kids." She frowned at Dana Sue. "You bring that up every time I see you. You need to let it go. Don't make it into something it wasn't."

"Well something helped you get through this afternoon," Dana Sue said. "Having a man in your life would do that."

"Maybe it was just having you guys here," Helen suggested.

"I don't buy it," Dana Sue said again.

"Do you want her to be miserable, Dana Sue?" Maddie asked. "If she says she's okay, we should take her word for it and be happy for her. This was a tough afternoon and she got through it without coming unglued. I'd say that deserves a toast."

As Maddie lifted her glass, she suddenly winced and sucked in a deep breath.

"What?" Helen said at once, rushing to her side. "Are you okay, Maddie?"

"I'm not sure, but that could have been a contraction," Maddie admitted.

Helen regarded her with alarm. "How can you not be sure? You've had four other kids. Shouldn't you know a contraction when you're having one?"

"I've had a few twinges off and on for a few hours now," Maddie said. "I thought it was because I overdid it helping Cal move some things around in the new playroom upstairs." She took a deep breath, then nodded. "Yes, I'm sure that's all it was. See, I'm fine. Nothing to worry about."

Dana Sue said worriedly, "Maybe we should go to the hospital and let you get checked out, anyway. You shouldn't be moving furniture this late in your pregnancy. I'm surprised Cal let you."

Maddie rolled her eyes. "Are you kidding? He let me carry a few toys across the room. When I tried to move the rocking chair, he went crazy and insisted I sit down in it and just tell him where I wanted everything else."

"But you're feeling okay now?" Helen asked. "No more twinges?"

"None," Maddie said, then groaned and grabbed her stomach. "*That* was definitely a contraction." She grinned through her obvious pain. "This little one is obviously full of surprises."

Helen looked at Dana Sue. "What do we do now?"

"You haul her out of that chair and get her to the car," Dana Sue said calmly. "I'll call Cal to meet us at the hospital. If her contractions are that close together, we don't have a lot of time."

Helen let Maddie grab on to her shoulders, then half lifted, half tugged her onto her feet. When she was upright, Helen gazed into her eyes. "You are not having this baby in the backseat of my car, understood?"

Maddie gave her a wry look. "Then I suggest we don't waste a lot of time standing around here chatting. I barely made it to the hospital with Jessica Lynn. Something tells me this one's going to be even more impatient."

She took a step, then uttered a curse.

"What?" Helen demanded.

"My water broke," Maddie said. "We might want to pick up this pace."

Dana Sue snapped her cell phone closed. "Cal's on his way to the hospital. Let's get this show on the road. If he gets there before us, he's going to have a full-blown panic attack."

"He warned me not to go out this afternoon," Maddie

said. "He's going to be furious if this baby is born anywhere other than a delivery room."

"Can you waddle any faster than that?" Dana Sue inquired, drawing a nasty look from Maddie. "Okay, okay.
You're doing the best you can."

Five minutes later they had Maddie stretched out on the
backseat with Dana Sue riding with her, while Helen drove.
Every time Maddie let out a scream, Helen's hands
clenched a little more tightly on the steering wheel and she
slammed her foot down a little harder on the accelerator.

They made the half-hour drive to Regional Hospital in
record time, but Cal was faster. He was waiting at the
emergency room entrance, a frantic expression on his face.
An orderly with a wheelchair was waiting with him.

"We need to get your paperwork taken care of," the orderly said.

"No time," Maddie said, her teeth clenched. "Delivery room now!"

"But—"

"Do it," Cal said. "The paperwork can wait."

"I'll handle that," Helen said. "Just go."

She spent twenty minutes placating an annoyed admis-
sions clerk, then went to find Dana Sue. She'd no sooner
found her in the waiting room of the obstetrics unit when
Cal came out of the delivery room, looking dazed.

"It's a boy," he told them, as if it were news. They'd
known that much for months. "He came out howling."

"Probably objecting to my guacamole," Dana Sue said.

"Congratulations," Helen told Cal, her emotions a wild
mix of delight, wonder and envy. Could she be right here
by this time next year? Perhaps, if she put her mind to it.
Could she do it without someone like Cal beside her? Of

course, she told herself staunchly. She would have her two best friends at her side. Even Cal and Ronnie would stick by her. Erik, too, more than likely. That would be more than enough. She was sure of it. Sure enough to start planning the next step first thing tomorrow.

Karen stood in the doorway to the kids' bedroom and stared at them in the moonlight that spilled through the window. Having them home again and knowing that this time it was for good had filled her with so much joy she'd barely reacted when Mack spilled milk all over the kitchen floor and Daisy threw a tantrum because Karen wouldn't let her have candy before dinner.

In fact, she'd waited in dread for her head to start pounding or her shoulders to tense, which had become so commonplace before they'd gone to stay with Helen, but she'd taken both incidents in stride. She hadn't even needed to make conscious use of the calming techniques Dr. McDaniels had taught her. She was simply too happy to let anything get to her tonight.

When Daisy and Mack had gone back to Helen's after the last visit, Karen had redecorated their bedroom. Mack had barely noticed the changes, but Daisy had been thrilled. The bare, merely functional room had been transformed into something special. Its walls were now the same buttery shade as the walls at The Corner Spa. In fact, the paint had come from there. When Dana Sue had heard she wanted to decorate the kids' bedroom, she'd offered the extra paint they'd stored after their remodeling of the old Victorian house that was now one of the region's best day spas.

Dana Sue and her husband had even spent an afternoon helping Karen paint. They'd also scouted a couple of secondhand shops and found some furniture, which they'd painted white, and a deep-yellow toy box with red, blue and green polka dots and stripes. With any luck, Mack and Daisy's toys would wind up inside it at least some of the time, rather than strewn all over the apartment.

Frances had made new curtains for the room from a polka-dotted fabric that coordinated with the toy box. She'd had enough material left over to make matching throw pillows for the beds.

Karen had bought colorful decals, which she'd scattered over the walls. She wanted the cheerful decor to represent their future—bright and new for all of them.

Exiting the bedroom, she found Frances tidying up in the kitchen after their dinner of her homemade mac-and-cheese, fresh peas and one of Erik's apple cobblers with vanilla ice cream.

"Kids get settled in okay?" Frances asked.

"They're already sound asleep. I hope you know how much I appreciate all your help with getting their room ready. Daisy loves it and I'm sure Mack does, too."

"Maybe we should tackle your room next," Frances suggested. "You've spent too long living here as if it's just a temporary roof over your head. You need to turn it into a real home."

"In other words, it's time to make lemonade out of those lemons," Karen said wryly. "You're right. I was so busy being resentful about being reduced to living in a tiny, two-bedroom apartment, I never wanted to do a thing to make it nicer. I just wanted out."

"Being happy where you are is never a bad thing," Frances told her. "Nor is it conceding defeat."

Karen frowned at the comment. "Meaning?"

"I think you've been afraid if you did anything to turn this place into a home, it meant you were accepting the raw deal fate handed you when your husband left. It meant you were giving in, or maybe giving up. You can still have ambitions, sweetie, but this is reality for now. Make the most of it."

"I think I get that finally," Karen said. "I just hope my kids haven't paid too high a price."

"Mack and Daisy are fine. Living with Helen was a grand adventure for them, but they belong here with you. Didn't you notice how excited they were when they got here this afternoon? Best of all, you're strong again and ready to handle whatever's next in your life."

"You think so?" she asked. "You really think so?"

"I *know* so. I saw it tonight at dinner. When Mack dumped that milk on the floor, you didn't bat an eye. And I don't know if you noticed, but there was relief in Daisy's eyes when you just mopped it up without a word."

Karen sighed. "She heard me lose it way too much, didn't she?"

"Probably so, but you can't fix the past. You can only do things differently from here on out. Any idea what you'd like your future to hold?"

"I'll be happy just to keep things on an even keel for now," Karen told her. "I need to remember how to be a good mom."

Frances frowned. "I suppose that's fine for now," she agreed. "But you need dreams, Karen. You need goals for yourself. You deserve to find happiness, too."

"If my kids are okay, I'm happy," she insisted.

"I'll accept that for the moment," Frances said. "But you need to give some thought to your future. Promise me you'll do that."

"I promise," Karen said, giving her a hug.

"Okay, then," Frances said, evidently satisfied. "Now let me leave, so you can get a good night's sleep. If you need anything at all tomorrow, you let me know. Don't be afraid to lean on people, Karen. That's what got you into trouble before. You were trying to handle everything on your own."

Karen gave Frances another fierce hug. "I honestly don't know what I'd do without you."

Frances beamed at her. "Then isn't it wonderful that you'll never have to find out?"

"I love you."

Frances brushed a lock of hair back from her face. "And you're like one of my own, Karen. Good night, sweetie."

"Good night," Karen said softly, tears stinging her eyes.

Right this second, her life seemed to be close to perfect, but it was good to know that the next time it started to fall apart, there was someone she could count on right across the hall. For so many years she'd wondered how different her life would have been if she'd ever had a real mom, a real home she could count on. Now, in so many ways, she'd found the answer to that.

Maddie had been home from the hospital for two weeks and Helen had stopped by to visit every single night. Holding baby Cole Maddox in her arms was solidifying the epiphany she'd had the day Maddie talked about the warm safe place her baby had in her body.

And just now she'd finally admitted to Maddie that she'd come to a decision. She wanted to get pregnant and have a child, no matter what anyone in Serenity thought of her for doing it. She could weather the gossip, and if she gave her child a loving home and surrounded him or her with a huge extended family, surely the child would never feel shortchanged.

Maddie searched Helen's face. "You're sure about this? You've actually decided you want to have a baby the old-fashioned way? I thought having Karen's kids underfoot might have scared you off."

"I thought so, too, at least those first few days, but it got better. I was good at the whole mom thing, better than I'd anticipated." She looked Maddie squarely in the eye and added passionately, "That yearning for something I've been feeling all these months turned into something fiercely maternal. This is right. I know it is."

"But, sweetie, there's a huge difference between playing mom when there's an end in sight and being in it for the long haul," Maddie cautioned.

"I know that," Helen said impatiently. "I've heard it often enough lately. But I'm ready to take it on. I *want* to take it on."

"And marriage? Do you see a dad in this picture?" Maddie asked.

"Honestly, I can't visualize that," Helen admitted. "I'm forty-two. If I haven't met someone in all this time I'd be willing to marry, why on earth would I think I can do it in the next few months or even in the next year?"

"Yes, it would put a courtship on a fast track," Maddie agreed, looking amused. "That shouldn't be a problem for a single-minded woman like you."

"Unfortunately, men tend to be more skittish when it comes to something like this, particularly if I were to mention on the first date that my biological clock is ticking so loudly it can be heard in Georgia."

"That might put them off." Maddie's grin spread.

"So what do I do?"

"Isn't there any man you're attracted to who might make a good husband, a good father?" Maddie asked. "You're not exactly known for giving men much time to make a good impression, but maybe now's the time to run down that list and give a few of those suitors you've dismissed another chance." She gave her a sly glance. "And then there's Erik. Dana Sue's convinced there's something brewing between the two of you."

At the reminder, the all-too-recent memory of a sizzling kiss surfaced in Helen's mind like a beacon in the darkness. Maybe she didn't have to find a man to marry her. Maybe she didn't need to find someone interested in becoming a full-time father. She had a career. She had resources. She was perfectly capable of raising a child entirely on her own. So maybe what she really needed was a man willing to sleep with her, no strings attached. Erik certainly seemed to qualify.

There was no question that he was attracted to her, and vice versa. Nor was there any question that he was even remotely interested in being married or in being a dad. He'd been abundantly clear about that, as well. He was the perfect candidate. He was someone she liked and respected, someone for whom she had feelings. Thus the whole experience wouldn't feel quite so calculated and impersonal. She would honestly be able to tell her child one day that his or her dad was a decent, good man and that she had deep, loving feelings for him.

If need be, once she was pregnant, she could draw up whatever legal papers were necessary to assure Erik that she would never ask for child support, that his role in the child's life could be as limited as he wanted it to be. If he wanted no involvement whatsoever, so be it. She couldn't help thinking that would be a loss for him and his child, but he'd been so adamant about not wanting to be a dad that she assumed that would be his response.

In essence that would make him a sperm donor, albeit in a more direct and tantalizing way, but she honestly couldn't see a downside to it. Erik would get great sex for a while, which was all he apparently wanted from a relationship. She'd get a baby. Wasn't that equitable?

"What on earth is going on in that head of yours?" Maddie asked after several minutes. "Was it what I said about Erik?"

"No, absolutely not," Helen insisted, praying she could keep Maddie from making that leap. She forced a smile. "But I may have a plan, after all."

"Really? What is it?" Maddie asked, looking far more worried than relieved.

"It's probably best if you don't know," she told her. And it would definitely be best if Dana Sue didn't know. She might get all weird at the idea of Helen using Erik to get the baby she wanted.

Heck, there was a possibility Erik might get a little weird about it himself. What if she suggested it and he shot her down? What if she just seduced him and told him later? She wasn't crazy about what such a deception said about her. And it would probably confirm every negative thing Erik had ever thought about her, destroying the easy camaraderie they'd discovered lately. That dismayed her a little more than she cared to admit, but this driving need to have a child of her own outweighed any dismay.

And she would make absolutely certain that a child of hers had everything he or she could ever possibly need—

love, a good education, a wonderful home. Those were the only things that really mattered.

What about a father? a nagging voice in her head demanded. Lots of kids did just fine without a father in their life, she argued with herself. She had. In fact, after seeing how her mom had struggled in one dead-end job after another to give her a decent life after her dad's death, Helen had been driven to make sure she could always provide for herself and any family that might come along. That determination was what had gotten her into this fix in the first place. She hadn't allowed herself to be sidetracked by anything that wouldn't contribute to her financial security and success.

Satisfied with her logic, she stood up abruptly. "I need to be somewhere," she told Maddie.

"But Dana Sue and Jeanette will be here any minute now," Maddie said. "We were going to talk about expanding the spa."

"Apologize for me," Helen said. "We'll make up for this next week."

"But you're the one who wanted to talk about opening a second spa," Maddie protested, even as Helen put baby Cole back into her arms. "This meeting was your idea."

"It can wait," Helen said. "You, Dana Sue and Jeanette can bounce the idea around and let me know what you think."

Maddie's eyes narrowed. "Something tells me you're about to do something impulsive. That's never a good thing with you."

"It's not impulsive and I don't need to talk about it. I've thought about it from every angle. I've probably analyzed it to death." Okay, not the part about Erik, but maybe it was better not to overthink that. She might start to doubt the wisdom of her plan, and there was no time for doubts.

"Well, you know Dana Sue and I will support you, no matter what you do," Maddie said, though her brow was creased with worry.

Helen hugged her. "I know, and you have no idea how much that means to me. Thank you for not telling me I'm crazy."

Maddie grinned. "Did I say that?"

"No, but you heard me and you didn't utter those words, so I'm taking that as a good sign."

"Could I say anything that would stop you from doing whatever it is you're about to do?" Maddie asked.

Helen shrugged. "Probably not."

In fact, right this second, she couldn't think of anything that could derail her plan. And somewhere between here and Sullivan's she'd decide just how much of her plan to reveal to Erik and how much to keep to herself.

13

The sheet of fondant was ready to be draped over the top layer of the three-tiered wedding cake when Erik turned to Tess, who'd been watching him intently.

"You do it," he said.

Her brown eyes widened in dismay. "I can't," she said, though she was clearly tempted.

"Of course you can. How many times have you practiced this?"

She shook her head and backed up a step. "But that was practice. This is the real thing. What if I ruin it?"

"You won't," he said confidently. "But if you do, it's not the end of the world. We'll do it over. Come on, Tess. You've practiced enough. You have to do it for real sometime."

Just as she was about to drape the smooth sheet of icing over the cake, the door to the kitchen burst open and Helen breezed in. Startled, Tess dropped the icing on the floor, then looked at him with a chagrined expression.

"I'm sorry," she said, gesturing toward the mess. "I told you I couldn't do it."

Erik sighed, regarding Helen with exasperation. "Did it ever occur to you to knock before charging in here at this hour?"

"No more than it occurred to you to ask me for a key to my house that time," she retorted. She dangled a key from her finger. "My key to Sullivan's. I've had it since Dana Sue opened."

He shook his head. "Why didn't I know that?"

"Because it's not your restaurant?" she suggested sweetly.

"Whatever," he muttered and bent down to help Tess, who was mopping up the remains of the fondant.

When he stood up, Helen was regarding him with a hint of uncertainty. "Is this really a bad time?"

He bit back a grin. "What do you think? You just scared poor Tess half to death and came close to ruining Jane Downing's wedding cake."

"Jane Downing is being married for the fourth time," Helen said. "I'd say this marriage is as doomed as her cake. Not a big deal." She turned to Tess. "I'm sorry for scaring you, though. I'm Helen Decatur, a friend of Dana Sue's and, despite his snide attitude, a friend of Erik's as well."

"Helen is the attorney I told you about, Tess," Erik added. "She said she'd help you with Diego's situation."

"Would you?" Tess asked as if not quite daring to hope.

"Absolutely. I would have been by to talk to you much sooner, but I had Karen's kids and, to be honest, I was a little overwhelmed."

Tess gave her a shy smile. "Children are a lot of work."

"They are, indeed," Helen said. "Why don't we let Erik finish up that cake and you can tell me what's happened with your husband?"

"Good idea," Erik said, relieved to have time to remind himself why he should not be attracted to Helen and why he should not act on his very powerful desire to kiss her. He'd resolved not to act on his feelings until and unless she came to him and made it clear she was interested in a no-strings relationship. When she'd walked through the doorway a minute ago, a part of him had immediately leaped to the conclusion that he was about to get the answer he'd been lying awake nights thinking about.

"Would you rather speak in private?" Helen asked Tess.

To his disappointment, since he'd hoped for some space so he could reclaim his composure, Tess declined.

"Erik knows what's happened with Diego," she told Helen. "I don't mind if he hears us."

Helen pulled two stools close together and climbed on one, which hiked her narrow skirt halfway up her thighs, giving Erik an intriguing glimpse of bare skin. He couldn't seem to keep himself from following the curve of her leg down to her trim ankle and the latest pair of sexy heels she was wearing. The woman did love her shoes. He couldn't recall ever seeing the same pair twice. He might not know much about designer shoes, but he did know quality. It was plain that habit cost her a fortune.

Apparently she caught the direction of his gaze, because she held one foot out. "Manolo Blahnik's," she said as if that would mean something to him.

He grinned at her. "They look good on you." They were also very tough on his resolve. Those shoes were all about seduction.

"I thought so," she agreed, then turned to Tess. "Erik says you had an attorney who billed you and never did any work. Is that true?"

Tess nodded. "Jimmy Bob West. He was the only attorney I knew."

Erik saw Helen stiffen visibly. His determination to stay

far removed from the conversation failed him. "You know this attorney?" he asked.

"We've crossed paths a few times," she said. "Jimmy Bob's no saint, but I never thought he would sink that low. Tess, tell me exactly what he told you, how much he billed you and what he did."

As Tess went through the sad tale, Helen took notes, her forehead creased in a frown. There was real anger in her eyes by the time Tess finished.

"You'll have your money back by the end of the week," she assured Tess. "One way or another."

"But what about Diego? He is what matters," Tess said. "I have all of his papers proving he is here legally. How do we get his deportation reversed?"

"I'll take care of that, too," Helen promised. "And if I bump up against too much bureaucracy, I know exactly who can untangle all the red tape. It may not happen overnight, Tess, but we will get your husband back here."

"I don't know how to thank you," Tess said. "That would be like a miracle for me and my children." She glanced at the clock on the wall. "It is very late. I need to be home." She regarded Erik worriedly. "I was no help to you tonight."

"You'll get your chance another time," he assured her. "You're good at this, Tess. It's just a matter of practice."

"I'm off tomorrow," she said. "I think I will practice baking a very special birthday cake for my mother as a surprise. If it turns out well, I will bring you a picture." She gave him a considering look. "We should create an album, you know. So people can see all the beautiful cakes you have made. We could have a Web site, too. My brother could create it. He's majoring in Web site design and computer skills at junior college. There is nothing he can't do." Her face shone with pride.

Surprised that Tess had put so much thought into the business side of things, he nodded thoughtfully. "That's a terrific idea, Tess. I'll speak to Dana Sue about it. Have your brother give me a call, okay?"

"I will," she said. "Thank you again, Ms. Decatur. I really appreciate what you're doing for me."

"I'm happy to do it, Tess," Helen said. "Good night."

After Tess had gone, Erik studied Helen. "You're not just happy to help because you care about Tess and Diego, are you? It has something to do with this Jimmy Bob West."

She grinned. "You're very perceptive. I want to nail that sleazebag's hide to the wall. What he did to her was unconscionable."

"He's not opposing counsel on some divorce you're handling, by any chance?"

"He is, indeed. Our last encounter in the courtroom was just my first warning volley. Lawyers like Jimmy Bob give all of us a bad name."

"Yet, you seem to take pride in being referred to as a barracuda," Erik noted.

"A barracuda's one thing. He's a bottom-feeder, the lowest of the low, an unethical son of a gun."

"In other words, you don't like him."

"I don't have to like every attorney I cross paths with," she said. "But I do prefer to respect them. I can hardly wait to have a little chat with Jimmy Bob as soon as I've done some research into this situation."

Erik grinned. "Now that I've put you on the scent for blood, what actually brought you by here tonight? I assume you knew Dana Sue wasn't here, since she told me she was having a meeting with you and Maddie. Don't tell me you skipped out on them just to see me."

She looked vaguely chagrined that he knew about the meeting. "I left early," she said, sounding oddly defensive. "It occurred to me it might be the perfect time for us to talk without being under Dana Sue's watchful eye."

"Interesting," he said. Helen looked surprisingly ill at ease, he thought. "Something in particular on your mind?"

"Don't get excited," she said. "I just haven't had a good sparring match lately."

"Really? And that's the only reason you came by? So we could match wits?"

"Something like that."

He shook his head. "Not buying it, sugar. You had some other agenda. Come on. Spill it."

To his astonishment, a burst of color flooded her cheeks. "You're blushing," he said, startled.

"I am not. It's probably a hot flash."

He winced at that. If she was having hot flashes, he definitely didn't want to know about it. Wasn't she a little young for them, though? He tried to recall what he'd read about menopause during his EMT training, but since most of his courses had focused on emergency medicine, not much came to mind.

He did like the fact that he'd somehow managed to throw her off-kilter. He decided to keep her there.

"It's okay to admit you came by because you couldn't go another second without seeing me," he said. "You don't have to be embarrassed because you find me irresistible."

She leveled an indignant look directly into his eyes, then glanced away. "This was a mistake."

"What was a mistake?"

"Thinking I could spend more than fifteen minutes with you without wanting to strangle you."

He bit back a grin. "We spent a whole night together not that long ago and I don't recall you wanting to strangle me then."

"Did you miss my reaction to the fact that you conned Dana Sue into giving you my key?"

"Oh, that," he said dismissively. "You weren't really upset about it."

"Yes, I was."

"But you got over it," he countered. "You just made a big deal out of it because you thought you should."

She scowled. "I made a big deal out of it because what you did was sneaky and underhanded."

Suddenly, the color that had remained in her cheeks washed right out, leaving her complexion pale. "I need to go," she said, grabbing her purse and heading for the door.

Erik stepped in front of her, worried by her pallor. "Are you okay? You're not feeling sick, are you?"

"No. I, um, I just remembered something I have to do."

He recognized tap dancing when he heard it. "Something to do?" he echoed doubtfully. "At this hour?"

"Yes. I should have done it hours ago." She pushed past him. "I'll see you."

He stared after her. What was up with that? One minute she was the same old feisty Helen, the next she was taking off like a scared rabbit. It was evident from the way she'd avoided meeting his gaze that she'd been lying through her teeth. And the only thing she had to do was get away from him.

He shrugged off his confusion. It was just one more reminder that she was way too complex and complicated for him. If he ever did break down and let another woman into his life, he wanted one who was serene and easy to read. Helen was anything but.

So why couldn't he get her out of his mind?

Well, that had certainly been a disaster, Helen thought as she drove away from Sullivan's. The moment she'd accused Erik of being sneaky and underhanded over a key, of all things, it had struck her that what she was planning was a thousand times worse. And yet, now that the idea of having him father her child had taken hold, she couldn't seem to abandon it.

At home she went through her bedtime routine by rote, missing the chaos Daisy and Mack's presence produced underfoot. She reached for the phone to call them, but a glance at the clock told her it was too late.

In bed she made mental lists of all the pros and cons of involving Erik in her plan to have a child of her own. The positives outweighed the negatives, or maybe she'd only weighted it that way so she could go through with it. In the end, though, she would have the child she desperately wanted. Wasn't that the only thing that mattered?

But what about what Erik wants? a nagging voice countered. He couldn't have made it any clearer that he didn't want children. After wrestling with that very hard truth for most of the night and the next day, she managed to convince herself that he'd be okay once he knew she didn't expect anything from him. In the meantime, she'd just have to find some way to live with the guilt of knowing she was deceiving him about the real reason she was initiating an affair with him.

Exhausted and cranky after a couple of sleepless

nights and countless frustrating calls to deal with immigration bureaucracy in an attempt to resolve Diego's immigration status, she left home on Wednesday morning and headed straight for Jimmy Bob's office. She was in the perfect mood to take him to task over what he'd done to Tess.

The law offices of West & Davis were located in Serenity's newest business complex, a cluster of single-story, pale-pink brick buildings with black shutters. It had been built a few years ago by a partnership of several of the town's professionals as a tax write-off. Maddie's ex-husband was one of the partners. Bill Townsend's suite of offices for his pediatrics practice dominated one entire building. West & Davis occupied another. The third building housed the more modest suites of a dentist, an accountant and a local developer. One of the growing real estate companies had just taken over the entire fourth building.

It was early enough that the parking lot was mostly empty. Helen immediately spotted Jimmy Bob's shiny new BMW convertible parked in front of his office. The spaces most likely used by his staff were still empty, as was his partner's assigned space, which meant she could raise a real ruckus with Jimmy Bob without fear of being overheard.

Briefcase in hand, she strolled inside and walked straight into his office without bothering to knock. Jimmy Bob's gaze shot up and alarm flared in his eyes before he carefully covered it with a phony smile.

"Helen, good to see you. Did we have an appointment this morning?"

"No. I was hoping you could spare a few minutes before your day gets too crazy."

"Well, of course I can. Have a seat. You want some coffee? Made it myself from a special blend I order online. Have to say it's the best in town."

"Then by all means," she said. "I'd love a cup."

He poured it for her, then went behind his imposing desk in a tactic that was meant to intimidate. "This is about the Holliday case, I imagine. Is Caroline ready to settle?"

She regarded him incredulously. "With your client on the ropes? I don't think so," Helen replied. "I think you'll find Brad's hidden assets quite fascinating. I know we have. So has Judge Rockingham, which is why he went along with that second delay I requested. Suddenly he seems to be as eager to get to the bottom of Brad's finances as we are."

She gave him an innocent look. "It must be making things a little tense for the three of you on the golf course, though."

He winced. "Look, I had no idea Brad had been keeping things from me," Jimmy Bob said. "I hope you know that. The judge was in the dark, too. He's livid and he let Brad know it. I always tell my clients that full disclosure is necessary in situations like this."

"I'm sure you do," Helen said, though she was certain of no such thing. That was a battle for another day. "I'm here about another case."

Jimmy Bob looked puzzled. "Are we representing opposing sides in another divorce?"

"No, this is about Tess Martinez."

For an instant his expression was blank, but then he nodded slowly. "Of course. I remember Tess. A very sad situation. She claimed her husband was deported even though he was here legally."

"She didn't just claim it, Jimmy Bob. It's the truth."

"They all say that," he insisted with a shrug. "Most of the time it's a lie."

"It isn't a lie in the case of Diego Martinez. He has his papers, Jimmy Bob. I know Tess showed them to you. And I know she paid you to represent her and fix this so her husband could come home to his family."

He frowned as he looked over the papers Helen had picked up from Tess on her way over here. "Excellent forgeries," he concluded. "That's why I couldn't do anything for her."

"Either you're incredibly lazy or you're an idiot, or maybe you're just low-down scum," she said. "I was able to check out this information with a few phone calls." Okay, it had taken two days, but still. "It's all completely legitimate. Diego's papers are in order. He should have been back here months ago. Instead, you took Tess's money and then blew her off."

He squirmed uncomfortably. "She's taking you in, Helen. I never picked you to be one of those softies who believes every sob story."

Helen stared at him. "So you're saying I'm gullible and you were just doing your civic duty by taking money from a client and then doing absolutely nothing to help her?"

"There was nothing I could do," he insisted.

She shook her head. "That's amazing. Because the person I spoke to at Immigration says we can have this straightened out by the end of the week and Diego home with his family within a few weeks at most."

"No way," Jimmy Bob said, his face red. "This town doesn't need any more of these border jumpers coming in to take jobs that belong to our own people, Helen. What is *wrong* with you?"

Helen merely shook her head at his outrageous comment. "There's nothing wrong with me, but there's a whole lot wrong with an attorney who would cheat someone out of their very limited funds, then do absolutely nothing to help them."

"I'm telling you, you're being conned," he blustered.

"The federal government doesn't seem to agree," she said. "But rather than sit here and argue with you about the merits of Diego's case, I'll be happy if you'll just write a check to Tess for the amount she gave you. She and Diego can use that to get settled when he gets back here. If you're smart, you'll add a little interest to keep me from spreading this story far and wide."

"That's blackmail," he accused.

"We can certainly debate that in front of the bar association's ethics committee," she offered.

Jimmy Bob locked gazes with her. When Helen didn't flinch, he finally pulled a checkbook out of his desk and wrote a check. She glanced at the figure and nodded in satisfaction. "Thank you. I'll see you in court in a few days. I think we can get the Holliday case wrapped up this time, don't you?"

"I'll do my best to convince Brad of that, but he's furious about this last maneuver of yours. I don't know that I've ever seen him so angry. He's been on a rampage, making all sorts of ridiculous threats."

Helen's gaze narrowed. "Threats?"

Jimmy Bob waved his hand dismissively. "Nothing to worry about. He's just blowing smoke."

"You sure about that?"

"Of course I am. Brad's been a respected member of this community most of his life. He's not going to do anything stupid." Jimmy Bob shook his head. "Doesn't mean I can get him to listen to reason when it comes to settling this case." He paused and gave her a considering look. "You know, Trent and I have been thinking about adding another partner. You interested?"

"In working with you?" Helen asked. Was he kidding?

"Why not? You're smart. You're tough. I admire that."

"While I appreciate the compliment, Jimmy Bob, I'm afraid I don't have the stomach for working with you."

To her surprise, he grinned. "That's exactly what I like about you, Helen. You don't pull punches. Think about the offer."

"No need to," she assured him.

"Not even if it meant you could spend your spare time trying to reform me?"

She laughed at that. "Something tells me you're beyond redemption, Jimmy Bob." She waved the check before tucking it into her briefcase. "But you did the right thing this time. I appreciate it."

He walked her to the door. "You take care, you hear."

"You do the same."

As she drove away, she couldn't help wondering if Jimmy Bob was the scumbag she'd always thought him to be, or just a good old boy who got a kick out of working all the angles to see who'd call him on it. Thinking of the check she'd gotten for Tess without too much of a protest from Jimmy Bob, she was beginning to think it might be the latter.

Karen had been conscientiously going to The Corner Spa every afternoon for an hour during the break between lunch and dinner at Sullivan's. As much as she'd hated the exercise at first, she realized that she always felt better afterward. She was never going to run in a marathon or lift her own weight in barbells, but the modest goals and challenges Elliott set for her were making a difference in her overall stamina and fitness.

She'd been disappointed when he'd declared her ready to do her workouts on her own, but she'd understood that his time was valuable. He had other, paying clients who deserved his full attention. Still, she watched with a certain amount of envy as he coached those other women, while she trudged away on the treadmill or rode an exercise bike.

She sighed as he bent close to a new client, whispering encouragement as he once had to her. She reminded herself he was just doing his job. Despite the sparks she'd felt, it was obvious she'd been just another client to him. Why had she allowed herself to make such a big deal of their time together? Because she was an idiot, that was why.

She finished her cooldown stretches, then headed for the locker room. Suddenly Elliott stepped into her path.

"You weren't pushing yourself today," he said. "What's going on?"

She flushed under his intense look. "I was distracted, I guess."

"Something you want to talk about?"

Not with him, anyway. She shook her head.

"Then how about going to a movie with me this weekend?"

The request, coming right after she'd convinced herself she'd only imagined Elliott's interest, caught her completely by surprise. "A movie?"

He grinned. "I've been known to sit in the dark occasionally and stare up at images on a big screen. It's relaxing."

"And here I thought you never sat down for a second."

"You still haven't answered me," he said. "How about a movie?"

Karen was tempted, but there were so many complications in her life she wasn't sure she could handle any more. Maybe she was better off sticking with the fantasy. "I'm not sure it's a good idea," she said at last.

Elliott looked genuinely disappointed. "Another time?"

Deciding to explain the reason she was turning him down, she asked, "Do you have a minute for a break? I'd like to talk to you about this." She wanted him to understand that her refusal wasn't about him. Maybe then she wouldn't be slamming the door for good.

"Sure, I can take a break," he said readily. "I'll get us a couple of bottled waters and meet you on the patio out back."

"Give me ten minutes to shower and dress."

"That'll work."

Karen was grateful for her short hair. She was able to shape it while it was still damp and look halfway presentable when she joined Elliott outside. Several women studied her with interest when she sat down at his table.

He handed her the bottled water, then leaned back in his chair. Though he was totally focused on her, he still managed to look completely relaxed and at ease. Karen envied him for that.

"Elliott," she began hesitantly, "I didn't turn you down because I don't like you. I…" She tried again. "My life is complicated and—" She stopped. "No, actually it's a mess. Or it has been. I have two kids. My ex-husband hasn't paid child support since he left. My kids have been sick a lot. I've missed work. I've been totally stressed out. In fact, one of the reasons I'm even here is because my shrink thought the exercise would help with the stress and Dana Sue arranged for a free membership. That's my life in a nutshell."

Elliott's gaze remained steady as she blurted everything

out. When she was finished, he simply nodded. "I knew all that, or most of it, anyway. I didn't know about the dead-beat dad, but I'd heard all the rest."

"And you still want to go out with me?" she asked in amazement.

He chuckled at her reaction. "Here's what I see. You're a beautiful woman who's had a tough time. You're a good mom. You're working hard to put your life back together. Your kids are back home now, which proves just how hard you've worked. What's not to admire and like about that?"

"But why would you want to get caught up in all my drama?" she asked, genuinely bemused.

"Didn't I mention you're gorgeous? And funny?"

Karen laughed. "You hadn't mentioned the part about me being funny," she teased. "*Now* I get it."

"Look, it's just a movie. We can make it a family thing, if that would be easier for you than worrying about a sitter. I like kids. I'd better. Between my brothers and sisters, I have ten nieces and nephews. They're always around at my folks' place. My mom takes her duties as their *abuela* very seriously."

Karen thought about that. "Daisy, she's my five-year-old, has been begging to see the new animated movie. Could you stand it?"

"My nieces tell me it's great and they're very good judges of animated films," he said.

Karen made an impulsive decision for the first time in ages. "I have to work on Saturday. Would Sunday afternoon be okay for you?"

"Sunday afternoon would be fine. We can go for pizza after the movie."

"You are a very brave man," she said.

"Heroic, perhaps?" he teased.

She laughed. "Maybe."

But, she admitted to herself, he was showing all the signs of being outstanding hero material.

Erik couldn't figure out what the devil was going on. Suddenly every time he turned around Helen was in the kitchen at Sullivan's, and she didn't seem to be there to see Dana Sue. In fact, he was getting this odd vibe that she was there to flirt with him, which made no sense at all. They'd talked about the fact that neither of them were looking for any kind of serious relationship. While there was no mistaking the flirtatious undertones of their conversations, she had yet to say or do anything that would suggest she was ready to move to another level. In fact, the messages she was sending out were so mixed he had yet to unscramble them. Didn't mean he wasn't getting a kick out of trying, though.

More peculiar than Helen's behavior was the fact that Dana Sue didn't seem to be behind any of it. If anything, she seemed just as puzzled by Helen's presence as he was.

After she'd shown up every single night for a week, Erik decided to call her on it. Dana Sue had gone home with Ronnie after Helen had volunteered to stay and help him clean up the kitchen. Right this second she was apparently on a mission to polish every piece of chrome in sight.

Erik hitched himself up onto a counter and watched her work, a frown furrowing her brow, her hair curling about her face from the steam that had filled the room when he'd opened the dishwasher. She'd kicked off her shoes, another pair of those high-heeled sandals that drew attention to her shapely legs. Her hips swayed in time to some tune she was singing, mostly off-key. He couldn't stop the grin that spread across his face as he listened to her slaughter the lyrics and the tune. It was yet another unexpected side to a very complex woman, who was as fascinating as she was infuriating.

Apparently sensing his gaze on her, she turned slowly. "What are you looking at?"

"You," he said.

"Why aren't you cleaning?"

"Because it's more fun watching you do it."

"If I'm that entertaining, maybe I should request pay."

"Since you managed to keep Karen on the payroll, convinced us to hire Tess and nudged Dana Sue to bring in more part-time help, there's not enough left in the budget to pay you, too.

"Tell me something." His tone was serious. "Why are you hanging around here so much lately? Are you bored? Did you run out of high-profile cases all of a sudden?"

To his surprise, her gaze locked with his. "Maybe it's the company."

That took the wind right out of his sails. He hadn't expected her to be so direct. Then, again, he didn't know why not. Helen was one of the most direct women he'd ever met. She never minced words. The surprise was that she'd taken so long to get to this point.

She tossed her sponge in the direction of the sink, then crossed the kitchen to stand directly in front of him. She put a hand on his chest. "We've kissed a few times now. I can't seem to get that out of my head," she said, sounding a little breathless. "How about you?"

He shrugged, not ready to admit to just how hard it had been to shake the memory of their kisses. "I haven't had to work too hard at forgetting," he claimed. "You said you wanted time to think things through. I figured you'd let me know when you had."

She looked skeptical. "Really? You haven't thought about those kisses at all? Maybe I'm remembering them all wrong. Could we try it again? This time without me throwing a pie at you first, of course. Or having a couple of kids around to keep things from getting out of control."

When she leaned closer, Erik put his hands on her shoulders and studied her. He wanted to be really sure about this, needed her to be sure, as well. Something told him that this time one kiss was going to lead to another and then to a whole lot more.

"What's really going on here, Helen?"

Her lips twitched. "I thought my communication skills were pretty well-honed. I want you to kiss me again, Erik. Or I can kiss you. It doesn't really matter which way it starts."

He grinned. "Haven't you heard? Men like to take the initiative."

"Then do it," she said.

But instead, he ran a thumb along her cheek, then along the curve of her jaw. Her skin flushed beneath his touch. "You're such a contradiction," he murmured, beginning to lose his grip on the common sense that was yelling at him to stay away from this woman. As direct as she was being, there was more going on, something he had a hunch he should know before he got in any deeper. Still…

He stroked a hand down her arm, the skin like velvet. "Such a contradiction," he repeated. "Hard as nails in some ways, but so damn soft in others."

She held his gaze, waiting, silent for once. Then she licked her lips and he was lost. That mouth of hers had tormented his dreams for a while now. It had only gotten worse once he'd kissed her and knew just how soft her lips were, just how passionately she would kiss him back. He'd lied about forgetting all that. He'd thought of little else for weeks.

"This is such a bad idea," he murmured, just before he leaned forward and claimed her.

Two hours later, when he woke up in his bed, the sheets tangled around them, her body curved into his, the idea seemed a whole lot better than it had at first glance.

14

Helen wasn't sure what she'd expected when she'd deliberately set out to seduce Erik tonight, but it certainly wasn't the wave of guilt that washed over her not five seconds after she'd had one of the most mind-shattering orgasms of her life. Her conscience, which usually remained silent given the relatively honorable life she'd always led, was screaming so loudly it drowned out the part of her that wanted to bask quietly in the moment. She'd even lied to his face about birth control, implying he didn't need to worry because she had taken care of it. Things had been so hot and wild at the time, he hadn't questioned her more closely.

"What's going on in that head of yours?" Erik asked, propped up on one elbow beside her, his other hand resting on the bare curve of her hip.

"I was just thinking that we should have done this months ago," she said. It wasn't a total lie. She'd thought that several times as he'd been making love to her. They'd wasted weeks on a dance that had had an inevitable outcome. How had she escaped the power of the chemistry between them until tonight?

Erik grinned at her. "You weren't ready months ago. Neither was I."

Helen wanted to argue that she'd been waiting her entire adult life for a man to pay so much attention to her pleasure, but she remained silent. Such a comment, which would have come naturally under other circumstances, rattled her now. She hadn't expected to feel so connected to this man after sleeping with him just once. She hadn't expected to feel anything more than a momentary release, a mutual satisfaction. Somehow she'd convinced herself that she could be intimate with Erik for however long it took for her to get pregnant and yet somehow remain detached. Tonight had pretty much destroyed that illusion. She might be able to walk away when the time came because she had to, but she wouldn't be detached.

"You're still thinking too hard about something," he said, scrutinizing her face. "Talk to me. Try the truth this time."

Instead, she reached for him. "Talking is a waste of time," she said right before she kissed him.

Erik pulled back, his gaze locked with hers. For a moment, she thought he was going to argue, but then he honed back in on her mouth.

Her body sang, she thought with amazement, as he stroked and caressed and probed, lingering here, skimming there, taunting and teasing until every inch of her was shouting for yet another magnificent release.

"I love watching the way your eyes turn dark when you're about to come apart," he said, gazing into her eyes.

"Are they dark now?"

He nodded.

"Then what are you waiting for? I want you inside me, Erik. Now, please."

"Not just yet," he said, and began his exploration of her body all over again, taking his time, clearly savoring every touch.

Helen had never allowed herself to let go completely with another man. Maybe it was because she was a control freak. Maybe it was simply because she was terrified to be that vulnerable.

Erik wasn't giving her any choice. He seemed to know her body as if he'd been studying it for years. He knew when she was achingly close to release, only to have him slow things down. He knew just how long to let the heat cool before turning it up again. In fact, to her frustration and delight, he was an expert at the teasing seduction.

Each time, he took her a little higher, then let her back down again until she was ready to take charge herself and end the torment.

"Now," she commanded, her unyielding gaze locked with his.

"Now?" he asked innocently. "You think so?"

"Yes!" Her hips writhed as he played his fingers over her damp heat. For this instant, her urgency had nothing to do with getting pregnant and everything to do with getting to that pinnacle that he was cleverly keeping just beyond her reach. It was all about the two of them and a connection so powerful it would have terrified her if she'd had the ability to think clearly.

"Okay, then," he said at last, hovering above her. "If you're sure."

"I am so sure," she whispered, lifting her hips.

When he entered her this time, she felt the most amazing sense of completion, as if she'd been waiting for this her entire life, not just for the past half hour. She bucked, trying to draw him deeper inside, but Erik controlled the rhythm, steadying her to accept his pace. Slow, then fast, then slow again until she was practically mindless with need.

The first wave of pleasure caught her by surprise, a quick, intense burst that erupted at her core, then rippled through her. While she was still savoring that, the sensations deepened in intensity, gathering force like the eruptions of a volcano, each one washing over her in wave after sensual wave.

When Erik's body finally tensed in release, Helen was already shuddering, every inch of her body covered in a sheen of perspiration. It took only one quick brush of his finger, one touch of his mouth to her breast, and she came apart with him in a dazzling explosion that left her heart thundering in her chest and her mind reeling.

Never so at a loss for words in her life, she looked into Erik's eyes. The moment demanded something, some expression of appreciation, or at the very least an awestruck "Wow!" She couldn't even manage that.

"You okay?" he asked, regarding her with concern. "You look a little dazed."

"Dazed doesn't begin to cover it," she whispered.

He grinned with smug, male superiority. "Really?"

"You know you're good at this. You must."

"It's been a while. I thought I might have lost my touch."

"It hasn't been that long. This is the second time tonight."

He laughed. "I meant before tonight."

"Well, obviously it's all come back to you," she said.

"You didn't do too badly yourself."

"I can do better," she said. "I was a bit out of practice, too."

"Any better and we'd both be dead," he commented. "Now for the tricky part."

"Which is?"

"Are you going to stay the night or are you going to scamper out of here like a scared rabbit?"

She didn't much like the imagery, especially as she'd considered making up an excuse to leave. "What makes you think I'm scared?"

"I can see it in your eyes."

"Well, I'm not," she protested. "I'm staying."

To his credit, he didn't gloat. He merely nodded. "I'm glad. You hungry? I could fix something."

Helen considered the offer. "You know, I never eat this late, but I'm starved."

"Good. Me, too. You stay here. I'll be right back."

"All this and he cooks, too," she murmured as he climbed out of bed. "What did I do to deserve this?"

"I think we both know the answer to that," he said wryly. "Back in a minute."

When he'd left the room, Helen glanced around. She'd noticed very little about his house when they'd arrived. They'd come here, not because he'd insisted, but because it was closer than hers by a block. By then, they'd both been intent on getting out of their clothes and into his bed. Now she had time to look at the very spartan decor. The dresser had no pictures on top, just a small TV at one end. The nightstand beside the bed had only a lamp on it, aside from the candle Erik had grabbed from a table in the living room as they'd passed through it.

The flame from that unscented candle was the only illumination in the room now, keeping most of it in shadows, but even so she could tell he'd done nothing to make the bedroom his own. She even wondered if he'd rented the place furnished, since the furniture had that sturdy, uninteresting look to it. Even the room's one chair was utilitarian—a place to toss clothes, rather than the kind of comfortable chair a man might choose if he intended to relax in his room watching late-night TV or a ball game.

In fact, even without getting a good look at the living room, she had a feeling this was the home of a man who'd never really intended to stay in Serenity. She was surprised by how much that bothered her. Obviously, in one regard, it'd be more convenient for her if he did decide to leave at some point, yet just the idea of that happening made her heart contract with pain.

She was still pondering that when he returned carrying a tray with two plates. He'd made a frittata, mixing the eggs with slivers of onion, peppers and tomato, along with a combination of cheeses, then baking it in the oven and cutting it into thick, fluffy wedges.

"This is amazing," she said, when she'd taken her first bite.

"Don't sound so shocked. I *am* a chef."

"I know, but I can't even imagine having enough ingredients in the refrigerator to make something like this."

"I noticed your cupboard was nearly bare the night I was there to camp out. You don't cook at all?"

"I can follow a recipe under duress," she admitted. "But my lack of skill in the kitchen is a very good thing for Sullivan's. I'm your best customer."

"True enough," he said, still regarding her curiously. "If you don't cook, which I assume means you don't enjoy it, why are you so willing to pitch in at the restaurant?"

"It's Dana Sue's. I'd do anything to help out a friend."

"And The Corner Spa? I know for a fact that you're not an exercise nut. Did you provide the seed money for that because Maddie needed work?"

"In a way," she replied. "And in theory, it was supposed to encourage me to exercise. The doctor was all over me about my blood pressure."

"It's high?" he asked, alarm in his eyes. "Why didn't you mention that?"

"It *was* high," she said. "It's under control now. I manage to make myself do enough exercise to relieve at least some of the stress. And I have a little pill to do the rest. No big deal. Why would I mention it to you? It's not exactly relevant to this." She gestured at the tangled sheets.

He frowned at her glib tone. "You're too young for a problem like that. You need to take better care of yourself."

"I'm trying, especially lately."

"Good," he said, then fell silent. When he spoke again, he sounded uncertain. "How do you want to handle this?"

"Handle what?"

"You and me," he said, then gestured at the rumpled bed as she had a moment earlier. "This."

"We could pretend it never happened," she suggested, only partly in jest.

"That implies it's not going to happen again," he said. "I think we both know otherwise."

Helen shivered at the implication. "Do we?"

"I do. Don't you?"

"It would be a shame not to repeat something that incredible," she admitted, grinning at him.

"Okay, then, do we tell Dana Sue or not?"

"Absolutely not," she said at once, which had his frown deepening.

"Okay, I have one reason why that makes sense, but something tells me you have an entirely different reason," he said.

Helen wasn't about to explain that Dana Sue might immediately put two and two together and come up with her baby plan, so she said, "Isn't it obvious? She would make way too much out of this. Besides, I don't think I could stand to have her gloating about it. She's been predicting it for months."

He laughed. "Yeah, the gloating would be hard to take. So, for now, we keep this just between us?"

"Agreed," she said.

"Any idea how we're going to pull that off?" he asked.

"No kissing, no touching, no lingering looks in public," she suggested. "And I'll act like I'm furious with you. That shouldn't be hard. You usually do or say something on a daily basis to infuriate me."

"I'll be sure to continue," he promised.

But despite Helen's conviction that secrecy was the right way to go, she couldn't deny feeling a little pang that she couldn't share this with her two best friends.

But share what? she asked herself. It wasn't as if she'd started a relationship that might lead somewhere, one that Dana Sue and Maddie would be elated to hear about. She'd started an affair that she hoped would result in a pregnancy. That was something best left unsaid. She knew in her heart that neither of her friends would congratulate her for that. Right this second she wasn't sure she was very proud of herself, either.

Erik was in the storage pantry at Sullivan's when he heard Maddie talking to Dana Sue. Though Dana Sue knew he was nearby, she didn't seem to censor herself or warn Maddie that they might be overheard. Dana Sue took it for granted that he'd be discreet. He'd already learned far more of the intimate details of Maddie's post-pregnancy recovery than he needed.

"Do you have any idea what's going on with Helen?" he heard Maddie ask. "I haven't seen her for a couple of weeks now. It's not like her to avoid us."

"You think that's what she's doing?" Dana Sue asked, sounding surprised. "I just assumed she was busy. You know how she gets when she's working on a big case. She goes into hibernation. The final hearing in the Holliday case is coming up soon and she's determined to get Caroline everything she deserves."

"I don't think that's it," Maddie said. "She has been consumed with the Holliday divorce lately, but Caroline tells me that's just about wrapped up. And she's already handled Tess's problem with Jimmy Bob West."

"I know," Dana Sue responded. "Tess is ecstatic. Diego's back home and working again already. She thinks Helen hung the moon."

"Okay, then, with those two things under control, Helen should have some free time. Where is she? Have you even spoken to her?"

"Now that you mention it, no," Dana Sue replied. "She was popping in here just about every day for a while, but suddenly that stopped."

"Well, what do you make of it?"

"New man in her life?"

"Why wouldn't she tell us about that?" Maddie demanded. "She tells us everything."

Erik decided it was time to make an appearance before Dana Sue's agile mind leaped to a conclusion it would be best to avoid. He'd known Helen's absences were going to spark speculation. He also knew she'd opted to avoid Sullivan's rather than risk Dana Sue spotting some slip that would reveal their new relationship—

she hadn't been that confident that either of them could stick to their plan.

Emerging from the pantry with bags of flour and sugar, he smiled at Maddie, who was beginning to regain her shape after her pregnancy. He thought she'd looked amazing while pregnant, but he had a hunch she was happier with her more slender figure.

"How's the new mom?" he asked. "You're looking fit."

"I'm feeling great," she said. "But I'm bored out of my mind. Dana Sue and Helen insisted I let Jeanette run the spa for six weeks. I've been antsy for four of those weeks, even with Elliott coming by the house to make me do these horrendous workouts for the past couple of weeks."

"Which means you took exactly one week to relax after having your son," he said after a quick calculation.

She grinned unrepentantly. "About that."

Erik caught Dana Sue frowning at him.

"How much of our conversation did you hear?" she demanded. "Not that I think you'd ever repeat a word of it, but I need to know."

"Sugar, I have more important things to do than eavesdrop on you."

"That's never stopped you before," she retorted. "How much?"

"Okay, all of it. Why? If you know I'm trustworthy, why do you care?"

"Then you heard us talking about Helen. What do you know about what she's up to these days? Has she been confiding in you?"

"Hardly," he responded, keeping his gaze averted. "Why on earth would she confide in me?"

"Because every instinct in me tells me you know something you're not saying. Otherwise you'd have been back in here ten minutes ago. It doesn't take that long to get a few things from storage."

"It does if someone I know goes in there and rearranges everything," he countered, seizing on the chance to change the subject and fix a nagging problem at the same time. "Why do you do that, by the way? I have a system."

"So do I," she replied. "Mine is the one that counts."

"Not when it comes to baking," he replied.

"Okay, that's it. I'm out of here," Maddie said. "Once you two start debating control issues, innocent bystanders are in the way." She hugged Dana Sue. "Let me know if you catch up with Helen."

"You do the same," Dana Sue said.

Maddie gave Erik a peck on the cheek and whispered, "Stick to your guns. The desserts are the best thing on the menu."

"I heard that," Dana Sue said.

Maddie grinned. "Then keep it in mind when you're discussing the arrangement of the stockroom. Erik might actually have some valid points."

"He might," Dana Sue conceded grudgingly.

When Maddie was gone, she eyed him intently. "You want to fight about the pantry or tell me what you know about Helen?"

"Let's fight about the pantry," he said.

"Then you *do* know something about Helen," she concluded.

"I did not say that," he insisted.

"You didn't have to," she said smugly. "It was written all over your face. That's okay. I'll let it pass this time. I'll get the information out of you when your guard's not up."

"My guard is always up around you," he assured her.

But just in case he was wrong about that, he'd be extra vigilant. Or maybe he'd just dump the problem in Helen's lap and let her deal with her friends. She was just as eager to keep the two of them out of their love life as he was.

Karen had been doing really well for several weeks now. Maybe it was because the kids had been on their best behavior, almost as if they understood that they might be separated again if things didn't go smoothly. Or maybe it was because all her sessions with Dr. McDaniels were paying off. She hoped that was it, because sooner or later the kids were bound to do something that would test her limits.

They'd also taken to Elliott from the very first time he'd come by. He was endlessly patient with Daisy's long descriptions of her days at school. In fact, he seemed genuinely interested in the details of kindergarten, the art projects she brought home and the boy on whom she'd developed a crush. As for Mack, Elliott had miraculously managed, over three visits, to get him weaned from sucking his thumb, a goal that Karen had despaired of accomplishing.

Frances had given Elliott a thumbs-up, too. "He's a very thoughtful young man," she'd told Karen. "Hot, too," she'd added with a wink.

Despite all the votes of approval, Karen was still keeping Elliott at arm's length. She had a feeling that sometime soon he was going to call her on it, perhaps even tonight when they were going to dinner alone, while Frances kept Daisy and Mack.

A tap on the door announced Frances's arrival. She took one look at Karen, still wearing her ratty old chenille robe, and shook her head. "Why aren't you ready? Elliott will be here any minute, won't he?"

"I can't decide what to wear," Karen said.

Frances gave her a knowing look. "I think you're scared."

"Scared of what?" she asked, a defensive note in her voice.

"The fact that this man finds you attractive and wants to spend time with you. You've done everything in your power to make him turn tail and run, but nothing's worked, has it?"

Karen frowned. "I haven't tried to run him off," she protested.

"Really? Well, you assigned him to break Mack of sucking his thumb as if the child's life depended on it," Frances said. "I'm sure that was designed to make him think twice about what he was getting into with a mother of two young children. What's next? Do you plan to leave him in charge of Daisy's birthday party next week? I hate to tell you, sweetie, but Elliott strikes me as a man who can handle a dozen six-year-olds with one hand tied behind his back."

Karen sighed. "You're probably right. I thought he was joking about all those nieces and nephews teaching him a lot about kids, but it seems to be true."

"Then why are you trying to run him off?"

Karen sank onto the edge of the sofa. "Do you really think that's what I've been trying to do?"

"I think every date you've had with him has been some sort of test. What are you going to do when he's passed them all, instead of disappearing?"

"I wish I knew," Karen said with a sigh. She glanced at Frances. "He really is a good guy, isn't he?"

"Seems to be," Frances said. "Besides scared, how do you feel about him?"

"I like him," Karen admitted. "I really like him."

"Then give him a real chance. You two need more nights like tonight, just the two of you, so you can really get to know each other." She smiled at Karen. "And don't worry about what time you get home. I can fall asleep right here on your sofa."

She blushed at the implication. "Frances! I am not going to stay out all night."

Frances's smile spread. "That's up to you, of course, but I wanted you to know it wouldn't be a problem if you did."

"Would you have told your daughter that?" Karen inquired curiously.

"Heavens, no!" Frances said with a laugh. "But she was twenty the last time she lived under my roof, and when it came to dating, she did what she pleased without me giving her any extra encouragement."

"Did you approve of her staying out all night?"

"Not really, but she was old enough to make her own decisions, same as you. I was wise enough to keep my opinions to myself."

"I don't ever want you to think less of me," Karen said. "You're like a mother to me."

"I'm proud you feel that way and I'm more than happy to offer advice whenever you ask for it, but I won't judge you, honey. Not ever. Now go and get ready before that man finds you in that robe. It really *might* scare him off. If he gets here before you're ready, it'll just give me a few minutes to see what his intentions are."

Karen laughed. "I'll hurry."

"No, please. Take your time. I don't get many chances to spend time with a man that gorgeous."

"Neither do I," Karen said.

"Then it's time to start enjoying every minute of it, don't you think?"

"I think you're absolutely right," Karen said.

But when she walked into her bedroom, she found the clothes she'd pulled from the closet as she'd tried to decide what to wear all in a heap on the floor with Mack sitting in the middle of them. Daisy was sitting in front of her mirror testing her makeup—all of it. She'd applied lipstick, powder, blush and eyeshadow with abandon, strewing the containers everywhere.

Karen's weeks of hard-won serenity fled in an instant. A bubble of anger rose in her chest at the mess.

"Daisy, what were you thinking?" she shouted. Daisy, who'd been gazing into a mirror with a pleased expression only a second before, promptly burst into tears at Karen's sharp tone.

Then she whirled on Mack. "Look what you've done to Mommy's clothes," she screamed at him, which sent him fleeing from the room on unsteady legs.

A moment later, Frances was in the doorway, a crying Mack clinging to her hand. "What on earth?" she began, then looked around. "Oh, my."

Weeks of progress vanished as an overwhelming sense of failure washed through Karen. Her room was in chaos and worse, her children were in tears, all because she'd yelled at them for doing what kids did.

"It's okay," Frances said, though it wasn't clear whom she intended her words to soothe. "Daisy, you and Mack come with me." She gave Karen an encouraging smile. "Don't worry. I'll be right back to help you deal with this. You get dressed. I can take care of the cleanup."

"But you shouldn't have to. It's not your mess," Karen said despondently.

"Well, truth be told, it's not yours, either, but I doubt we can count on the culprits to straighten this up to our satisfaction. It won't take but a minute. Get dressed, Karen. Then go on your date and leave the rest to me."

"I shouldn't have yelled at Daisy and Mack," she said wearily. "I've upset them."

"Yelling is a common enough reaction. You'll apologize. Now, hurry. I'll go check on them."

Karen was still shaking from the rush of adrenaline that had pumped through her when she'd first walked into the room, but she managed to salvage an outfit from the pile on the floor and get her own makeup on with fingers that trembled.

Just as she walked into the living room, she heard Daisy tell Elliott, "Me and Mack made Mommy mad."

She sounded so forlorn Karen's heart ached.

"But I'm not mad anymore," she told Daisy, stooping down as her daughter ran into her arms. "It's okay, sweetie. I shouldn't have gotten so upset."

"I didn't mean to make a mess," Daisy whispered against her cheek.

"I know."

"I just wanted to be pretty like you."

Her own eyes welling with tears, Karen cast a helpless glance toward Elliott. He promptly scooped Daisy out of her arms.

"You are even more beautiful than your mom," he told her. "When you're older, boys will be lining up at the door. You'll be the most popular girl in school."

Daisy's eyes shone. "Really?"

Elliott nodded. "Really."

Daisy gave him a considering look. "Maybe I'll grow up and marry you, instead."

Elliott grinned. "Trust me, by then, I'll be so old you won't want me."

"Then maybe you should marry my mommy, instead," Daisy suggested.

Elliott's gaze caught Karen's. "Maybe I should," he said quietly. "One of these days we might have to talk about that."

Karen's heart thumped unsteadily as his gaze sought hers. Surely he wasn't serious! They'd barely shared more than a good-night kiss up 'til now. How could he possibly be considering a leap like that?

"I think we'd better go," she said, struggling to keep her voice even.

She put a hand to Daisy's cheek. "I love you, baby." Then she picked up Mack and planted a smacking kiss on his cheek. "Love you, too, little man. I won't be late," she said pointedly to Frances.

"Enjoy yourselves," Frances replied. "We'll be fine."

Karen practically dashed out the door, anxious to tell Elliott that he shouldn't be making promises like the one he'd just made to Daisy.

But just outside the door, he caught her hand. "I meant what I said," he told her, his gaze locked with hers. "We are going to talk about marriage eventually. I know what I want, Karen, but I'll give you a little time to catch up."

"You can't possibly know a thing like that," she protested, unable to stop the trembling his words had set off. She wasn't sure what scared her more, the anticipation he'd stirred in her or his absolute certainty. "This is our first real date."

"All those other times we've gotten together with the kids told me everything I needed to know," he insisted. "Those occasions were real. I know what it would be like to have a family with you. What could possibly be more important?"

"But I'm a terrible mom. I made my kids cry," she whispered, ashamed of the scene he'd walked in on.

"You're being way too hard on yourself," he told her. "Do you think you're the first mom to lose her temper when her kids misbehave? My mom has the patience of a saint, but she was tested beyond her limits more than once. And believe me, my sisters have raised their voices to their kids more than once."

He met her gaze. "You didn't lose control, did you?"

She thought about it and realized she hadn't. She hadn't felt that gut-deep loss of control she had a few months back. "Not really."

"Okay, then. You're not a terrible mom. Can we agree on that?"

She smiled. "I suppose."

"Good." He touched a finger to her lips. "We don't need to talk about the rest of it now. I just thought I ought to be clear about where I see us headed."

She frowned at him. "Well, just so you know, I'm now a nervous wreck."

"Why?"

"Because I don't want to mess up what could be the best thing that's ever happened to me," she said candidly.

His hand cupped her cheek. "You couldn't if you tried."

Karen wasn't convinced of that. But maybe, for now, it was enough that he believed it.

15

The hearing for Caroline and Brad Holliday's divorce was finally going to happen. Helen had accumulated enough material on Brad's finances to assure Caroline and her children a secure future. She had no illusions, though, that the proceedings would go smoothly. She doubted Jimmy Bob had had much luck in getting through to his client. Brad would go down fighting to hold on to every penny.

In the courtroom, Helen turned to Caroline. "Are you ready for this?"

"It's really going to end today?" Caroline asked, her voice unsteady. "No more of their tricks?"

"Not this time," Helen told her. "The paper trail on Brad's hidden assets finally caught Jimmy Bob's attention, to say nothing of infuriating Judge Rockingham. Jimmy Bob knows if they don't end this now, there's no telling what else we might unearth."

Caroline swallowed hard and regarded Helen guiltily. "Brad called me last night."

Helen held on to her temper by a thread, though she wasn't particularly surprised. It was exactly the kind of stunt a man on the verge of losing would pull. "Oh?" she said, her tone neutral.

"He wanted to talk."

There was a sinking feeling in Helen's heart. "About?"

"A reconciliation."

Helen bit back a groan. "What did you tell him?"

Caroline sat up a little straighter. "That he could come over to talk, but that a reconciliation was out of the question," she said.

But before Helen could breathe a sigh of relief, Caroline asked uncertainly, "Was that the right thing to do?"

"Only you can answer that," she told Caroline. "How did it feel when you told him that?"

"Lousy," Caroline admitted. "Somewhere inside I remembered the man he used to be, the man I loved. If I could have that man back…" Her voice trailed off.

"He doesn't exist anymore," Helen told her gently. "At least that's not the man I've seen, but if you're having second thoughts, we can stop this proceeding. It's not too late. Do you honestly think there's hope for your marriage?"

Caroline looked across the aisle at her husband, who was huddled with Jimmy Bob. He glanced over at Caroline, his expression hard. Apparently Caroline caught the implication, because she stiffened in response.

"It was all a ploy to soften me up, wasn't it?" Caroline said with dismay. "Brad figured if he could get me to take him back for a few weeks or even a few months, we'd have to start this process all over again. It was just a gigantic postponement tactic, wasn't it?"

"What do you think?" Helen asked.

"I saw it in his eyes just then," Caroline said, chagrined. "He's angry that it didn't work. I could hear it in his voice when I told him on the phone that I wasn't interested in a reconciliation. Last night wasn't about getting back together or he would have come over and tried to convince me. It was just an attempt to get under my skin so I'd feel all warm and fuzzy toward him."

Helen clasped her hand and gave it a squeeze. "Isn't it a good thing that you're smart enough to see through that?"

Caroline glared across the aisle, then turned back to Helen, her resolve clearly steadied. "Take him for every cent I deserve," she said.

Helen grinned. "It'll be my pleasure."

Three draining hours later, they had hammered out the terms of the settlement with Brad Holliday gnashing his teeth and protesting over every nickel and dime. Fortunately, Jimmy Bob had seen the handwriting on the wall and was able to keep the process on course, warning Brad from time to time that his attitude was getting in the way of him winning any points at all.

"She'll never see a penny of this," Brad shouted at one point, only to have Judge Rockingham stare him down, his patience with Brad clearly at an end.

"Then you'll be in a cell facing contempt charges," the judge assured him. "Am I making myself clear enough about that, Mr. Holliday?"

"Absolutely, Your Honor," Jimmy Bob said, shooting a quelling look at Brad, who looked as if he wanted to break something. His color was high and his fists were clenched.

Helen thought of the threats that Jimmy Bob hadn't taken seriously and wondered if she should request a restraining order to protect Caroline. She leaned toward her client.

"Caroline, is there any chance that Brad will try to take his anger out on you over this decision today?"

Caroline looked shaken by the suggestion. "No, of course not," she said at once.

"I could ask for a restraining order," Helen told her.

"No," Caroline said. "It really isn't necessary."

Helen nodded. "If you're sure, but let me know if you change your mind."

Even without a request from Helen for a restraining order, apparently Judge Rockingham recognized that Brad's temper was unpredictable. When the hearing ended, he told the bailiff to find an officer to escort Brad from the premises and another to see to it that Helen and Caroline weren't accosted on their way out.

"Do you have someone who can stay with you for a few days?" Helen asked Caroline, picking up on the judge's concern. If Rockingham read a danger in his golf buddy's demeanor, then they needed to take it seriously. "I don't think you ought to be alone."

"I agree," Jimmy Bob said, surprising her. "Better yet, stay with a friend, Caroline, or take the kids on a trip for a week or so. Brad will cool down eventually, but right now, I wouldn't trust him not to do something crazy. Like I told Helen, he's been saying a lot of stuff the past few days. Most of it's nonsense he doesn't mean, but there's enough anger in him that I'd be careful if I were you."

Helen nodded. "It's good advice, Caroline."

Caroline looked uneasy, but she was clearly ready to stand her ground. "Sooner or later, I'll have to deal with him," she argued. "Brad's never been violent."

"He's never been pushed this far before, either. Better to deal with him later," Jimmy Bob insisted. "I've known him a long time and I've never seen him like this." He faced Helen. "You're not too popular with him right now, either.

I know I told you I thought he was all talk, but it's better to be safe. Watch your back, okay?"

Helen shivered at the genuine concern she heard in his voice. "I will," she promised.

She was with Erik most nights lately, at her place or his. She'd talk to him about staying at his place for a while until Brad Holliday cooled down and began to see things more clearly.

"Caroline, what about you?" she persisted.

"I think you're both worrying about nothing," Caroline said. "Brad's angry, but he'd never hurt me. Still, I'll go visit my sister for a week or two just to put your minds at ease. She's been wanting me to come, but I didn't feel like I could before now."

"Perfect," Helen said. "Be sure you call the office and give Brenda your contact information. Do you want me to come home with you while you pack a bag?"

"That's not necessary," Caroline said.

The officer who'd escorted them from the courthouse glanced at Helen. "I'll stay with her, Ms. Decatur."

"Thanks," Helen said. No matter what Caroline said, she trusted Jimmy Bob's perception of Brad's mood better than that of the woman who still wanted to find some good in him.

As she watched Caroline drive away with the patrol car right behind her, she still felt uneasy. Turning to Jimmy Bob, she saw that he looked worried as well.

"How dangerous do you think Brad is?" she asked him.

"I'd like to believe we're all overreacting," he told her. "But Brad lost a lot in that courtroom today. I'm not just talking money and assets, either. I'm talking about the huge blow to his ego. Remember how this whole thing started, with him wanting to prove he was still a man? I'll be honest with you. A man in Brad's state of mind won't handle any of this well." He met her gaze. "I'll say it again—watch your back, Helen."

She shuddered at his somber tone. She'd handled dozens of difficult divorces, some of them even nastier than this one, but for the first time in her career, she genuinely felt afraid. If Brad was as unstable as Jimmy Bob and Judge Rockingham thought he might be, who knew what he might be capable of doing?

Erik kept stealing glances at Helen. She'd arrived at Sullivan's just before closing time, given Dana Sue a hug and him a peck on the cheek that had Dana Sue's eyebrows lifting.

"You okay?" Dana Sue had asked immediately, but Helen had shrugged off the question.

She was fine, she'd insisted, but then she'd grabbed a scrubber and started in on the pots and pans piled in the sink. It was a task she usually shunned, especially when she was wearing one of those smart suits she wore to court. Tonight she hadn't even bothered with an apron.

Dana Sue sidled close to him. "What's that about?" she whispered, glancing pointedly at Helen as she attacked a particularly greasy pan in which Dana Sue had baked lasagne.

"I have no idea," Erik admitted. "But I don't like it. She's obviously upset and she's way too quiet."

"Maybe you should go," Dana Sue suggested. "She might open up to me."

"No way," he countered, his gaze never leaving Helen.

Dana Sue regarded him with a puzzled expression. "Erik, what's going on with you two?"

"We're friends," he said tersely. "If she's this upset, I'm not about to walk out of here 'til I know why."

"Well, neither am I," Dana Sue replied.

Just then, Helen whirled around and glared at them. "You two can stop whispering behind my back now. Dana Sue, go home."

Dana Sue regarded her with astonishment. "What?"

"Please," Helen begged. "I'll talk to you tomorrow." Suddenly a look of alarm flared in her eyes. "Erik, you need to walk Dana Sue to her car."

"I don't need anyone walking me out," Dana Sue argued.

Helen's tense expression warned Erik that she was close to the breaking point. "Get your purse, Dana Sue," he said. "I'll go out with you."

"But—"

"Just do it." He cast a pointed look at Helen. Her spine was rigid. She looked as if she was about one argument from coming unglued. Dana Sue apparently saw the same thing he did, because she finally nodded.

Outside in the parking lot, she gave him a helpless look. "Call me if you need me," she instructed. "I don't like this. I don't like it one bit."

"Me, neither. One of us will fill you in tomorrow. I promise."

With one last glance back at the restaurant, she climbed into her car. She'd started out of the parking lot when she stopped and rolled down her window. "Take good care of her," she ordered. "Promise me."

"I will."

"And be prepared to answer a whole lot of questions about why she's turning to you, instead of to me or Maddie."

He managed a half smile at her indignation. "I figured that would bother you as much as anything."

"Well, why wouldn't it? She's been our friend forever."

"Do you really think this is the time to debate which of us is a better friend to her?" he asked.

"No." She sighed and drove off.

When Erik got back inside, Helen had kicked off her shoes and was sitting on a stool, her shoulders slumped, her expression glum.

"You ready to tell me what's going on?" he asked quietly.

"Could you just hold me?"

"Sure. I could do that," he said, moving close to take her in his arms. Her trembling alarmed him. "Come on, sugar, spill it. What happened today to put you in this mood?"

"I won a really good divorce settlement for Caroline Holliday," she told him, her voice muffled against his chest.

He was still confused. "Isn't that a good thing?"

"You'd think so, wouldn't you?"

"What am I missing?"

"Her husband, or soon-to-be ex-husband, has kind of gone off the deep end."

Erik tensed. "Meaning?"

"His lawyer, the judge, everyone seems to think he might go after Caroline," she said, then looked up at him, an unfamiliar hint of fear lurking in the depths of her eyes. "Or me."

"Good God!" he said. "Then what the hell were you doing on the streets alone this late at night?"

"I'm not scared," she insisted, though everything about her said otherwise. "I just wanted to see if I could maybe stay at your place for a few days. You know, 'til this blows over. It's not like I'd be moving in permanently or anything."

"Of course you can stay with me," he said at once. "You didn't even have to ask."

"Yes, I did. It's not as if we've ever talked about living together or anything. I didn't want you to get some crazy idea that this is a ploy to change things between us."

Erik sighed. "Helen, I think I know you well enough to see when you're scared out of your wits."

"I am not," she protested indignantly.

He grinned at her. "Okay, then. Not scared, just very cautious."

"Exactly. Discretion is the better part of valor. Isn't that the saying?"

"Uh-huh. Do you need to go home and pack your things?"

"I have a suitcase in my car," she told him. A flash of anger lit her eyes. "I hate that I'm letting this jerk chase me out of my own home."

"Just remember what you told me not five seconds ago," he said. "Discretion and all that."

"I suppose."

"What about Caroline? Is she safe?"

"She left for her sister's. She took the younger kids with her. Her oldest's at college. Hopefully Brad will cool down before they come back."

Of course, Erik thought, that meant Helen was the only immediate target on this jerk's radar. Not good.

"Come on," he told her. "Let's go home."

He'd keep her safe there if he had to stand watch night and day. Of course, that would all have to take place between dodging Dana Sue's and Maddie's inevitable questions. Those were going to be flying fast and furious first thing in the morning.

* * *

Helen couldn't believe she'd allowed Jimmy Bob and Judge Rockingham to work her into such a frenzy. She'd never been afraid of anyone in her life. She'd always been able to take care of herself, but for some reason Brad's reaction in court and his friends' response to it had spooked her completely.

She'd gone home at the end of the day, determined to fight her fear and not be chased out of her own home, but within an hour or two of darkness falling, she'd been jumping at her own shadow. When a car backfired on the street, she'd barely stopped herself from diving behind the sofa. That was when she'd packed a bag and headed for Sullivan's.

"Did you eat dinner tonight?" Erik asked when she'd unpacked the last of her things and put them into a drawer he'd cleared out for her. Her suits were hanging in his nearly empty closet, next to a few of his dress shirts and a couple of dark suits. She'd lined her shoes up below, three pairs of her favorite kick-ass spiked heels.

When she looked up from the drawer filled with lingerie, Erik was watching her from the end of the bed, a worried frown on his face. She went over and sat beside him, leaning into his side.

"Stop worrying about me," she told him. "I'm sure Brad's too smart to do anything at all."

"Then why are you so scared?"

"To be honest, I feel kind of silly. I should probably just go on home."

"Not a chance," he said tersely. "Not for a few days, anyway, 'til we see what this guy's going to do. Maybe I should have a talk with him."

She shook her head. "If he starts thinking everyone in town is lining up against him, it'll only make matters worse."

"It might also scare some sense into him," Erik countered. "Bullies, especially men who bully women, don't like it when people get in their face, especially someone who's bigger and stronger."

She smiled at him. "You don't even know Brad Holliday. He could be twice your size."

"True, but I can be pretty impressive when I'm ticked off."

He glanced sideways at her, a grin tugging at his lips. "Is he bigger?"

"No, but I love that you were willing to take him on anyway," she said. "What I would love even more is something to eat. You said something about food a minute ago."

"Are you sure you didn't wrangle an invitation over here just so I'd feed you on a regular basis for free?"

"Nope, but that is definitely a side benefit," she told him. "Anything good in your fridge?"

He lifted a brow. "What do you think?"

"Anything chocolate?"

"You want dessert first?"

"I want dessert and then you," she told him, enjoying the immediate heat that sparked in his eyes. "In fact, I can't imagine anything that could take my mind off Brad Holliday any faster than that combination."

He stroked a finger along her jaw, then tucked a strand of hair behind her ear. "Is this a hot-fudge-sundae crisis or will a brownie do?"

"Both, if you have them," she said. At his amused expression, she said, "Okay, I've been craving chocolate all day long."

"And me?"

"Lately, I seem to be craving you twenty-four/seven."

"Good to know I rank at least slightly higher than a sundae," he said, then covered her mouth with his.

When he finally released her, she was breathless and needy. "Maybe the sundae could wait," she murmured, pulling him back. She was getting to be an expert at juggling her priorities.

Helen was in her office by eight in the morning, escorted there by an insistent Erik, who'd flatly refused to let her go alone. For the moment, she was enjoying this protective streak, but she had a hunch it was going to wear very thin before long. While it was nice and unexpected to be pampered, she was too used to taking care of herself.

She'd been at her desk for barely fifteen minutes when Dana Sue and Maddie burst in, scaring ten years off her life.

"What is wrong with you?" she demanded, glowering at them while she fought to regain her composure.

"That's our question," Dana Sue said unrepentantly, taking a seat across from her. "You were a wreck last night and I want to know why."

"And why did you turn to Erik instead of us?" Maddie asked.

Dana Sue nodded. "In fact, that might be the more interesting question. I called your house 'til three in the morning. Where were you last night after you left Sullivan's? Please, please tell me you were having mad, passionate sex with Erik."

Helen frowned at the clever guesswork. Since she couldn't bring herself to outright lie to her friend, she merely said, "And that would be your business because...?"

"Because you meddled in our lives and now it's our turn," Maddie said. "Is there something going on between you and Erik?"

Helen gave the two of them a stern look. "That's too personal."

Dana Sue scowled at her response. The scowl slowly gave way to a huge grin. "That's a yes, isn't it?" she said triumphantly. "You're not going to admit it—though I can't imagine why not—but the two of you are together. I know I'm right. I knew it when Erik went all protective and weird last night."

"If it's true, why won't you just say so?" Maddie asked.

"I'm not confirming that it's true," Helen said.

"You're not denying it, either," Dana Sue responded. "I knew it! I just knew the two of you would be perfect together. Why are you hiding it? Are you ashamed because Erik's not some hotshot lawyer or something?"

Helen was horrified that one of her best friends could even think such a thing. "Absolutely not. I am not, nor have I ever been, a snob. Besides, you, of all people, know what a great guy Erik is."

"She jumped to his defense," Dana Sue said to Maddie. "I'd say that's more confirmation."

Maddie, however, didn't seem convinced. "I hate to throw a damper on your enthusiasm, Dana Sue, but I think there's something else going on here," she said.

"Don't be ridiculous," Helen said hastily, worried that Maddie might put things together and come up with a bombshell that could ruin everything. "Maybe Erik and I—

assuming there's anything going on between us—just don't want the two of you in our business."

"That's reasonable," Dana Sue said. "Especially since he works for me. So, let's back up a minute. What had you so freaked out last night?"

Helen filled them in on the Holliday divorce aftermath. "There's a chance, albeit a really tiny one, that Brad could do something crazy," she concluded. "Listening to Jimmy Bob's warnings after court let out made me a little skittish. I'm okay this morning. It was crazy to let myself get so worked up over nothing."

"I imagine Erik got worked up right along with you," Dana Sue said. "That man has a protective streak a mile wide. He watches over Annie like a hawk. He keeps an eye on every bite of food I put in my mouth. It's a little tiresome, but really sweet."

Helen thought of the way he'd hovered over her this morning until she'd kicked him out of her office with a promise to keep the doors locked 'til Barb got in. Maddie and Dana Sue had used their keys to get in. The Sweet Magnolias had one another's keys to everything.

Maddie's lips twitched. "That must be why he's still sitting in the parking lot outside," she said.

Helen stared at her. "Erik is outside now?" She went to the window and peeked out. Sure enough, he was hunkered down behind the wheel of his car making a pretense of glancing at the morning paper. She shook her head. "I thought he'd left. This is crazy. I'm going out there right now—"

"No, you're not," Maddie said. "He needs to do this, and frankly, I'm not convinced you're as safe and invincible as you seem to think you are. Some men are capable of doing all kinds of irrational things when they think they have nothing left to lose."

"I agree," Dana Sue said, then grinned. "Besides, what woman wouldn't want a man like Erik taking care of her? I say you should milk this for all it's worth. Who knows what might develop?"

"Just be careful," Maddie cautioned. "And I'm not just talking about Brad Holliday, either."

Helen shivered under the impact of her gaze. For the second time that morning, she sensed that Maddie had figured out exactly what she was up to with Erik and wasn't exactly overjoyed about it.

And if Maddie thought she was behaving abominably by involving Erik in her baby plan, then Dana Sue was definitely going to hit the roof. Helen just had to pray that it wouldn't cause an irreparable rift in their lifelong friendship.

16

There was an air of excitement in the kitchen at Sullivan's and none of the tension that usually surrounded a busy night in the dining room. In fact, the restaurant was closed to the public. They'd refused all reservations and posted a sign on the door to prevent walk-ins.

"Do you think she knows?" Tess whispered to Dana Sue.

Erik grinned. "Trust me, Helen knows."

Dana Sue scowled at him. "How could she possibly know we're throwing her a surprise birthday party, unless you blabbed?"

"Hey, this was my idea. Why would I blab? I'm just saying she's not easily fooled. She's smart," he began, then ticked off more reasons they would never pull this party off as a complete surprise. "She's observant. She's suspicious by nature." He grinned at Dana Sue. "And none of you can keep a secret worth a damn."

"I resent that," Dana Sue said. "I have kept my mouth shut about a whole lot of things through the years."

Erik couldn't help being a little intrigued. "Such as?" he inquired.

Dana Sue frowned at him. "Oh, no, you don't, you

sneaky devil. I'm not going to slip up and tell you any of Helen's deep, dark secrets. Pry them out of her, if you must know."

"Helen has deep, dark secrets? Interesting," he said. It would be a great topic for later tonight, once he had her well distracted, something he'd grown increasingly efficient at accomplishing.

Dana Sue regarded him with a wary expression. "Don't you dare imply to her that I've already told you," she warned. "Maybe I should give her a heads-up, so you can't get away with any sneakiness."

Tess observed all this back and forth in fascination, then focused on Erik. "Is there something going on between you and Ms. Decatur?"

Erik winced. Of course, truthfully, she was probably the last to figure it out. He had a hunch Dana Sue and Maddie had known for weeks now, certainly since Helen had moved in with him. Dana Sue, especially, had been amazingly quiet on the topic of him and Helen, which meant she'd concluded her matchmaking efforts were no longer needed. He doubted, though, that she was aware of the no-strings clause in the relationship. If she were, she'd be all over him.

"We're friends," he told Tess, stressing it in a way that had Dana Sue's lips twitching with barely contained amusement.

"Is that what they're calling it these days?" Dana Sue asked. "Friends with benefits, perhaps?"

"Get out of here," he ordered in mock anger. "You're in my way."

"No, actually I'm in your face, and you hate that," she countered cheerfully. "But I will go and check on the dining room to see how Maddie and Jeanette are coming with the decorations."

After she'd gone, Tess continued to study him. "I can see it," she said eventually. "You and Ms. Decatur. You would balance each other."

Erik felt a need to discourage her from thinking there was anything permanent about what he and Helen shared. "We're opposites, Tess. That might work in the short term, but never for the long haul."

Tess shook her head. "You're wrong about that. People said Diego and I were too different, but it works." A smile blossomed on her face. "In fact, it works very well. I will never be able to repay Ms. Decatur for bringing him home to me."

"She was happy to do it, Tess."

Karen breezed into the kitchen then, followed by some muscular hunk of a man Erik had never seen before.

"Erik, Elliott Cruz," Karen announced. "Elliott, this is Erik. You can get acquainted later. I'm on a mission. Dana Sue wants the pink cloth napkins, not the green, and she wants them now."

Erik chuckled. "Tell her if she insists on turning the decor into some girly thing, all of us guys are going to bail on you."

"You tell her that if you're brave enough," Karen countered. "Me, I'm finding the pink napkins."

"I know where they are," Tess said. "I'll show you."

While the two women left to look in the linen supply closet, Erik studied Elliott, whose gaze followed Karen from the room.

"Elliott Cruz," Erik said, drawing the man's rapt attention away from the direction Karen had gone. "I've heard that name before."

"I'm a personal trainer at The Corner Spa," Elliott said. "That's how I met Karen."

"And now you have a thing for her," Erik guessed.

Elliott gave him a wry look. "You could say that. We've been dating for a few weeks now."

"Ah, so that's why she's been smiling so much," Erik concluded. Then his protective streak kicked in. "You serious about her? Because if you're not, I have to tell you, she doesn't need the heartache."

"Oh, I'm serious," Elliott said without hesitation. "Karen's the one who refuses to discuss the future. She thinks I don't have any idea what I'm getting into."

"But you do?" Erik said, liking the man's honesty and willingness to put his feelings out there. He'd done that once, but never again.

"It's a little hard not to know when she's constantly trying to make me see the worst side of being around her and the kids. When Mack regressed to his pre-potty-trained days, she had me give him a refresher course."

Erik barely managed to bite back a laugh. Karen hadn't mentioned that. "How'd that go?"

Elliott shrugged. "I have five nephews. I talked to my sisters. It was a breeze. So was having Daisy throw up all over the place when she ate too much at the county fair. Then Karen vanished during Daisy's birthday party and left me for fifteen minutes with a bunch of giggling six-year-olds trying to pin the tail on a donkey. And asked me to take Mack to the emergency room when he cut his knee on a piece of glass at the park." He gave Erik a resigned look. "You get the picture, I'm sure."

"I doubt Karen planned all that for your benefit," Erik said.

"True, but make no mistake, each incident was a test," Elliott said.

"How'd you do?"

Elliott shrugged. "It's all just part of life with kids. You deal."

Erik envied him his totally unflappable attitude. He'd had his share of experience with his own nephews, which was one reason he didn't want any more kids in his life. Those precious but rambunctious children, who ranged in age from three to twelve, were more than enough. And he got to go home at the end of an exhausting day and fall asleep in his own bed without fear of being interrupted by any one of the hundred crises that came with kids. At one time, when Sam had been alive to share it all—the joy and the burden—he'd thought otherwise, but now he was content with the way things were.

Before he could comment on any of that, Karen and Tess returned with an armload of pink napkins.

"Come on," Karen told Elliott. "You can help me fold them."

Elliott's gaze narrowed. "I do not make little swans," he informed her.

Karen grinned at him. "You will by the time I'm through with you."

Elliott cast a woeful look back over his shoulder at Erik as he followed Karen to the dining room. Erik couldn't seem to work up any sympathy for him. He almost wished he were as smitten with Helen, rather than just in lust with her.

Of course, being in lust with Helen was pretty darn incredible. There were nights when they lay tangled together under his sheets that he couldn't imagine his life any other way. Maybe he was just a little smitten, after all. One of these days he'd have to think about nipping that in the bud before it led him down a path he didn't want to travel. He couldn't afford to risk his heart.

* * *

Helen was about to wrap up her paperwork at the office and call it a night when Barb stuck her head in the door.

"You about finished?" her secretary asked.

"Yes, thank goodness."

"Then let's go have a drink," Barb suggested.

Helen frowned at her. "Don't you have to get home?"

"I have time. I thought we could toast your birthday. I have a present for you, too, but I'll give it to you when we get there."

Helen stared at her in surprise, then glanced at the calendar on her desk to confirm that it was, indeed, her birthday. She'd completely forgotten. She was forty-three today, and the truth was she didn't feel much like celebrating. With every day and week that passed without any sign she might be pregnant, she grew more and more discouraged. She was all too rapidly running out of time. She didn't need to be reminded of that.

"I don't know—"

Barb cut her off. "No excuses. Birthdays need to be celebrated. And I know you don't have plans for tonight or you would've mentioned them."

Caught, Helen conceded reluctantly, "Okay, one drink." Why not? She'd been avoiding alcohol for some time now on the chance she might be pregnant, but what was the point? She deserved a glass of champagne to mark the occasion.

"Where do you want to go?" she asked Barb as she got her purse.

"Only one place in town that's classy enough for a birthday celebration," Barb insisted. "We'll go to Sullivan's. Maybe I'll even spring for dinner."

"Fine," Helen said, then considered the fact that she'd

heard nothing from Dana Sue and Maddie all day. Usually they were the first to call with birthday wishes. Of course, with all those two had going on in their lives, it was little wonder they'd forgotten. Still, they were her best friends. They'd never missed a birthday in all the years they'd known each other. She was reminded yet again that lately they'd had entirely too little time together. Part of that was her fault. She'd been avoiding them so she wouldn't have to answer questions about her relationship with Erik.

The parking lot at Sullivan's was jammed as usual, but Helen finally managed to find a space in the alley out back. "We can go in through the kitchen," she told Barb.

Her secretary frowned. "I don't think Dana Sue would want you parading people through her kitchen on a night as busy as this one obviously is. We can walk around front."

Helen started to argue, then shrugged. Maybe Barb had a point. Helen knew how chaotic it got in there all too well.

Around front, Barb opened the door and held it for her. The instant Helen stepped inside, the room exploded with flashing lights and what sounded like a hundred people shouted, "Surprise!"

Clasping her hand over her mouth in shock, she whirled around and scowled at Barb. "You knew about this?"

"They couldn't have done it without me." Her secretary looked entirely too pleased with herself. "I was the one you'd least expect to be leading you into a trap."

"You're a very sneaky woman," Helen accused, but she wrapped her in a hug. "Thank you."

"Don't thank me. The party wasn't my idea."

Dana Sue and Maddie appeared then.

"Were you really surprised?" Dana Sue demanded.

"Stunned," Helen assured her. "I can't believe you two

did this. I was just feeling down because I thought you'd both forgotten."

"What you really can't believe is that we pulled it off without giving you even a hint of what we were up to," Maddie said. "As for forgetting, surely you know us better than that."

"I thought I did."

"By the way, you shouldn't be thanking us, at least not entirely," Dana Sue added. "The party was Erik's idea."

Helen's gaze few across the room to where Erik was standing just outside the kitchen door. "You did this?" she mouthed.

He shrugged, then gave her a sheepish nod.

"How on earth did he even know it was my birthday?" she asked Dana Sue.

"He told me he saw it on your driver's license the morning you left your wallet at his place," Dana Sue said pointedly. "I'd like to hear the story behind that one day soon. I know you've been staying over there because of Brad Holliday, but being forgetful? That's the real shocker."

"I agree," Maddie said. "Now, get in here and say hello to everyone."

The packed room was filled with old friends and former clients, as well as attorneys and judges, including Lester Rockingham and Jimmy Bob West, who was keeping his distance from Tess.

"Brad hasn't been bothering you, has he?" Jimmy Bob asked when Helen greeted him.

"Not so far," Helen said. "It's been a couple of weeks. He's got to be over it by now."

"I wouldn't be too sure of that," Lester Rockingham said. "He's still refusing to play golf with us. Won't even take my calls, in fact. If he figures Jimmy Bob and I betrayed him, there's no telling how he feels about you."

Erik approached just in time to hear the warning. He stiffened visibly. "You really think this guy's a danger to her?" he asked the two men.

"I'm just saying she needs to keep her eyes open," Jimmy Bob said.

"Why not just throw him in jail?" Erik demanded.

"No grounds," the judge responded. "He hasn't even made any overt threats, much less acted on them. It's just a gut feeling Jimmy Bob and I have that he's going to have a meltdown one of these days. I hear he's sitting at home with a bottle of booze and stewing about how the court and Helen here wronged him. That's never a good thing."

Erik frowned at Helen. "Then you're not moving back to your place yet and that's that," he said.

Though Jimmy Bob seemed a little startled, he nodded. "Makes sense to me to stay where you're not alone and where Brad's less likely to look for you."

Helen wasn't sure how she felt about more people knowing about her current living arrangements. It meant there were that many more people who would know the truth if she eventually turned up pregnant. They'd all have questions and, more than likely, want to paint Erik as the bad guy if they didn't marry. She hadn't meant for that to happen.

"I'll think about it," she told them all. "I need to say hello to some more people."

As she walked away, Erik was right on her heels. "Okay, why did you go all stiff and weird just then? Was it because I mentioned you'd been staying with me?"

"I just thought we'd agreed that the fewer people who knew about that the better," she told him. She decided to tap-dance around her real reason for wanting their relationship to remain underground. "Do you really want Brad to know exactly where to find me?"

Erik immediately looked guilty. "I hadn't thought about that," he said. "Then, again, maybe it's a good thing if he knows there's someone looking out for you."

"I don't want to count on that," she said, then stood on tiptoe to press a kiss to his cheek. "Thank you for thinking of the party. I never had a surprise party before, at least not one that was a real surprise."

"Never?"

She shook her head. "I'm too nosy. I always found out."

"I was sure you were going to find out about this one, but I'd have blamed Dana Sue and Maddie for not being able to keep a secret," he said.

"They really are lousy at that," she agreed. "But I haven't seen too much of them for the past couple of weeks. I've been otherwise occupied."

"Really?" he said, drawing her into his arms. "Pleasantly occupied?"

"Amazingly occupied," she said, lifting her mouth to his.

When he finally released her, he regarded her with an odd expression. "That's the first time you've kissed me— I mean really kissed me—in public."

"It's my birthday. I'm allowed to be impulsive and throw caution to the wind. Besides, most of the people here have figured out that something's going on between us, anyway. We may as well acknowledge it, at least among friends. Keeping it to ourselves isn't working all that well, anyway."

"And Brad?"

"He won't find out from any of these people," she said.

Erik glanced across the room to where Maddie and Dana Sue were watching them with interest. "I just hope you're prepared for the consequences of all this new openness," he warned. "In fact, the primary consequence appears to be heading this way. I think I'll retreat to the kitchen to put the finishing touches on your cake."

"Chicken," she called after him.

"Cluck, cluck," he responded, laughing as he disappeared from view.

"Why don't you two just admit what's going on?" Maddie demanded.

"I have no idea what you're talking about," Helen said.

"That act's not working anymore," Dana Sue countered. "You're having an affair. That much is plain. What I want to know is when you're going to take it to the next level."

"Which would be…?" Helen asked.

"Marriage," Dana Sue responded.

Helen shook her head. "Not in the cards," she said flatly.

"That's ridiculous," Maddie declared.

"Why on earth wouldn't you want to get married to a man like Erik?" Dana Sue asked. "He's perfect for you."

"This is a party," Helen retorted. "And I am not discussing my love life with you now."

"Tomorrow, then," Dana Sue said. "Be at the spa at eight or we'll come looking for you. Won't it be interesting if we find you in Erik's bed?"

Helen sighed as the two of them walked away. This whole scheme of hers was suddenly spinning out of control. She didn't have a doubt in her mind that Maddie and Dana Sue's questions were going to be tough to handle. And she couldn't think of a single way to avoid them.

Karen saw that Elliott fit right in at the party. Of course, it made sense since he worked with Helen, Maddie and

Dana Sue at the spa, but he'd also gotten along with Maddie's husband Cal, Dana Sue's husband Ronnie and even Tess's Diego. Apparently he'd had quite a chat with Erik in the kitchen, too.

That should have pleased her. Though she worked for Dana Sue, she'd come to think of all of these people as friends. For the first time in her life she had a real support system and knew she could make it on her own. She didn't want to risk that for a relationship with a man who might shatter her hard-won independence and wind up leaving the way her ex-husband had.

"You've been awfully quiet," Elliott said as he drove her home. "Didn't you have a good time at the party?"

"I had a wonderful time," she said. "It was so much fun seeing Helen's face when she walked in. I think she was genuinely surprised."

"She obviously loved the picture you gave her of Daisy and Mack," Elliott said. "It made her cry."

Karen frowned at the reminder. "Happy tears, I hope, but I'm not so sure."

"Why would it have been anything else?"

"Just a feeling I have," she admitted. "I think she wants her own family."

"Then perhaps she and Erik will get together. There's definitely something going on between those two."

"There's a lot of chemistry, that's for sure," she conceded.

He glanced over at her. "Like there is with us."

Once again, she frowned. "Elliott, please. I don't want to talk about us."

For once he didn't let the subject drop. "Why not, Karen?" he asked. "We're good together. More than good."

It was true. He was amazing with her kids and kind and

loving toward her. But the idea of allowing herself to give in to the feelings he stirred in her scared her.

She reached for his hand. "I know you can't possibly understand where I'm coming from, and I'm sorry. I like you, Elliott. I love spending time with you."

"But what? You're not in love with me?"

"I didn't say that. I don't know what I feel."

He pulled to a stop in front of her apartment building and cut the engine. Staring straight ahead, he asked, "Do you want to end this?"

"No," she whispered, tears welling up in her eyes. "But I can't promise you anything. It's not fair to keep you waiting around, either."

"You're not making any sense," he accused. "Are you confused? Scared? What?"

She took a deep breath, then blurted, "All of that. I just started getting my life back on track. I finally feel as if I have some control over it. Falling in love, well, it means giving up some of that control. I don't know if I can do it again."

He tucked a finger under her chin and forced her to face him. "I do get that, Karen. I really do. I know what you've been through. It's probably too soon for me to be pushing you like this. I just need you to know where I'm coming from. I can wait, if you'll just tell me that there's a chance for us. If there's not, if you can't see yourself ever trusting another man not to hurt you, then tell me and I'll leave you alone. I won't spend years trying to prove I'm not like your ex-husband."

"I want to trust you," she said softly, her cheeks damp with tears. "I've seen the gentleness and kindness in you."

"Then give us a chance," he said quietly. "That's all, just a chance. But if you know you'll never be able to open up your heart, please don't just go through the motions."

It would be so easy to say yes, she thought. It would be so easy to start a relationship and see where it led. But the panic that rushed through her just thinking about it proved it was too soon.

Slowly, she shook her head. Touching a hand to his cheek, she said, "I can't, Elliott. I'm not ready to take that kind of risk. If I were, you'd be the man I'd choose, but I can't."

He sat back with a heavy sigh. "Okay, then. If that's really the way you want it, I'll back off."

Holding back tears, she nodded. "I think that's best."

"I'll walk you in."

"You don't have to do that."

"Yes, I do," he said, getting out of the car and coming around to open her door.

He said absolutely nothing as they walked to her apartment. At the door, she lifted her gaze to his. "I'm sorry."

"So am I."

She unlocked the door, but when she would have walked inside, he stopped her. "You're a terrific woman, Karen. I know you're just discovering that about yourself, but it's been obvious to me since the day we met. I hope someday you'll believe in yourself enough to let a man into your life."

Then he turned and walked away, leaving her alone on her doorstep…and feeling lonelier than she had in years.

17

Karen tiptoed into her apartment, trying not to wake Frances, who'd fallen asleep on the sofa with the television tuned to a late-night talk show. Unfortunately, by the time she'd peeked in to check on the kids, Frances was wide-awake and filled with questions.

"How was your evening?" she asked, fully alert and eager for answers.

"Fine," Karen murmured, not anxious to talk to a woman who could read her like a book. She knew Frances would be distraught over her breakup with Elliott. She'd said at least a hundred times how lucky she thought Karen was to have found him.

"I'll tell you all about it tomorrow," Karen promised. "Since you're awake, why don't you get home so you can sleep in your own bed, instead of being all cramped up on my sofa?"

Frances ignored the suggestion and regarded her suspiciously. "Come here where I can get a better look at you," she commanded. "Have you been crying?"

Since her cheeks were still damp, Karen could hardly deny it. "It's no big deal."

"Tell me," Frances demanded. "What did Elliott do?"

Her immediate indignation on Karen's behalf made Karen smile. "He didn't do anything," she said. "It was me. I broke things off with him."

Frances looked stunned. "Why on earth would you do a crazy thing like that?" Even before Karen could reply, she said, "It's because you're scared, isn't it? I should have seen this coming. The more time Elliott spends around here, the more distant you've become."

Karen acknowledged the truth with a nod. "He's ready for more, Frances. He wants a real relationship with a future and I can't promise him any of that. I can barely think ahead to tomorrow."

"Is this about sex?" Frances asked, her indignation returning. "Was he pressuring you to sleep with him?"

Karen felt weird having this conversation with Frances. She'd never talked about intimate topics like this with any of the women who'd been her foster mothers. She'd learned everything she knew about sex from kids in school and even at that, she'd hardly been prepared for marriage. Still, this was Frances, who listened and didn't make judgments.

"No," she admitted. "It wasn't like that at all. Believe me, there's a lot of chemistry there, but this was all about an emotional commitment. Elliott is ready to make that. I'm not."

"I see. It would have been easier for you if it had just been about sex, wouldn't it?"

Karen nodded. "Sleeping with him would be amazing, I'm sure of it. But any more? I just don't see it happening. I'm barely standing on my own two feet," she told Frances. "You've been here. You know how it was just a few months ago. I can't risk all the progress I've made. I'm stronger now, but I don't want to backslide and wind up being dependent on another man."

"But wouldn't it be nice to have someone to lean on, someone you could count on?"

"Of course," Karen conceded. "But it could just as easily turn out differently. Once upon a time, I thought I could lean on my husband. Look how that turned out."

"Elliott is nothing like your ex-husband," Frances said with fierce certainty. "He would never walk out on the mother of his children. Just look at how patiently he's put up with all your attempts to make him go. He's solid and dependable. He's a family man. You can tell that by how close he is to all his sisters and their kids. Not every man his age would be so eager to take on a woman with two young children, especially a man who can have his pick of women. I imagine a lot of the women at the spa have set their sights on him, probably with no strings attached, but Elliott chose you, Karen. That speaks volumes to me. It tells me he values you and respects you."

"I know," Karen said wearily. "Like I said, this is about me. I don't trust my own judgment anymore."

"Then give it time," Frances said. "You don't have to make a decision about your future tonight."

"It's too late," Karen told her, a catch in her voice. "I just didn't think it was fair to lead him on when I might never be ready for more. It's over, Frances. I made sure of that."

Frances gave her a sympathetic look. "Oh, honey, nothing's over until that man goes off and marries some other woman. If you're right for each other, you'll work it out. If he lets you go without a fight, then he's not the man I think he is."

Karen gulped back a sob as she thought about never

spending time with Elliott again. Daisy and Mack were going to be devastated, too. They adored Elliott. "I hope you're right. I hope I didn't make the biggest mistake of my life."

"Not a chance," Frances said. "When I look at Elliott, I see a man who's deeply in love and knows you're worth waiting for."

Karen thought of the bleak expression of finality she'd seen on Elliott's face tonight and prayed she'd misread it. Hopefully Frances, with her years of experience with human nature, was the one who'd read the situation correctly.

Erik went into Sullivan's early, hoping to get a head start on his dessert preparations for the day. He was trying a new recipe and it required the kind of concentration he could seldom manage once the kitchen started to bustle with all the food prep for lunch.

Unfortunately, he'd barely begun to assemble his ingredients—flour, sugar, cream and a dark, rich chocolate— when someone pounded on the back door. Muttering a curse, he went to open it and found Cal Maddox and Ronnie Sullivan out there.

"I would have used my key," Ronnie said as he walked inside, "but I don't like to do that when someone's here. I scared ten years off Dana Sue's life one night when I showed up and she wasn't expecting me. Came close to getting whacked on the head with a cast-iron skillet, too. That woman's self-defense skills are scary."

Erik grinned, despite the untimely interruption. "She does have her moments, doesn't she?"

"Enough chitchat," Cal grumbled. "Where's the coffee? Ronnie promised there'd be coffee."

"Over there," Erik said, gesturing toward the full pot he'd brewed when he arrived. "So what are you two doing here?"

"Blame our wives," Ronnie said. "They're worried about Helen. They think you might need backup in protecting her."

"And Maddie wants to know what your intentions are," Cal added, giving Erik a commiserating grin. "I suggest you form your answer carefully or run like hell."

Erik ignored Cal's question since it seemed to be a lot trickier than the implication that he couldn't keep Helen safe on his own. "As long as Helen behaves sensibly and listens to reason, I think we have the whole protection thing under control."

The two men exchanged a look of skepticism.

"We're talking about *Helen*," Ronnie said at last. "I've known that woman most of my life. She's smart, but she's also stubborn. She thinks she can control the universe. She probably figures she can hogtie Brad Holliday and deliver him to the sheriff with one hand tied behind her back."

Erik grinned. "I'm sure she does."

"And that doesn't worry you?" Cal asked. "Seems to me that suggests she'll take chances."

Erik was forced to admit that since that first night when she'd come to him and asked to stay at his place, she'd been getting increasingly reckless about where she went and when. He had a hunch she'd stopped looking over her shoulder, despite the warnings Jimmy Bob West and Judge Rockingham had repeated just last night.

"You could have a point," he said at last. "But she's independent. What am I supposed to do?"

"I have one idea," Cal volunteered. "I know Brad. His youngest son played ball for me the first year I was here. Brad was one of those dads from hell who thought every call from the umpire that went against his boy was wrong. Figured he was a better coach than me, too. He made that kid's life miserable 'til we had a little chat one night and I threatened to ban him from the games if he didn't keep his mouth shut."

"What's your point?" Ronnie asked. "That he's a bully? That's not comforting."

"No, my point is that bullies often back down when somebody bigger and tougher gets directly in their face," Cal explained patiently. "I suggest the three of us have a little come-to-Jesus conversation with Mr. Holliday."

Ronnie grinned, looking a bit too eager for Erik's peace of mind.

"I'm in," Ronnie said. "How about you, Erik?"

"Much as I would like to pummel some sense into this guy, I see a downside," Erik replied. "Helen is going to be furious if we take on her battles for her."

"Better a furious Helen than one who's in the emergency room," Ronnie said. "Jimmy Bob pulled me aside last night. There's not a lot about Jimmy Bob I trust, but his concern for Helen was genuine. He convinced me it could come to that."

Erik flinched at that. "Then we need to get a protective order right now," he said. "Rockingham will issue it."

Just as he uttered the words, Helen walked into the kitchen. Apparently she'd been less hesitant than Ronnie about using her key and had come in through the front door.

"Judge Rockingham will issue what?" she said, frowning at the three of them. Even if she hadn't heard a snippet of their conversation, finding them assembled at Sullivan's this early in the morning on a weekday would no doubt have made her wary.

"A restraining order to keep Brad Holliday away from you," Erik told her, convinced it was smarter just to be straight with her. "I want it done before the end of the day."

Helen immediately shook her head. "No way. All that will do is get Brad even more worked up. He's already convinced that the justice system is against him."

"Well, we have to do something," Erik said.

"Plan A," Cal muttered.

"Plan A, it is," Ronnie agreed.

Helen locked gazes with Erik. "What is Plan A?"

"Don't worry about it," he said, holding her gaze unflinchingly. "We have it under control."

"Now why doesn't that set my mind at ease?" she asked.

"I can't imagine," Erik said with a shrug and turned his attention to the two men.

"I'll call you later with details," Cal said, swallowing the last of his coffee and heading for the door.

Ronnie was right on his heels. "Good luck, pal. See you soon."

After they'd gone, Erik faced Helen, whose expression had darkened.

"Start talking," she commanded.

"What about?"

"Don't pull that nonsense with me," she said. "What are the three of you up to? It better not have anything to do with me or Brad Holliday."

"We're just taking some precautionary measures," he said blithely, stepping closer and giving her a kiss he hoped would prove distracting.

"Good morning," he murmured when he released her. "How'd you sleep last night?"

She punched him in the arm. "Don't think for one second that kissing me is going to make me forget about whatever it is you all are planning."

"You're not even a little distracted?" he asked. "I must be losing my touch."

"Your touch is just fine, thank you, but so is my memory. Talk, pal. Now. And if I don't like what I hear, you'd better put a stop to Plan A."

"It's not a big deal," he assured her. "We're not going to haul Holliday into a back alley and beat him to a pulp."

"Well, that's reassuring," she said dryly. "Because if that was the plan, then you shouldn't count on me to bail you out of jail. I'm not big on vigilante justice. In addition, I think you're all overreacting. Brad may be mouthing off, but he hasn't done anything. He hasn't even set foot near me."

"You sure about that?" Erik asked. "Have you been watching who's around when you're on the streets? Have you looked to see if anyone's tailing your car?"

"Now you're being melodramatic," she said.

He heard the slightest tremble in her voice, which was enough to convince him that she hadn't been that observant.

"Am I being melodramatic?" he asked. "I'm not the only one who thinks the man's a danger to you. So do people who know him a whole lot better than you or I do."

"They *think* he could be dangerous," she corrected. "There's a difference. The more time that passes, the less worried I am."

"And *that* worries me," Erik told her. "You need to be on guard all the time."

"I don't want to live like that," she said.

"Then let us follow through with Plan A. I promise none of us is going to get hurt, Holliday included, and maybe it will keep you from being hurt, as well."

"Or it'll make Brad even more furious with me," she suggested. "Can't you all just leave this alone?"

He shook his head. "I don't think so. Sorry."

"But I'm not asking for your help," she said with obvious frustration. "I don't *want* your help."

Erik shrugged. "Too bad. You have it anyway."

"Men!" she muttered in exasperation. "Do what you have to do, but don't blame me if it backfires. Just keep in mind that I'm the one who's likely to pay the price if it does."

She headed toward the door, her spine rigid. Erik wanted to say something to reassure her, but nothing came to mind. Once they'd confronted Brad Holliday, he'd have a much better idea if they'd warned him off or made matters worse. Until then, he and Helen would simply have to agree to disagree.

Helen marched into The Corner Spa and headed straight for the back patio, where she knew Dana Sue and Maddie would be waiting. Obviously they'd put their husbands up to that little gabfest she'd walked in on at Sullivan's. Maybe they knew what Plan A was and whether it really involved a back-alley brawl.

"There she is," Maddie said cheerfully as Helen approached. "And she's not looking one day older than she did before her birthday."

Helen scowled at her. "I appreciated the party, but I don't want to talk about being older. Besides, we need to discuss what your husbands are up to. I found them at Sullivan's conspiring with Erik."

Maddie and Dana Sue exchanged a look.

"Interesting," Dana Sue said. "She stopped by to see Erik before coming here. Why do you suppose that was?"

"Because he's sexier!" Helen snapped. "Now stop evading and answer me. I know they were over there working up some scheme to deal with Brad Holliday. What did you say to your husbands to get them all worked up? Did you exaggerate the threat?"

"There was no exaggeration. They already understood the situation," Maddie soothed.

"But you encouraged them to hatch some scheme, didn't you?" Helen said. "Are you crazy? You know how guys are. Somebody is going to get hurt and if that happens, it's on your heads."

"Cal won't let that happen," Maddie assured her. "He's the voice of reason. So is Erik."

Dana Sue frowned. "You left out Ronnie."

"Deliberately would be my guess," Helen said. "He's always been a hothead."

"Not anymore," Dana Sue insisted. "Not since he got back to town and we remarried. You know that's true."

"Which only means he's overdue for doing something crazy," Helen retorted.

"Hold it," Maddie said. "These are all grown men. They're just trying to look out for you, Helen. They can handle themselves."

Far from reassured, Helen sat back in her chair. "Well, I hope you're right."

"Let's move on to a far more interesting topic," Dana Sue suggested. "How serious are things between you and Erik?"

"It's a fling," Helen said. "No big deal."

Dana Sue's expression darkened. "I don't like the sound of that. Are you just toying with him, Helen?"

"No more than he is with me," she assured her. "Two consenting adults, Dana Sue. We both knew the score when we started this."

"Did you really?" Maddie asked pointedly. "Erik knew the score?"

Dana Sue's narrowed gaze shifted from Helen to Maddie. "What are you suggesting?" she asked, her expression quizzical.

"Nothing," Helen said hurriedly. "Maddie doesn't know anything you don't know, right, Maddie?"

Maddie's gaze clashed with hers, but Maddie was the first to blink. "No, I don't know anything for a fact."

Dana Sue seized on the very evident loophole. "But you're speculating about something, making an educated guess, aren't you?"

Helen held Maddie's gaze until she shook her head.

"I know better than to speculate about Helen," Maddie said eventually. "She's too unpredictable."

Helen forced a smile as she tried to cover her relief. "I'll take that as a compliment."

"I'm not sure you should," Maddie said darkly.

It was definitely time to get out of here before the conversation got any trickier. "Well, I need to get to work," Helen said briskly, rising to her feet. "Dana Sue, what about you?"

"I'm going to stick around," Dana Sue said to Helen's dismay.

"Okay, whatever," Helen said. "I'll see you."

She had no choice but to trust that Maddie would stay silent after she'd gone. Whatever Maddie knew—or thought she knew—was not something Helen wanted her to share with Dana Sue.

As Helen left The Corner Spa to walk to her office, she noticed a car slowly turn the corner, then keep pace with her. The driver stayed in her peripheral vision, but never got far enough ahead for her to see who was behind the wheel. A chill crept up the back of her neck.

"You're only jittery because of all that talk about Brad," she muttered under her breath. "This is probably just some little old lady who never goes over five miles an hour, that's all."

Still, when she finally turned onto the street her office was on, she picked up her pace. When the car made the same turn, it took everything in her to make herself stop and turn back.

"Nervous, Ms. Decatur?" Brad Holliday called out to her, his expression cold. "You should be."

Before she could reply, he hit the gas and drove off.

"He's just a bully, that's all," Helen told herself staunchly as he disappeared around the next corner. "He just wants to scare me."

Well, he'd accomplished that, she realized as she stared after him. Bile rose in her throat and for a minute she thought she might be sick, but she forced herself to take a few deep breaths, then walked the rest of the way to her office.

She knew she should call the judge or the police, but she couldn't make herself do it. What had Brad done, really? Told her she ought to be nervous. Big deal. It wouldn't be enough to get a restraining order. And a restraining order wouldn't keep him away if he was determined to get even with her. She'd seen the ineffectiveness of that flimsy piece of paper too many times.

Maybe Plan A, whatever it was, wasn't such a bad idea, after all.

For the next week Helen was so jittery she had to force herself to leave Erik's house or the relative safety of her office, where no one got past Barb without an inquisition. Only stubborn pride kept her going about her normal routine.

When she realized in the middle of the following week that she'd missed her period, her immediate thought was stress, not pregnancy. Then she added in the vague nausea she'd experienced on a few mornings lately. Could it possibly be...?

The second Erik left the house, she grabbed her day planner and looked at her calendar. Each time her period had come right on schedule, she'd secretly shed a few tears and made a little mark. With fingers that shook, she flipped through the pages, back one week, then two, then three.

"Oh, my God," she whispered, when she'd flipped back six weeks to find the little mark she always made on the top corner of the page.

She'd been so busy, so caught up in her unexpected feelings for Erik and, more recently, so nervous about Brad Holliday, she hadn't even thought about the baby plan she'd put into effect a few months back. Initially obsessed with those damnable little marks, lately she'd completely lost track. Or maybe she'd simply lost hope.

Now, though, she was late. Seriously late.

"Oh, my God," she said again. "I'm pregnant!"

Caution immediately had her correcting herself. "I might be pregnant."

Thankfully, in anticipation of this day, she'd bought several at-home pregnancy tests at a Charleston pharmacy and hidden them in her suitcase in the back of Erik's closet.

Pushing aside her clothes, she dragged out the suitcase and fumbled with the lock, then took the kits into the bathroom. She was shaking so hard, she could barely hold the box still long enough to read the instructions.

While she waited for the results, she took another test for good measure. And then a third.

The first positive reading brought tears to her eyes. The second brought on a jubilant shout. The third had her sitting down hard on the lid of the toilet and holding a hand over her stomach.

"Baby, if you're really in there, I am going to take such good care of you. I promise."

Five minutes later, she'd scheduled an appointment for the following week with the obstetrician she'd liked the best. If he confirmed what three at-home tests had told her, her life was about to change dramatically.

And so was her relationship with Erik.

Helen was acting weird and Erik didn't think it could be blamed entirely on their disagreement about how Brad Holliday should be handled. *That* had become an almost daily bone of contention.

Tonight, though, she'd had this funny little half smile on her face ever since he'd come home, but when he'd asked what she was thinking, she'd blown off the question.

"You weren't that happy this morning," he said, still studying her suspiciously.

"Actually I was," she said. "Then my mood changed when Maddie called to tell me that you, Cal and Ronnie were getting ready to execute Plan A. I remembered how annoyed I was with you three and your macho plan."

"But I gather you've put that behind you now," he said.

"What makes you think that?"

"You're here. If you were really ticked off, you'd have gone to your place." He searched her face. "Unless, despite all your disclaimers to the contrary, you're still scared of

Holliday and that outweighs your annoyance with me. To be honest, I'd find that reassuring."

"Oh, for heaven's sake, do we have to keep talking about Brad Holliday?" she demanded.

"Nope."

In fact, the less said about the man the better. Erik didn't want to answer questions about when he, Cal and Ronnie intended to implement Plan A. In fact, they'd settled on confronting the man at his home on Saturday morning. Erik didn't much like the idea of waiting two more days, but they'd already waited a week and he'd agreed that confronting him at work would be counterproductive. A public confrontation would be just one more thing to infuriate a man whose hold on his temper was already tenuous.

"Can I bring you anything?" he asked Helen. "I thought I'd have a glass of wine before bed."

"Nothing for me," Helen said, then held up a glass. "I have some water."

That was odd, too. Helen usually joined him in a glass of wine at night. It wasn't worth making a big deal about, though.

When he came back into the living room, he settled on the sofa beside her. "How about watching a movie? There's an old Katharine Hepburn–Spencer Tracy film on tonight. I know you love those."

"Not tonight. I'm tired. It's been a long day." She stood up. "I think I'll go on up to bed."

"Wait," Erik said, frowning. "Are you still upset with me about Holliday?"

"No. I told you it was up to you. Do whatever you have to do."

"But you still disapprove?"

"I still disapprove," she confirmed, "because he's *my* problem. It's up to me to solve it."

"Couldn't you just think of us as backup?"

"Backup's one thing," she told him. "Interference is something else entirely."

"You really are upset about this, aren't you?"

"Gee, you think?"

"I can talk to Cal and Ronnie," he said against his better judgment. "We can hold off for a while. Is that really what you want?"

She regarded him seriously. "It's really what I want."

"Then I'll talk to them," he conceded. "None of us is trying to undermine your independence, you know. We just want you to be safe."

She sighed then and sat back down. "I know that. I just don't like thinking that I'm so vulnerable I need protecting."

"Isn't it better to be safe than sorry? I'd never forgive myself if something happened to you when we might have been able to prevent it."

He couldn't quite read the strange expression that flitted across her face. Something he'd said, though, had obviously resonated with her.

"Go ahead with whatever Plan A is," she said, the about-face catching him completely off-guard. "Just swear to me that none of you will put yourselves in danger."

"We won't," he promised.

He wanted to ask why the change of heart, but he didn't dare. Deep down he believed that moving ahead with the plan was too important to risk losing her hard-won approval. Better to put the fear of God in Brad Holliday now than have to kill him if he ever laid a hand on Helen.

18

Upstairs Helen thought about Erik's concern for her safety and wondered how he'd feel if he knew he might also be protecting their child. In the midst of their argument, she'd suddenly realized she couldn't think only of herself anymore. She had to take whatever precautions were necessary to make sure that no harm came to this baby she might be carrying.

Until this mess with Brad Holliday had started, she'd planned to slowly break things off with Erik the instant she found out she was pregnant. Brad's threats, however unlikely he was to carry them out, made it necessary for her to stay with Erik awhile longer. She sincerely hoped this Plan A would erase the threats and she'd be able to go back home and then end things with Erik in a way that wouldn't hurt him too deeply.

From the beginning of their affair, she'd tried to convince herself he'd be glad to be free of the drama she'd brought into his life, but she knew she was deluding herself. Neither of them was going to walk away from this relationship entirely unscathed, no matter how badly she wanted them to.

She knew tonight's one-eighty about Plan A had startled Erik, but she'd managed to get away before he could start asking uncomfortable questions. She'd counted on his being so relieved by her acquiescence he'd stay silent, and he had, giving her just enough time to bolt.

By the time he came into the bedroom, she was on her side, facing away from him, feigning sleep. She listened to the familiar sound of his clothes being tossed in the general direction of a chair in the corner of the room, then the shower running. When he finally slid beneath the sheets beside her and pressed a quick kiss to her cheek, she almost regretted her charade.

It would have felt good to fold herself into his embrace, to talk quietly about their day, maybe even make love, and then let the steady beating of his heart soothe her to sleep. She'd gotten too used to that lately. Alone for so many years, she hadn't expected to grow accustomed to the little intimate moments that make up a relationship. She was going to miss all of them dreadfully when she went back to her own home and her solitude. The solitude, at least, would be temporary.

Eventually, there would be a baby to hold and love and care for, and that would be its own kind of fulfillment. She touched a hand to her still-flat belly and tried to imagine the tiny life growing inside. She was completely awestruck by the idea of it. Please, God, let her not be wrong about this. Let there be a baby.

"Helen?" Erik whispered. "Are you awake?"

Giving in to her desire for him, she murmured, "Yes."

He rolled toward her and pulled her against him, his bare skin against her back, his heat and male scent enveloping her, awakening her. When he cupped her breast, she thought she noticed a new sensitivity, as pleasure immediately shot through her.

Just like that, she was wide-awake and filled with need. As if he sensed it, Erik's touch went from gentle to impatient, his urgency and her own sudden heated response, catching her off guard.

They came together in a raw burst of passion, breath mingling, hands anxious and determined, hips meeting in a mindless parry and thrust that spiraled out of control in little more than a heartbeat. The fierce explosion that ripped through her triggered his and seemed to go on forever.

That perfectly attuned connection made her wonder— when she could finally think again—how they'd come to know each other's bodies so well. If only their hearts were as well-matched, she thought wistfully before she fell asleep in his arms, the whir of the ceiling fan and its gentle breeze carrying her off to some imaginary hideaway on a romantic tropical island. If only, she thought again. If only...

Helen was plowing through a huge stack of court documents when Barb buzzed her. Sounding alarmed, she announced that someone from Regional Hospital was on the phone.

"What about?" Helen asked.

"Caroline Holliday."

Helen snatched up the phone. "This is Helen Decatur."

"Ms. Decatur, this is Emily Wilson. I'm an emergency room physician at Regional Hospital. Caroline Holliday said you recently represented her in a divorce proceeding."

"Yes. Why? What's happened?"

"She was brought in here, barely conscious, about an hour ago. She'd been beaten. She told officers her ex-husband was responsible, but they haven't located him yet. I have a detective here who'd very much like to speak to you. Can you come?"

"I'll be there within the hour," Helen said, her heart pounding. This was her fault, dammit! Why hadn't she done more to protect Caroline? A restraining order might not be the most effective tool in the world, but she should have demanded one that last day in court when they'd all witnessed Brad unraveling before their eyes. Instead, she'd listened to Caroline say she was going to remove herself from Serenity for a couple of weeks and felt satisfied. Obviously, she'd come back—and to this.

"How is she?" Helen asked, her heart in her throat.

The doctor hesitated, then said, "You're not a family member, so I shouldn't be releasing any information, but Caroline specifically wanted you to know how out-of-control her husband was, so I'll tell you the truth. She's in surgery right now. She has a ruptured spleen, other internal injuries, a broken arm and quite a few cuts and bruises. Brad Holliday was one very angry man."

Helen gasped. "Oh, my God," she whispered. "Will she make it?"

"The best surgeons on staff are with her now. It's in their hands and in God's. I think the only thing that kept her conscious was her determination to warn you. I don't want to tell you what to do, but you shouldn't be alone. Caroline was adamant that you need protection."

"I'll have it," Helen said. "Please take good care of her. This is my fault."

"Because you got her away from a bully?" the doctor asked incredulously.

"No, because I infuriated him in the process," she said,

riddled with guilt. Surely there'd been another way to protect Caroline's interests. She should have found it. In her worst nightmare, she'd never imagined Brad becoming this violent. Even when he'd confronted her on the street just days ago, she still hadn't imagined how deeply disturbed he was. How could she have ignored all the warnings?

"Please let the detective know I'm on my way now and tell him he can get more information from Judge Lester Rockingham and Brad's attorney, Jimmy Bob West."

"I'll pass that along," Dr. Wilson promised.

Helen was shaking when she hung up. She glanced up and realized Barb had come into her office while she'd been on the phone.

"How bad is it?" Barb asked.

"She's in surgery. I need to get over there."

"Surely, you're not going alone," Barb said. "Have they arrested Brad?"

"Not yet, apparently."

"Then you need to take someone with you," Barb insisted.

Helen glanced at the clock. It was just before noon. Erik would be swamped at the restaurant.

Barb apparently figured out what she was thinking because she said firmly, "I'm calling Erik. I don't care how busy he is. He's going to want to go with you. Pick him up on the way. Promise me, Helen."

Too rattled to argue, Helen nodded. "Tell him I'll swing by to get him. I'll pull into the alley."

Ten minutes later she turned into the alley behind Sullivan's and found Erik and Dana Sue both standing there. Dana Sue looked terrified, Erik deeply worried. He yanked open the car door and climbed in.

"You okay?" he asked tersely.

She could only nod. Glancing at Dana Sue, she said, "I'll call you when we know more."

Dana Sue scowled at Erik. "Don't you dare let anything happen to her," she ordered.

"Not on my watch," he assured her.

"We need to go," Helen said, then stepped on the accelerator and shot out of the alley.

"Slow down," Erik commanded. "Try not to get us killed driving over there."

"Would you feel better if you were behind the wheel?" she snapped.

"Based on what I've observed of your driving in the last ten seconds, yes."

She knew he was right. She was too shaken to be behind the wheel. She pulled into a parking lot, slammed her foot on the brake and cut the engine. "Be my guest," she said, getting out and walking around to the other side.

Erik got out and snagged her wrist before she could take his place in the passenger seat. He held her gaze and his tone softened. "It's going to be okay."

Tears stung her eyes. "I hope so, but you didn't hear what the doctor said about Caroline's injuries. It's not good, Erik. She might not make it."

His eyes darkened. "It could have been you."

"But it wasn't," she said. She didn't mention that Caroline and the police thought she might very well be next.

Once they were on their way again, she couldn't bring herself to admit aloud how relieved she was that Erik was now behind the wheel, that he was with her. Even though she could almost feel the tension radiating from him, his strength and mere presence steadied her.

"Thank you for coming with me," she said at last.

He glanced at her. "Your idea or Barb's?"

"Both," she admitted with a half smile. "She was a little more certain that interrupting you at the height of lunch hour was the thing to do."

"You can call me anytime, day or night," he said. "When the choice is between you and baking some fancy dessert, you're going to win hands down, okay?"

She studied him. "You really mean that, don't you?"

"Of course. Why do you even have to ask?"

"Because you've always been so clear about not wanting any emotional entanglements," she told him candidly.

"We're friends, Helen, and friends will always come first with me."

Friends, she thought, leaning back against the seat and holding in a sigh. It was good that he'd reminded her of that. Not that being friends was a bad thing. Not at all. And being friends who slept together was amazing. But there was a clear limit to the relationship, one that told her yet again that he would want no part of this child who might be growing inside her.

Regret washed through her. Regret that the man she'd chosen to father her child would never give that child the same fierce loyalty and protectiveness he gave her. What a tragic and terrible loss for both of them!

Erik glanced over at Helen as he made the turn into the emergency room parking area at the hospital. Her hands were clenched into white-knuckled fists in her lap, and her face was drawn with lines of tension. He guessed that she was blaming herself for what had happened to Caroline Holliday, rather than placing the blame squarely on the man responsible.

When Barb had quickly explained what was going on, he'd felt an overwhelming surge of anger toward Brad Holliday and panic that Helen would be his next victim. He'd been yanking off his chef's jacket and heading for the door before he'd hung up the phone, Dana Sue right on his heels as he explained what was going on. Neither of them had hesitated even a second over the decision that Helen's safety took precedence over anything going on at Sullivan's.

"If we run out of whatever's ready now, we'll serve ice cream," she'd told him. "Just go and keep Helen safe."

On the drive to the hospital, he'd kept his eyes peeled for any suspicious cars, worried that Holliday might have followed Helen from her office. Hopefully the man was scared out of his wits by what he'd done to his ex-wife and was so anxious to avoid the police he wouldn't come anywhere near Helen.

Even though Erik hadn't spotted anyone following them or lurking in the hospital parking lot, he instructed Helen to stay in the car 'til he opened her door.

He cut off her protest. "Just common sense, sugar. Don't get your back up."

She sighed. "I know, but hurry."

He lifted a brow. "We made it here in under thirty minutes. I'm hurrying."

He moved quickly around to her side of the car and shielded her body as she exited. With one arm around her and his gaze darting from side to side, he walked her into the emergency room. A uniformed officer and another man in a rumpled suit that reminded Erik of old *Columbo* shows were hanging around the triage desk.

"We're here about Caroline Holliday," Erik told the nurse on duty, drawing the attention of the men.

"Are you Helen Decatur?" the plainclothes officer asked. "I'm Detective Myers."

Helen nodded. "I'll answer all your questions, but I need to find out how Caroline's doing first." She turned to the nurse. "Is Dr. Wilson available?"

"I'll see if she's free," the nurse said. "I'll send her over to the waiting room."

"Thank you," Erik said, when Helen looked as if she wanted to barge back into the treatment area and search for the doctor herself. He steered her across the hall.

"I'll get coffee," he told her.

"It's pretty disgusting," the uniformed officer said with a grimace.

"I'd rather have herbal tea, anyway," Helen said.

"Fine. I'll get tea," Erik said. "Don't leave her alone for a minute, okay?"

"Not a chance," the detective assured him.

Erik went off to find the cafeteria or a vending machine. Hospital noises and smells were as familiar to him as the aromas in Sullivan's kitchen, but ever since Sam had died they made him queasy. He had to fight with himself to keep from heading straight back to the parking lot, where he could suck in fresh air and maybe get a grip on his composure.

It didn't take him long to find a vending machine, which spewed out a pitiful-looking cup of weak coffee for him. He bought that, then found Helen's tea in the cafeteria.

As he was passing the triage desk, the nurse beckoned to him. "Dr. Wilson is with another patient right now, but she said to tell Ms. Decatur she'll check on Mrs. Holliday's status and be out to fill her in as soon as possible."

"Thanks," Erik said. "I'll let her know."

When he got to the waiting room, he heard Helen summarizing the scene on the day Caroline Holliday had been granted her divorce and the concern the judge and Brad's attorney had expressed for her safety and Helen's. Taking a seat beside Helen, Erik handed her the tea with a roll of his eyes. "Be grateful you opted for that," he said after taking a sip of his coffee.

"You're drinking it," she noted.

"I'm desperate. Any caffeine will do."

Helen shook her head. "Shouldn't you have gotten decaf?"

"It wouldn't matter," the officer said. "Desperation is the only reason anyone would drink that stuff. I'm in here just about every night following up on an accident or a domestic violence incident and I've been pleading with 'em for two years to try to get one of those big coffee chains to open up a franchise by the E.R. It'd make a fortune."

Beside Erik, Helen's eyes immediately brightened. "Maybe it doesn't have to be a big chain franchise," she said, her gaze on him. "What do you think, Erik? It could be a Sullivan's café like the one we have at The Corner Spa."

Detective Myers regarded her with surprise. "I've had the coffee at that restaurant. Best around."

Helen grinned. "He's one of the chefs," she said, gesturing toward Erik.

For a few minutes the tension dissolved as the four of them talked about Sullivan's food and coffee, but the instant a harried-looking woman in green surgical scrubs walked into the waiting room, the mood immediately turned somber.

"Hey, Doc," Detective Myers said. "Any news?"

"Good and bad," she said with a nod in Helen's direction. "Thanks for coming."

"What's the good news?" the detective asked.

"She made it through surgery," Emily Wilson said, but her expression remained grim.

"But?" Erik said.

"She's not coming around the way we'd hoped and her blood pressure hasn't stabilized. In fact, it's dropping."

"She's still bleeding," Erik guessed before the others could react.

The doctor nodded. "That's what we're afraid of. The surgeon was sure he'd found all the bleeders and tied them off, but he could have missed something. Her internal organs took quite a beating."

"Is he going back in?" Erik asked, aware of Helen's gaze. "There may not be a lot of time to wait it out."

"He'll make a decision in the next half hour," Dr. Wilson confirmed. "You seem to have a good grasp of all this."

"I was an EMT for a while," he said.

The detective stared at him. "And now you're a chef. I'll bet there's a story in that."

Erik shrugged. "Not a very interesting one," he said.

"I'll keep you posted," Dr. Wilson told them. "Detective, have you been able to reach her kids?"

"I tracked down her oldest son. He's rounding up the others. They should be here soon."

"The sooner the better," the doctor said.

Beside Erik, Helen shivered. He draped an arm around her and gave her shoulder a squeeze. "Maybe we should go," he suggested.

"No," Helen said at once. "I need to stay. If you need to get back, take my car. Maddie or somebody can pick me up later."

"Not a chance," Erik said. "If you stay, I stay. I just

thought you might not want to be here when her children get here."

Helen shook her head. "They may have questions I can answer."

"Or they may blame you for triggering all this," he countered. "Remember, they love their mom *and* their dad."

"He's right," Detective Myers said. "In these circumstances, people sometimes aren't rational. I have the background information I need from you for now. Go home." He met Erik's gaze, though he continued to speak to Helen. "Just make sure someone's with you at all times until we find this guy, okay? He's clearly lost his grip."

"Someone will be," Erik assured him.

"I'll notify your sheriff that he needs to keep a watch on your house and your office," he said.

"She's spending a lot of time at my place," Erik said. "Most of the time she's not alone there." He gave him the address.

"I'll make sure he knows about that, too," Detective Myers said. "You can't take this lightly, Ms. Decatur. I know Mrs. Holliday was worried, and when I spoke to the judge and Holliday's attorney, they expressed concern for you, too. The last thing any of us wants is for you to wind up here in the same shape Mrs. Holliday is in."

"I get it," she said, her face pale. "I'll be careful."

The two policemen walked them to Helen's car. It appeared to be a casual gesture, but Erik noted that they were very much on alert, checking out the parking lot in every direction, then waiting until Erik pulled out of the space and drove off before going back inside.

"I should have stayed," Helen said as they turned onto the highway.

"No," Erik contradicted. "This is for the best. You can go back when Caroline's in a room and needs company. Now what she needs are your prayers."

Helen didn't look entirely convinced, but she fell silent. In fact, she was so quiet for so long that Erik began to worry, until a glance told him that she'd fallen asleep. Obviously the news and the frantic drive had taken a toll on her.

At his place, she let him fix her some soup and a salad. She ate three spoonfuls of the soup and no more than a bite or two of the salad.

"Could you call the hospital and check on her?" she asked Erik, when she'd pushed aside her food. "You seem to understand all the medical stuff better than I do. Then you can tell me what's going on in plain English."

"Sure." He placed the call and was able to get Dr. Wilson on the line. "Any news on Caroline Holliday?"

"They went in again and found the bleeder," she told him. "Her blood pressure is almost back to normal, so I'm guardedly optimistic. She still has a long way to go, though. Her body went through a lot of trauma. Her kids are with her, all but her daughter. Apparently she can't believe her dad would do something like this. She's somehow convinced herself someone else had to be responsible and that her mom's just using this to get even with her dad."

"Deep denial," Erik said. "Not that uncommon. Mind if I check back with you to keep tabs on Mrs. Holliday's condition? Helen's really worried about her."

"Sure," she said. "By the way, Detective Myers told me Ms. Decatur suggested opening a Sullivan's Café here at the hospital. I really hope you think about it. It might make the hours I spend here less exhausting if I could get a decent cup of coffee or a decent meal once in a while."

"I'll talk to my boss about the idea first thing tomorrow," he promised. "She might go for it."

He hung up and found Helen pacing impatiently in the living room.

"It took you long enough," she muttered. "Did you and the doctor have a good time catching up?"

He assumed it was worry, not jealousy that had put that tone in her voice, so he said mildly, "Caroline's improving. They did a second surgery and that seems to have stopped the bleeding. Dr. Wilson is more optimistic."

"It didn't take that long for her to tell you that. What else did you talk about?"

He looked at her in surprise. "I know you can't possibly be jealous since you're the one who wanted me to call her," he said.

She frowned. "Of course, I'm not jealous."

"Good, because that's not the kind of relationship we have, right?"

She sighed. "No, of course not. Sorry."

"You're worried. I get that," he said quietly. "Let's watch that movie I brought home yesterday. It'll take your mind off all this."

She regarded him with obvious ambivalence, but she finally nodded. "Okay."

He grinned. "You always love it when Katharine Hepburn twists Spencer Tracy around her little finger."

Her expression brightened. "Yes, I do," she said more cheerfully.

For just an instant, he wondered if he would ever tire of the amazing twists and turns her mind took. He doubted it. But down that path lay a future he wouldn't allow himself to contemplate.

19

Helen was almost out the door the next morning when her cell phone rang.

"I want you to stop by the spa," Maddie ordered. "I want to hear exactly what went on yesterday. Why didn't you call me? I could have driven you to the hospital."

"It made more sense to call Erik," Helen said. "I know you're tough, Maddie, but you have five kids now. I couldn't take a chance on anything happening to you because you were with me."

"I suppose that makes sense," Maddie agreed, though she still sounded miffed at being sidelined in a crisis. The Sweet Magnolias had always stuck together. "But I still want to know what happened. How soon can you get here?"

"Erik's going to drop me at the office," Helen explained. "I really need to catch up."

"That can wait. Have him drop you here instead," Maddie instructed. "Elliott can take you to the office. I think Erik would agree that Elliott's an adequate bodyguard."

"Fine. I'll see you in five minutes," Helen agreed, knowing that Maddie wouldn't be happy until she'd seen for herself that Helen was okay. Though Helen hadn't seen the morning paper, she imagined that between the news reports and the Serenity grapevine, Brad's attack on Caroline—bad enough in reality—had been exaggerated a thousandfold.

In the car, she explained the change of plans to Erik. "You won't have to wait around. I know you need to get to Sullivan's. Maddie promised that Elliott would give me a lift to the office."

Erik frowned. "You won't suddenly decide that it's too much trouble and take off on your own, will you?"

"No," she promised. "Believe me, hearing the details about what Brad did to Caroline, I'm no more anxious to take chances than you are to have me take them."

"Okay, then," he said, pulling to the curb in front of The Corner Spa. "Call me when you get to your office. I want to know if there's any sign of a sheriff's deputy outside, okay? If adequate protection's not being provided as promised, then we're going straight to the judge. No arguments, okay?"

"Yes, worrywort," she said lightly and kissed his cheek. "I'll call."

Inside, she found Maddie in her office with a dozen towels spread out on her desk.

"Feel these," she commanded. "Tell me what you think."

Helen shrugged and picked each one up. Some were rough, some too thin. Two were thick and luxurious, but probably outrageously expensive. "I assume we're changing towels," she said.

"We compromised quality for cost in the initial buy," Maddie said. "Those are wearing out." She pointed to the thin ones. "Jeanette thinks we should spend a little extra and get something that'll last longer. Besides, we want our clients to feel truly pampered when they come here. I'm constantly surprised by how many women in this region are willing to pay big bucks for a day of luxurious indulgence. Workouts are just that—work. But the spa treatments are a pleasure, something they think they deserve or something they want to give their friends. Did you see how far ahead of projections the sales of the gift certificates were? And just imagine what'll happen when the holidays roll around. We need to do our part to make the whole thing a fantasy come true."

"I trust you and Jeanette on all that," Helen assured her. "Do you have a price comparison on these two?" She fingered the more luxurious ones, relieved to be chatting about something so mundane, rather than Brad Holliday.

Maddie shoved a piece of paper across the table. "You're holding the two Jeanette preferred, but that cost makes me cringe."

"You need to weigh how much would be saved by not having to replace them as soon. She was right about the robes, wasn't she? Those have held up, while the lower-cost towels haven't."

"True," Maddie admitted. "Okay, which of those two?"

Helen shrugged. "I can't tell that much difference and the price is comparable. Is one vendor more reliable than the other?"

"We used one for the robes and he's been excellent to work with."

"Then go with him. He might even give you a price break since you'll be dealing with him exclusively on more items," Helen said, placing the towels back on the desk. "You didn't drag me over here to involve me in the day-to-day decisions around here, though. That's your territory. Are you just trying to lull me into a false sense of complacency before you start asking the tough questions?"

Maddie grinned. "You know me too well."

"Okay, shoot. Let's get this over with."

"Are you pregnant with Erik's baby?" Maddie asked, stunning Helen.

"Where did that come from? I thought you wanted to talk about Brad and what he did to Caroline Holliday," she said irritably.

"I know that's what I told you on the phone, but I thought I might get an honest answer out of you about Erik if I took you by surprise."

"Why would you think I'm pregnant?"

"As you pointed out on the phone, I have five kids. I know the signs. You've turned green a couple of mornings in here and you're more irritable than usual. Are you saying I'm right?"

"I haven't said anything," Helen muttered. "And I'm not going to."

"Why not? Because you know this is all going to blow sky-high the second you do own up to what you've done, don't you?"

"Maddie, stay out of it," Helen pleaded. "Let me handle it."

Maddie held up her hands. "Believe me, I would be more than happy to let you handle this if I thought you had the slightest clue how to go about it."

"I have a plan," Helen told her.

"And that's been the problem all along," Maddie accused. "You had a plan that didn't take into account how anyone else might feel, especially Erik. Dana Sue, too."

"I *did* take Erik's feelings into account," she said defensively. "He and I have a clear understanding about the limits of our relationship."

Maddie regarded her with blatant skepticism. "Somehow I doubt that conversation included a discussion about you getting pregnant with his child. Am I wrong about that?"

Helen sighed. "No, you're not wrong."

Maddie's gaze turned worried. "Oh, sweetie, what on earth are you going to do now?"

"It'll work out," Helen said confidently.

"Will it really? Do you think Dana Sue is going to be overjoyed about it?"

"It's not her business. It's between Erik and me."

"Right now, it's all about you and what *you* want," Maddie contradicted. "Erik's had no say in any of this. When do you plan to tell him?"

"I'm not even a hundred percent certain there's anything to tell yet," Helen said. "I'm seeing the doctor on Monday. Then I'll decide what to do. It's gotten a little complicated because of the whole thing with Brad Holliday. Erik will have a conniption if I try to move out of his place and distance myself from him while Brad might still be a threat."

Maddie stared at her in shock. "*That's* your plan? You're just going to move out and say nothing about being pregnant?"

"Erik doesn't want a wife. He doesn't want kids, so yes, that is the plan. He doesn't need to know about any of this. I can handle the pregnancy, the baby, all of it on my own."

"You're delusional," Maddie snapped. "The man can count, for heaven's sake. Don't you think he might take one look at you in, say, five months' time and conclude that the child you're carrying could be his? What a terrific thing to do to a man you claim is a friend, if nothing else. And from what I've seen, Erik cares about you. Really cares about you. Did you consider the possibility that he might be happy about this news?"

"He won't be," Helen said, though her confidence was shaken by Maddie's words.

Maddie looked worried. "Oh, Helen, what were you thinking?" She waved off the question. "Never mind. It's plain you weren't thinking, at least not very clearly."

"Thanks for being so supportive," Helen said coldly.

"I will always be supportive of you," Maddie answered. "But I won't stand by and watch you make an idiotic mistake. Tell Erik and then tell Dana Sue, before you lose two of the best friends you've ever had. You owe them the truth, Helen. And they need to hear it from you before someone else figures out what I have and spills the beans."

Maddie's harsh words shook her in a way that even Brad's threats had not. "I can't lose them," she whispered. "They mean the world to me."

"Just not enough for you to be honest with them," Maddie chided. "I mean it, Helen. Talk to them or *I* will."

She stared at Maddie with shock. "You wouldn't."

"I would," Maddie said, her tone unyielding. "I know it's not my place, but I can't sit by and watch you ruin your life without doing everything in my power to stop it. Give Erik a chance to step up and do the right thing. He might surprise you." She leveled a look at Helen. "You have until Tuesday."

"Tuesday?" Helen echoed.

"You'll know for sure by then. Don't waste a second sharing the news, okay? I mean it."

Helen read the determination in Maddie's gaze and

knew she meant every word. Maddie wouldn't care how much she infuriated her if she thought she was doing the right thing in the long run.

"It's too soon to tell anyone," Helen said, grasping at any straw to try to get Maddie to back down. "You know there's a high risk of miscarriage at my age. You didn't even tell any of us about your last pregnancy until you were well past the first trimester."

"Don't try that excuse on me," Maddie said. "I told Cal because the father has a right to know from the very beginning. You need to tell Erik for the same reason."

"But if I do lose this baby, then I'd never get another chance, not with Erik anyway."

"That's a risk you'll have to take," Maddie said, her gaze unflinching.

Helen sighed. "Come on, Maddie, this needs to be handled on my timetable, not yours."

"Tuesday," Maddie repeated firmly. "I'll get Elliott now. He can take you to your office."

"When did you learn to play hardball?" Helen asked with grudging admiration.

"I've spent most of my life around you," Maddie retorted. "It was bound to rub off."

"I should have known I'd live to regret my influence over you," Helen said. "I'll be in touch."

Maddie nodded. "See that you are."

Helen couldn't seem to stop the smile that tugged at her lips. "You can stop the tough-guy routine now. You've made your point."

In fact, she'd made it so effectively that Helen wondered if she'd be able to salvage anything out of this mess she'd created. The only thing keeping her from sinking into despair was the thought that in just a few months, she'd be holding her own child in her arms. That would make any of the consequences she suffered worth it.

Karen was walking into The Corner Spa for her morning workout when she spotted Elliott leaving with Helen. A streak of pure jealousy shot through her. She was so absorbed in watching the two of them, in noting the way Elliott bent down to listen more intently to whatever Helen was saying, that she bumped straight into Maddie, who was coming out of her office.

"I'm so sorry," Karen murmured.

Maddie followed the direction of her gaze. "I thought you'd broken things off with Elliott."

"I did," Karen admitted.

Maddie regarded her with sympathy. "But now you're regretting it?"

"I might have been a little hasty," Karen said. "But it looks as if he's moved on."

Maddie shook her head. "I don't know what's wrong with all the women I know," she lamented. "Not one of you has a grain of sense."

Karen stared at her. "Excuse me?"

"Never mind," Maddie said with a dismissive wave of her hand. "Elliott's not interested in Helen and, believe me, she is definitely not interested in him. He's giving her a ride to her office because some guy has threatened her and she's not supposed to go anyplace alone right now."

The relief that washed over Karen was telling. "I see," she said softly.

"If you want him, do something about it," Maddie advised. "Helen's the least of your worries. Elliott is surrounded by temptation all day long. As far as I can tell, he's shown no interest in any of the women around here who throw themselves at him, but that could change in a heartbeat."

"What should I do?"

"Tell him how you feel. Be honest. People don't seem to be using that strategy nearly enough these days," Maddie said heatedly.

Karen looked taken aback. "Are we still talking about me and Elliott?"

"Not entirely," she admitted. "Just remember what I said. Directness and honesty are traits to be valued in any relationship. The lack of either one can doom you."

Karen nodded. "I'll keep that in mind."

Maddie gave her shoulder a squeeze and headed for the treatment area.

Fifteen minutes later when Elliott walked back in the front door, Karen spotted him at once. She shut off the treadmill on which she'd been doing a halfhearted workout and stepped down, then marched across the room until she was almost toe-to-toe with him. It was the first time she'd forced a confrontation since they'd broken up.

She put her hands on his shoulders, stood on tiptoe and planted a kiss on his mouth that would have shot the temperature in the steam room up another fifty degrees. When she stepped back, he looked dazed.

"I thought we'd broken up," he said eventually.

She shrugged. "I changed my mind. I think that was a bad idea. How about you?"

His lips twitched. "I always thought it was a bad idea."

"Then can we go out on Sunday? Just the two of us?"

He shook his head and her heart plummeted.

"We can go out on Sunday only if you bring the kids

along. It's my niece Angela's first birthday. There's a family celebration."

Karen stared at him. "And you want us to go with you?"

"I do," he said solemnly.

"Your family will have questions," she warned him.

"Believe me, I know that even better than you do. Are you prepared for that?"

She thought about it, thought about Frances's insistence that Elliott was a family man who'd stick by her side through thick and thin. Maybe this was her chance to see that firsthand. Hopefully it would tell her everything she needed to know before she opened her heart all the way.

She lifted her gaze to his and nodded. "I think I am."

"Then I'll pick you up at noon. No need to bring a present. I'll get something from all of us."

"From all of us?" she echoed. That would be a declaration of sorts.

He nodded. "Is that a problem?"

"No," she said slowly. "No, it's not a problem at all."

For the first time, he gave her a full-fledged smile, then touched her cheek. "I'm glad you changed your mind, *querida*."

It was the first time he'd used the endearment. It touched a place inside her that had been cold and lonely for way too long. "Me, too," she said. "But let's not get too far ahead of ourselves, okay?"

"How far is too far?" he asked. "Just so I understand the rules."

Suddenly feeling more daring than she had in years, she told him, "No rules. Let's just improvise."

"Slow-track improv," Elliott concluded. "I can do that. In fact, I'm looking forward to it."

So was Karen. It didn't mean she wasn't scared. Nor did it mean the future was certain. But she was looking forward with anticipation, rather than panic and dread. It was a darn good feeling.

Helen got dressed after her examination, then went into the obstetrician's office. She hadn't been able to read anything from Dr. Matthew Dawson's expression while he'd been poking and prodding her.

In his office, she sat across from him while he made notes in her chart. Her pulse scrambled wildly as she waited for the words that would confirm whether or not she was finally going to have the baby she wanted so badly.

Eventually he looked up, his expression grave. Once again, her pulse went crazy. Wouldn't he look happy if she were pregnant? Or at least neutral?

"You've been really anxious to get pregnant, haven't you?" he said at last. "We talked about it the last time you were here."

Unable to speak, she nodded.

"Well, the good news is, you've gotten your wish. You're definitely pregnant."

Helen heard a *but* in there, a very worrisome *but*. "Why do I get the feeling you're not as happy about that as I am?"

"I'm not unhappy," he told her. "I'm just concerned. Your blood pressure's not as low as I'd like to see it at this stage. With your history, it's going to be very tricky for you to safely carry this baby to term."

"I've been under some unexpected stress the past few days, but I'll work harder to get it back down," she promised eagerly. "I'll do whatever you tell me. I want this baby more than anything."

"Enough to agree to complete bed rest if I decide it's necessary?" he inquired skeptically.

"Absolutely," she said at once. She would find some way to work it out. She'd divert her clients to other attorneys. She'd hire a housekeeper. Whatever it took. Nothing was going to endanger this chance to become a mother.

"You say that now," he said, "but you're a very driven woman, Helen. That's how you got yourself to this point. Stress is part of your daily life. How are you going to eliminate that?"

Seeing Brad Holliday arrested would certainly help, but she didn't want to get into that. The doctor would probably recommend she spend her entire pregnancy on some nice, quiet island.

"I'll take yoga classes. I'll meditate. I'll exercise."

"All things you've been promising me for months that you'd do," he reminded her.

"And I have," she said. "At least most of the time."

"Your blood pressure says otherwise."

"I'll do better," she promised. "Really. I'll be a model patient. Nothing means more to me than having a healthy baby."

To her relief, he seemed to believe her as he wrote out prescriptions. "One's for a prenatal vitamin. The other's for a stronger diuretic than the one you've been on. We need to avoid water retention. Take them. And do all of those other things you promised. I want to see you again in two weeks, rather than a month. We're going to need to monitor you closely if you're to carry to term."

"Can you tell how far along I am?"

"I'd say a month, maybe six weeks at the most. We'll do an ultrasound next time and we'll know more." For the first time, he smiled. "Congratulations, Helen. I'll do everything I can to see that you have the healthy baby you want. You just need to do your part. Avoid stress above all else. Understood?"

"Yes," she assured him.

She just had two stressful conversations to get through and hopefully by then Brad would be in jail. From then on, she intended to eliminate anything even faintly stressful from her life.

She decided she'd start by talking to Dana Sue. Once Dana Sue had calmed down, she might have some ideas about how she should tell Erik. And no matter how badly either of them reacted, Helen had to put it behind her. From now on this baby was her number-one priority. Period.

For three months Erik had been caught up in a situation he couldn't explain, all but living with a woman who didn't seem to have any expectations outside the bedroom. Helen wasn't demanding. She didn't seem to be interested in staking some sort of claim. All she cared about was the kind of hot, steamy sex men dreamed about. In fact, he was just about worn-out from all the late nights. As incredible as it had been, he couldn't help thinking that there was something going on he didn't totally understand, especially over the past week.

He knew Helen had been annoyed with his protectiveness despite her own concern that Brad Holliday might come after her, but it was more than that. She'd been quieter than usual, more withdrawn, especially since Caroline Holliday had wound up in the hospital. He would have chalked it all up to fear, but Helen was the kind of woman who faced fear head-on. He was beginning to get a sinking feeling that this had more to do with him.

He was on his way into the kitchen at Sullivan's when he heard raised voices coming from Dana Sue's office. He recognized his boss's and then Helen's. Unable to stop himself, he walked closer to the door.

"Dammit, Helen, what were you thinking?" Dana Sue shouted. "How could you do something like this? Maddie knows, doesn't she? That's what she's been so annoyed about lately."

"Maddie guessed, but I don't see what you're getting so worked up about," Helen replied stiffly. "You knew all along that Erik and I were spending time together. Heck, we've been living together ever since Brad Holliday became a threat."

"Of course, and I couldn't have been happier," Dana Sue said. "You two are great for each other. I've been waiting for weeks now to have one of you admit you were falling in love. Instead, you come in here, tell me you're pregnant and that you're dumping him. You've used him, accomplished your goal, and that's it? How could you, Helen?"

Erik stood rooted in place as Dana Sue's words sank in. Helen was pregnant? How the hell had that happened? She'd told him... What *had* she told him? He searched his mind, trying to remember a single conversation they'd had about birth control. Surely way back at the beginning they'd talked about it, he thought. Then he recalled one hastily uttered claim from her that everything was okay, that he didn't need to worry. He'd taken her at her word. Why wouldn't he? Helen was supposedly one of the most trustworthy people in town.

And now she was pregnant? And if he was correctly interpreting the gist of her conversation with Dana Sue, that had been her plan all along? She'd apparently wanted a baby and chosen him to help her make one, despite his oft-repeated statements that kids were not in the cards for him.

A blind rage swept through him. Before he could think about it or reconsider, he pushed open the door and stalked into Dana Sue's cramped office. Both women regarded him with dismay. He faced Dana Sue first.

"Out," he said tersely.

She scrambled from behind her desk, gave him one last sympathetic look and left.

After her initial shock, Helen faced him with a surprisingly calm expression. "I gather you heard."

"Enough," he said. "Maybe you ought to start from the beginning, though, and spell it out for me. I want to be sure I have all the facts straight."

"It's nothing for you to be upset about," she began in a reasonable tone that made him want to start breaking things.

"Maybe you should let me decide just how upset I want to get," he retorted. "You're pregnant, is that right?"

She nodded. "But I don't expect anything from you. I'm happy about this, Erik. Really happy. I've wanted a baby more than anything for a long time now."

"More than anything," he echoed, ice in his voice and in his veins. "But you saw no need to mention that to me?"

"Actually we have talked about it, at least in a general way," she reminded him.

"A general way?" he echoed. "Oh, yes, I do remember that. But I don't recall a single mention of the role you intended for *me* to play. Didn't you consider that perhaps I ought to have at least *some* say?"

She swallowed hard. "I see your point. I probably should have discussed it with you."

Erik saw red. "Probably?" he all but shouted, then fought to bring his temper under control.

She regarded him earnestly. "Erik, I swear to you that I can give this baby everything it needs. You're under no obligation to be part of his or her life at all. It's not as if I did this to trap you or something."

"Which doesn't exactly deal with the real issue, does it?" he said. Clenching his fists to keep from grabbing her and shaking her, he said, "And if I *want* to be a part of the baby's life?"

That seemed to rock her back on her heels. "What?"

"I asked you how you feel about me being involved in the baby's life."

"I told you it's not necessary," she said. "I know you don't want children."

"And yet here we are," he said sarcastically, "with you pregnant with my baby."

"But there's no reason for you to feel obligated," she insisted again. "This is my baby. I take full responsibility for what happened."

"It happened because you made it happen," he said. "Isn't that right?"

She winced. "I suppose you could say that. I knew it was a possibility." At his scowl, she said, "Okay, I did everything possible to make it happen, which is why I'm taking responsibility and expecting nothing from you."

"It doesn't work like that, sugar," he said grimly, not sure if he was more furious about her decision to have this baby without consulting him, or about her willingness to shut him out of their lives as if he'd been nothing more than some anonymous sperm donor.

Granted he hadn't ever planned on becoming a father,

not after losing his baby when his wife died. The pain of that loss had stuck with him and was something he couldn't bear to risk repeating.

Nor had he thought about marrying again, especially not to Helen. Their casual relationship with no demands, mind-blowing sex and mind-challenging conversation had suited him just fine. Now, suddenly, all of that had changed and he didn't intend to be shut out of her life or their child's.

He grabbed the chair from behind Dana Sue's desk and set it down right in front of Helen, then straddled it. Given the room's lack of space, she had no wiggle room at all. She had no choice but to stay where she was and listen.

"Here's the way it's going to be," he said, looking at her intently. Despite the shock he'd felt when he'd heard the news, he was as certain of what needed to happen next as he'd ever been of anything. "You've gotten your way apparently. You're pregnant. Now I'm going to do what *I* want. Are you listening, Helen? I really need you to hear every word of this."

She nodded, her eyes wide, her expression shaken.

"You and I will get married," he said flatly. "We will go through this pregnancy together. After the baby's born, if you still want to be some kind of supermom on your own, we'll talk about a divorce, but I will have shared custody of our child. That's it."

She regarded him with an unmistakably panicked expression. "You can't be serious."

"I'm as serious as a heart attack."

"But why?"

"Because I lost one baby and there wasn't a damn thing I could do about it. I won't lose another. And if you think I'll change my mind once I've had time to think things through or that you'll just postpone and delay your way out of making a commitment, think again."

"You can't *make* me marry you," she protested. "We're not in love."

"You should have thought of that before you hatched this cockamamie scheme of yours," he said mildly. "Console yourself with this. At least you know the sex will be great."

He got up and left the room.

It was only after he was in the kitchen—and Dana Sue had bolted in the direction of her office—that he realized he wasn't nearly as upset about the idea of marriage as he'd thought he'd be. He might be shaking with rage over being duped. He might be panicky at the thought of losing yet another child. Helen was, after all, forty-three and at a high risk for carrying a baby all the way to term.

But as his temper cooled, he knew that being with Helen for the rest of his life was something he'd wanted for a long time now and been too scared to go after. It seemed fate— with a very deliberate and calculating assist from Helen— had stepped in and forced his hand.

20

"Oh, my God, what have I done?" Helen said when Dana Sue came back to check on her.

"Offhand, I'd say you've stirred up a hornet's nest," her friend said without much sympathy. "I'm a little surprised to find you in one piece. I thought I saw steam rising from Erik when he came back to the kitchen. I've never seen him like that before. Just how mad was he?"

"He says he's going to marry me," Helen said, regarding Dana Sue with bewilderment. "I don't think he's going to take no for an answer."

For the first time since Helen had broken the news of her pregnancy, Dana Sue's dire expression softened. "Well, now, that's an interesting turn of events, though not entirely unexpected."

"It's not funny and it is totally unexpected," Helen grumbled. "I didn't want to trap him into marrying me. That was the last thing on my mind."

"Maybe it shouldn't have been," Dana Sue told her. "Surely you know the kind of guy Erik is. He's solid and dependable and protective. You've seen that firsthand in the way he looks out for me and Annie. Didn't you stop for one second to think about how he'd be with a baby involved, especially *his* baby?"

"Okay, I get that he feels a little protective about the baby, especially with what's happened to Caroline Holliday, but marriage? Isn't that going too far?"

"Obviously he doesn't think so," Dana Sue replied.

"But what about love?" Helen asked wistfully.

Once more Dana Sue regarded her with a complete lack of sympathy. "Another of those things you should have thought about before you decided to take matters into your own hands. Besides, you two have strong feelings for each other, anyone can see that. Call it whatever you want, but it seems close enough to love to me. Even though I'm not one bit happy about the underhanded way you went about this, I still think this is the best thing that could have happened to you. Otherwise, you two might've danced around your feelings for years. You're both too stubborn for your own good. Seems to me this is exactly the push you both needed to get you where you should be."

"But none of this was about getting married," Helen protested.

Dana Sue grinned. "Well, it is now." She reached for the calendar on her desk. "So, let's pick a date. If there's going to be a wedding, I need time to plan. And I assume, given your pride in your appearance and your preference for designer clothes and fancy footwear, you won't want to be the size of a whale when you walk down the aisle. In that case it had better be soon."

Helen scowled at her. "There's not going to be a wedding," she said grimly.

Dana Sue merely smiled. "Wanna bet? I'd suggest you get with the program, or the most important day of your life will happen and you won't have control over one single detail."

"No wedding," Helen repeated.

Dana Sue went on as if she hadn't spoken. "Tell you what, we can meet Maddie at the spa tomorrow morning and start making lists. You'll love that. We can go over all this with her at eight. I can't wait to see her face when you tell her the news."

"She won't be as shocked as you might think," Helen muttered. "She tried to warn me I was going about this all wrong, even though she couldn't get me to acknowledge what I was doing."

"I still hate it that she figured this out and I didn't have a clue," Dana Sue groused. "I must have been so wrapped up in what was going on in my own life with Ronnie that I never saw this coming. I'm going to have to watch that, especially if you're going to get into the habit of trying to keep things from me."

"It wasn't like that," Helen argued. At Dana Sue's arched brow, she amended, "Not exactly anyway. I just knew you'd try to talk me out of it or warn Erik and ruin everything."

"Maybe if I had found out, you wouldn't be about to marry a man who's furious with you," Dana Sue suggested.

"I keep telling you that we are *not* getting married," Helen countered.

"I think you need to get over that refrain," Dana Sue said. "Nobody's going to buy it, not once they've crossed paths with Erik and seen the determination in his eyes, anyway. Let's just get together with Maddie tomorrow and put this wedding together the way you want it." Her mood visibly improved. "This is going to be so much fun."

"Forget the wedding," Helen said again. "Ganging up on me is not going to work. And since when do you and Maddie side with an outsider against one of your own?"

"When it's the right thing to do," Dana Sue said without hesitation. "You and Erik are good for each other. You'll be terrific parents, too."

"You make it sound like we'll be some happy little family holding barbecues in the backyard," Helen grumbled. "You said it yourself, Dana Sue. He's furious with me. That's what this is about. Nothing good can come from a marriage that starts like that. I won't do it. None of you can bully me into it."

But even as she said the words, she, too, recalled the determination in Erik's eyes—the same determination Dana Sue had obviously seen—and shuddered. Maybe she should look up the law on whether a woman could be forced to marry against her will. She was pretty sure it was on her side, but if there was some loophole she didn't know about, there wasn't a doubt in her mind that Erik would find it.

Barb had a stack of messages waiting for Helen when she got to her office the next morning, after skipping the little tête-à-tête that Dana Sue had planned for eight o'clock. She had a hunch she was going to pay for that act of rebellion, but she hadn't been up to facing her two best friends and their current mission to see that she got properly married to a man who was forcing a wedding only because he was angry.

"Ten of those messages are from Erik," Barb said, her expression filled with curiosity. "He seemed edgy. Is something going on?"

"I moved out of his place yesterday," Helen said. "And I didn't take any of his calls last night."

Barb stared at her in shock. "Why on earth would you do that, especially now with Brad Holliday on some sort of rampage?"

"It was the right thing to do," Helen said. She'd had her things out of his place by seven o'clock, long before he was likely to be home from Sullivan's. If she hadn't had a such a busy schedule for the next couple of weeks, she would have packed and headed for some tropical island to relax until Erik's temper cooled down and he dropped this whole marriage insanity.

Helen had been a little surprised that Erik had gotten so upset over her departure. Surely he'd known they couldn't go on living under the same roof. She'd said as much in the note she'd left so he wouldn't worry that Brad had kidnapped her or something. Apparently that had only given him another reason to be angry with her, as the tenor of his messages revealed. Barb had clearly picked up on that, as well, because she was scowling at Helen.

"That man is the best thing that ever happened to you," Barb scolded her. "Why would you want to sabotage that?"

"Look, things happen. People change. Emotions can't be trusted. It was time to move on."

Barb's eyes suddenly filled with understanding. "In other words, you got scared. He wanted more than you were prepared to offer and you panicked."

Helen didn't see any reason to share the whole truth with Barb, even though her secretary was more friend than employee. Right now, the fewer people who were in on the mess she'd made of things, the better.

"Something like that," she agreed. "Now, if you're all through digging around in my personal life, I think I'll go in my office and get some work done."

Barbara regarded her with a disappointed expression. "Whatever you say," she said stiffly. "Just tell me what you want me to do when Erik—"

Helen cut her off. "I'm not taking his calls."

"But—"

"Don't argue with me," she said, noting that Barb simply shrugged and gave in to Helen's command.

Two seconds later she understood why her secretary had capitulated so easily. Erik walked in practically on her heels and slammed the door shut. Obviously Barb had been trying to tell her he was on his way over. Helen concluded she really did need to start listening to people, instead of issuing orders.

"What are you doing here?" she asked, giving him one of her haughtiest glares.

"You never used to ask dumb questions," he said, taking a seat on the sofa and patting the space beside him.

Helen deliberately walked behind her desk and sank wearily into her chair. "Go ahead. Say whatever's on your mind. I know you're mad."

"And worried," he said. "Let's not forget that a crazy man could be stalking you, yet you decided to take off from someplace where you might be safe. Since when did you turn into the kind of woman who would take foolish risks just to avoid a confrontation, especially one you know you can't avoid forever anyway?"

Helen shivered. Somehow, in her haste to get away from Erik's before things got worse than they already were, she'd discounted the danger Brad Holliday presented.

"I'm sure the police knew where I was," she replied. "They're supposed to be keeping an eye on me."

"That makes me feel all warm and fuzzy, sort of the way I felt when I couldn't reach you for hours on end."

Even under the unmistakable edge of sarcasm, she could hear real concern in his voice. "I'm sorry you worried," she said sincerely. "That's why I left you a note, so you'd know where I was. I just thought it was for the best that I go home."

"Best for whom?"

"Both of us," she told him.

"And the baby? Is it best for the baby that you could have been putting your life at risk just so you could get away from any uncomfortable questions I might ask?"

"It's not your questions I'm worried about," she retorted. "It's your demands."

"Running away won't change that," he said quietly. "We *will* get married, Helen."

The emphatic note in his voice left her shaken. "But why?"

"Because my child is going to have my name. It's going to grow up with a mother and a father, no matter what kind of patchwork, nutty relationship we manage to have."

Helen shook her head and sighed. "Who would have thought you'd be so traditional? A few days ago, all you cared about was great sex and some lively conversation from time to time."

He gave her a wry look at her assessment of their relationship, then shrugged. "Okay, I'll admit it. It surprises the hell out of me, too. But that's the way it is. Get used to it. Who knows, you might turn out to be traditional, too."

A part of Helen yearned for just that, but she didn't see

how it was possible when a marriage started off as uncon-
ventionally as this one would if Erik forced it on her. And
even if it somehow lasted, she would always wonder if he
loved her or if he was just making the best of a situation
he hadn't chosen, a situation she'd thrust upon him in her
blind rush to get something she wanted.

He leaned forward and regarded her intently. "Let's
forget the whole marriage thing for a minute. There's a
safety issue here for you and the baby. You need to come
back to my place, Helen. Now's not the time for you to
be living alone."

"I'll be fine," she insisted.

"You won't even consider it?" he asked in frustration.

"No."

"Then let me move into your place," he suggested.

She gave him an incredulous look. "I think you're missing the point. I'm trying to pull off a clean break."

He actually smiled at that. "And I've already told you
that's not going to happen. Right now, the only thing
you're going to accomplish is knotting my muscles up
like pretzels."

She frowned. "How am I going to do that?"

"Have you tried spending the night in the front seat of
a car?"

She stared at him incredulously. "What? Are you crazy?
You're actually telling me you're going to sleep in your car
in front of my house?"

"You're not giving me a choice. My back will have
kinks in it for months after being out there last night. I'd
prefer not to repeat the experience, but until Brad's in custody or you and I are married and living together, then I
have to keep an eye on you somehow."

"Oh, for heaven's sake," she complained. "You know you're being ridiculous, don't you?" Still, she had to admit that it was rather sweet of him to care that much.

"I don't see it that way," he said. "Nothing is happening to you or the baby on my watch."

Her gaze clashed with his, but he didn't flinch. "You're serious, aren't you?" she said, resigned.

"You bet."

"Fine. I'll come back to your place, but I'm staying in the guest room."

He shrugged. "Up to you."

Apparently satisfied, he stood up and headed to the door, then turned back. "By the way, the wedding's the last Saturday of the month. Dana Sue and I've agreed on that much. We'll hold the ceremony in the park and the reception at Sullivan's. I've made all the arrangements."

He was gone before she could react. She wasn't sure which made her more furious, that he'd had the gall to make plans without her, that he'd involved one of her best friends, or that he didn't seem to care what her reaction was. He just assumed she'd go along with them.

She was still seething with indignation over that when Dana Sue and Maddie breezed in, armed with bridal magazines, color swatches and albums of floral arrangements. Obviously they'd joined forces with Erik.

"Since you didn't show up at the spa, we went ahead and narrowed down the choices," Dana Sue said cheerily. "It'll save time. We only have three weeks to pull this off if you're going to be your fashionable, svelte self. After that, your body will start to change and your dress might require too many last-second alterations."

"So, you chose the date based on my dress size?" she

asked incredulously. "That may be even more absurd than the idea of us getting married at all."

"Sweetie, I think that ship has sailed," Dana Sue said. "Erik's pretty determined."

"Since when is this wedding all about what Erik wants?" Helen asked petulantly.

"Having a baby was all about what *you* wanted. Seems fair he gets a turn," Dana Sue replied. "Besides, he seems a little more into it than you are. I've said it before, but I'll say it again—maybe you ought to get with the program."

"I'm getting a little sick of all you pushy people telling me what to do!" Helen snapped. "If there's going to be a wedding—and I haven't yet said there will be—then *I* will make the decisions."

She reached for the magazine with the most little yellow Post-its sticking out. "What have you marked in here?"

"Gowns," Maddie said eagerly. "There's a Vera Wang in there that would look fabulous on you." She gave Helen a sly glance. "And the shoes pictured with it are to die for."

"Show me," Helen commanded. They were finally beginning to talk her language. There was nothing like buying an outrageously expensive pair of shoes to improve her mood, though given the week she was having, she might need to buy a few dozen pair.

Tess was hanging over Erik's shoulder as he sketched out the wedding cake he had in mind for his own reception. It had the advantage of being something that could go from three tiers to five or more, depending on just how persuasive Dana Sue and Maddie were with Helen. If she got on board, the guest list could grow. If she didn't, well, three tiers was as small as he intended this cake to be.

Anything smaller would look as if they'd picked it up at the grocery store.

"Those will be orchids?" Tess asked of the flowers he'd drawn flowing down one side of the simple cake.

He nodded. "That's what I was thinking. Do you like it?"

"Very elegant," she said. "Like Helen." She gave him a knowing look. "You don't seem very happy for someone who's about to get married."

"It's complicated," he said, which was an understatement if ever he'd uttered one. So far, the bride was still digging in her heels and refusing to marry him at all, though Dana Sue had told him last night that Helen had found some shoes she liked.

"The wedding dress came in a close second," she'd said. "I think with a little more coaxing we can get her over to Charleston to try it on. They're holding it for her. Thank goodness, she's the size of the sample, so we won't have to wait for it to be custom-tailored."

"Maybe we should forget about a formal wedding," Erik had suggested. "Just do a civil ceremony."

"Absolutely not!" Dana Sue had declared. "Helen might balk and complain about all this, but she'll never forgive us, herself or you if she doesn't have the wedding of her dreams, even if it is on short notice and under duress."

"It will hardly be the wedding of her dreams if she's fighting us every step of the way," Erik said.

"Which is why you need to get busy and work your magic on her," Dana Sue told him. "Underneath all this belligerence and rebellion, she loves you, Erik. She's just scared to admit it, because she's afraid she's trapped you into marrying her. It's time for you to correct that impression."

"I'm not sure I can," he'd said, but the truth was, he wasn't any more ready than Helen to put his heart on the line. The two of them were one hell of a pair, both filled with enough doubts, insecurities and bullheadedness to take up a week's worth of Dr. Phil episodes.

When he snapped back to the present, Tess was looking at him with concern. "You should tell her how you really feel," she advised him, almost as if she'd been reading his thoughts. "Deep in your heart, you love Helen. Anyone can see that."

"But despite what Dana Sue thinks, Helen's not in love with me," he said, not denying Tess's claim about his own feelings. "She's made that clear."

Tess rolled her eyes. "Are all men such idiots, I wonder."

Erik frowned at her. "Meaning?"

"The woman is so crazy about you she glows when you're in the same room."

"I think she's glowing because she's pregnant," he said before he remembered that Tess hadn't been told that part of the story.

Now her eyes lit up. "A baby," she repeated with wonder. "But that is perfect. It will all work out, Erik. If she's denying her love for you, it's only because her hormones are all over the place. I was the same way with both my pregnancies. I loved Diego one minute and hated him the next. It's a miracle he put up with me, much less stuck around to go through it a second time."

Erik didn't think Helen's hormones had anything to do with her determination not to marry him. He was pretty sure she'd made that decision way back when her head had been clear and her hormones were behaving normally.

Unfortunately, Helen was stubborn. Once she made a

decision, any decision at all, she clung to it, no matter how wrongheaded it might be.

Fortunately, she'd met her match in him.

"You're stressing me out," Helen declared as Dana Sue and Maddie dragged her into a Charleston boutique that overflowed with designer wedding gowns. "I'm not supposed to be under any stress at all. You know that. My doctor is going to be furious with you."

Maddie gave her a chiding look. "We're here now. Just relax and enjoy yourself. You love to try on clothes."

"I love to try on clothes I'm going to wear," Helen corrected. "I am not going to wear a wedding dress, because there is not going to be a wedding."

"Oh, give it up," Dana Sue said impatiently. "That line is getting old. You're getting married in less than three weeks. You may as well look beautiful even if there are only fourteen wedding guests there to see you walk down the aisle."

Helen frowned. "You've invited fourteen people to this wedding without even consulting me?"

Maddie and Dana Sue exchanged a look that Helen couldn't quite interpret.

"We assumed you'd want me, Cal and the kids there," Maddie said. "Well, maybe not the baby, since he's fussy. I think Jessica Lynn could be a flower girl if she doesn't have to walk too far. She's still a little unsteady."

"And Ronnie, Annie and I will be there," Dana Sue added. "Plus Tess and Diego, Karen and Elliott and Barb. That should do it." She gave Helen a knowing look. "Unless you'd like something more elaborate. We could arrange for your mother to fly up from Florida, no problem. And

of course, you know just about everyone in town, plus all
the lawyers, judges and clients you've worked with. Say
the word and we'll turn this into a full-blown event."

Helen was about to tell them what they could do with
their guest list when a tall, elegant woman in a simple designer suit and Manolo Blahnik shoes came out of the back
to greet them. She beamed at Helen.

"You must be the bride," she said at once. "Your friends
described you perfectly. I have several dresses that will
look amazing with your figure. Shall we get started?"

Helen wanted desperately to balk, but there was something about being in this tastefully decorated salon with its
silk-upholstered antique chairs, soft lighting and bouquets
of fresh flowers that awakened a long-buried dream. Like
a lot of little girls, she'd imagined her wedding down to the
last detail, from the flowers and candles on the end of each
pew in the church to the swell of organ music as she made
her entrance. Up 'til now the only trips she'd made to a
bridal salon had been for Maddie and Dana Sue's first
weddings. It hadn't been the same. A tiny part of her had
yearned for a day like today when it was *her* turn.

Over the years the dream had been refined and simpli-
fied. The pearl-encrusted dress she'd once imagined had
evolved into a sheath of shimmering satin. The elaborate
flower arrangements had given way to single sprays of
delicate white orchids. The setting had moved from the
church she rarely attended to the gazebo in the town park
with the azaleas in full bloom, the lake sparkling with sun-
shine and swans gliding across the water.

Eventually, though, the dream had faded altogether.
She'd convinced herself there would never be a wedding,
just as she'd resigned herself to not having children. Now,

it seemed, all of that would change—if only she gave in to Erik's insistence on moving forward with this ceremony.

But how could she do that? How could she agree to marry a man who'd never professed to love her, whose only goal was staking his claim on the child she carried? How could she marry knowing that divorce was almost inevitable?

When the clerk returned with the first gown, it was exactly what she'd imagined herself wearing down the aisle, the shimmering fabric draping low across her breasts and clinging to her hips. Helen lost focus for a minute and a powerful longing swept through her as she skimmed her fingers over the fabric.

"Where can I try it on?" she asked, aware of the conspiratorial smiles Maddie and Dana Sue exchanged. She glared at them. "Don't get any ideas. It doesn't mean anything."

"Of course not," Maddie murmured, but her eyes were filled with triumph.

A few minutes later Helen walked out of the tiny dressing room to stand in front of the triple mirror. The dress's hemline in front came just barely to her ankles, showing off the shoes the clerk had persuaded her to try. In back, there was a short, flowing train. In it she looked as slender and delicate as a calla lily.

The clerk approached and added a simple, twisted band of matching silk that secured a veil to her hair and suddenly she was the bride of her dreams. Staring at her reflection in the mirror, she was enchanted. She swallowed hard, fighting the allure of it, as tears stung her eyes.

"You want to do this," Maddie whispered, coming to her side. "You know you do. The whole thing, with lots of guests and your mom here."

Helen tore her gaze from the mirror to meet Maddie's eyes. "But I want it to be *real*," she said, a catch in her voice.

"It *is* real," Dana Sue said, joining them. She gave Helen a wry look. "Maybe the proposal left a little to be desired—"

"It left a *lot* to be desired," Helen interrupted. "It was a command, not a proposal at all."

"My point is," Dana Sue said impatiently, "that doesn't mean the wedding and the marriage can't be everything you want them to be. You can make this work, sweetie. I know you can."

Maddie nodded. "Have you ever known a Sweet Magnolia not to do whatever it takes to get exactly what she wants? I know you want Erik. Despite how this started, you love him. Take a risk and admit it."

Helen shook her head. "I don't think I can. I've messed up too badly. How will he ever be able to trust me again? Without trust, what kind of relationship can we possibly have?"

"You'll do what you and Maddie told Ronnie and me to do when we got back together after he betrayed me," Dana Sue said. "You'll earn back his trust one day at a time. Erik is offering you a lifetime to do that. That's a pretty good deal when you think about it."

Helen considered Dana Sue's words as she once again studied her reflection in the mirror. If she said yes, she could be the bride she'd always wanted to be. If she said yes, she had a chance at least to have the family she'd wanted, as well. She'd already risked a lot to get to this point. Surely she could take one more risk to have it all.

Drawing in a deep breath, she turned to the clerk. "I'll take the dress," she said in a steady voice.

"You don't want to see the others?" the clerk asked,

clearly stunned that any woman would seize the first wedding gown she'd tried on.

"I want this one," Helen confirmed. It seemed there were a few decisions she could still make impulsively, after all. Now she just had to pray she wouldn't live to regret it.

21

After dropping off the packages from her shopping trip, Helen decided it was time to visit with Caroline Holliday. She'd been calling the hospital daily to check on her and had even spoken to her once on the phone, but she'd been putting off seeing her in person. She wanted to blame the omission on the chaos of her life ever since Erik had found out about the baby, but that was too easy. The truth was she hadn't wanted to see firsthand the violence that Brad was capable of. It would make his threats against her too real.

To everyone's frustration he still wasn't in custody. She wanted to believe he'd taken off for good, left the country, perhaps, but she couldn't count on that.

Maddie, who'd insisted on coming home with her so she wouldn't be in the house alone, eyed her warily. "You look like a kid who's just had a treat and knows it's now time for some yucky medicine. What's going on?"

"I need to drive to Regional Hospital to see Caroline," she said. "I'm not looking forward to it."

"I'll ride with you," Maddie said.

"There's no need," Helen said, then noticed the stubborn set of Maddie's jaw.

"Did I imply you had a choice?" Maddie inquired sweetly. "If we're going, let's go. I'll call Cal and let him know where we're headed."

"This is ridiculous," Helen grumbled. "Brad hasn't come near me since that day he followed me to the office."

Maddie's eyes widened. "Brad followed you? Did you tell anyone? Where was the sheriff's deputy who's supposed to be keeping an eye on you?"

"The sheriff doesn't have enough manpower to watch me twenty-four/seven," Helen said.

"Then you need to hire private security," Maddie told her.

"I'm not getting a bodyguard. Besides, it was only one time. I haven't seen him since. He's probably long gone."

Maddie frowned. "You don't believe that any more than I do."

"Debating this isn't accomplishing anything," Helen said. "Let's just go."

"Fine," Maddie said, but in a way that suggested the subject wasn't finished.

After leaving Maddie in a waiting room at the hospital, Helen was startled to find a deputy stationed outside Caroline's door. She introduced herself, then asked, "Have there been more problems with her ex-husband?"

"No, I'm just here as a precaution. The family hired me. Her son didn't want to take any chances 'til Mr. Holliday's in custody."

Helen nodded. "I can understand their concern."

She tapped on the door, then walked into the room. It was filled with afternoon sunlight and too many flowers. From a chair in the corner, Caroline looked up when Helen entered and gave her a wobbly smile. Given the yellowing bruises on her face and the cuts on her jaw and cheeks, it was a poignant effort. Helen had to blink back tears.

"How are you?" she asked, crossing the room to drop a light kiss on Caroline's battered cheek.

"Glad to see *you* in one piece," Caroline replied. She shook her head. "I hope you're being careful, Helen. I had no idea Brad was capable of anything like this. He'd never laid a hand on me before. He rarely even yelled when he was angry. When he came to the house the night I got back from my sister's, I let him in. I thought he just wanted to talk or to pick up some of his things. Instead, he hit me before the door was even closed. He didn't stop 'til one of the neighbors heard me scream and ran over."

She swallowed hard and met Helen's gaze. "He had a gun," she whispered. "I have no idea where or when he got it, but I think he was planning on using it to…" She shuddered. "If my neighbor hadn't come when he did…"

"It's okay," Helen said. "It's over and you're okay."

"It won't be over and I won't feel safe until he's locked up," Caroline said. "You shouldn't, either." She clutched Helen's hand. "Please be careful. Promise me."

"I won't take any chances," Helen promised, especially now that she knew about the gun. She'd deluded herself into thinking she'd be a match for Brad in a physical confrontation, but the gun changed everything. Her hand went protectively to her stomach. From now on she would swallow her stupid pride and take all the protection that was offered.

Erik was chopping vegetables for a hearty stew when Dana Sue returned from the shopping trip to Charleston. He'd been on pins and needles since she'd left with Helen and Maddie, wondering if Helen had balked yet again about going forward with this wedding. As determined as he was, he hadn't quite figured out how to get her down the aisle if she really refused to go.

Ever since she'd moved back into his place, she'd been quiet and distant, speaking to him only when he forced the issue and then in a tone icy with disdain. Since he wasn't especially cheerful himself, he'd let it pass, but the tense atmosphere couldn't be good for her or the baby. If it kept up, he might have to back down and let her go, if only for the sake of the pregnancy. He knew from his own background and from Dana Sue's fierce warning that stress was dangerous for Helen, especially at this early stage of the pregnancy. The last thing he wanted was to contribute to anything that could lead to a miscarriage. Not only would it devastate Helen, but him, as well.

For now he studied Dana Sue's expression and tried to gauge how the trip had gone. She was giving away nothing.

"Well?" he finally prodded. "Are you guys still speaking? Did she burn down the bridal salon when she figured out where you were taking her? What?"

Dana Sue's lips twitched, then curved in a full-fledged smile. "She bought a gown."

"A wedding gown?" he asked, stunned. "Really?"

Dana Sue shook her head. "You really don't know anything about women at all, do you?"

"Meaning?"

"Once she put on the perfect dress, the one she'd been dreaming about her whole life—well, her entire adult life, anyway—it was a done deal. She wasn't going to turn her back on that."

"So this is all about giving her a chance to wear a dress she likes?" He wasn't sure how he felt about that. Maybe he should just be grateful that it meant she'd at least walk down the aisle.

Dana Sue patted his cheek. "Don't pout. On the surface this might be all about the dress, but she would never in a million years get married if she didn't want to. She's spent her entire professional career handling nasty divorces. She would not go into a marriage if she didn't think she could find some way to make it last. It wouldn't matter how much any of us pushed her, you included."

A tiny spark of hope flared inside him. Maybe they could get past her antagonism and his anger about her deception, after all.

"Would you mind a word of advice?" Dana Sue asked.

"We both know you're going to give it, so why ask?" he teased.

"Sometime before the day of the wedding, you might consider a real proposal. I don't think you want her to spend the rest of her life remembering you demanded she marry you. It kind of takes the romance out of it."

"This isn't about romance," Erik reminded her.

Dana Sue leveled a look straight into his eyes. "Isn't it?"

"Look, there's a baby involved," he said. "That's all it's about." Maybe he was being stubborn, maybe it was about saving his pride, but he refused to admit to anything more than his determination to be a part of his baby's future.

She shook her head and gave him a pitying look. "You are so dense. You love the woman. Tell her before it's too late. It'll make all the difference, Erik, for both of you."

He frowned. "Too late for what? Do you think she's going to back out at the last minute?"

"No. I think if Helen goes through with this ceremony without hearing those words, she's going to have doubts about your feelings for years to come, no matter how often you say them after the fact. She needs to hear them now, Erik. She needs to know this isn't all about you making sure you have legal rights to your child."

"But—"

"Listen to me," Dana Sue said. "For all of her success and all of the respect she's earned in the courtroom, when it comes to love, Helen's as insecure as anyone else. She's never really opened her heart to anyone except her mom, Maddie and me. Believe me, Maddie and I had to work for her trust, too, even way back in elementary school when we first met. She was already scarred from her dad dying and her mom having to struggle so hard."

"But Helen's the one who forced this to be about custody," he retorted. "She's the one who was going to deny me the chance to be with my own child. I had to do something."

"You're absolutely right," Dana Sue agreed a little too readily. Her gaze clashed with his. "Is being right going to keep you warm at night?"

Erik thought about that over the next few days, but every time he tried to broach the subject of his feelings with Helen, the words lodged in his throat. He simply couldn't get past the depth of her betrayal and his own fear of risking his heart again.

And after each failed attempt to open up and express his emotions—as tangled and confused as they were—he noticed that Helen seemed to withdraw a little further. They were like strangers living under the same roof, not at all like two people who were to be wed only two weeks from now, or two people who'd been sharing intimate, spectacular sex only a few weeks ago.

Deep down, Erik knew that someone was going to have

to break this impasse or they were doomed, but for the life of him, he couldn't summon up the courage to be the one.

On more than one occasion, as he lay alone in his bed at night with Helen just down the hall, he wondered if they shouldn't call off the ceremony, but then he thought of his child and his resolve returned. He would see this through for the baby's sake. And maybe someday, somehow, he and Helen would find their way back to each other.

The wedding definitely wasn't a scene out of *Brides* magazine. Oh, the setting by the lake was spectacular. Just as Helen had envisioned, there were plenty of flowers in full bloom, even though it was well after azalea season, the swans were gliding across the water and the fourteen guests—she hadn't bent and allowed her friends to make a bigger production of the ceremony—all seemed to be disgustingly pleased. Cal and Maddie were holding hands. Dana Sue had her arm linked through Ronnie's. And Annie was stealing besotted glances at Ty.

In contrast, Helen stood stoically beside Erik, wishing she were in some wedding chapel in Las Vegas with an Elvis impersonator as the minister. It would have been more fitting, given what a joke this ceremony was.

More than once she'd thought Erik was about to open up to her and share his real feelings. Even if he'd shouted at her some more, it would have been better than the grim determination and silence that greeted her each morning across the breakfast table. She'd almost forced the issue, but her courage had failed her. She was disgusted with herself about that, too. She'd faced down high-powered opponents in the courtroom. She'd outtalked and outnegotiated most of them. But she couldn't seem to initiate a conversation that mattered with the man she was about to marry, a man she'd cared enough about to choose to be the father of her child.

A thousand times she'd told herself to back out of this farce, but here she was, waiting to say the words that would tie her to Erik forever—or at least until one of them could wriggle out of it.

"Do you promise," the minister began.

It was all so much *blah-blah-blah* as far as Helen could tell. Still, she said, "I do," when it was called for because anything else would cause a scene no one in town would forget for the next century.

His own vows were spoken with only slightly more enthusiasm.

And then it was over and their small group was moving on to the reception at Sullivan's that Dana Sue insisted they have. Erik had even baked one of his spectacular wedding cakes with a vanilla fondant frosting and a profusion of white orchids spilling down the sides. When Helen saw it, she almost burst into tears. Somehow he'd seen into her heart and gotten the cake exactly right.

For the first time since he'd found out about the pregnancy, Erik looked at her with something other than anger or cool indifference.

"What's wrong?" he asked, actually looking worried. "Do you feel okay?"

Swiping at a tear that leaked out, she could only nod.

"Is it the cake?" He followed the direction of her gaze. She nodded. "It's so beautiful."

His expression softened. "Wedding cakes are my specialty. How could I make ours anything less than perfect?"

Then, to her dismay, she burst into tears, mentally blaming her reaction on hormones and not the sweetness of his gesture. Erik took her hand in his and dragged her into the kitchen, then pulled her into his arms. She felt a sense of relief out of all proportion to the embrace. Maybe he didn't hate her, after all.

"It's okay," he said, awkwardly patting her back. "It's going to be okay, I swear it."

"How can it be? I've made such a mess of things. No marriage is supposed to start like this."

She felt his chest heave with a sigh.

"I've done my share of idiotic things lately, too," he confessed. "I'm sorry."

She looked up at him, seeing the regret on his face even through the blur of tears in her eyes. "I never meant to hurt you or make you angry," she told him.

"Me, neither," he said. He touched her cheek, wiped away the dampness. "Let's just start from today and see how things go, okay? Can we try to do that?"

"You sound as if there's all the time in the world to figure things out."

"By my calculations we have just over six months 'til the baby comes," he said. His lips twitched with the faint beginnings of a smile as he added, "Since one of us has an obsessive-compulsive personality, surely that's enough time to reach a few conclusions about where we go from here."

Helen recognized an olive branch when it was extended to her. "Deal," she said, holding out her hand.

Erik ignored her hand and settled his mouth on hers, instead. It was the first time he'd kissed her since he'd found out about the baby. The kiss was a reminder that not everything was bad about this predicament they were in. Desire blossomed inside her like the promise of a new beginning, but before she could let it sweep her away, she remembered something else, and a sob caught in her throat.

"What?" Erik asked.

"We're not even going on a honeymoon," she whispered. Not taking advantage of the one thing between them that was so right seemed like a terrible way to begin their life together.

"I wasn't sure you'd want to be alone with me," he admitted, then grinned. "But I took a chance, anyway."

Her eyes widened. "What kind of chance?"

"I booked us a suite in Paris for a few days."

Her mouth dropped open and she stared at him in wonder. "Paris? How did you know I've always wanted to go there?"

He laughed at that. "Wasn't a shopping trip to Paris supposed to be your reward if you met your goals in that deal you had going with Maddie and Dana Sue a while back?"

"You knew about that?"

"You have no idea the things I know," he said. "So, do you want to go or not?"

"I have court on Monday morning," she lamented.

He shook his head. "No, you don't. Barb spoke to the judge and rescheduled, just in case you said yes. She moved all your appointments for the rest of the week, as well. We'll come back on Thursday and you can do a little catch-up in the office on Friday and you'll have the whole weekend to recover from jet lag. How does that sound?"

"It sounds amazing!" she said, clasping her hands behind his head and giving him a kiss. "Let's do it."

Just then Dana Sue stuck her head into the kitchen and grinned. "You know about Paris?" she guessed.

Helen nodded.

"I thought that would make you happy."

"Were you in on it?" Helen asked her.

"It was Erik's idea," Dana Sue said. "He simply asked me what I thought. I just told him I hoped he had a huge limit on his credit card."

Helen bristled. "He won't need it. I have mine."

Erik shook his head. "We're married now. I can buy you a couple of those fancy blouses you love so much." His eyes lit up. "Maybe even some sexy lingerie."

Annie stepped into the kitchen just as he said that and Dana Sue made an elaborate show of covering her daughter's ears and elbowing Ty back out of the kitchen.

"Mom!" Annie protested, standing her ground. "I know guys like sexy lingerie." She grinned at Erik. "I'd love to see the look on your face when you go shopping for it, though."

"I'll be off at Le Cordon Bleu taking a cooking class," he said.

"You're supposed to do things *together* on your honeymoon," Annie scolded.

Erik winked at her. "Can you see Helen in a cooking class?"

"About as easily as I can see you in a lingerie boutique," Annie teased. "Come on. You have to stick together. Promise me. I want pictures."

Helen listened to the banter with a sense of wonder. It was surprisingly relaxed and normal, almost the way it had been between Erik and her before he'd found out about the baby. Maybe they could recapture that connection again, after all.

"How was the wedding?" Frances asked when Karen and Elliott got home that evening.

"Tense," Karen said. "But something happened during

the reception. I don't know what, but things seemed to be better." She turned to Elliott. "Did you notice that?"

He shrugged. "I wasn't paying much attention to Helen and Erik," he said. "I had other things on my mind."

Suddenly Frances was on her feet and bustling around the living room gathering up her things. "I'll see you two tomorrow," she said.

Karen frowned. "Don't run off. Stay and have some wedding cake. I brought a piece home for you."

Frances winked at Elliott. "I'll have it at home with a nice cup of tea. You two have more important things to do."

"No, we don't," Karen protested. "We're just going to sit here and unwind."

"Enjoy yourselves. That's what I'm going to do at my place—unwind. Mack and Daisy were a handful tonight. I'm a little tired."

Karen regarded her worriedly. "Were they too much for you?"

"No, of course not," Frances said. "Good night."

She was out the door before Karen could ask any more questions.

"That was odd," she said to Elliott. "She loves to stay and hear all about whatever we've been doing. I really hope the kids didn't wear her out."

"I think she was just trying to be subtle."

"Subtle?"

"She knew I wanted to have you all to myself," he explained.

Karen met his gaze and suddenly she knew what was on his mind, what had been on his mind for weeks now. "This is about you and me, isn't it?"

"Let's sit down," he said, drawing her to an easy chair

and pulling her onto his lap. "I couldn't stop thinking about us today."

"That's just because we were at a wedding. Everyone feels a little misty and romantic at a wedding, even one as rushed and crazy as this one."

"Does that include you?" he asked. "Did you give any thought to where we're headed?"

"I thought we'd agreed to move slowly," she said, though her pulse was racing in anticipation.

He traced the outline of her lips. "I've changed my mind. I know what I want. I want us to be a family, Karen. I don't want you to have to struggle anymore. If we're partners, I can share things with you, take some of the burden off your shoulders. I love your kids as if they were my own. I'd even like to adopt them, if it could be worked out and it was something all of you wanted."

The picture he painted held tremendous allure, but she was still hesitant. She knew her feelings for him were deep, that it might even be love. And she trusted that his feelings for her were solid and true. The kids adored him. Frances, the closest thing she had to a mother, approved. So why was she hesitating?

Ironically, it was because of one of the things she'd so admired about him—his attachment to his family. Staunch Catholics, they were unhappy that she'd been divorced and had made no pretense about their disapproval. She'd seen it written all over his mother's face and his sisters' when she and Elliott had shown up at his niece's birthday party.

"Your family won't be happy," she said at last. "And I can't bear to be the cause of a rift between you."

"I'll deal with my family," he stated. "They'll come around."

"Elliott, my being divorced strikes at the very core of their beliefs," she reminded him. "I should have anticipated that before I even met them. So should you."

"You could have your marriage annulled," he suggested.

"I'm not Catholic," she reminded him. "I wasn't married in the Catholic church. It was a civil ceremony."

"Then the church won't even recognize it as a marriage, anyway," he said. "Look, I don't know all the church law on this, but it doesn't matter to me. I love you. You're the woman I want to spend the rest of my life with. We'll work it out. We can meet with a priest and he'll tell us what needs to be done."

He made it sound so simple, but there was one thing he wasn't considering, the one thing that mattered most to her. "I won't do anything that will suddenly turn my children into bastards," she said fervently. She met his gaze. "I won't *do* that to them, Elliott. I won't. As useless as their father has turned out to be, he *was* their father. They were legitimate. I grew up not having a clue who my father was. It made me feel unwanted and ashamed. My mother abandoning me, emotionally at first and then physically, only added to that. I never felt good enough. I know now that I am a good, decent person, but I had to fight to accept that. I don't want my kids to ever struggle with that kind of insecurity."

"But they'll have *me*," Elliott said, his hand on her cheek, the touch meant to be reassuring. "Together, we'll see to it that they know who they are, that they're loved and respected and cherished. If we can work it out, I'll even legally adopt them. It won't be the same for them as it was for you, I promise."

Karen wanted to believe it could be that way, wanted to

believe she hadn't come this close to finding the man of her dreams, only to have him slip away.

"We can talk to the priest," she said at last. "I'll listen to what we'd have to do to be married in your church and to win your family's approval. That's as much as I can do for now."

His eyes filled with relief. "Then we're engaged?"

"No," she said adamantly, then tempered her tone at the flash of hurt in his eyes. "Maybe engaged to be engaged."

A smile tugged at his lips. "That'll do for now. It will all work out," he said with a certainty she was far from feeling.

She recalled the condemnation in his mother's eyes when she'd realized Karen was divorced. His sisters had been kinder, but no more enthusiastic about the relationship. Karen knew that winning them over was going to be an uphill battle.

Then she looked into Elliott's eyes and saw the love shining there and thought that maybe, just maybe, it was a battle worth fighting.

Helen returned from Paris with seven new pairs of shoes, six new designer suits and a whole suitcase filled with sexy French lingerie. She also came home with new hope for the future of her marriage. The honeymoon had been a brief, but idyllic four days. She'd even learned to make a roux at the exclusive culinary school, though when she would ever need to do that escaped her. It had been fun, though, seeing Erik in his element. And as Annie had insisted, they'd come home with pictures. Hundreds of them, it seemed, including one of a red-faced Erik amid a dozen mannequins dressed in lacy bras and panties.

Right this minute, those pictures were spread out over table on the patio at The Corner Spa as Maddie and

Dana Sue pored over them. Helen ignored their envious sighs as she held out a foot and admired one of her new pairs of shoes, high-heeled mules with a pointed toe in a leather so soft it felt like butter. She figured she only had a few more weeks before she'd be too ungainly to walk in shoes like these.

Maddie glanced over and caught the direction of her gaze. "Did you do anything over there besides shop for shoes?" she inquired.

"Of course we did. You're looking at the pictures to prove it." She grinned wickedly. "And there were quite a few things we did that I don't care to discuss. There are no pictures of any of that."

"So things are good again between the two of you?" Maddie asked, her eyes filled with concern.

"Not perfect, but improving day by day," Helen replied. "It'll take a while before Erik trusts me again, and I'm not sure how things are going to be after the baby arrives."

Dana Sue frowned. "What do you mean by that?"

"He told me from the start we could end the marriage then if that's what I wanted," she said, her voice hitching despite her efforts not to think that far ahead.

"He told you that because you were so determined to raise the baby on your own," Dana Sue said with exasperation. "Erik loves you."

"He's never said that," Helen said. "Not to me."

Dana Sue sighed. "I told him that was going to come back to haunt him," she muttered. "Look, while he's working on the whole trust thing, maybe you need to try to take a few things on faith."

Maddie gave Dana Sue a wry look. "You're talking to a woman who sees things as black or white."

"Funny," Dana Sue said, her gaze pinned on Helen. "I always thought she was a woman who understood that actions speak louder than words. How many times have you told a client not to listen to all the sweet words her lying, cheating husband utters, but to watch what he does?"

Helen had no idea what to say to that, so she gathered up her photos and stood up. "I need to get to the office. Barb says my calendar's jammed starting Monday and there's a pile of messages, even though I was gone less than a week. I need to make a dent in all that today."

Maddie looked alarmed. "Don't you dare try to do too much on your first day back. A whirlwind overseas trip is hard enough on your body. You don't need more stress."

"It's just one day," Helen reminded her. "I'll have the whole weekend to recuperate while Erik's busy at the restaurant."

"I'm just saying—" Maddie began, but Helen cut her off.

"I know what you're saying," she said, bending down to give her friend a hug. "And I love you for worrying, but I won't do anything foolish, I promise."

"Okay, then," Maddie said. "But I'm calling your office later. Barb will tell me if you're misbehaving."

"Only if she wants to lose her job," Helen retorted as she picked up her briefcase and headed toward the patio exit, rather than going through the building.

"Hold it," Maddie hollered after her. "You need to go through the spa. Elliott's going to walk you to your office."

"I saw him when I came in. He's already with a client," Helen said. "I'll be fine."

Maddie frowned. "Helen, please. It's still not safe for you to go anywhere alone."

For a brief flash the image of Caroline as she'd last seen

her appeared in her mind, along with a reminder of the promise she'd made, not just to Caroline, but to herself.

"Okay, fine, I'll get Elliott," she said, making a U-turn and heading into the spa.

"If he can't break free, I'll drive you," Maddie called after her.

Helen chafed at all this protectiveness, but she knew it was justified. She resolved to call the sheriff the instant she reached her office and demand to know the status of their hunt for Brad. If she sensed that Brad wasn't a high enough priority for them, then she was going to put her own detectives to work tracking him down. It was time for this to end.

22

With Elliott at her side, Helen walked back to her office, trying to take some pleasure in the gorgeous day. Elliott's grim demeanor wasn't helping. He obviously took his body-guard duties seriously. His gaze was directed up and down the street as they walked and he answered all her questions in monosyllables without once glancing at her. Helen finally gave up trying to have a conversation with him.

As they walked along Main Street, she spotted Ronnie inside his hardware store and waved to him. At Wharton's, she told Elliott to wait while she poked her head inside to say hello to Grace and Neville.

"I brought you something from Paris," she told Grace. "I'll bring it by later."

Grace's arms were loaded down with plates of scrambled eggs and pancakes. "You had a wonderful honeymoon, then?"

"It was amazing," Helen confirmed, knowing that half the town would be chattering away about that before the morning was out. Maybe it would put a stop to the rumors probably circulating about her walking down the aisle under duress.

Once they reached her office, she grinned at Elliott. "Your job here is done," she told him. "You've delivered me safely."

"Why don't I go inside with you?" he suggested.

"Barb's here," she said, spotting her car in the driveway. "I'll be fine."

"Okay, then. You need me to go anywhere with you, all you have to do is say the word, okay?"

"Thanks, Elliott."

As he started to jog back toward the spa, she opened the door and went inside. Barb glanced up from the phone call she was on and beamed at her, then mouthed, "Welcome back."

When Helen would have picked up her messages and gone on into her office, Barb gestured for her to wait as she wrapped up her call.

"I just wanted to alert you that there's a client waiting in your office," Barb told her. "He said it was an emergency and since you didn't have anything on your calendar for today, I told him he could come in if he didn't mind waiting 'til you got here."

"Who is he and what kind of emergency?" Helen asked, annoyed because she'd counted on having the whole day to catch up on her cases.

Barb glanced at a note on her desk. "He said his name is Bryan Hallifax."

"I don't recall a Hallifax family in Serenity."

Barb shrugged. "He didn't say if he lived here in town. I didn't recognize him, either."

"And the emergency?"

"Something about his wife threatening to take his kids away from him," she said. "She hit him with this right after he got back from a business trip and he panicked. He didn't give me a lot of details."

"Okay, whatever. I'll deal with him, but no more calls and definitely no more appointments."

"Got it," Barb said. "I'm sorry about this, but he was so frantic."

Helen gave her shoulder a squeeze. "Don't worry about it. I know what a softie you are."

When she opened to door to her office, she didn't immediately spot the man. It was only after she'd closed the door that she saw him standing in the shadows. When he turned, her heart leaped into her throat. It was Brad Holliday, his eyes filled with rage and satisfaction at having caught her off guard.

Helen instinctively started to yank the door back open and yell for Barb to call the police. But then she saw the gun in Brad's hand and froze. It was trained on her.

"Good," he said when she stepped away from the door. "You're a smart woman."

"What do you want, Brad?"

"Justice, satisfaction," he suggested, then shrugged. "We'll see how it goes."

Helen moved cautiously until she was behind her desk, where she could sit down. Hopefully the solid desk would offer some protection for the baby if Brad decided to fire the gun. Unfortunately, she'd never installed the panic button that some attorneys insisted on having on the floor beside their desks. She dealt with divorces, not criminal law.

She forced herself to look directly into Brad's eyes. They were filled with hate. Still, she managed to keep her tone even and reasonable. "Brad, don't you think you're in enough trouble after what you did to Caroline? Do you really want to make things worse?"

He gave her a wry look. "Like you said, I'm already in a lot of trouble. What's a little more? I don't have much to lose. You took everything from me."

Helen knew better than to engage in an argument with someone who wasn't thinking clearly. Some instinct, though, made her want to get through to him, maybe save him from himself.

"Brad, you know that's not true," she said quietly. "You still have plenty of money. You have your kids."

"They hate me now."

Helen knew the sons were angry, but his daughter was another story. "Your daughter doesn't hate you. She's trying very hard to believe in you, but if you do something to me, that will be it. She won't be able to ignore the truth—that you're not the man she thought you were."

His laugh was bitter. "But don't you see? I'm *not* the man she thought I was. And it's all because of you." His expression hardened. "Now I want you to know what it's like to have your life ruined." The gun in his hand wavered as he spoke, but it was still pointed at her.

Helen was beginning to doubt her ability to make Brad lower the gun, and a cold fist of fear formed in her belly. She scanned her desk looking for anything heavy enough to serve as a weapon. A crystal paperweight, an award from the bar association, could probably do some damage and it was within reach. She knew she'd only have a split second to throw it at him and pray her aim was accurate. Maybe if she kept him talking, she could get her hands on it before he realized what she was up to.

Sweat rolled down her back as she rested her hands on

top of her desk, hoping the sight of them in plain view would make him lower his guard. "Brad, you really don't want to do anything you can't take back. Why don't you put the gun down and let's talk? Maybe I can help you find a way out of this situation you're in."

"You're a helluva lot better than Jimmy Bob," he said, "but even you aren't clever enough to fix this. My life's over."

"Come on. It doesn't have to be that way. You'll serve a little time, maybe even get probation for what you did to Caroline," she said, deliberately minimizing what was likely to happen. "Then you can have a fresh start."

He shook his head. "You can't fast-talk your way out of this, hotshot."

Helen's hand had been inching toward the paperweight and now closed around it. It felt solid in her grip, but was it enough?

Just then Barb tapped on the door. Brad's head jerked in that direction and Helen took advantage of his distraction to hurl the paperweight directly at his head. It hit with a glancing blow that wasn't nearly enough to cause serious injury. He whirled around and shot without taking time to aim. The bullet splintered the wood on the corner of the desk. Outside the door, Barb screamed.

Helen dove beneath her desk, but not quickly enough. A second shot grazed her arm, sending a bolt of searing pain through her. A third shot went wild and shattered a window.

"You bitch!" Brad yelled, just as the first sirens split the air.

It took Helen a second to realize they weren't police sirens at all, but the building's security alarm, set off when the window shattered. Nonetheless, the sound was enough to make Brad bolt from the room.

Then Barb was there, helping Helen into her chair, murmuring apologies even as she used a towel she'd grabbed from their restroom and tried to stem the bleeding.

"I had no idea," she said over and over. "I'm so sorry. I should have asked more questions. God, what was I thinking?"

Helen squeezed her hand. "Barb, it's okay. How could you know? You'd never met Brad."

"But I should have been more suspicious. Everyone in town knew you were off on your honeymoon this week. The second he called for an appointment on a day you were only supposed to be catching up, I should've guessed he was up to no good."

"Barb, you can't second-guess the motives of every potential client."

"But that man almost killed you!" she said. "I'll never forgive myself for that." She glanced around, her expression panicked. "Where are the police, dammit? And the paramedics? You're bleeding!"

Just then from outside, another shot rang out, followed by a collective, horrified gasp—the onlookers who'd apparently gathered when the alarm went off.

"What happened?" Helen asked Barb, even as she rocked back and forth, clutching her bloody arm and trying to ignore the pain.

"I don't know," Barb said, pressing the towel to the wound, her expression grim. "The EMTs should be here any minute. Just take deep, slow breaths—you're hyperventilating. Come on, sweetie. Slow breaths. That's it."

"Oh, God, my baby," Helen whispered, her hand on her still-flat stomach.

"Hush now. Your baby's going to be just fine," Barb reassured her.

Finally, after what seemed an eternity, the EMTs arrived. When Barb started to move out of their way, Helen grabbed her hand and clung to it. "Don't go."

"I'm not going anywhere. Let me call Erik and I'll be right back."

"No," Helen said. "He'll just worry."

"He has a right to worry, don't you think?" Barb scolded.

Helen must have answered a hundred questions, first for the EMTs, who were insisting that she go to the hospital, then for the police, who were surprisingly tight-lipped about whether Brad was in custody or not.

It seemed like hours, but was probably no more than minutes before Erik arrived. Kneeling down in front of her, he took her hands in his.

Expecting a lecture about her recklessness, Helen was surprised when he turned the full force of his fury on the police. "Where the hell were you? Someone was supposed to be watching her at all times!"

The officer closest to them, a fresh-faced kid new to the force, winced. "The sheriff thought you all were still on your honeymoon. No one notified us you were back."

Erik turned pale. "Then this is my fault," he said, lifting his gaze to meet hers. "It's because of me you were shot."

"Don't be crazy," she began, but before she could say another word, he was on his feet and out the door. She stared after him in confusion.

"Ma'am, we need to get you over to Regional Hospital to be checked out," the EMT told her. "The wound's not deep, but I gather you're pregnant. You should probably see an obstetrician while you're there."

Helen nodded, then glanced up at Barb. "I need Erik."

"He'll be there. I'll see to it. You go with the EMTs. I'll follow. I'll call Maddie and Dana Sue, too. They'll want to know about this."

"You don't need to bother them," Helen said, but Barb merely shot her a look that said she was the one making the decisions for the moment. Helen didn't waste any more breath arguing.

Docilely, she let the EMTs carry her to the ambulance on a gurney. They managed to shield her view of all the activity still going on on the street. Maybe it was just as well. She suddenly felt drained.

Inside the ambulance, she closed her eyes and tried to block out the worry that was crowding out everything else, even the pain. She didn't understand that bleak expression in Erik's eyes right before he'd taken off, but somewhere deep inside, she knew she was responsible for putting it there. He felt guilty. She got that, no matter how misguided she thought he was. She also suspected the depth of that guilt cut to the heart of why he'd never wanted to marry or have children.

She knew suddenly and with absolute clarity that she could lose him over this. And the realization scared her to death.

Erik was mindlessly stirring a triple batch of brownie dough when Maddie and Dana Sue converged on him in the kitchen at Sullivan's. They looked a little like avenging angels, and he seemed to be the target.

Not that he was surprised. He'd known that sooner or later someone would tell them what had happened to Helen and how he'd abandoned her. He simply hadn't been able to make himself stay. Her pain, the blood, all of it had brought back too many heart-wrenching memories.

Worse than that had been the crushing fear that he would lose this wife, this baby. Even though his medical training told him Helen would be fine, he'd panicked. There was no way of getting around that. He was human. Maybe it was time they all understood that. He was nobody's hero.

"Why are you here?" Dana Sue demanded.

"Someone has to think about the restaurant," he retorted as he kept right on stirring. "We open in a couple of hours for lunch."

"Let them eat fast food or grab a burger at Wharton's," Dana Sue snapped. "That's what they did before Sullivan's existed. They can do it again for one day."

Erik frowned at her. "You don't mean that."

"I most certainly do," Dana Sue said. "Your wife was just shot by a maniac. Nobody in this town gives a damn about brownies right now. Everyone's worried sick about Helen and the baby. If you think brownies are more important, then there's something wrong with you. You should be with Helen. At the very least you should be on your way to the hospital."

"I was with her. She's in good hands," he insisted, though his pulse still jolted when he thought about how close he'd come to losing her.

"That's it?" Dana Sue said incredulously. "You spend two seconds with her, then turn her over to strangers?"

"They weren't strangers. She knew everyone in that room," he muttered defensively. And they'd all been capable of handling the crisis that had leveled him.

Maddie, who'd been silent up 'til now, finally spoke up. "Erik, you don't have any reason to blame yourself for what happened," she said, studying him intently. "And right now blame's not what's important. You need to get to the hospital and be with your wife."

Dana Sue yanked the bowl of brownie mix away from him. "Go, dammit! I'm capable of making the stupid brownies for once. I did it often enough before I hired you."

"I'll drive you," Maddie said.

A part of Erik wanted to argue. A part of him wanted to stand his ground, to hide out right here in a world that made sense to him, but deep in his gut he knew both Maddie and Dana Sue were right. His place was with Helen. He'd just lost his mind for a little while when he'd realized how close he'd come to losing her. The sense of déjà vu had been overwhelming.

"Okay, let's go," he said at last.

Dana Sue looked triumphant, but Maddie merely looked relieved.

"We'll call you from the hospital," she promised Dana Sue.

"And I'll be back in time for the dinner rush," Erik told her.

"You most certainly will not be," Dana Sue said. "Especially if they release Helen from the hospital. You'll need to stay with her. Tess and Karen can fill in. I'll call them right now and explain what's going on."

"We'll play it by ear, then," he said, which was as much of a concession as he was prepared to make.

In the car, Maddie glanced at him. "You okay?"

"I'm not the one who was shot."

"They say when you love someone, it's possible to feel their pain."

"Oh, please, spare me the psychobabble," he said. "But I understand what you're trying to say." He swiped a hand over his eyes. "When I got the call from Barb, you have no idea what went through my mind."

"Oh, I think I have some idea," Maddie responded. "I suspect it was a lot like what Dana Sue and I were thinking—What if it's more serious than Barb is saying? What if we lose her?" She met his gaze. "Am I close?"

Erik smiled, relieved to know he wasn't alone with a heavy load of guilt. "On the money."

"I imagine Barb's feeling the same thing about now," Maddie went on, "since she's the one who let Brad into Helen's office. But the truth is, all the blame should be directed at Brad. He's the one who lost his grip on reality just because his divorce didn't go the way he'd anticipated. He was the one with the gun. He shot himself when he saw the police closing in. None of that is the behavior of a rational man. Accept what he did, maybe even pity him, but then let it go. Nothing matters now except making sure that Helen and the baby are okay."

"That all sounds very mature and rational, but I still feel this overwhelming sense of guilt." The deputy's words echoed in his head. "Did you know I never thought to let the sheriff's department know we were back from Paris? If I had, there would've been someone keeping an eye on her."

"You'd just come back from an incredible honeymoon. You can be forgiven for not thinking about a threat that was made weeks ago in anger. All of us had at least some reason to believe the danger was past."

"You didn't," he corrected. "You insisted that Elliott go with her to the office."

Her lips curved slightly. "I'm a mother. I worry about everything. Ask my kids. Even though Ty's away at college, I worry about whether he's wearing a sweater when it's chilly or whether he's brushed his teeth at night or has eaten a decent meal. It's all force of habit."

"I don't imagine you call him to ask about all those things, though, do you?" Erik asked, pretty certain the nineteen-year-old star baseball prospect wouldn't take kindly to such questions from his mother.

"Are you crazy?" she asked, laughing. "He'd never come home again. I just drive Cal crazy asking *him* if he thinks Ty is doing all those things. Periodically, I catch Cal telling Ty that I've been pestering him about stuff like that. They commiserate over how nutty I am, what a *mom* I am."

Just then she pulled up in front of the emergency entrance. "You go in. I'll park the car," she told him. "Helen needs you right now more than she needs me."

"I'm not so sure about that," Erik said. "I did a fairly lousy job of handling this particular crisis."

"Maybe, but you have a lot of other things going for you, including the fact that you love her to pieces. That's what matters. Maybe you can finally tell her that."

With Maddie's words resounding in his head, he went inside to find his wife.

His *wife.* Calling her that still had the power to amaze him.

"I'm looking for Helen Whitney," he told the nurse at triage. "Or Helen Decatur. I'm not sure how she registered."

"Just married," the nurse guessed. "She couldn't decide, either. She's in cubicle eight. I think she'd be happy to see your handsome face about now. She's waiting for the obstetrician to get here."

Erik's heart sank. "Is there a problem with the baby?"

"Not that we know of. It's just a precaution after the trauma she's been through. Dr. Wilson recommended it."

Erik nodded, relieved that Emily Wilson had been on duty. At least hers would have been a familiar face for Helen. "Thanks," he said as he started toward the back.

"By the way," the nurse called out, "she's registered as Helen Whitney. Guess she took those vows seriously."

Erik couldn't stop the smile that crept across his face as he went in search of Helen. If she'd wanted to disavow their marriage because of his failure to protect her or because he'd bolted from her office, she would've stuck with her maiden name. Maybe he had one more chance to get this right, after all.

The pain medicine had made Helen groggy, but she knew the instant that Erik came into her cubicle and took the seat beside her.

Fighting to open her eyes, she managed a faint smile. "Hi. You came. I wasn't sure you would."

"Maddie and Dana Sue were pretty persuasive," he admitted.

Her smile wobbled. "Did they beat you up?" she asked, actually sounding a little worried that they might have.

He laughed. "No, they didn't need to go that far." His expression sobered. "How are you feeling?"

"Dopey. They patched up my arm."

"Any twinges with the baby?"

She shook her head. Her hand instinctively went to her stomach. "I think she's okay, but the doctor's going to make sure."

He gave her an odd look. "She?"

"Or he," she said. "Just not 'it,' okay?"

"Understood. Look, you need to rest. I'll be in the waiting room with Maddie."

He started to stand up, but Helen latched on to his hand. "No," she commanded. "Don't leave me again, please. I'm scared, Erik. Really scared. And nobody will tell me what happened to Brad. He didn't get away, did he?"

"You don't need to worry about Brad ever again."

"Why? Tell me."

"He shot himself. He's dead," he said, sitting back down beside her. He kept her hand in his, his thumb idly caressing her knuckles, his thoughts seemingly far away.

Her relief that Brad was gone lasted only a moment. "Erik?"

He looked into her eyes. "What?"

"Why did you take off back at my office? You know none of this was your fault, don't you? You weren't there. There was nothing you could have done to stop it."

"I'm not so sure about that," he said. "But Maddie convinced me that maybe there's enough blame to go around."

"But there was something more going on with you, something that went deeper than what happened today. I could sense it."

His expression shut down. "It's nothing for you to worry about," he told her. "All that matters is making sure you and the baby are okay. Close your eyes and rest 'til the doctor gets here."

When she would have probed a little more deeply, he gave her a warning look. "I mean it," he said. "Rest or I'll leave."

She sighed and closed her eyes. Maybe he thought he could stall her now, but he surely knew he wouldn't be able to stall her forever. She was a pro at interrogation, at least when she was at the top of her game. In a few days, fewer if she concentrated hard on making a quick recovery, she'd get the answers she was after.

Karen and Tess exchanged a look as Dana Sue flew around the kitchen snapping out orders. Finally Karen grabbed her by the shoulders and marched her toward a stool.

"Sit," she ordered. "You need to calm down and eat something."

"I can't eat," Dana Sue grumbled, but she accepted the dish of chicken salad Karen handed her. "Why haven't we heard anything from the hospital?"

"Probably because they don't know anything yet," Karen soothed. "I'm sure Helen is fine. Maddie would have called immediately if things were bad, so you could get over there."

"I suppose," Dana Sue said, eating a bite of the chicken salad and then another. Finally she looked up, a curious expression on her face. "This is different. What did you add to it? Dill?"

"Just a little," Karen said. "Is it okay?"

"It's fabulous."

"I was thinking of adding toasted walnuts, too, or maybe almonds. What do you think?"

Dana Sue took another bite. "Almonds, I think. I love walnuts in salads, but they're best sprinkled on the top. People need to know they're in there. Otherwise, they're liable to think they're biting down on a piece of bone. Almonds aren't quite as crunchy."

"Good point," Karen said. "Anyway, I thought it might be a nice change from the pineapple chicken salad we do now. We could rotate them seasonally or something."

"I've been thinking about that myself," Dana Sue said. "I think we ought to have a new menu each season with some of the favorites, of course, but a few new dishes as well. We'd still have specials, too, but I think change might keep our regulars coming in— You know, in case they get tired of the same old things."

"I have some ideas if you want to hear them," Karen

said, barely able to contain her excitement. At Dana Sue's nod, she pulled a stool up next to her.

"Fresh tomatoes are still available. We've never tried a tomato and buffalo mozzarella salad. Or a bruschetta. Those are terrific in warm weather and we have another couple of months of that, at least."

"It would be a change from the house salad or sliced tomatoes and onions," Dana Sue agreed. "Do you think our customers are ready for that kind of change?"

Karen nodded eagerly. "Sure. Just look at how much they loved the gazpacho. Sullivan's is known for being innovative. People can make a plain old salad or sliced tomatoes at home. They don't need us for that."

Dana Sue grinned. "Good point. Okay, what else?"

"Last summer Erik made a lot of cobblers, but what about fruit tarts instead?"

"I love it," Dana Sue said, clearly catching her enthusiasm. "He can do a wonderful pastry, then add a thin layer of custard and top it with fresh fruits and berries. They'll taste great and look fabulous if we finally get that big color-photo spread in one of the regional magazines." She studied Karen. "You're good at this. I hope I tell you that enough."

"You do," Karen said.

Dana Sue studied her. "And things are better at home now, aren't they? Your life has settled down?"

Karen nodded. "I finally feel as if I'm back in control. Elliott's helped with that. He's been a rock. Frances, too."

"Are you and Elliott getting serious?"

"He is," she admitted. "But there are complications."

Dana Sue regarded her with concern. "Oh? Anything you want to talk about?"

"No," Karen said. "I don't want to bring my problems to work, not anymore."

"Maybe you could think of it as sharing them with a friend," Dana Sue said.

"You're still my boss," Karen reminded her.

Dana Sue frowned slightly. "We're a team, Karen. You and Tess and Erik are all like family to me. Okay, it's a *work* family, but the feelings are there, just the same. I care about what's going on with you, I really do. I know it might not have seemed that way a few weeks ago, but even when Erik and I were stressed out and annoyed because you weren't here, we still cared about you."

Tears stung Karen's eyes. "I know, it's just that I need to know I can solve my own problems. Maybe that'll change one day, but for now it's important to me."

Dana Sue reached over and squeezed her hand. "As long as you know I'm here if you need me, I can respect your need to do things your own way." She stood up. "Now we'd better get back to work or the dinner crowd will be dining on leftover cheese grits from lunch. They might be great with a slice of ham, but they sure won't go over as a main course."

Before she walked away, she turned back to Karen. "Thanks for distracting me and keeping me from climbing the walls."

"No problem. It was survival instinct."

Dana Sue winced. "I was that bad?"

"Pretty much, but not to worry. I'm sure we'll hear something from the hospital soon and you'll really be able to relax."

After that, they all fell back into their usual routine, including Tess, who'd made herself scarce while Karen had been talking to Dana Sue.

It was nearly five before the phone rang. Dana Sue grabbed it on the first ring, mumbled replies Karen couldn't hear, then hung up. But when she turned around she was smiling. "Helen and the baby are both okay. Erik and Maddie are bringing them home. They didn't even insist on her staying overnight for observation." Dana Sue grinned. "Probably because they figured they'd never hear the end of it if they tried."

"Thank God," Karen said as Tess sketched a cross over her chest.

"Amen to that," Dana Sue said. "Now, let's get busy, ladies. The hungry hordes will be here any minute. And if I haven't said it before, thank you both for pitching in and picking up the slack today. You're angels."

The sincerity in Dana Sue's voice filled Karen with happiness and pride. Only a few short months ago, she'd been on the verge of losing this job. Now she knew she was capable of making a real contribution here. And it did feel as if she'd found more than a job—she'd found a family. Add in Daisy and Mack, Elliott and Frances, and her life was full.

Erik knew he'd accused Helen of being obsessive-compulsive, but when it came down to it, where the baby was concerned, he had her beat by a mile. The thought of another pregnancy, another baby, cast a shadow over everything. Ever since the close call with Brad Holliday, he found himself watching Helen just about around the clock. He went to every doctor appointment, but he wasn't half as reassured as she seemed to be when she received a clean bill of health. He'd asked so many questions on their last visit that the obstetrician had joked that next time he'd schedule two appointments, one for each of them.

If Helen woke in the middle of the night with a craving, he saw to it she got whatever she wanted. If she looked tired, he couldn't rest 'til she was in bed or on the sofa with her feet up. He dreaded a time when the doctor might insist on complete bed rest, because he knew with absolute certainty he'd have a fight on his hands. Helen was incapable of staying still that long. Thankfully, though, she'd kept her blood pressure in check so far.

When he first saw the baby on a sonogram, the last of his anger at the circumstances of the baby's conception drained away, and he was completely captivated by this child he'd never expected to have. The power that tiny baby had over him was astounding.

They'd agreed they didn't want to know the sex ahead of time, but Erik was convinced it was a boy. Helen seemed just as convinced it was a girl. They spent hour after hour debating names. Their first list had taken up two pages. Now they'd whittled it down to ten possibilities for a boy and eight for a girl. All of it had made this baby real for him, something he'd vowed not to let happen. He hadn't wanted to start loving it too much. He hadn't wanted to start eagerly awaiting the moment when it arrived in this world.

Helen put up with his attentiveness with surprising docility. In fact, as the weeks wore on, her hard edges seemed to fade and she seemed to enjoy being pampered, even if she did regard him with curiosity when he insisted on taking care of the simplest tasks.

Finally, when she was six months along and still in apparently perfect health, she reacted as he'd expected her to react much sooner. She lost patience and openly rebelled at his protectiveness.

"Okay, enough's enough. What's going on here?" she

demanded when he'd jumped up to get the pen she said she needed to jot down notes for her closing statement in court in the morning. "You know I can walk across the room for a pen. I'm perfectly capable of getting myself a glass of water, too, even if it does mean I'll be waddling down the hall to the bathroom ten minutes later. I know Ronnie went a little crazy when Dana Sue was pregnant, and Cal almost drove Maddie insane with his hovering, so I've tried to be tolerant. But you've taken this to new heights, Erik. Why? It has to stop."

Erik shook his head. "It's not going to stop," he said tersely.

"Then I'll ask you again, why? It's not just about me, is it? Or even our baby. There's something else going on. I guessed that when you took off after Brad shot me. I let you get away with not answering me back then, but I've had it. Talk to me."

Erik wasn't entirely sure why he hadn't blurted out the story long before now. He'd hinted at it back when he'd first found out she was pregnant, but both of them had been so upset that day his comment about his already losing one baby had apparently gone right over her head.

Of course, after Sam had died, everyone had tiptoed around him, not even mentioning her name most of the time, so he'd gotten used to keeping his feelings bottled up inside.

Worse, everyone had pretended the baby had simply never existed, but she had been as real to him as if he'd held her in his arms. He'd felt her stirring in Sam's belly. Though he'd felt incredibly silly doing it, he'd sung lullabies to her and even read her stories. He knew that she kicked up a storm when Sam ate spicy food and rested peacefully at the sound of his voice.

Even now, nearly seven years later, his emotions were

nearly as raw as they'd been back then, especially lately. He gazed into Helen's eyes, saw her expectation. She was going to wait him out this time. Keeping quiet about the details of Sam's death and his child's was no longer an option, not if they were to have a prayer of making this marriage work.

"You know I was married before," he began, trying to keep his voice steady.

Helen nodded. "And she died, right?"

"Yes, she died," he said, his voice strained.

Sympathy washed over her face. "You've never said what happened. She had to be so young. Was she sick or in an accident?"

Both were natural assumptions given the age Sam had been when she'd died. Erik hesitated to voice the truth, especially with their own baby due in a few months. The timing for this revelation sucked, but it was no one's fault but his own.

"I'm not sure I ought to be telling you any of this now," he began. "It's the wrong time."

"I need to know," she said. "Please."

Still he hesitated, but her gaze remained steady. The questions clearly weren't going away. "Okay, here it is. Sam was pregnant. She went into premature labor. She started bleeding and I couldn't get it stopped. You know I was an EMT, and I was right *there*. I did everything by the book. Everyone said so."

He closed his eyes, fighting the memory or maybe trying to avoid the worry he was bound to cause her. Finally he forced himself to meet her gaze, prepared for the shock and dismay he would find there once he said the rest. "Before we got to the hospital, she'd already lost too much blood. Nothing I tried worked, and Lord knows, I tried everything. By the time the ambulance came and we got Sam to the hospital, she'd bled to death. We lost the baby, too."

He felt the same sense of helplessness now. "I know I'm making you a little nuts with my hovering, but I can't stop it, Helen. I won't."

"Oh, Erik, I'm so sorry," she whispered. "I can't even begin to imagine how painful that must have been for you."

She reached for his hand and pulled him down beside her, then placed his hand on her belly, where their baby was kicking up a storm as if aware that a point needed to be made.

"See, we're fine," she told him softly.

Erik stretched out beside her, his hand still resting on her taut stomach.

Not this time, he pleaded with God. *Don't let me lose this woman or this child.* Somewhere along the way he'd fallen in love with Helen. This unborn child, like another one, had crept into his heart. He'd started to count on them being a family. If that changed, if he lost them, he wasn't sure he'd be able to fight his way through the anguish a second time.

23

As she approached her ninth month, Helen felt like a blimp. Her feet were so swollen she couldn't wear a single pair of the dozens of outrageously expensive shoes in her closet. She'd been wearing a pair of old sneakers with no laces for two weeks now. Fortunately, given the size of her stomach, she couldn't see the disgusting things.

Indian summer had arrived with a vengeance, dragging on and on until everyone in town was grumbling that they'd be having a heat wave on Valentine's Day if it kept up. The heat only added to her misery. She was cranky and impossible, which actually seemed to be surprisingly advantageous in most of her divorce negotiations. Either the husbands or the opposing counsel or both were terrified she'd go into labor right before their eyes, or maybe they remembered their own wives' pregnancies and treated her with a fair amount of respect for her condition. She'd been winning concessions right and left lately.

She had one more court date in Charleston next week and then she'd be sticking close to home 'til the baby arrived. Even now, she was doing her best to rest a lot, primarily because Erik completely freaked out if she didn't. Now that she understood what he'd been through, she tried really hard not to add to his stress by doing anything he thought might put her or the baby at risk. And arguing with him only added to her own stress levels, something his constant blood-pressure monitoring had proved time and again.

This morning, though, she'd insisted on lumbering out of bed and walking to The Corner Spa for her meeting with Dana Sue and Maddie. For once Erik hadn't fought her. He'd showered and walked with her, depositing her at the front door with strict instructions to get a ride to her office or to call him to come and get her.

"I don't want you walking any more in this heat, understood?"

"Believe me, I'm not the least bit interested in losing another gallon of fluid by walking anywhere once the temperature climbs another couple of degrees," she told him, then walked inside where the spa's air-conditioning was pumping away. It was heavenly. She closed her eyes and took a deep breath, then headed for Maddie's office.

En route, she noticed that the spa was strangely empty. Normally at this hour of the morning, the treadmills were in use and the air was filled with the clanking of weights and the groans of protest from a couple dozen women. Today the only sound she heard was music. Even stranger, it wasn't the classical music or jazz Maddie preferred, but something from way back, something about "the cutest little baby face."

When she walked through the door to the café, the room exploded with sound.

"Surprise!"

Helen gasped, stunned that her friends had managed to pull off yet another surprise party for her so soon after her birthday. She stared at the sea of familiar faces—Maddie and Dana Sue, of course, then Jeanette, Barb, Karen, Tess and a handful of other former clients. It was when she spotted Caroline Holliday that tears sprung to her eyes. It was the first time she'd seen Caroline since the woman had left the hospital and moved to live closer to her sister, taking her two youngest children, both teenagers, with her. She'd told Helen that they hovered around her in a way that worried her.

"I know they're grieving for their dad and blame themselves for not protecting me," Caroline had said in a phone conversation a few weeks after she'd left the hospital. "They're terrified now that something will happen to me and they'll be all alone. I thought being closer to my sister and her family would help them realize that they will always have people they can count on, but it's not working."

Helen had told her about Dr. McDaniels and recommended that she contact the psychologist if things didn't improve. "She's great with teenagers. She made all the difference in the world with Dana Sue's daughter, Annie."

Now Caroline gave Helen such a huge smile that Helen just knew that things in her life were finally improving. She could hardly wait for a few moments alone with her to hear the latest. Right now, though, a dozen or more faces were watching her expectantly.

"Quick, find her a place to sit," Maddie said, taking Helen's arm. "We don't want her toppling over before she opens presents."

"Very funny," Helen said as she sank onto the chaise longue they'd brought in from the patio.

Maddie grinned at her. "You look very regal stretched out there. Okay, what's your first command? Food or presents?"

"The food better be more interesting than oatmeal, which is all Erik lets me have in the morning," she grumbled.

Dana Sue chuckled. "I was in charge of the food. What do you think?"

"Then bring it on," Helen said.

An hour later, she was stuffed from eating Dana Sue's cheese and mushroom omelet, a half-dozen miniature orange-cranberry muffins and drinking what must have been half a gallon of sweet tea. She'd lumbered to the closest restroom twice and was pretty sure it was almost time for another trip, but the lure of the pile of presents across the room was too much to resist.

"Not yet," Maddie said, catching the direction of her gaze. "We need to play at least one game."

"Baby shower games are silly," Helen said, still eyeing the huge boxes across the room. "I've always hated them."

"Nonetheless, we want you to have the total baby-shower experience," Dana Sue said. "You've waited a long time for this."

"Oh, for heaven's sake," Helen said. "Pick one and let's get it over with."

Maddie laughed. "Nice to see you've mellowed during your pregnancy."

Helen immediately shut up and dutifully went along while they played some silly guessing game about the size of her stomach and another one involving baby names, none of which would ever be pinned on her child, not if she had anything to say about it!

When they'd finished the second game and she'd made yet another trip to the restroom, Maddie declared it was time for Helen to open the gifts.

"But we all want you to know how difficult you made

things by refusing to find out the sex of the baby ahead of time," Maddie said.

Helen frowned at her. "In the old days no one ever knew. People still had perfectly successful baby showers. I'm sure you all rose to the occasion."

Dana Sue handed her the first package and read the card. "This one's from Tess," she said.

Helen fingered the elaborate yellow bow. "It's too beautiful to open."

Dana Sue rolled her eyes. "You've been wanting to get to this part for an hour. Stop dillydallying."

Helen felt a bit like an overindulged kid opening presents on Christmas morning. She smiled in delight, then tore off the bow and wrapping paper. She lifted the top on the box to find a beautiful christening dress inside. There was no mistaking that the delicate white fabric had been tucked and embroidered by hand. The attention to detail was amazing.

"My mother made it," Tess said shyly. "We wanted to give you something special for bringing Diego back to me."

Tears stung Helen's eyes. "It's exquisite," she whispered, her voice choked. "I never expected anything like this. I'd hug you if I could stand up."

Tess's eyes shone. "I'm glad you like it. My mother will be pleased."

"Tell her I am in awe of her skill with a needle," Helen said. "I want you all to come to the christening, then you can see how the baby looks in this."

"Now this one," Dana Sue said, handing her another package. "It's from Karen."

This one had three baby rompers in pale green, yellow and lilac. "I thought the lilac might be pushing it if it's a boy," Karen said. "But it was too cute. I thought you had to have it."

There were more outfits, a hand-knitted baby blanket from Frances and several more practical presents. Caroline Holliday had brought an engraved silver baby cup and matching spoon.

"I know people don't do that much anymore," she said. "But even if you never use them, they're wonderful keepsakes."

"Oh, trust me, Helen's baby will use them. There will be no tacky plastic utensils for this child," Maddie said. "That saying about someone born with a silver spoon in his mouth will fit this child perfectly. I predict he or she's going to be spoiled rotten. If Helen doesn't cater to its every whim, Erik will."

"And why shouldn't we?" Helen asked. "This is going to be one amazing baby."

"Which is why Maddie and I bought you this," Dana Sue said, struggling to fight a smile as she handed Helen another package.

When Helen opened it, she found a book advising parents on how to cope with their gifted child.

"Just in case you find you can't keep up with the little genius," Maddie teased.

Helen feigned a frown. "As if," she retorted.

"Oh, wait, there's one more thing," Dana Sue said. She went to the door and called out to Elliott, who'd made himself scarce during this ladies-only function. "Could you bring that other gift in for me?" She grinned at Helen. "It's from Ronnie and it was too big to wrap, at least in a way that wouldn't tell you right off what it is."

A moment later, Elliott came in with a huge, awkwardly

wrapped package, which he set in front of Helen. Then he went to stand behind Karen to watch Helen open it, his hand resting lightly on Karen's shoulder. Helen noticed Karen glance up at him. The girl's eyes shone with so much love it made Helen want to weep. Then again, just about everything made her want to weep these days.

Her attention returned to the gift, and she reached for the huge bow and pulled it away, then tore at the paper. Inside was a hand-carved cradle, so beautifully crafted it took her breath away. A parade of tiny ducks that almost looked alive decorated the headboard. Each spindle on the side was equally delicate. And at the foot of the cradle, a mama duck and a papa rested close together, their obviously loving gazes directed toward their brood at the opposite end of the cradle.

Everyone in the room erupted in *oohs* and *aahs* at the sight of it, Helen's gaze flew to Dana Sue. "Wasn't this Annie's cradle?" she asked.

Dana Sue shook her head. "No, we're keeping that one for her, but it's just like it. Ronnie said it was the one thing he ever did that you seemed to approve of, and so he wanted you to have one. He's been carving it for months now, ever since we found out about the baby. He knew how much you loved the one he did before Annie was born."

Yet again, Helen's eyes welled with tears. She and Ronnie hadn't always gotten along. In fact, they'd been at serious odds after he'd cheated on Dana Sue, but Helen's attitude toward him had mellowed once she'd finally seen how much he still loved Dana Sue and his daughter and the lengths he'd been willing to go to in order to get them back. That he would make something this thoughtful and amazing for her child proved that he was ready to put their differences behind them, as well.

"Warn him I'm going to kiss the daylights out of him when I see him," Helen told Dana Sue, who was beaming proudly.

"I think he's counting on it," Dana Sue said. "Just don't get too carried away or I'll have to kill you."

Helen leaned back on the chaise longue, overcome with emotion. "I don't know how to thank you all, not just for all the presents, but for sticking by me. I know I can be a pain sometimes."

"Sometimes?" Dana Sue taunted.

"Most of the time," Maddie chimed in.

"But we love you," Dana Sue added. "Always."

"And the rest of us might not be daredevil, troublemaking Sweet Magnolias, but we love you, too," Caroline Holliday told her. "And we are so grateful that you've been there for us when we've needed you."

"Amen to that," Tess said quietly.

It was the first time Helen really realized just how deeply she'd touched the lives of some of the people she'd worked for over the years. For her it had been mostly a job she was determined to do well, but for some of the women in this room, she'd actually changed their lives for the better.

And to think, there were so many more wonderful years to come.

Karen was all too aware that nothing Elliott had said and none of the overtures she'd made had accomplished anything with Maria Cruz or her daughters. Their continued disapproval of Elliott's relationship with her was starting to take a toll. Just last night they'd fought about it again when Karen had refused to attend a Cruz family gathering. Earlier in the day she and Elliott had been so close during that moment at Helen's shower when she'd opened the cradle from Dana Sue and Ronnie. He'd squeezed her shoulder in a gesture she'd known meant he was thinking of a time in the future when they would have their own child on the way, when they would be as joyous as Helen and Erik were now.

Later, though, when he'd told her about the dinner his mother had planned for that evening, Karen had balked. Nothing Elliott had said could persuade her to change her mind. Surely he had to see that things were far from perfect in their world. Sooner or later his mother would find some way to destroy what they had.

"I won't subject myself or my children to another night of being treated like second-class citizens," Karen had finally said.

"We have to keep trying," Elliott had replied reasonably. "Otherwise, what? You're going to cut them out of our lives?"

"Not *our* lives," she'd said. "Mine. They're your family. I would never ask you to avoid them."

He'd frowned at her then. "That's no solution."

"It works for me. What's the alternative? Do you have one?"

He hadn't been able to offer one and eventually he'd gone on to the dinner at his mother's house without her.

Karen knew they couldn't go on like this. Elliott was too close to his family and he loved her too much. Eventually, if they couldn't come to some kind of accord, it would tear him apart. She'd break things off with him before it came to that.

But first, maybe there was one thing she could try that she hadn't. Dressing in her one good dress after she'd taken the kids to school and day care, she spent extra time on her hair and makeup, then grabbed her purse and drove across town to the comfortable old Victorian house where Elliott and his sisters had grown up under Maria Cruz's watchful eye.

As she parked in front of the house, she could imagine what it had been like years ago. Toys had probably been strewn about the yard then, even as the grandchildren's toys were now. The swing that hung from the oak tree in the front yard looked new, but Karen guessed there had been one years ago, too.

She picked her way carefully up the sidewalk, avoiding toy trucks, a tricycle and a scattering of plastic blocks. Even as she stepped onto the front porch, the screen door swung open and Maria Cruz leveled a suspicious look in her direction. Karen would have found it daunting any other time, but today it only steeled her resolve to have it out with this maternal tyrant.

"I was hoping we could talk," she said, not looking away from those dark eyes that bore not even a hint of welcome.

"And your phone did not work?" Mrs. Cruz inquired. "I would have told you not to come."

Karen allowed herself a small smile. "Which is exactly why I didn't call first."

That seemed to startle the older woman. Eventually she shrugged. "You are here now. You might as well come in," she said grudgingly.

"Thank you," Karen said, careful not to sound victorious.

For a woman who wielded so much power in her family, Maria Cruz was surprisingly petite, almost fragile. Her hair was still thick and black and worn pulled into a severe bun at the back of her head. The style suited her stern persona, but did nothing to flatter her sharp features.

"We'll go to the kitchen," she announced, leading the

way. "I have cookies in the oven. Adelia is bringing her children by after school."

"The cookies smell delicious," Karen said. "My neighbor bakes cookies for Daisy and Mack."

Mrs. Cruz frowned. "Isn't that something you should do yourself?"

Karen tried not to take offense at the suggestion that she was somehow shortchanging her children. The woman had made it plain more than once that being employed, rather than being a stay-at-home mom, was yet another of Karen's failings. "I do sometimes, but Frances enjoys having children around to bake for, much the same as you do, I imagine."

The possibility that Karen might actually be thinking of her neighbor's needs rather than being neglectful seemed to take Mrs. Cruz by surprise. "You make a good point," she said, then waved Karen toward a chair. "Sit. I'll pour us both a glass of tea."

When she'd filled two glasses and set them on the table, she peeked into the oven, then closed the door. Finally she sat down opposite Karen and gave her a challenging look.

"Why are you here?"

"I'm sure you can guess," Karen said, deciding to be totally direct and candid. "I know you disapprove of me because I'm divorced. Maybe for other reasons, as well. But I love your son, Mrs. Cruz. You've raised him to be a wonderful, thoughtful man. And you've taught him how to love with everything in him. He holds nothing back." She looked directly into Mrs. Cruz's eyes. "He loves me."

When the woman made a disparaging sound, Karen held up a hand.

"You know he does," she insisted. "And I know it troubles you. Somehow, though, we have to make this work for

Elliott's sake. It's not fair for him to feel he has to choose between us."

"You say you love him and yet you would make him do such a thing?" Mrs. Cruz demanded, practically quivering with indignation. "What kind of love is that?"

"I'm not the one forcing him to choose," Karen said mildly. "*You* are. If you and I can't make peace, then I will walk away. He thinks we can simply coexist, if it comes to that, but I know better. For every holiday, every family celebration—your family's or ours—Elliott would be filled with sorrow that we aren't all together. Is that what you want? Do you want me gone so badly that you would make your son miserable to accomplish it?"

Mrs. Cruz's gaze faltered at that. "You are willing to leave, rather than cause problems between my son and his family?"

"I don't want to," Karen said. "He's everything I ever dreamed of in a man, but if it comes to that, yes. He loves you. He respects you. Family means everything to him. You should know, because you taught him that. I won't take that away from him, even if it means losing the best thing that ever happened to me."

For just an instant, Mrs. Cruz's expression softened. "He's a good son. Since my husband died, he's been the man of the family. We all count on him."

"I know you do. And he'll be a wonderful husband and father," Karen said. "He can be all of those things, but only if you and I can make this work."

"You're divorced," Mrs. Cruz said, her face set stubbornly. "It is a sin."

"Isn't it a sin for the father of my children to abandon me?" Karen asked her. "Isn't it a sin for him not to pay one dime of child support? Do I stay married forever to a man like that, a man who would walk away from his own children?"

Elliott's mother visibly struggled with what Karen was telling her. "He left you alone with two babies?"

Karen nodded. "It wasn't like it was for you when Elliott's father died. My husband was not well-to-do. He left no insurance as your husband did. I've worked because I have to, and I love what I do."

"The father sends no money for his children?" Mrs. Cruz asked, her expression incredulous.

Again, Karen nodded. "There was a time when I believed marriage was forever, too. I meant it when I spoke those vows, but my husband did not. After he'd gone, after I realized he was never coming back, would never be a father to his children, I filed for divorce. He wasn't a good and decent man, Mrs. Cruz. He was nothing like your son. If Elliott and I marry, it would be in your church and it would be forever. He wants to adopt my children and make them his. We would have the kind of family I've only been able to *dream* about 'til now."

She gave the older woman an innocent look. "And you would have two more grandchildren to adore you. They need you as much as they need a dad. They need aunts and uncles and cousins. I want that for them, but not at the expense of causing a rift between you and your son."

Slowly, Mrs. Cruz nodded. Her expression had softened some, but was still far from the doting gaze she reserved for her son and daughters and grandchildren. "I'll tell Elliott to bring you and the children to dinner on Sunday," she said at last.

Karen remained skeptical. "You'll give us a chance? A real one this time?"

"I want my son to be happy," she told Karen. "So do you. It seems like a place to begin."

A faint spark of hope stirred inside Karen. "Thank you."

"So you will come?" Mrs. Cruz asked, sounding surprisingly hesitant.

"We will," Karen assured her.

The gesture might not be huge, but it was enough for now. Elliott's mother might not be crazy about her or about the situation, but at least she'd accepted that they had one major thing in common: their love for Elliott.

When the contraction sent a sharp, searing pain through her belly, Helen gasped and guided the car off the road, cursing this one last case that had taken her all the way to Charleston.

No! she thought. She couldn't be going into labor, not almost three weeks early and not here on an isolated road miles from the nearest hospital. Not when she was all alone with no one around for miles. The thought of what Erik would do if anything happened to her or this baby swam through the haze of pain and made her feel stronger. She could handle this, she told herself staunchly. She had to.

Eventually the pain eased and she fumbled in her purse for her cell phone. Please, let there be a signal, she prayed as she punched in the number for Sullivan's. A moment later, Dana Sue answered.

"Thank God," Helen murmured. "It's me. I'm about twenty miles outside of Serenity. I'm on Route 522 in the middle of nowhere and…" Her voice caught on a sob. "I think I'm in labor."

"I'll get Erik," Dana Sue said at once.

As desperately as she wanted him with her, Helen could

only think of the anguish he'd suffered when he'd watched his wife die in childbirth. "Don't," she pleaded. "You can't tell him. Maybe this is just a false alarm. Those Braxton-Hicks pains, you know what I mean."

"Doesn't matter," Dana Sue said. "Erik needs to know."

Helen thought about it. "Okay, you're right, but he can't come out here, not alone, anyway. Please, Dana Sue. I know you don't understand, but I can't put him through that. If something goes wrong…"

"*Nothing* is going to go wrong," Dana Sue countered with reassuring certainty. "I'll close the restaurant and come with him myself. Don't you dare try to drive any farther, okay? And if you need me again, call my cell. We'll be there in half an hour, maybe a little longer. Less, if I let Erik drive."

"Then don't let him drive," Helen ordered, then gasped as another pain roared up and left her clutching her belly, the phone dropping, forgotten, on the floor of the car.

When she could, she smoothed her hand over her tight stomach. "I know you're impatient," she told the baby. "You're just like me that way, but could you hang on just a little longer, please? Your daddy and Dana Sue are on their way with help. You don't want to be born on the side of the road. It'll be so much nicer if you arrive in a nice, clean hospital surrounded by people who know what they're doing and who have a nice warm blanket to wrap you in."

The baby responded by sending another contraction ripping through her. God, she was as bad as Maddie. She'd felt some strange back pains earlier in the day, but she'd thought they were just the result of being cramped up in the car for the drive to Charleston. Damn her high threshold for pain! Apparently she'd been in labor for hours without realizing it.

"This is not good," she whispered, looking at her watch.

The contractions were way too close together and way too strong to be some kind of false labor. And like so many things in her life, it seemed apparent she was going to give birth in a hurry, too.

Between contractions, she managed to get out and crawl into the backseat of the car where she could lie down, albeit awkwardly.

An endless thirty minutes later, she heard a siren, then spotted dust swirling up in the distance. "Thank God," she said, gritting her teeth against another wave of pain.

Then Erik was there, barely a minute ahead of the EMTs, his face drained of all color, Dana Sue beside him looking almost as worried.

"How are you doing, sweetheart?" Erik asked in a voice thick with emotion.

As glad as she was to see him, she frowned. "How do you think?" she snapped, grabbing his hand with a grip that could have broken bones.

"Let's get you to a hospital, then," he said, his tone light, but tension radiating from him.

"I don't think there's time for that. The contractions are pretty close together."

He stared at her in confusion. "How long ago did the pains start?"

"This morning, I think."

Erik muttered a curse.

"I'm sorry," she whispered, still clinging to his hand.

"No, no, it's not your fault," he said. "You didn't know. You've never been in labor before. Sometimes those early contractions can fool you."

Two EMTs rushed over to the car, but when they tried to shoo Erik out of the way, Helen protested.

"My husband's a trained EMT," she said, her gaze locked with his. "I want him to deliver our child."

Erik looked horrified. "No. I can't. These guys know what they're doing."

"So do you," she said quietly. "I believe in you. We're going to do this together, you and me."

Just then the opposite door opened and Dana Sue crawled in. "I guess that makes me your breathing coach," she said cheerfully, winking at Erik.

He locked his gaze with Helen's, his eyes filled with so much worry, so much love, she was almost blinded by it.

"You're sure?" he asked.

"Absolutely," Helen said. "Not a doubt in my mind. And the baby seems to be pretty convinced, too."

"Maybe we could make it to the hospital," he suggested, sounding a little desperate.

Helen shook her head. "I already told the baby to wait," she whispered to him when she could catch her breath. "She doesn't seem to be interested in that idea."

A faint smile tugged at his lips. "Obviously he's already a little rebel. It doesn't bode well for the teenage years."

"Then she's probably going to need both of us around so we can back each other up," Helen suggested, watching his face closely.

"Looks like it," he agreed. "You okay with that?"

She swallowed hard as the desire to push nearly overwhelmed her. "Um, Erik, I don't think we can have this conversation now," she said between pants.

He immediately moved into place and went into action. Moments later, he commanded her to push.

Suddenly she felt the baby coming and was filled with exhilaration. She waited to hear the baby's first tiny wail. When it didn't come, she cast a panicked look at Erik, but he was working, his movements sure and confident. The other EMTs were close by, nodding at his actions, ready to step in if needed, but Erik clearly had this under control.

Then, at last, there was a loud, healthy howl and relief flooded her. Her eyes swam with tears.

"Girl or boy?" she asked, trying to raise herself so she could see.

A moment later Erik was holding a bundle wrapped in a blanket. "Mom," he said, shifting to place the baby in Helen's waiting arms, "I'd like you to meet your daughter. And unless I miss my guess, she's full-term, not a preemie. Goodness knows, her lungs sound fully developed."

"Sarah Beth," Helen whispered, looking with wonder at the squalling, pink-faced baby in her arms. She glanced back at Erik, who couldn't seem to tear his awestruck gaze away from the baby. She nudged him with her elbow. "A girl really, really needs her dad." She lifted her gaze to meet his. "I need him, too."

Erik touched a finger to the baby's cheek, then to hers. "Sugar, don't you know by now how much I love you? You couldn't get rid of me if you tried."

She searched his expression to see if there were any doubts, but he looked as if he meant it. "You're sure?"

A slow smile spread across his face. "Absolutely, positively. We might have taken a few detours and backroads, but it feels to me as if we're meant to be a family."

In a gesture that mirrored his, Helen touched her baby's petal-soft cheek. Then she reached over and caressed her husband's faintly stubbled cheek, as well. "Feels that way to me, too." She glanced at Dana Sue, who was openly crying. "How about you? You think the world is ready for another Sweet Magnolia? We're family, too."

"Just think about it," Dana Sue said, smiling through her tears. "Annie, Katie, Jessica Lynn and now Sarah Beth. Serenity will never be the same."

"Something tells me it'll be better than ever," Erik said. "I can hardly wait to see what happens next."

Helen exchanged a look with Dana Sue, then smiled down at her precious baby girl. "Amen to that."

From *New York Times* bestselling author

SHERRYL WOODS

The Sweet Magnolias

February 2007   **March 2007**   **April 2007**

SAVE $1.00 off the purchase price of any book in *The Sweet Magnolias* trilogy.

Offer valid from February 1, 2007 to April 30, 2007. Redeemable at participating retail outlets. Limit one coupon per purchase.

52607602

5 65373 00076 2   (8100) 0 11383

MSWSMT07

MIRA®

New York Times bestselling author

ANNE STUART

Museum curator Summer Hawthorne considered the
ice-blue ceramic bowl given to her by her beloved Japanese
nanny a treasure of sentimental value—until somebody
tried to kill her for it.

The priceless relic is about to ignite a global power struggle
that must be stopped at all costs. International operative
Takashi O'Brien has received his directive: everybody is
expendable. Everybody. Especially the woman who is getting
dangerously under his skin as the lethal game crosses the
Pacific to the remote mountains of Japan, where the truth
can be as seductive as it is deadly....

ICE BLUE

"A master at creating chilling atmosphere
with a modern touch."
—*Library Journal*

*Available the first week of April 2007
wherever paperbacks are sold!*

www.MIRABooks.com   MAS2478

SHERRYL WOODS

32415	A SLICE OF HEAVEN	___ $6.99 U.S.	___ $8.50 CAN.
32363	STEALING HOME	___ $6.99 U.S.	___ $8.50 CAN.
32336	WAKING UP IN CHARLESTON	___ $6.99 U.S.	___ $8.50 CAN.
32238	FLIRTING WITH DISASTER	___ $6.99 U.S.	___ $8.50 CAN.
32149	THE BACKUP PLAN	___ $6.99 U.S.	___ $8.50 CAN.
32048	DESTINY UNLEASHED	___ $6.50 U.S.	___ $7.99 CAN.
66815	ABOUT THAT MAN	___ $6.50 U.S.	___ $7.99 CAN.

(limited quantities available)

TOTAL AMOUNT	$ _____
POSTAGE & HANDLING	$ _____
($1.00 FOR 1 BOOK, 50¢ for each additional)	
APPLICABLE TAXES*	$ _____
TOTAL PAYABLE	$ _____

(check or money order—please do not send cash)

To order, complete this form and send it, along with a check or money order for the total above, payable to MIRA Books, to: **In the U.S.:** 3010 Walden Avenue, P.O. Box 9077, Buffalo, NY 14269-9077; **In Canada:** P.O. Box 636, Fort Erie, Ontario, L2A 5X3.

Name: _____
Address: _____ City: _____
State/Prov.: _____ Zip/Postal Code: _____
Account Number (if applicable): _____

075 CSAS

*New York residents remit applicable sales taxes.
*Canadian residents remit applicable GST and provincial taxes.

MIRA®

www.MIRABooks.com

MSHW0407BL